BLOODMAN

Published by Thomas & Mercer
P.O. Box 400818
Las Vegas, NV 89140

ISBN-13: 9781612182131
ISBN-10: 1612182135

BLOODMAN

ROBERT POBI

THOMAS & MERCER

For my mother and father,
who taught me to swing for the fence.

One need not be a chamber to be haunted;
One need not be a house;
The brain has corridors surpassing
Material place.

— Emily Dickinson – *Poem 670*

But fix thine eyes below; for draweth near
The river of blood, within which boiling is
Whoe'er by violence doth injure others.

— Dante Alighieri – *The Divine Comedy,
Inferno* – Canto XII

1

Day Four
Montauk, Long Island

Two hundred feet below the rolling metal surface of the Atlantic, a handful of ghosts skittered along the ocean floor in a jerky seesaw roll, furling and unfurling in a diluvial ballet. They were dragged forward by the storm raging overhead, still together after miles of progress across the rock-strewn bottom. Soon the gentle slope of the sea floor would change pitch, the earth would drop away into black, and the ghosts would tumble down into the deep. There they would be picked up by the Gulf Stream to be dragged up the Eastern Seaboard, past Massachusetts, finally washing out into the North Atlantic. Maybe they would be consumed by the creatures that swam in the dark world of the cold waters – maybe they would simply decay and be forgotten – but it was certain they would never be touched by daylight or warmth again.

Debris littered the ocean floor around them and the sounds of the world coming apart at the seams echoed overhead. An army of lawn furniture, scabs of roofing tiles, plywood, tires, an old Barbie doll, golf bags, a dented refrigerator, oil paintings, a battered Dodge Charger – banged along in the current with them, heading straight out to sea. Of all the detritus, the Charger moved the slowest, tumbling over and over on its side, one door gone, the lights somehow still glimmering like the eyes of a dying robot. Barbie moved quickest, staying upright with the help of her buoyant plastic injection-molded breasts and the bubble of air trapped in her ancient, empty head.

The ghosts were given no special treatment, no consideration by the storm; they collided with appliances, snagged on rocks, were inelegantly covered with weeds and plastic bags and rips and tears in their skin like the rest of the garbage.

But unlike the other flotsam being herded out to sea, they were not the product of the hurricane; they had been created by something much more malevolent, and much less predictable, than weather.

2

Day One
Montauk, Long Island

Jake Cole stood at the door, looking down at the tattered mat he had last seen the night he had walked out more than a quarter of a century ago. Staring at the rug, he felt a minor sizzle in the circuitry as a burst of the old emotions came back but he very much realized that he was no longer afraid. Or angry. Or any of the other things that had finally given him the courage to leave. But the sensation was there, if only in the abstract.

The rug had aged, faded, and started to fray on three sides. Anyone else would have thrown it out. But not his old man. He had never paid attention to things like rugs. Or manners. Or his son. No, the only thing Jacob Coleridge had ever given a shit about was color. The rug was purple, only his father would have called it *Pantone 269*. The flowers were once white – *blue-white, son*. Purchased by his mother in a tourist shop in Montauk before she died and his father's drinking got out of control and started crawling around in his skull like a poisonous spider, turning whatever kindness was left to pyrotechnic meanness.

Fuck it, Jake thought. "It's purple and white," and wiped his feet on it. He unlocked the big deadbolt and pushed the door open – his fingers splayed out on the dark teak – then stepped inside.

Without his father here he felt like he was invading the old man's kingdom; besides being an extremely private man, Jacob Coleridge Sr. was a control freak extraordinaire. But Jake wasn't an interloper; he had been summoned – beckoned, if you wanted to be exact – to make decisions for a man who was no longer capable of making them for himself. According to the doctor Jake had spoken to at the hospital, his father had set himself ablaze during an Alzheimer's-fueled fit of confusion, coming as close to killing himself as anyone would want to get. And the hardcore hermit and workaholic had finally run out of time. He would never paint again. At that his son thought they might as well take him out behind the hospital, perch him on the edge of the dumpster, and blow his head off because without his painting, Jacob Coleridge wasn't even there.

With perfect muscle memory, Jake's fingers reached into the dark and found the heavy Bakelite switches just inside the door. *Flip, flip, flip.* The three Verner Panton Plexiglas globes that lit up the main foyer cracked to life. Jake stood in the doorway for a minute, the big aluminum Halliburton forgotten in his hand, and gazed around the room. In twenty-eight years it hadn't changed – and not in the nomenclature of a real-estate agent telling you that it needed updating, although that was part of it; no, the stasis of the space was more visceral than that. The room was a stage set out of Dickens.

Jake walked past the Nakashima console in the entry – a big undressed slab of walnut – and dropped his keys on the dusty surface beside the wire-frame model of a sphere that had been there as long as he could remember. Dust and spiderwebs stuck to the polished metal surface in a fuzzy skin, and when Jake dropped the keys, the flesh of the sculpture moved, almost flinched, an optical illusion in the late-afternoon light. He moved into the body of the home.

The house had been one of the first all-glass dwellings built on the point. A marvel of modern design, with a heavily canted roof, California redwood beams, and a kitchen straight out of a Scandinavian design lab. His father's reference library was there, swallowing up the wall around the slate fireplace. The surfboard coffee table was littered with dusty coffee mugs, scotch bottles, and unopened elastic-bundled copies of the *New York Times*. A forest of stubbed cigarettes filled a big ceramic ashtray with a bite-sized chunk sloppily glued back in place that sat on the floor. The sofas were in the same positions, the leather polished to a fine sheen, the arm of one chair hastily – and probably drunkenly – repaired with duct tape. His mother's Steinway, unused since the summer of 1978, sat in one corner, one of Warhol's *Shot Marilyns* – a gift that Andy and that six-foot-three blonde he used to travel with had dropped off one weekend – hung lopsided over the dusty top.

Jake walked slowly through his father's life, examining the last quarter-century. Obviously, Jacob had been riding the dementia train for some time; this didn't just happen overnight. It took some doing. Some *serious* doing. And the closing number had been one for the family album – a human torch dancing around the living room, punctuated by a crash through a plate-glass window topped off with a dive into the pool. Sure. *All systems go. Houston, we have no problems.*

The general mess that used to lie on top of the order had burrowed down, into the bones of the place, so that disorganization was now the rule. Like a wrecking yard, entropy seemed to be the governing law of mechanics. The bottles, always a must in any room inhabited by the great Jacob Coleridge, were strewn about like empty shell casings. Jake bent over and picked one up. His old man's taste had gone from Laphroaig to Royal Lochnagar – at least he hadn't gotten cheap in his later years.

The weird part was the knives – yellow utility knives scattered throughout the space, always within reach. Jake picked one up, spun the wheel, and slid the blade out of the handle. It was rusty. They must have been on sale, Jake thought, and put it back down.

One of the twelve floor-to-ceiling panes that opened onto the ocean had been replaced with a sheet of exterior-grade plywood, the edges painted a bright green. This was where his father had gone through the glass on his way to the pool – clothes burning, fingers melting like candles. The pool sat in the middle of the weathered gray deck, a now green rectangular pond, the inside painted by Pablo Picasso and his father one drunken weekend in 1967.

Leaning against the back of the sofa was a Chuck Close portrait that someone had slashed the eyes out of – no doubt with one of the utility knives – the secret graffiti of one Jacob Gansevoort Coleridge Sr. Why would his old man do that?

Jake paused to examine a note taped to one of the remaining big front windows. Across a chunk of sketch paper, in the bold draftsman's block letters of his father's hand, it said, *YOUR NAME IS JACOB COLERIDGE. KEEP PAINTING.*

Jake froze, his eyes crawling over the rough surface of the sketch paper, trying to decide if he was ready for this. The answer wasn't long in coming. *Not really.* But this wasn't one of those *choice* things, this was one of those *do* things. There was a difference. He went into the kitchen.

He checked the fridge. Three cans of light beer, steaks that had passed being fit for consumption – human or otherwise – some time ago, a dozen Styrofoam soup containers half-filled with sludge well on its way to being petroleum, a lone wrinkled lemon that looked like an ancient abandoned breast, one shoe, a ring of keys, a dried-out chunk of sod, a couple of paperbacks, and a pair of utility knives – one in the vegetable drawer, one in the butter compartment. Jake closed the fridge and scanned the rest of the kitchen.

There were no dirty dishes to speak of, just a mottled layer of crumbs, dust bunnies, and paint-crusted fingerprints that looked like they had been there since before the Internet existed.

He opened a random drawer and found some paintings stuffed inside, small canvases stacked like books, dreary irregularly shaped blobs of black and gray that grimaced up at him, daring him to keep looking.

His father's work had always been dark – in composition and theme – an early trademark among the proto-flower children of his generation who painted in beautiful colors and optimistic brushstrokes. But these little pictures were lifeless fields of gray and black with a red striation running through them, like veins just under the surface. They weren't classic. They weren't modern. When he thought about it, he realized that they probably weren't even sane. Then again, what else could you expect from a man who kept chunks of lawn in the fridge and torched himself on a Thursday evening?

He looked around and wondered what had happened to the man he had left. The brilliant Jacob Coleridge had been reduced to leaving himself notes and painting mindless blobs of madness. Of all the things he had expected of his father, meaninglessness had never even been considered. Jake dropped the canvas back into the drawer and pushed it shut with his knee.

It was amazing how things could just turn to shit. Thirty-three years of misery had lived here. The house stunk of it. Maybe the best thing he could do would be to light up one of the newspapers, lob it into the living room, and close the door, leaving it to the fire. Let the whole place disappear from memory. Maybe that's what the old man had been trying to do himself. Maybe he had finally had enough of his own company.

"Stop it," he said aloud, and with the sound of his own voice came the realization that he was doing exactly what he had promised he wouldn't – feel sorry for himself. He left the kitchen and crossed a hardwood floor littered with dozens of small Persian area rugs, overlapped at weird transepts like foreign postage stamps on a package.

He went to the big sliding doors that opened up to the ocean, and stood there, his hands in his pockets, his mind trying to be somewhere else. Anywhere else but here, in this home, in this place he swore he would never come back to. He watched the water and took control of his breathing. He reached into his pocket, pulled out a pack of Marlboros, and fired one to life with the sterling Zippo that Kay had given him.

He took in a lungful of smoke and focused on the ocean out beyond the beach. Staring at the water, he remembered the hurricane that was on the way. Another Cape Verde. The town was already preparing for it; he had seen the signs as he drove through on the way to the house – shutters going up, cars being loaded, bottles of water and flashlight batteries being horded by the crate. The grinning orange face of the CNN anchorwoman on the screen of the silent hospital-room television had held a little extra twinkle of malice in it when she had pointed to the massive swirling eye of the beast on the satellite images. It was a big one, bearing down on New England with an ETA of a little over fifty hours. Plenty of time for him to cross the Ts and dot the Is on whatever forms the hospital needed and still get the fuck out of Dodge. He focused on the horizon, trying to see past the clear sunlit day to the approaching storm, but all he saw was the static blue sky of a Winslow Homer watercolor. But bad things were on the way. Something about coming home made it necessary. Good old-fashioned luck, it seemed.

Jake finished his cigarette, dropped it to the floor, crushed it into the carpet with the heel of his boot, and turned away from the photorealistic painting of the Atlantic to the scratched negative of the house. He took his iPhone out of his pocket, dialed without really looking at the screen, and dropped into the thick leather sofa in a cloud of dust.

Three ... four ... five rings. He checked his watch. Jeremy would be with the sitter and Kay would be at practice, her phone turned off and—

"Kay River," she answered, the distant caw of the orchestra resonating thinly in the background.

"Hey, baby, it's me. I just wanted to hear that you and Jeremy were doing all right."

"We're good. Don't worry about us. How's your dad?"

Jake thought back to the sedated man he had seen at the hospital an hour ago. The white points of mucus in the corners of his eyes. The labored breathing. His hands, melted off and swathed in bandages. "Older would be the appropriate response." He focused on the waves beyond the pool, hitting the beach, the music accompanying Mother Nature nicely. "Campioni?" he asked, trying to place the arrangement.

Kay laughed. "Good guess. Luchesi."

"Sorry. I try."

"I didn't marry you for your ear."

"I know." An image of Kay flowered in his head, her freckles and smile swirling into a mental hologram.

"Are you at the hospital?"

"Finished an hour ago and just got to my dad's place. It's a mess. Don't know if I can stay here." His eyes crawled over the room, taking in the details. With the garbage and art it looked like a ransacked tomb in the Valley of the Kings, minus a sarcophagus. "Or want to."

"You can. And should. This is what you need, even if you don't know it, Mr. Know-it-all."

Why was it she always knew how to make him feel better about the demons? All he said was, "Okay."

"Look, I have one more rehearsal tomorrow that wraps up early. Jeremy and I could catch the bus out there. I can spare a few days. I don't want you going through this by yourself."

His eyes left the bright moving canvas of the beach beyond the window and found the broad porcelain ashtray with the hastily repaired chunk. That had happened what? Thirty-one years ago now. His hand unconsciously went to the base of his skull and he felt the lump of scar tissue, the one that still lit up if he stared at bright lights too long or got stuck in traffic.

"—ake? Are you there? Jake? Are you—"

He pinched the bridge of his nose. "I guess I'm more tired than I thought. I'm going to grab a nap, maybe get some food."

"That sounds like a good idea. Eat some protein. Sardines and cream cheese on multigrain, okay?"

He smiled, and it was a welcome change from the grimace welded to his skull since the hospital had called. "Thanks, babe. I miss you already."

"I miss you, too. Call if you're feeling lonely, even if it's two in the morning. Deal?"

"Deal. Bye, baby."

He dropped the phone to the littered surface of the coffee table. Motes of dust sprouted, and Jake realized that if Miss Havisham had been a booze hound, she would have hit it off with his old man. As long as she was good at hiding under beds and locking doors when the wolfing hour took hold of her man.

He went up the center-strung staircase and as he climbed higher, he saw garbage strewn over the top of every piece of furniture in the main room, from empty soup cans and unread copies of *Awake!* magazine to the more esoteric stripped Barbie doll and an old oil filter. At the top of the stairs he paused, surveying a house that had looked so much larger when he was last here.

The light coming in through the big rectangles of glass that opened onto the Atlantic washed away a lot of sins, blanching dust and debris with a broad stroke of blue-white that made him squint. The Persian carpets, overlaid and crosshatched waffles of color, were plastered over with scraps of life like the rest of the house. Jake saw the charred footsteps his father had left in his Alzheimer's dance, the winning combination in a Twister game for pyromaniacs, over by the sheet of plywood that replaced the one big pane. Jake unconsciously read their pattern, starting just left of the fireplace, sambaing a good four in front of the piano, then turning quickly right for five steps in a foxtrot, finally lurching left again, spinning in place for the finale, and crashing through the glass and out onto the deck where he had run for the pool, flopping in the sludge like a sick fish. With all the booze in his blood, it was a wonder he hadn't simply detonated, sending the house up in one white-hot mushroom cloud.

Outside, through the plywood-interrupted view, he saw his father's studio sitting at the edge of the property, overlooking the beach. The windows were dark, the shingles half gone, the remaining ones blackened and crooked – another component in the heavily stylized mental picture Jake was quickly constructing.

He thought about checking out the rest of the place, then realized that he wasn't really interested. The dirt and utility knives had been enough. At least for now. He clomped back down the stairs, his harness boots thudding with each heavy step, and realized that he was more tired than he had admitted to Kay. He picked a stack of small canvases off the sofa and leaned them against the coffee table. They looked dark and bloody like the batch in kitchen drawer – gray, unsettling.

Jake took out his firearm, a big stainless Smith & Wesson M500, and slid it under the cushion at the head of the sofa. Then he took off his boots, swung his legs up onto the sofa, and was asleep before his body had warmed the leather that covered the pistol behind his skull.

The shrill chirp of his cell phone jarred him from his sleep and he snapped upright. "Jake Cole," he said reflexively. His leather jacket was still on and he felt like his head was filled with hot soot. It was dark out and he checked his watch. Eleven thirteen.

"Special Agent Jake Cole?"

He took a deep breath and uh-huhed. Scratched the chunk of scar tissue at the base of his scalp.

"This is Sheriff Mike Hauser, Southampton SD. Got your number from the New York bureau office. Sorry to call at this hour but I got a problem and for some reason you're five miles from where I need you." The tone and word choice told Jake a lot about the man at the other end. Trim. Fifty. Flat-top. Sig Sauer P226 for a sidearm. American flag pin on his lapel. Ex-jock.

There was a pause and Jake realized that he was supposed to tell Sheriff Hauser that it was fine that he had called. That sure, he would listen. That, yessir, he was there to help. He reached under the cushion and slid the heavy revolver out. He checked the cylinder – a habit he had learned a long time ago – and tucked it into the pressure holster on his belt. All he said was, "How'd they die?"

The pause dragged out a little longer, and Jake recognized the pregnant silence of a man trying to build up courage. This silence told Jake a lot more about him. Hauser swallowed audibly, then said, "They were skinned."

And the little current of emotion that he had refused to acknowledge a few hours ago came to the front of everything, blocking out the ocean and the moon beyond. It froze in his head and his blood pressure surged in one electromagnetic pulse that rattled his gray matter.

That old motherfucker fear was coming out to play.

3

Jacob Coleridge Jr. – now Jake Cole – downshifted from fourth gear into third and hit the gas. The 426 Hemi growled as the legion of water-cooled ponies dug into the asphalt and the '68 Charger screeched through the corner, launching his pack of cigarettes across the dashboard. As he cleared the apex of the curve, the lights swung out over the shoulder and lit up one of the drift fences stretched across the beach that bordered the highway. There was a bright blue strobe of fence and sand and a brief glimpse of the Atlantic beyond, then the long expanse of his hood was through the corner and he was barreling up 27, almost due east, on his way to see the dead.

It was a weeknight and there was no traffic on the Montauk Highway. The gentle slalom of road brought Jake back to his sixteenth summer, driving up to Billy Spencer's place in Billy's ancient Corvette after their shift at the Montauk Yacht Club, pockets filled with two- and three-dollar tips that added up to just enough money to last the weekend. They'd rip up the coast with the torn canvas top folded down, listening to The Clash and smoking weed.

The windows were open and the cool night air buffeted the cabin. The wind that had been chopping up the surf had died down and all that was left was a strong thrum of air that pulsed along the coast like a heartbeat, pumping fresh air in from the ocean. Something metal in the back seat clinked rhythmically, probably the buckle on Jeremy's baby seat, but the sound was muted by the static of the moment.

Jake was trying to get into character. He did this every time he went to work – every time, in fact, he was forced to face the dead, the mutilated, and the dishonored that made up his clientele.

It was an armoring process, only it was internal. Unlike most of the men he worked with in the bureau, the immediate threat was not to his body. As the first man on the scene of some of the most violent murders on the planet, Jake was continually at risk of being damaged by flak from the bloody human sculpture he decoded. Instead of a Kevlar vest and a riot helmet, he protected himself with a carefully tailored personality shield positioned to prevent the soft parts of his psyche from being damaged. Before Jake walked onto a murder scene, he wrapped parts of himself up and put them away in a secure area of his mind so they wouldn't be part of a process that both repulsed and fascinated him. And when it was over, when he walked out of work, he was able to function without tension rot getting to him. At least that was the theory.

Lately, getting into the zone took a little force, and tonight the switch-line in his head that he depended on to let him go from a full stop to a full go seemed to be misfiring. With anyone else he would have understood it. Empathized with it. But he didn't allow these things for himself. He couldn't. He resented the image of his father, sedated in his hospital bed, contaminating his thoughts; he needed that space right now.

When he thought about it, it wasn't just his father – it was the entire act of being here. Being *back* here. Stepping into the house. Seeing that goddamned cracked ashtray with the glued bit still sitting on the floor. Stepping over and around those grim little canvases that a once-great painter had scabbed together during a redline descent into madness. Smelling the ocean. Driving the Montauk Highway. Thinking about Spencer and the old Corvette. The sod in the fridge. The algae-infested pool. All of it.

Jake took a breath and pushed the extra mental inventory aside and concentrated on getting into the zone. He focused on his driving, on the road opening up in the bright glare of the headlights, and on keeping the car between the lines on the pavement. He punched the gas, double-clutched up into fourth, and felt a batch of mice let loose in his stomach as the car crested a small hill on the road that wove up the coast like a black serpent. His body strained against the seat belt as the Dodge peaked, then dropped down into a trough on the snake's back, pushing him into the leather. He hammered down on the gas and the car lurched forward in a high-pitched wail that converted petroleum into momentum.

A few minutes later he spotted the Christmas-tree pulse of emergency lights up ahead, off the road and partially obscured by the dark teeth of tree trunks. He didn't ease off the gas until he was a hundred yards from the gate, then rapidly downshifted from fourth to second. He hit the brakes and fishtailed into the entrance, the seat belt digging into his hips, the Hemi angry at the loss of juice to its heart.

Two imposing stone pillars that supported massive wrought-iron gates flanked the driveway. A pair of Southampton black-and-whites guarded the opening, a visual opera of sharp red, white, and blue flashes. Jake swung the Charger through the gate and stopped short as one of the uniformed officers scrambled up to his window, a Maglite hanging loosely from his hand.

Knowing cop protocol, he didn't bother to look up – an eyeful of flashlight beam could set off one of his headaches.

"You Special Agent Cole?" the unseen officer shimmering at the edge of his peripheral vision asked and Jake's software pulled up an image to go with the voice. When the beam of the flashlight was off his face he looked up.

"Spencer?" he said, and felt the corners of his mouth curl up with the closest thing to a smile he was capable of when on the job.

The cop took a step back and the flat expression on his face evened out into a question mark that flashed in the cruiser lights. "It's Officer William Spencer." And with his last name, the tone dropped off as he recognized Jake in the pulsing blue and red.

"Jakey? What the actual fuck!" The cop's face switched to smile mode and it was a lot friendlier, even in the alternating Christmas glimmer of the roof rack. His eyes slid over Jake and his mouth managed a pretty good smile, which even after all this time surprised Jake because he had knocked half of it out back in second grade. Spencer swung the flashlight in the car, then over the baby seat in the back.

Jake stopped the emotions he knew he would not be using in the next little while and held up his badge. "Your sheriff sounded pretty grim on the phone fifteen minutes ago."

Spencer ignored him. "You back about your old man?" Then, after nodding *of course* to himself, said, "What's with the name?"

Jake drew in a chestful of sea air and let it settle to the bottom of his lungs. This is what he hated about coming back. They asked about his past. "The name Jacob Coleridge was more of an obstacle than a blessing out in the world." Being the son of the famous painter had come with its own kind of baggage, none of it good. Except maybe the art-school groupies who had slept with him as a way to somehow absorb some good old famous DNA, even if it was once-removed.

Spencer's smile short-circuited and he nodded like he understood. "You're the guy Hauser called?" It was worded as a question but meant as a statement.

Jake nodded and stared up at the former oyster-shucker. In the blaring lights of the cruisers his eyes still flashed blue and red, ornaments that couldn't make up their minds. "I'd hate to be you," Spencer said.

The pulsing eyes were a little unsettling and Jake turned his focus onto the glowing slant of the roof just over the slight hill of the drive; it was an old Long Island landscaping habit to keep the house hidden from the road with a berm. He watched the slate roof lit up by the lights of the emergency vehicles he knew were encamped in the drive, fanned out in varying degrees of importance. "Where have you put the media?" Jake knew that with the storm rolling in, every national news program would have its people out stalking the coast for impending disaster stories. And they wouldn't miss a double homicide, no matter how deep the local police tried to bury it.

Spencer shook his head. "No media. Sheriff hasn't called anyone and I don't think he's going to."

Jake put that down on the list after American lapel pin.

Officer William Spencer tapped his sidearm with the lens of the big flashlight. "Cameraman tries to get in there, I have a trespasser on the premises."

Jake shook his head. "No, Billy, you don't. You come get me. We clear?"

Spencer let the question rattle around in the silence for a few seconds before he said, "Sure. Yeah."

"The media is going to be important with this investigation. We want them working with us, not against us. They show up, you come get me."

Spencer smiled, and they were good again. "You were called for a reason."

"I've done this before. The bureau was requested by the local SD and the New York office knew I was staying out at the house. I guess the powers-that-be thought I needed to be here." He turned back to Spencer, whose flashing-ornament eyeballs had somehow become less disturbing. "Just a lucky coincidence, I guess."

"You're a smart guy, Jake. At least you used to be." Spencer's mouth opened up and his teeth began to flash along with his eyes in the glare of the cruiser. "No such thing as coincidence." His mouth pursed up and he looked down, as if he was embarrassed. "You know that."

Jake hated platitudes and clichés, but something about the way Spencer said it raised a flag somewhere in his head. "Drop by," he said, and roared off down the driveway.

19

4

Unlike the Wyeth clan, the next generation of the Coleridge blood-line couldn't draw a stick figure without fucking it up. Jake was, however, able to do some remarkable things inside his skull. His one true talent – even greater than his father's gift – was the ability to paint the final moments of people's lives. And this uncanny and often frightening gift made Jake Cole very good at hunting monsters.

The people he worked with thought of it as an esoteric art form, some sort of weird channeling from places best left alone – deranged, psychotic, tortured places. Jake found the nuances in what made individual crime scenes unique. And in this unique-ness he decoded the stylistic fingerprint – the murderer's signa-ture. Once this signature was committed to memory, he would recognize it on sight. In the real world art market, if applied to paintings, a gift like his would have been worth millions of dollars a year in the economy of the business. In the search for killers, it was priceless.

He walked through the high arched doorway, intricately carved in a French motif. The house immediately spoke to him. Of wealth. Education. Breeding. Death. And ... and? And something else Jake couldn't quite nail. He had never been here before – he had eidetic memory for surroundings and had no recall of the property – but back, buried behind the personality traits of the home, there was something he knew. A distant chatter that he could not quite recognize.

Sheriff Hauser looked exactly like the mental portrait that Jake had painted in his skull, right down to the American flag pin in his lapel. He stood an easy six three in his engineer boots, weighed in at a healthy two-forty, and had the prerequisite flattop and bland good looks of his ilk. Although now, standing in the beach house of dead people he had promised to protect and serve, with two bloody skinned human bodies splattered all over the floor, Jake saw stress vibrating beneath the sheriff's composure. The tight lines of concern looked like fissures in a garden statue that had been left to the elements for too long. Without knowing how he knew, Jake was sure the man had played football; there was something in the way he moved his shoulders, the way he swiveled his head, that said quarterback. But for all his presence, Jake knew that it wouldn't take much to put a few holes in Hauser's thin skin of togetherness, and he'd have to go outside to throw up.

Jake pushed into a conversation the sheriff was having with a spacesuited photographer from the Medical Examiner's Office.

"Sheriff Hauser? Jake Cole." Jake extended his hand.

Hauser didn't take it, but looked Jake over. His mouth tightened a little and Jake wondered if he had met another tight-assed small-town sheriff who would end up being his own worst enemy on the case. Hauser surprised him. "Cole? Sure. Sorry. I ..." He let it trail off and wiped the back of his hand across his mouth. "I'm not firing on all eight right now. I guess that's the last thing I should be saying to the FBI, huh?"

"I appreciate the honesty." He looked over Hauser's shoulder, at the bedroom door thrown wide, the interior of the chamber lit up in space whites from the utility lights. He told himself to wait another minute, until after Hauser was up to speed on his new PR function. "What are you doing about media?" he asked, skipping small talk.

Hauser shook his head. "No media."

"Half the news crews in the country are within fifty miles of here. Official FBI policy is to work with the media. Establish a relationship and you'll be surprised how the news can do more good than bad."

Hauser pulled off his rubber glove and massaged his eyes with a thumb and forefinger. "I don't have a lot of experience with this kind of thing."

Jake gave the sheriff a thirty-second talk on putting together an effective media plan that would be a useful tool in the investigation. He suggested Hauser as the public information officer – as far as PIOs went, Jake thought the man would present well on camera. After his quick lecture and promises of help, Jake pointed at the bright rectangle of utility lights and excused himself.

He slid past Hauser and walked to the door, pushing two of the sheriff's people out of the way as he moved. No one protested or said a word when Jake was on site – something about him told people to get out of his way.

He saw them on the floor and his brain did what it did, the computational software automatically gathering details and comparing them against the vast databank in his mental vault. The noise in the room stopped. The people moving behind him disappeared. And there was no light save for the harsh truth of halogen on the dead. He stood there for a few seconds that could have been minutes or hours or days and inventoried everything he saw in a mental data download.

Immediately – quicker than immediately if that was at all possible – he knew. *Knew.* With a certainty that was as inexplicable as what he did.

Now he understood the background chatter he hadn't quite recognized when he had walked in. It had been the scent of familiarity. He knew this work. It was him.

Him.

Jake stood there, the minutiae of the scene humming in his skull. He knew what had happened. How it had happened. How long it had taken.

The world was gone – just gone – and there was no sound except for the howling of the child. The screams of the woman on the floor. Jake heard the celery-bite crunch when her ribs were kicked in. He heard the snap as her jaw broke when she was hit with the pommel of the hunting knife that would be used to skin her. He listened to her screeching above the sound of her skin coming off her body. And her gurgled intimate prayers for it all to stop. For death to come for her.

And then, just as quickly, it was gone. He was back at the threshold and a voice off to his left made a joke. Someone laughed. Jake was jolted out of his work, out of himself, and he turned.

A big trooper with a shaved head had the tail end of a smile hanging on his lips.

Jake kept himself from yelling but made sure everyone in the house heard him. "Does this look fucking funny to you, asshole?"

The trooper, whose nametag identified him as Scopes, locked his eyes on Jake. The look on his face was half resentment, half embarrassment.

"Do you know what happened here?" He waited, and the house went silent. Everyone stopped what they were doing. "A woman was skinned alive. She was held down, forced to watch a little boy mutilated while the fucking kid probably broke the sound barrier with his screeching. And he bled to death before his murderer was finished with him. He would have twitched a lot at the end. Then the motherfucker dropped the kid to the floor like a broken toy and kicked the woman's ribs in. While she was gasping like a fish, trying to find some breath to pray or scream for help, he scalped her. Then he probably winded her again, and she almost lost consciousness. And while she was sinking away from the world, he sliced all the meat off of her face. Then he waited. And when she woke up, he probably let her scream for a few minutes so he could get a nice memory-image to jerk off to later. Then, because he liked the sound of her voice too much at this point, he held her down with his foot and sliced all the skin off of her while she went through degrees of agony that would take your brain apart. So if you find something even remotely funny here, I am personally going to take you outside and beat some fucking sense into you and if you think I am not serious," Jake took a step toward Scopes, a good half-head taller, and easily the biggest man in almost every room he entered, "say something just a little bit stupid."

Scopes dropped his eyes. "I didn't—"

"Shut the fuck up. I don't want an apology. I want you to get the fuck out of my sight. And if you decide to build up enough balls to come after me later, liquored up and full of rage, you have an open invitation. Are we clear?"

"I'm sorry." His face went a little pale, then shifted to a deep red that showed the veins in his neck.

"Go do something useful and I'll consider this forgotten."

Scopes nodded and grudgingly went outside.

Jake turned, looked at Hauser. The sheriff's eyes were locked on the bedroom door and his skin had gone pale, greenish.

"You okay?" Jake asked, trying to be the other half of his personality.

Hauser still looked green, although he was starting to get his bearing back. The sheriff waved him away. "I'm sorry about Scopes. We all deal with stress in different—"

Jake shook his head. "Forget it."

Hauser swallowed, his lips a tight line that barely moved when he spoke. He swallowed again, trying to breathe through his mouth. The house smelled of metal, blood, shit, and fear.

Jake wanted to turn back to the bedroom, to the violated bodies on the thick pile rug. Back to the work. But that little voice in his head was chattering away now, rattling off the unifying factors in this case and the other one. The first one. The one that had made him decide to do this.

Hauser cut into his head. "The house is owned by Carl and Jessica Farmer and from what the neighbors tell us, they rent it out when they travel. Right now I assume these, um –" he paused, turned his head consciously away from the room of the dead – "people are – *were* – renters. We don't know their names. Not the woman or the child."

"He's her son."

Hauser looked at Jake and his eyes narrowed. "How do you know?"

"I just do."

Hauser started back up. "According to a neighbor, the Farmers are sailing in the Caribbean. They go every fall and winter and there's always new people coming and going."

Jake looked around, took in the art, the antiques, the expensive fabrics. The neat order was in stark contrast to his father's morbid cave down the beach. "It doesn't look like they need the money. There's twenty grand in Aubusson cushions in the living room. Why would they rent it out?"

Hauser shrugged, pulled the back of his hand across his mouth again. "I don't know. The rich are different." He paused and looked over Jake's shoulder, his eyes peering to the bedroom. "So far, none of the neighbors have seen any renters or heard a child playing. Maybe the woman and ... her child just arrived. Maybe they were the renters."

"You checking the Farmers' bank account?"

The sheriff nodded. "If rent was paid by check we'll have something tomorrow. Two days if it's an out-of-town bank."

"No purse? Mail? Prescription bottles in the bathroom?"

Hauser's blank expression slid back and forth as he shook his head. "No purse. No wallet. No luggage. Nothing distinguishing, nothing personal found."

"Clothes?"

Hauser shook his head. "No kid's clothes. No clothes for a woman that size. Or age, if you're right and she is the mother. Without her ... skin, it's hard to tell. Could be his grandma or—"

Jake shook his head. "She's the right age. Good musculature, not much subcutaneous fat." *What about the other things you saw?* the little voice asked from the dark.

A woman of about sixty-five, primped and perfect in a once-blonde pageboy haircut, came over. She was thin and wearing one of the antistatic spacesuits that Jake had seen on hundreds of crime scenes. Hauser introduced her as the medical examiner, Dr. Nancy Reagan. "No relation," he added very matter-of-factly and Jake hoped he wouldn't turn out to be one of those dumb cops who had somehow slid into the job because of family influence in the area.

"Is the FBI officially involved?" Reagan asked pleasantly, like a snake greeting a mouse.

He thought about the woman behind him, sprawled out and glued to the carpet with her own blood. "Yes."

The ME's smile went a little flat and she said, "Do I look incompetent to you, Special Agent Cole?"

"It's not a question of competence, it's a question of experience." Jake slipped back into character. "You mind if I have a few minutes in here with Madame X and the child?" he asked. "By myself."

Hauser swallowed for what must have been the hundredth time in two minutes and nodded. "Sure. No problem. I give out tickets. Sometimes I see accidents. Drunk kids in fights in town. Killings? Sure, this is America, there's enough of that shit to go around. Shootings and stabbings and beatings and drownings and suicides. But I have never even imagined that people do this kind of shit to one another. Not once." He glanced over his shoulder and his Adam's apple Ichabod Craned again. "Why would anyone skin a child? I can't … I just … I don't …"

Jake cut the sheriff off to prevent him from crying in front of his people. "I'd like Dr. Reagan's photographer to stay with me. Shoot what I ask him to. On my own flash card. You can have copies, of course. I'll also expect copies of your protocols." The ME's office had already gone through the place. Blood spatter patterns had been recorded, the crime scene cataloged by a photographer, and every surface dusted for prints or genetic evidence. But Jake wasn't looking for the things that the ME would be interested in – or even able to see. What Jake Cole wanted was to reach inside the fear he felt pulsing through the house and speak to the dead with that part of him that he never really understood.

Hauser snapped back to the here and now. "I'm staying."

"It's your investigation."

The sheriff lifted his head. "Everyone outside. Conway?"

A small man in one of the ubiquitous spacesuits with an expensive Nikon dangling from his neck came over, his feet swishing on the carpet. "Yeah?"

"This is Special Agent Jake Cole, FBI. Cole is doing us a favor here, so shoot whatever he tells you – *however* he tells you. Understood?"

Conway nodded. "No problem, Sheriff."

The house began to empty, the sheriff's people filing out with the ME's people in a silent white-suited crowd. Conway changed memory cards in his camera and adjusted the big Sunpak flash.

When they were alone, Jake leveled his gaze at Conway. "Let me poke around a bit but keep me in sight."

Conway shrugged like a man used to taking orders and cycled up his flash.

Hauser stepped back like he was at a nature preserve observing wildlife. He cocked his head to one side and watched, hoping that this would somehow put what had happened into some sort of a rational context.

Jake walked to the bedroom and stopped at the threshold. On the floor were the scabbed skinless sprawled-out figures of Madame X and her little boy. He walked through the door for a second meeting with woman and child. Mother and son.

These are not people, Jake told himself.

This is not a family.

This is a set of clues.

Left by an artist.

An artist you know.

You've seen.

This is his palette.

He stopped just inside the threshold and the jagged peal of the bells of bad memories started clanging away in his head. For an instant he wanted to reach out, to grab something for support, but like his brain, his muscles had frozen, the machine of his body unplugged from his CPU. He stood there, his eyes locked on the bodies spilled out of their skins onto the floor, his lungs cocked in a half-breath.

It is him, the voice in his head said, matter-of-factly.

And he was surprised that he was calm. That his feet were welded to the floor and that he was stronger this time. He felt Hauser's presence in the empty space behind him, a cold spot in the room. He could tell that the sheriff was holding his breath.

Jake filled his lungs with the sickly sweet air and for a split second it got away from him and he thought he was going to throw up. He didn't fight it, didn't try to suck it back or push it down, just let the feeling rumble around inside him for an instant and then it was gone like he knew it would be and he was back in the room. Back in the here and the now and the bedroom gallery with the art of the dead.

He recorded what he saw, took it down in pixilated form and committed it to the memory banks because this one was—

Him.

—important.

Him.

Jake didn't need to see any more to know. He already *knew*. The signature – *his* signature – was all over this place. That's what the secondary smell had been back in the living room when he had been talking to Hauser: the stench of familiarity.

Madame X was at the end of the bed, slopped all over the floor like a water balloon that had let go. She was facedown on the rug, one of her legs bent at the knee, a bloody foot smeared onto the edge of the mattress. There was a lot of blood on the carpet. On the bed. On the floor. The happy zigzag pattern of a weekend butcher at work.

Him.

"Did you check the drain? Tub and shower?" Jake asked Hauser, who had moved silently up behind him. "Pull the grilles and the P-traps?"

It was Conway who answered in a swish of mint. "Ran a swab down the drain, straight into the septic system. No municipal service out here. Didn't find a thing."

Are you sure that it is him? Hope whispered. But there was no mistaking it. Not this close. Not after everything that had happened. Spencer was right, there are no coincidences.

He squatted down on his haunches and leaned over the body of the woman. He had seen a lot of indignities in his time but the added horror of familiarity somehow made it more visceral, as if it had been meant for him to see.

Even before he examined her, he knew what he'd find.

All the skin had been removed from her body. He twisted his head like a cat going through a fence, peeked between the bloody stubs of her toes, bent down, looked into the crook of her arm, examined the base of her skull, and couldn't find a shred of skin anywhere. She had been peeled and thrown on the floor. Her flesh was etched all over with crescent-shaped incisions left by the tip of the knife. Without meaning to, he said aloud, "She was skinned with a single-edged knife with a recurve tip. Thick blade. Hunting knife, most probably." He looked at the work, at the technique, and it all came rushing back.

Him. It was almost a chime in his head now. A choral mantra.

"Why would he do that?" Hauser asked somewhere between a whisper and no sound at all.

"Do what?"

Hauser licked his lips so that his vocal cords would work this time around. "Um, skin her. Was he trying to conceal her identity?"

Jake shook his head and reminded himself that most people – police included – never get to see something like this. As far as stupid questions went, he had heard a lot worse. "It has nothing to do with that. We have her dental – mostly. And DNA. No, we'll find out who these people are and he knows it." Jake looked down at them and realized that he hadn't answered Hauser's core question, the big *Why?* "Some take feet. Some take internal organs. A lot take genitals. This guy likes skin. I don't know the *why* yet, only the *how*. The short answer is simply that it's his trip, his own little mental toboggan ride, so he sets it up in a way that makes him feel good." He turned to the woman. "He finds this beautiful."

The flesh under her face was puckered and cracked like pudding and her teeth were jagged nubs of white that she had gnashed off on the carpet. Her tongue was a few inches from her face; she had chewed it off and spat it out and it looked like a thick meat slug that had died trying to escape a building on fire.

He opened the closet and stopped. The hangers were empty. In the bright beam of the task lighting, Jake saw eight small indentations on the carpet. "Get these. With measurements."

"Get what?" Conway asked, staring at the rug.

Jake squatted down, pointed in turn to the eight indentations. Conway squinted. "I don't see anything."

Jake pointed them out again. "There, there, there, there. Then again *here, here, here, and here*."

Conway's face shifted into puzzlement when he saw them. "Holy shit. What are those?"

Jake tried not to roll his eyes.

"Suitcase feet," Hauser said from behind.

"Suitcase feet?"

"Someone took two suitcases out of the closet." Jake raised his finger, pointing at the bar above his head filled with the empty wire hangers. "And all the clothes."

"Why would they do that?"

"Just take the fucking pictures, okay?"

That was when Jake realized that something else was missing – toys. You didn't go anywhere with a child that size without toys. Even if you were only going for five minutes.

Jake turned away and went over the room with is eyes, taking in every object, surface, and detail, forming the space into a 3-D model in his skull that he could walk through later when he needed something. He ignored the coppery sweet smell of blood mixed with the bitter gag of feces and the smell of his own fear – ignored that he was in a room where a child had been skinned in front of his mother and she had been taken apart like a bloody present. He dismissed that Hauser's boys were outside probably contaminating the crime scene. He was even able to forget the photographer, squatting down on his static-free haunches and snapping photos, great drafts of incomprehension coming off him like steam. He was even able to forget the dead.

But he was unable to ignore the little voice that had begun chattering away in his mind like some fevered ghost on speed. *He's been waiting for you to come home, Jakey. You thought that he was gone. Maybe even dead. Didn't you?*

Well, guess what?

He's back.

And you, my friend, are fucked.

5

1,260 miles east of Nassau, Bahamas

Every now and then Mother Nature assembles a performance to show off a little. Or a lot. Scripture labels it Judgment, usually laid down by a vengeful God to keep Man humble. But through progress made in earth sciences, it is now known that natural catastrophes are nothing more than a synchronous assembly of coincidental atmospheric conditions. All that is necessary is patience and the right combination of events.

In mid-September, roughly 500 miles southwest of the Azores island chain, a massive thunderstorm stalled over the ocean. This stall was precipitated by three storm fronts moving in on one another, and they pinned the thunderstorm in place.

The water that fueled this malevolent beast had been lifted off the ocean by solar heating, driven up into the atmosphere in the form of condensation. The act of evaporation generated energy that quickly increased wind speeds over the tropical waters, and the faster winds caused increased surface evaporation, feeding the thunderstorm with even more condensation. This hoarding of fuel swelled the pregnant belly of the beast and the storm clouds mushroomed into the atmosphere, forcing more condensation to form, and a self-feeding monster was born.

The system, affected by the earth's rotation, began to spin, a massive heat-engine with an endless supply of fuel. The metamorphosis from large thunderstorm to hurricane was complete.

There was more heat.

More evaporation.

More wind.

More condensation.

More.

More.

More.

Then the atmospheric pressure dropped several millibars.

And the hurricane began to move west.

On its journey its eye dilated to the largest in history, outsizing Carmen by over sixty miles. In the tradition of political correctness, the storm had been identified as male, and given the title of Dylan.

Hurricane Dylan was now surging toward the American coast and the water in its path was hammered into eighty-foot waves by winds that neared 200 miles an hour. And he hadn't really started putting on his war paint.

He was saving that for landfall.

6

Day Two
Montauk, Long Island

Jake stood just above the ridge of foam and seaweed that the Atlantic had spent the night laying across the beach one wave at a time. It was still nice out, the Gulf Stream now bringing up a southern current that pulled the warm air along with it. The whole East Coast was having a good day, one of those fall mornings that let you know that summer was not yet gone. There was no taste of the hurricane that was pushing the warm front north.

He had been up early, and ate a piece of bologna on toast over the sink like he had back in his junkie days. It was funny, even back then, when his mind had been dialed to comatose most of the time, he had never become a slob. The apartment was always neat. Of course that was easy when you didn't own a second pair of shoes and the big-ticket items in the place were the stainless-steel fork and knife that lay proudly on the cardboard place mat on the kitchen counter. Beside the heat-blued spoon and the surgical tubing.

He had walked across the living room in his bare feet, drinking a cup of coffee out of an ancient A&W paper cup that he had emptied of its paintbrushes. Something about the wax and the heat of the coffee on his fingers and the faint smell of turpentine brought out that the world had changed irrevocably. He hadn't been here in almost thirty years and now, walking through the bright wedge of space, he realized it was as if he had never really left at all. Because our minds are not built to forget, but to ignore.

The craggy man with the flat black eyes and the tattoo he saw looking back from the big mirror beside the piano was nothing like the boy who had left here all that time ago. Twenty-eight years had been swallowed by the clock and the almost-broken piece of machinery he used for a body had changed its cells a full four times since leaving. Except for the electrical impulses stored as memories, Jake Cole was a different man.

Jake didn't remember getting the tattoo, or even thinking about it. Back then his money had been spent on coke and heroin; he never would have wasted budgetary considerations on something as inane as a tattoo. But one morning he had woken up in the tiny apartment on Spring Street, four months behind on rent and somehow not evicted. He had come to life in the middle of the kitchen floor, his head pulsing like an infection, shivering in a pool of rusty brown water from an overflowed toilet in the next room. He stood, and when he put his arm out to steady himself on the fridge that was no longer there, he saw it, covering his arm like a black silk shirt. The ink blanketed his entire body. From wrists to ankles, ending in a jagged line just below his larynx. Flat and healed at his feet – puffy, red, and fresh at his neck. And he remembered none of it. Four months erased from his life.

He had stood in front of the mirror for hours, the longest period he had could remember going without the nervous twitches without being high. The script was Italian and after deciphering a few names and phrases, he realized what it was.

The twelfth canto of *Inferno*, the first part of Dante's *Divine Comedy*. Jake knew the story, of course. When he had been a child, it had been his favorite book in his father's library. A massive leather-bound tome illustrated by Gustave Doré. He had never made any sort of conscious decision about the best parts, but staring at himself in the mirror, watching the ink that snaked over his frame, he knew that he had made the choice. And when he thought about it, the twelfth canto *was* the inevitable passage. The violent condemned to hell. The story of the Men of Blood. Like the ones he now hunted.

Like the *one* he now hunted.

After all this time. And just like finding himself back home, it all reeked of that fucking word destiny. Because some things were meant to happen. Some places were supposed to be revisited. And with that he realized that he hadn't yet gone upstairs.

Of course the upper floor was as bad as the downstairs, worse because the rising heat had no place to go and it had baked the smell of dust and dirt and despair into the walls. The floor up here was bare, the hardwood stripping dented and the varnish beaten through to now dirty raw wood. Along with more utility knives, a few miserable blobs of canvases were stacked up here, too, leaning against the wall. He stopped and picked one up, trying to figure out what had happened to his father's thinking. Were these exercises? How long had he been painting these things? How long had he been sick? Why had no one noticed?

He wondered what his father had been thinking while he had been painting these lifeless chips of noncolor. Jake had stopped caring about his old man years ago, but he had never stopped respecting his mind. Of all the shitty things you could say about Jacob Coleridge – and there were enough to fill a football stadium one filthy vowel at a time – you could not say was that he was talentless. Not like the rest of the hacks who had cashed in on being in the right place at the right time, back when showing up had been half the battle. When you added this hardwired brilliance to the equation the whole process of slapping paint to canvas had become something special to behold.

While the rest of them were measuring their progress with a backward-sliding pencil mark on the door jamb of self-parody, Jacob Coleridge had been reinventing the way people looked at the world. Looked at canvas and crusted pigment. Looked at themselves. He went deep into the arteries of the beast, until he was at its paint-pumping heart, and his work had been the most original and passionate to come out of the East Coast for a long time. Jacob Coleridge had not been a slouch, not even when it had been in style.

So what the fuck had happened to him in the past what – two? – five? – ten? years?

Jake turned one of the asymmetrical canvases clockwise, then counter-clockwise. His father had never believed in modern art, not as a rubric. And he certainly had never believed in the narcissistic self-indulgent crap that his son was now staring at. So what had happened here? Jake leaned the canvas against the wall and walked on down the hall.

His old bedroom and his mother's old office were both locked. The master bedroom had a pocket door that slid into the wall. It was cocked about four inches and Jake wrapped his fingers around the edge and tried to pull it open. It barely budged, as if it was mired in wet sand. He peeked through the crack, into the room, and saw that the door was barricaded – there was no other word for it. From the tight view he saw a chest of drawers, an old iron architect's table, and a giant gilded blackamoor pushed up against the panel. How the hell had his father gotten out of the room after doing that? And what had been going through his head when he had piled the furniture up?

Peeking through the gap, he saw more utility knives laid out on all the surfaces, always one within reach. The room smelled worse than the hospital did, and in the dark it was infinitely more gloomy, if that was at all possible. He'd open it tomorrow – or the next day – it really didn't matter.

After the tour of the upstairs, Jake headed down to the water. He walked barefoot, his tattooed arms almost the same worn blue as his FBI T-shirt with the cracked yellow letters. He held on to the empty cup; he was never able to litter, to leave any of himself behind. In his job, he had seen it get too many people in trouble. Kay always said that after Jake visited a place, it was as if he had never been there at all. He thought of it as simply another occupational hazard.

The cold sand was in direct contrast to the warm wind but he barely noticed. His mind's eye flicked between the 3-D model of the Farmers' bedroom and his father's accident. Coming here to deal with his father and walking into that house up the highway last night were not coincidences. This was bad no matter how he tried to look at it.

Jake walked up the beach, the cool sand squeezing up through his toes like gritty cake icing, the sensation stirring up vestigial memories. The beach had changed in the last quarter-century. A lot, in fact. Like the town itself, the point used to be a community of two distinct groups: the locals and the summer people. The smaller, more modest homes belonged to the locals and the bigger, newer places belonged to the summer people. Gentrification had swallowed all the available real estate in sweeping gulps, and the locals had been pushed farther and farther from the shoreline until the beach was a well-kept line of resort houses devoid of personality and Montauk risked becoming just another eyesore of the wealthy. Desecrated land with preened lawns and three-car garages that owners called *car houses*.

By the time Jacob Coleridge had moved to Montauk he had already made a name for himself. Pollock was dead, Warhol was a firm presence, and there was a huge gaping hole in the progression of American painting. Opposed to Pollock's color overload or Warhol's trite packaging, Jacob Coleridge laid down a grim vision in sweeping lines of crusted pigment that critics began to notice. Collectors quickly followed.

Like most artists, Coleridge began as a classicist and was, by the age of eleven, a skilled draftsman. He quickly outgrew the need for people to see meaning in his work and began each painting with a technically breathtaking illustration that he would deftly, and some would say criminally, cover with successive layers of pigment until only a small detail of the original photorealist work was left. Unlike the mass of American painters who wanted their work worshipped, Jacob Coleridge covered up the parts he figured people would want to see. The critics lauded him as the only non-narcissist in American painting. Many collectors had their works X-rayed so they could see what they were missing. Eventually he started painting with lead pigment, grinding it with linseed oil so that an X-ray machine would have a hard time getting through. And the more he told them to go fuck themselves, the more they paid for his work.

Jake edged along the surf line, absentmindedly kicking at the thick line of weeds and flotsam that snarled the shore, his inner detective looking for … what? Sea shells? Pirate treasure? Answers? A spotted sandpiper trailed behind him, picking up early-morning insects that his curiosity dislodged.

He hadn't come home to work – he had come home because his father had set himself on fire and burned off most of the meat of his hands – little more than charred black hooks now. The short of it was he had come home to set things straight so the old man could be placed somewhere. Then he was going to get back into his car, head for New York, and never come back here. It was a simple scenario when it was put in those terms. Only those terms had been blown to pieces when Hauser had called last night.

The sandpiper off his flank raced in and picked up a sand crab he had kicked up, skedaddling away with the coin-sized animal. The bird dropped it onto the beach and stabbed at its belly with controlled jabs of its beak. For a few seconds the crustacean made a valiant effort but it eventually succumbed to the superior fire-power and the bird pulled its guts out in a jet of color.

The lighthouse shone weirdly in the early-morning haze and Jake could see two fishing boats heading around the point, to the lee side of Long Island. He figured that every boat in the area would be somewhere else by nine a.m.

As far as he could see both up and down the coast he was the only one out. He turned his head back toward the house, a geometric wedge of black against a blue-orange sky, as if Richard Neutra had designed the Rorschach test. The light off the water bounced red and orange against the glass and the dark line of the horizon crept down the wall of windows that faced the beach. The house looked like it was rising out of the dune and Jake remembered watching the sun come up on the beach with his mother after a night spent eating Mallomars and watching old movie marathons on PBS.

Why was he unable to focus here? What was scattering his concentration? Was it the mess inside the house coming awake in front of him? Was it the memory of his mother? Was it that fucker who had taken the woman and child apart? Was it those creepy little paintings inside the house? Or was it just the plain old fucking fact that he didn't want to be here? That he wanted to be back in the city with his wife and son, away from a place he had tried to forget for most of his life. After all, how did he have any responsibility here?

As the sun rose, its light crawled down the dunes and Jake felt the damp start to burn off his body. He stood on the sand, watching the edge of the world somewhere off to the east, and he knew that he wouldn't be able to leave. Not now. Not for a while. I came back to take care of my father's life, he told himself. And now there's work to do. There's a monster here. A monster no one else can handle. A monster no one knows but me. A monster no one else can find.

Skinned.

I came here to help my old man. Not because he deserves it or because I give a shit. But because it is the thing a son should do. And what am I going to do about the past? Nothing. Because it's not something I can fix.

Skinned.

It's not a coincidence.

Skinned.

I don't want it to be *him.*

Skinned.

Not now.

Skinned.

Not after all this time.

7

Jake stood in the kitchen sipping his eighth cup of fine convenience-store no-name blend topped off with a shoplifted packet of sugar from the coffee stand in the Kwik Mart. His hair was still wet from a hot shower and he felt better. At least comfortable in the doubts department, for whatever the fuck that was worth. From forty feet the endless line of black script tattooed into his flesh looked like a well-tailored shirt. He considered it part of the new him, one that began when he had stopped speedballing his way through life on heroin and cocaine and baby laxative. The end of the before. The end of the drugs and the booze and the heart attack trifecta that he had somehow managed to cheat. The end of the bad times before he had found Kay and Jeremy. Before they buried a cardiac resynchronization appliance under his chest muscle, almost in his armpit, to keep his heart from simply forgetting to beat. Before he had decided that life wasn't shitty all the time. Before the new and improved Jake Cole.

He still missed the cocaine and the heroin. The booze, too.

But the coffee was good, and he raised his cup in a silent toast to the before, to the memory of his mother. To the good old days. Back before the whole thing had somehow just gone up in flames.

He was pouring another cup when the bell rang. He wondered if it was Hauser's men or the news – both would be dropping by sooner rather than later. Out of habit, he dragged the cold stainless revolver off the counter, put it into the waistband at the small of his back, and walked to the door with the mug of coffee in his hands and another bologna on Wonder Bread clamped firmly in his teeth. He chomped down on the soft bread and it molded to the roof of his mouth. He tore the welfare sandwich away from his teeth and opened the door in one movement.

The bright panel of sun flooded the dark front hall and the space went from dead grays to dusty wood and chrome. Jake squinted into the figure at the door, haloed in light, features obscured in shadow, only one known quantity: male. The image slowly materialized, like an old-timey dial-up Internet connection, pixels slowly morphing into focus. Jake didn't recognize the face behind the big Ray-Ban aviators, but he recognized the smile again, still amazed that it wasn't broken like he had left it the first time they had met.

"Jakey!" Spencer yelled and barreled through the door, enveloping Jake in a bear hug that lifted him off the ground. Jake wasn't small, but he was eclipsed by the mass of the man squeezing him.

"Jakey!" he hollered again, this time in Jake's ear.

"Yeah, yeah. Jesus, you trying to make me deaf?" Jake wriggled out of the clinch, spilling coffee and losing the tail end of the sandwich.

His old friend backed away and held up the gun that Jake had put into his waistband. "Not very trusting I see."

"Not particularly, no," Jake said flatly and took it back. When it was in his hand, he looked the man up and down, taking in what twenty-eight years had done. "You look good, Spencer." And he did. Better than the flashing blue-and-red Christmas monster at the entrance to the death house last night.

Spencer nodded, smiled. "Thanks. Yeah. You—" He stopped and looked Jake over, taking in the sinewy build, the tattoos. His eyes slid back to the pistol in Jake's hand. "—too." He paused. "Really." Paused again. "Different. But good, man. Wow." He grabbed Jake by the shoulders and held him at arm's length like a client sizing up a painting. "You look just the same. Charles Bronson."

Jake rolled his eyes. "Thanks. Really. Come on in." He ushered his friend into the house. "Coffee?"

Spencer lumbered by and the floor shook. "Sure. Absolutely. Yeah. Holy shit, this place hasn't changed at all. I mean *at all*." He walked through the hall and stopped at the geometric model on the console by the door. It was the size of a library globe. "I forgot about that thing. Now it's like I was here yesterday."

Jake followed his eyes to the stainless-steel sphere. "I know what you mean." Jake walked into the house, took his FBI T-shirt from the back of a chair, and slid it on. "What do you take in your coffee? I got sugar."

"Black's perfect. Unless it's some chocolate vanilla crap, then just get me a glass of water. Tap water. The bottled shit gives you Alzheimer's and cancer—" He stopped cold, reconsidered his words. "Aw, shit, Jakey. I didn't mean—"

Jake dismissed it with a shrug. "Fuck it."

The question of whether or not his father had drunk too much plastic bottled booze was asked by that creepy little voice he had already heard too much of in the past half day. He topped off his coffee, poured one for Spencer – into an old superhero mug that had held brushes for three decades – then slid it across the counter. "Thanks for coming by." And he meant it, which surprised him almost as much as hearing himself say it out loud.

"You scared the shit out of everyone last night. And I mean *everyone*." Spencer stopped and his face grew serious, almost grave. "Even Hauser, and he's a tough man to get to."

"Has Hauser briefed you on a media plan?"

Spencer nodded. "He'll be handling all releases. He called all the reporters on your list and three of them were already in the area on another story. You've gained a lot of trust from the department so far."

"You here on any sort of a mission?"

Spencer waved it away. "I haven't told Hauser I know you. Not yet. I wanted to be allowed to drop by and have a talk before I was prohibited from dropping by and having a talk."

"I appreciate it. Especially after Scopes."

Spencer's tone dropped an octave. "Everybody's heard about that, Jakey. Scopes is mean."

"My kind of mean?"

Spencer looked at him and thought about the question. It was purely academic. They had met in second grade, after Spencer had transferred in from another school. Spencer, in an attempt to carry over his title as resident bully, decided he wanted alms from some of the smaller children. At recess, Spencer informed the eight-year-old Jake that he had to pay fifty cents a day for protection. Jake listened calmly as he stapled a project on leaves together, five or six sheets of construction paper adorned with oak, maple, and elm leaves. When Spencer was through talking, Jake looked up at him, smiled, then knocked his mouth into a bloody mess with two rapid slams of the heavy steel stapler. While Spencer was on the floor, teeth and blood leaking from his face, Jake leaned over and asked, "Protection from what?"

They had stayed best friends until Jake walked out nine years later.

"Nobody's your kind of mean, Jakey." He took another sip of his coffee. "Can I ask you why you didn't let me know you were coming to town?"

It was an honest question – one Jake had expected. He thought about lying, about saying that he had been busy, that he had his hands full with his father's affairs, that he hadn't planned on staying around for long. But he had tried to give up lying when he had kicked the drugs and he had gotten pretty good at the truth. At least his version of it. "I spent a lot of time trying to forget this place. You remind me of what I had no intention of coming back to."

The big cop in the civilian clothes took another sip of his coffee and nodded seriously. "Thanks for not bullshitting me." He put the mug down. "So what *are* you going to share, Special Agent Jake Cole?"

"You first. How's your father?"

Billy's father, Tiny Spencer, had been a bike racer in the late sixties and early seventies, racing the American circuit for Suzuki. For eight years he traveled the country, chewing up racetracks with the likes of Halsy Knox and the rest of the death wishers. Then his almost record-breaking stint as a corporate rider ended on an August afternoon in Bakersfield, California. The crash tore both legs off at the knee and Tiny's racing days were over. So Tiny had bought a place in Montauk, because he hated Texas where he was from, and began building custom racing canopies in his garage. Within six months he was making more money than he had as a circuit racer. Jake recalled that the house had always smelled of fiberglass and solvent.

Spencer walked down into the living room and stared out at the ocean and Jake remembered how everybody who came here was

47

always drawn to the same thing – the big line of the Atlantic that didn't stop until it hit Portugal. "Dad died five years ago. Prostate cancer. He said it was from his ass sitting on wheels all those years. First bikes, then the chair." Spencer's shoulders slumped when he saw the weed-covered pool, lily pads and lush algae, a deep green against the perfect blue of the ocean beyond. "I remember when this place was like a TV show. Your mom wiggling around the place in Chanel, getting us sandwiches with the crusts cut off and letting us stay up late on Creature Feature Night. Mallomars and Pop-Tarts. And your dog, Lewis." He paused, and the silence said he regretted bringing it up. "Remember those days?"

Spencer's gaze shifted to the algae-lush surface of the pool, a monument to the past. "I remember that pool. Jesus, where did it go?" Of all of Jake's friends, only Spencer had permission to use the pool owing to that Pablo Picasso had decorated the bottom with a large winking cubist vagina. Spencer had been appreciative of the painting until he had seen his first vagina in real life; he had been perplexed at – and grateful for – its lack of ninety-degree angles.

Jake shrugged. There was no conceivable way to answer the question – rhetorical or not – without opening things he wanted to stay closed. Things like his dog.

Spencer took another sip of coffee to fill the dead zone in the conversation, then said, in a documentary filmmaker's voice, "*How did Billy Spencer become Officer William Spencer?* would be the next question. Hauser saved me. And I don't want any jokes. I am not a born-again anything, Jake. After you left I tried to keep things the same. Kept shucking oysters for the yacht club, chasing the summer girls. You know, the same old *same old*. But that only worked for so long. So I floated. For a decade. But you know how time has that funny little way of catching up with you? Yeah, well, one night I'm driving home from work and I'm hammered. Hauser pulls me over and has me get out of the truck. I can't even stand. He can arrest me. Have my truck towed. You know what he does? He gets in my Ford and parks it in a field off the road. Then he drives me home. It was one of those light-bulb moments you hear about; I realized that not everyone in this line of work is out to get people. Some of them – guys like Hauser, I mean – just want to make the place a little better. So a week later I wrote the police exam and did pretty good, well enough that they contacted me to see if I needed any encouraging to go to the interviews. After the interviews they went at me with a background check, psychological profile, polygraph test. I did the twenty-eight-week program, and Hauser hired me right out of the gate. Now here we are." A lifetime summed up in a few sentences.

They stopped speaking for a few minutes, both listening to the sound of the ocean. Jake finally asked, "What can you tell me about Hauser?" He pulled out a cigarette, brought it to life.

"Born here, played ball for Southampton High. Football scholarship to the University of Texas. First string quarterback for three seasons. Went pro. Number six draft choice for his year in the NFL. Played four solid games for the Steelers before he had his right knee bent ninety degrees against design. You'd probably like him if you got to know him. He's a capable guy, it takes a lot for him to go green like last night."

"Last night would be tough on anyone."

Spencer mulled the statement around for a few seconds, then held out his mug for a refill. "You seemed to be fine with it."

Jake heard it coming out in his voice. The worry. "It's what I do."

Spencer nodded like that had answered it all, but his face was still playing around with a few questions. "History? Wife? That kind of stuff," he said, changing the subject.

What could Jake say to that? *Heroin, a cardiac resynchronization therapy defibrillator sewn into my chest, drinking problem. NA, AA. Somehow got through it. Met Kay. Makes me laugh, makes me horny. A boy, Jeremy.* "Her name's Kay." *I figure out the event cascade at a crime scene faster than a team of battlefield anthropologists.* "I've been with the bureau for twelve years now." *Half of them clean.* "A son, Jeremy." *Who I call Moriarty because he thinks it's a cool name and I am terrified he will someday find out that I don't know if I am a good man.* "Live in New York. Kay plays with the orchestra – cellist." *I am on the road eleven months a year.* "I'm back because my father set himself on fire and smashed through the front window." *And pissed off that the bastard didn't have the courtesy to die.*

"I wish you would have said good-bye. Or sent a letter. Something. Anything. I went into the city to find you a couple of times."

Jake stared at Spencer, wondering if he was supposed to say something here because Spencer had paused, like he wanted some sort of dialogue. Jake rinsed his mug under the faucet and placed it in the rack beside the sink. A few drops of water beaded on its surface.

"Everyone figured you'd come back some day. And here you are. More than half a lifetime later."

Jake shrugged, as if that was some sort of an answer. He hoped Spencer would let it go.

"What'd you do when you got to New York?" Spencer pushed.

Jake remembered his visit to David Finch – his father's art dealer. Jake had asked for thirty-one dollars, so he'd be able to stay at the YMCA while he found a job, got on his feet. He promised to pay it back when he could. Finch had said no. That Jacob wouldn't approve. That he was sorry. And then he had closed the door in Jake's face.

Two nights of no meals and no place safe to sleep later, Jake had sold a little piece of himself – the first of many. And learned, with an odd mix of horror and pride, that he was a survivor. The next part of his life had faded and been forgotten. The drugs helped. For a very long time they had helped. "Got on with my life."

Jake's eyes left Spencer and slid down to the safari pool out on the deck. In a way there was something serene, almost meditative about it. Maybe it wasn't a sign of neglect after all. Maybe his father had been going Zen.

"What, exactly, do you do, Jake?"

"I paint the dead." He looked back to the pond/pool.

"Another great American artist," Spencer said, and poured his coffee down the drain.

8

His father's jaw hung slack, cheeks dented in as if an invisible hand squeezed his face. Charred gray stubble flecked his skin and white specks of mucus hung at the corners of his closed eyes and open mouth. The left side of his face was a black-red mess of scab and antibiotic ointment bisected by a long sutured scar that ran from eyebrow to chin. His hands were bandaged knobs at the ends of his wrists, bloody gauze clubs. He snored loudly, the tremor of his voice shaking the air in the room. Even in medicated sleep the man commanded attention.

The room was full of flowers of every conceivable color, hue, and proportion. It smelled like a jungle, and Jake wondered what his old man would say about the composition.

The pneumatic door closer hissed softly and Jake turned to see a nurse in hospital blues come in. She was small, compact, and there was something familiar about her. "Has anyone asked you about the mail?"

Jake's eyes swept back to his father, then to her brown stare, then down to her name tag. *Rachael*, it read. He would have much preferred a last name to go with the woman. "Mail?" was all he said.

She nodded. "The mail department called up and asked the station what they should do."

Jake looked at her, wondering what the hell she was talking about. "About what?" he asked.

"About your father's mail. It's piling up."

Jake sighed, tightened up his chest to process oxygen a little more efficiently, then shrugged. "Just put it in his nightstand. I'll take care of it."

The nurse stared at him for a few seconds, then her head began to shake side to side. She raised an eyebrow. "There's an *awful lot*, Mr. Coleridge."

"Cole. My name is Cole."

She paused for a second, as if her hard drive had crashed. "Um, there's nine sacks of mail for your father downstairs. I suspect that a lot more is coming. There will be more flowers, too."

Jake's brain was still hung up on trying to figure out what was so familiar about her. "Nine sacks?" he asked, jerking a thumb at his father. "For him?"

"Apparently so, yes."

Jake let out a sigh that he followed with a loose shrug. It was hard to forget that his father was famous but he had somehow managed it. But the world of the triple W would no doubt be abuzz with news of his father's accident. "Any suggestions?"

"Peter Beard stayed overnight once. His people took care of everything. We're not equipped to handle this much mail."

Jake smiled. "I don't have any people." *Or a desire to be here,* he wanted to add. "I'll get someone to come collect it." His father's snoring hitched with an interrupted breath, then stopped. "Do you have a pediatrics ward?" he asked.

Nurse Rachael nodded. "Of course, second floor. Why?"

"Take all of my father's flowers to pediatrics. Hand them out to the children. Throw the cards out."

The nurse nodded slowly as she tried to find something wrong in his directives. When she couldn't find a loophole, she smiled. "That's a wonderful idea." Suddenly, Jake realized what was so familiar about her.

Jake turned back to his father. "Has he been awake at all?"

Nurse Rachael nodded. "He was up last night, at the beginning of my shift." As if to accentuate the point, she suppressed a yawn with the back of her hand. "He was in pretty good spirits."

"Him?" he asked, not meaning to sound so surprised. Jake could not remember his father ever being in good spirits. The light etched his face with deep shadow, hollowed out his cheeks. He looked dead. Then the snoring started back up and the illusion was broken. "Did he say anything?"

"We talked a little. He asked for a drink and I got him a glass of water. When he took a sip he asked, 'What the hell is this piss?' Apparently he was hoping for scotch." She smiled. "He seems to like me. He gets agitated around the other nurses. But a little of his fear seems to leave when I'm here. He keeps telling me that I look like Mia."

Jake's vital signs fluttered and he felt a little more of the old fear come back. So his father had noticed it, too. "You do." He took in a breath and thought back to the days when you could smoke in a hospital room. Glory Days, Springsteen had called them. "Mia was my mother. My father hasn't spoken her name in thirty-three years."

Nurse Rachael – look-alike – nodded knowingly. "Divorce?"

Jake thought back to the last time he had seen his mother. It had been after a gallery opening in the city when he was twelve. She drove home by herself, leaving Jacob to his sycophants, his critics, and his booze. She sat down on the corner of the bed and he woke in a fog. Her hair was tussled from the open convertible and she was wearing a black cocktail dress and a pearl necklace. She smelled faintly of perfume and salt air.

She had leaned over and kissed him. Told him she loved him. That she was going back out for cigarettes. And a bag of Mallomars. They'd go down to the beach and watch the sun come up from the sleeping bag. She rubbed his back, then went out for smokes and cookies.

She never came back.

"No," he shook his head, and the loose image of that night fell apart. "My mother was murdered."

9

June 1978
Sumter Point

Jake was deep in the heat stage of REM sleep when she put her hand on his back, and his skin felt like a smooth sun-baked stone. She rubbed gently, feeling bones under the skin. Eventually he woke, rolled over.

She just watched him, waiting to see if he would make the rare transition from sleeping child to awake child; most of the time he would just smile at her, close his eyes, and drift off into wherever it was that he went when he slept.

"What time is it?" Jake stretched and his pajama shirt climbed up, exposing ribs and tummy.

She looked at her watch. "Four thirteen."

"Dad come back with you?"

His mother's face, a beautiful mixture of gentle shadows, smiled. "The show went well and he wanted to stay and talk. I wanted to come back to see you."

"You should have stayed," Jake said through a gaping yawn. "Did you have a nice hotel room? The kind with free soap?"

She smiled, rubbed his leg. "Yeah, the kind with free soap." She leaned over and kissed him on the forehead, something he was not yet embarrassed about – at least not in private. She had driven the coastal highway with the top down and she smelled of perfume and salt, that humid ocean smell that gets into everything by the water. "What did you do tonight, Jakey? Anything fun?"

"It was all right. Billy came over. We watched the Creature Feature. *Battle of the Gargantuas* was on but we didn't have any Mallomars. Billy decided that he wanted to sleep at home."

She ran her hand along his leg and kissed him again. "I have to run back to the Kwik Mart to get some cigarettes. I'm pretty sure they have Mallomars, too. You want me to get you some?"

It was the kind of thing his mother always did for him and he had to constantly resist the urge to abuse her kindness. Even at the age of twelve he could see that his dad did that enough for the both of them. "I'm okay, Mom."

"I'll be back in fifteen minutes. If you want, we can go down to the beach and watch the sun come up. I'll put some coffee in Dad's old army Thermos and we'll cuddle up under a blanket and pretend that we're the last two people on the planet and apes have taken over."

"Cool."

She smiled, stood up. "See? I'm not so bad for an old lady." She was thirty-seven.

She leaned down and kissed him again and he couldn't smell cigarettes on her and he knew that she was going to go to the store whether he asked her to or not. "Get a big bag," he said.

"You got it."

They found her car a mile from the Kwik Mart, pulled into the driveway of an empty summer rental.

There was no blood – no signs of a struggle – just her Pagoda sitting on the gravel with over half a tank of gas in it. A fresh pack of Marlboros sat on the middle console, a single cigarette missing from the pack. The bag of Mallomars and her purse were on the passenger's seat. Two cookies were gone but the $25,000 in cash from the gallery show was still in her purse. Nothing missing but those two cookies and a single cigarette.

What was left of Mia Coleridge lay on a red patch of gravel 200 yards away.

10

Jake sat in a vinyl and aluminum chair jammed in between the sink and the window, staring at – but not seeing – his father. His mind was walking through the rooms at the Farmers' house up the highway. He was in one of the guest rooms – an *empty* guest room – looking at the floor. He squatted down on his haunches and focused on something on the threshold. He had only seen it glimmer for a second, then he was past it, and it had become invisible. He leaned forward and the nearly straight line of a long strand of yellow hair, almost white, jumped off the topography of the wood grain.

He moved his mind's eye back and forth, taking it in. It was twenty-six or twenty-seven inches in length, and thin, wispy. It was well past yellow and on its way to white. He hoped Hauser's guys had bagged it.

Why hadn't he said anything last night? Because he was used to working with the bureau boys, and their forensic guys never missed things like that. In a way, it was a test. A test he hoped Hauser's people passed.

He'd see the medical examiner in a few hours and there would be a lot more in the way of answers. Until he talked with the ME, and examined Madame X and the child, all he had was the three-dimensional model in his head. More than enough to work with. Enough to kill a few hours with at least.

In his head, Jake left the room with the yellow hairs, turned, and walked on down the hall to the room where the murderer had spread Madame and Little X all over the floor. He stared down at them. Eyes massaging the scarlet mess for … for …

"Can I get a drink?" a voice said out of the darkness and the model fell apart. He was back in the hospital in the chair in the corner and he blinked once, fiercely, and saw his father staring at him.

He had lost none of the worldliness that had made him a favorite of critics and fans alike. He had never pretended to be polished or special. He believed he was what he was: a painter. And now he was a thirsty painter. "Well, dickhead, can I get a drink?" he asked again, his voice hitching up with a tremor of irritation.

Jake stood up. "A drink? Sure." Then he remembered Nurse Rachael's story about the scotch. "There's only water. No scotch." Staring his old man in the eyes now, he felt nothing, not even a glimmer of the old poison. And his father's snarl didn't push any of the scare buttons it used to. Then again, he wondered if he even owned scare buttons anymore or if they had all been lost along the way.

The old man smiled as if he were talking to a person of diminished capacity. "Of course there's no scotch. It's a hospital. You think they hand out scotch at a fucking hospital? What kind of a volunteer are you, anyway? Sitting there staring off into space. Aren't you supposed to be reading to me or scratching my ass or some such bullshit since I can't do anything myself?" He held up his hands, two clumsy stubs of white gauze, black-red where dark punches of blood had seeped through. "Why don't you—" And then he stopped abruptly, as if someone had pulled the plug to his vocal transformer. After a few seconds of examining Jake's face, he asked, "You look a little like Charles Bronson. My son looked a lit—" And then he stopped again, voice box on pause. He looked at Jake for a few heavy breaths, examining his features. "I can see it in your eyes," the old man said, something about him suddenly very still.

"See what?" Jake asked.

"The dead people have started showing up."

11

The room was cold and humid and the air tasted of steel and disinfectant. But the lighting was good and Dr. Nancy Reagan knew how to run a lab. There were only two permanent autopsy tables in the room, and Jake was grateful that they weren't in the middle of the busy season. He often wondered how little country offices managed to solve any crimes at all with the limited resources they had; the ME for the greater Manhattan area had sixty-five full-time autopsy tables and a four-floor lab that occupied an entire city block. Not to mention a backup network of nearly 1,000 folding units in the event of a natural disaster or pandemic situation.

Two bodies lay under semitransparent plastic sheets. Both were laid out straight now, the rigor mortis having either been eased or broken out of the joints. One body took up a lot less real estate under the sheet. Both looked black under the semitransparent polyethylene covers, only going to red where a wet bit pushed up against the plastic.

Sheriff Hauser stood at the foot of the two tables, his arms crossed tightly across his chest, his jaw clenching its way through half a pack of very strong mint gum. His hat was on a seat by the door and he stood a little lopsided – not very pronounced, but noticeable if you paid attention.

Dr. Reagan had a home-court advantage here and she pretended to be busy for a few minutes before heading over. Jake thought about going to her desk and picking her up by the elbow but decided that he'd let her have her literal fifteen seconds. Of all the links in the chain here, Reagan was second in importance only to Sheriff Hauser – and it was an arguable distinction at this point of the investigation.

Jake stood beside the longer body, his hands on his hips, his breathing down into the slow range, waiting for Reagan's power trip to blow itself out so they could all learn a little more about what had happened to Madame and Little X.

The ME finally stood up, straightened her lab coat, took a sip of coffee, and came over, her pumps – elegant and black – clack-clack-clacking on the cold linoleum.

She stared down at the autopsy report. "First off, Special Agent Cole was right. I don't have DNA confirmation yet but I do have a matched blood type that points to mother and child. AB negative."

"One person per hundred and sixty-seven individuals," Jake repeated from memory.

Reagan raised her eyes above the lenses of her glasses. "Female. Roughly five foot one inch tall. Age twenty-five to thirty-five. I'd lean to early thirties. Ninety pounds, postmortem. Pre? We can say roughly one-twenty, depending on how much subcutaneous fat she had. I'd go with very little. She was fit."

"COD?" Hauser asked.

Reagan's eyes stayed balanced above her glasses. "She bled to death. They both did."

Hauser nodded like he regretted asking, then lapsed into his former sullenness.

"Distinguishing physical history?" Jake asked, his hand slowly climbing for the head of the sheet.

The medical examiner shook her head. "Her right wrist has been fractured. It's an old break, most likely a fall. It was compound. Other than that, no previously broken bones. No wounds, operations, or deep-tissue scars on her body." Dr. Reagan flipped through her notes, and pointed to the corpse laid out on the stainless-steel table.

"Last night makes up for that," Hauser said, barely above a whisper.

Reagan took a deep breath, but there was nothing theatrical or pensive about it, she just wanted enough oxygen to run through her findings. "Three fractures to her jaw caused by a single impact with a pointed object – it left an octagonal indent in the bone. Her nose was broken and her left orbit was caved in. She was hit twice in the sternum, the first blow breaking the fourth through seventh rib on the left, the second snapping the third through seventh on the right. These strikes were probably used to keep her from making too much noise."

"No one would have heard her way out there anyway," Jake said flatly.

Hauser shifted in his boots, and looked over at Jake, thinking back to the sonofabitch he had been to Scopes last night.

"Race?" Jake asked, and locked his fingers around one of the plastic tarps. It felt like silk snakeskin.

"Her eyelids were gone. No skin between the toes. Nothing."

Hauser swallowed again, remembering that Jake had got down on the blood-caked carpet and peered between the woman's toes like some kind of perverted rubbernecker.

Jake peeled back the plastic sheet.

The sheriff saw Madame X, laid out like a blistering red roast. Her body had lost some of the humanity. He was grateful that it was no longer posed in the horror of agony, but in the *Now I lay me down to sleep* position that did absolutely nothing to soften the marks of violence on it. She still looked used, violated, and Hauser's gum was tinged with the acid bursts of spit from the back of his throat when he swallowed. He turned around and spat the gum into a garbage can with a single bloody latex glove stuck just inside the rim.

Dr. Reagan looked up at Jake. "We sent DNA samples out to the bureau this morning. Do you know what kind of turnaround times we're looking at?"

"Mitochondrial is twelve hours; we'll get race, haplogroup, and confirmation of mother–child relationship between the two victims. Nuclear will take about seventy-two and hopefully we'll find her in the system. Criminal record. Government employment. Diplomat. Missing person."

Hauser raised his head, cleared his throat. "I put a search out on every case of domestic violence in the past six months where there is a two- to four-year-old boy at home. Maybe she had a husband who beat her and she ran. Maybe he found her."

Jake shook his head. "This was not done by an angry husband."

Dr. Reagan paused patiently, and her eyes went to Jake's skin. She looked down at his hands, crosshatched in dark ink that swirled out of his sleeve, down over his wrists, over his metacarpals, ending along the first knuckle of his phalanges. In all her time as medical examiner, she had never had anyone who looked or talked like Jake Cole come through – especially not in the capacity of law-enforcement specialist.

Jake squinted at Madame X and took a flashlight off of a trolley to his right without moving his eyes. He leaned forward, flicked it on, and peered into her mouth. The splintered teeth glowed white and the dark black of the flesh went to a bright red under the harsh glare. "Dental records?"

"She shattered most of her teeth – the FBI labs said the dental reconstruction will take about two weeks. I can tell you that she had three fillings – two porcelain, one silver. Her teeth broke because they weren't that strong to begin with. She had a vitamin D deficiency at some point and she's never really recovered."

Jake rolled the sheet back and away from Madame X. Bits of dried blood and muscle tissue cracked off and rained down. Jake put the sheet at the foot of the stainless-steel table and stared at the deep Y incision in her chest, now fastened with bloody baseball stitches in a braided line.

Reagan removed the shroud from the boy.

Hauser closed his eyes once, hard, and when he opened them his mouth was a tight line that said he was back in cop mode. At least for a few minutes.

Jake ignored the child and kept his attention locked on the dead woman on the table. He thought about the hairs he had seen earlier in his head. "What about the blond hairs on the floor of the guest room? There were more in the living room in front of the window, too."

The effect on Hauser was instantaneous. "What blond hairs? I didn't see any—"

"I didn't see them until this morning."

Hauser was frozen in a position that said he was either going to run or hit someone. "You didn't go back in the house this morning. My deputy would have—"

Jake tried not to sound flippant. This was the part they never understood. "Not the real house." He lifted his hand, tapped his index against his temple. "I recorded everything I saw last night, then went through it this morning. And I found hairs."

Dr. Reagan gave him a hard brown stare. "They are equine."

Hauser, still stuck on disbelief, simply repeated the last word as if it were a question. "Equine?"

Jake thought out loud. "The Farmers are sailors – not horse people. I didn't see one ribbon or photo in the place that would make me believe that they were horse people. And if the hairs had come from the antiques, they'd be black."

"The antiques?" Hauser asked.

"Antique chairs and sofas are stuffed with horsehair." He turned back to Dr. Reagan. "Tox scan?"

Reagan flipped through the printout and the pages rattled. Jake saw a coffee ring flip by. "I appreciate the late night."

Reagan's subway-tile hue darkened a little, as if she were done holding her breath. "There are plenty of slow days." She stopped. "Toxicology. All negative. I did a CBC, a WBC, and a WBC differential."

Jake waved it away. "That's perfect."

"Her liver was pretty beat up, her gamma-glutamyl levels were high but aspartate levels were perfect, so it's an old problem. She gave up drinking a while ago.

"She had renal issues at one point – her kidneys had been stressed by something she used to take. Function was somewhere around seventy percent. I doubt she even knew she had problems unless she had a blood work done in the past little while. She smoked. Had at least one child. No venereal diseases. She was fit at the time of death – I'd say in super shape. No subcutaneous fat.

No fat deposits in abdomen, posterior, under the arms, or around the neck. Her heart was in stellar shape."

"What was she skinned with?" Hauser asked.

Jake stared down at the crescent-shaped ridges in the muscle. Without meaning to, he said, "Single-edged knife with a recurve blade. Heavy, probably a hunting knife."

Reagan looked at her notes and nodded. "About eight inches."

Hauser shook his head. "Not an ideal knife."

"Meaning?" Jake asked.

Hauser swallowed. "A small curve-bladed skinning knife would do the job in half the time."

Jake nodded. "What does that tell us?"

"That he had time?"

"Bingo."

Jake examined the thin ridges along her muscles where the tip of the knife had left its mark, removing a little more of who the woman was with each swish of the razor-sharp edge. "Vaginal wounds?"

Hauser had fallen back into a nervous silence, his lopsided stance a little more pronounced now. His eyes were no longer on the woman, but spent their time nailed to Jake.

Reagan shook her head. "Nothing. Wash, swabs, and pelvic exam were clean. Nothing was put into her vagina."

Jake was examining the bottom of Madame X's foot. He ran his index up the muscle as if he expected it to curl in a ticklish reflex. "Size six feet," he said softly. "Small."

Hauser's head tilted to one side in that canine way that was becoming familiar to Jake. His mouth opened up and in a monotone voice he said, "Female, roughly thirty-two years of age. One old break in her wrist. Slender athletic build. Good muscle mass. Light smoker. Weakened kidney function. Bad liver from an old alcohol problem. Three fillings and an old iron deficiency. Size six feet and her killer did not interact with her in a sexual manner."

Jake held up his hand. "Don't say that. We don't know yet."

Hauser pointed at Madame X. "No vaginal wounds, Dr. Reagan's words, not mine." Then, seeing his arm pointing at the dead, he let it drop to his side. "Was this about sex?"

"Not in any way you or I could relate to. But to the perp? That bastard got a massive endorphin rush out of it. It's too early to tell if this is sexual for him. Where's her skin?"

"I don't know. It wasn't there. We haven't—"

"Because it was taken. Maybe it was a little porn to jerk off to later so he can feel all big and powerful and in control of the storm raging inside the fucked-up fusebox that passes for his brain."

Hauser took a step back. "Jesus Christ."

Jake looked at Hauser, saw his hands twitching, his face going green like last night. "Go get some air. I'll fill you in when we're done." Then he turned to Dr. Reagan. "Can I get copies of her tox scans? Especially the GGT, ALT, and AST ratios," he asked, ignoring Hauser.

Hauser spun and darted out of the room.

The sound of a kicked garbage can was the last noise before the sheriff's steps disappeared into the stairwell. Jake ignored the sound of the metal lid rolling in faster and faster circles and turned to the smaller hump on the next table.

"Tell me about the child," he said.

12

22,216 Statute Miles Above the Atlantic Ocean

Sent into space during the height of President Ronald Reagan's Strategic Defense Initiative, the geostationary satellite began its life as a tool of the Cold War, using thermal imaging to track nuclear submarines via the heat generated by their reactors. Under the watchful eye of the Strategic Defense Initiative Organization, the satellite – internally designated *Loki* – was launched in early 1985. A few months later, perestroika began, and the Iron Curtain quickly started to show signs of metal fatigue. But Loki continued to track Soviet naval traffic in the Atlantic for eight more years, until the SDIO was retooled as the Ballistic Missile Defense Organization under President Clinton's administration. The satellite, written off the books as so much obsolete space garbage, was donated to the National Hurricane Center, and retasked to serve the people of the United States in spying on a less predictable adversary – Mother Nature.

Now, a quarter-century after it had been launched, and performing a task for which it had not been designed, Loki's unfeeling eyes stared down at the planet from its vantage point in space. Its taskmasters had focused its vast array of attention on a massive weather system that had somehow sprung to life nine days ago off the coast of Africa, gorging itself on heat and seawater, growing into a Category 5 hurricane – a hurricane now called Dylan.

Loki's data showed that in the past five hours, the distance from Dylan's center to his outermost closed isobar was nearly nine degrees of latitude. Dylan was now the largest Atlantic hurricane in recorded history, with a diameter of more than 1,200 miles. This data in itself would usually have been enough to cause a panic at the National Hurricane Center, but Dylan was not yet finished reaching into its bag of dirty tricks.

Dylan soon began to generate massive vertical winds. These winds carried particles of water off the ocean up through the body of the storm with a force stronger than regular evaporation by orders of magnitude. As these vertical wind-driven water particles, known to meteorologists as hydrometeors, were slammed upward, they rubbed against one another. This friction generated a charge in the water particles. The hydrometeors separated by weight and charge – the negatively charged (and heavy) particles dropped to the lower regions of the hurricane, and the positively charged (and lighter) particles rose to the top of the massive storm turbine. This separation of positively and negatively charged water molecules created a new weapons system for the hurricane.

Dylan had just gone electric.

13

Hauser slammed through the doors and chewed up linoleum with an efficient long-legged stride. He was trying to burn off the sickening thud that had blossomed in his chest just after Dr. Reagan had pulled the plastic sheet off the three-foot chunk of bled meat that used to be a living, breathing child. Hauser's hand was still clamped around the rubber grip of his Sig and the muscles in his long jaw pulsed like snakes under his skin. For the first time he could recall he wished he had chosen another type of work. Contracting, maybe. He had always liked taping sheetrock – the pay wasn't bad and you never took your work home with you at night.

And it beat the hell out of looking at skinned children.

A half-dozen reporters sprang up in his path, microphones out, the bright lights from the cameras actually heating his skin. Hauser stopped, took a deep breath, and tried to look calm. "I will have a press release for you in exactly thirty minutes."

"Have the autopsies been completed?"

"Do you have any suspects?"

"Can you release their names?"

Hauser stared down the cameras and said, "Give me half an hour to get a statement together. I promise that this will be the first release of many. Please make sure you all leave your coordinates – including your producers' coordinates – at the front desk. We *will* keep you informed." He turned away and plowed into his office, irritated at the gratitude he felt toward Jake for prepping him in how to deal with the media; without Jake's coaching, Hauser knew he would have already fucked his relationship with the news teams six ways past repairable. And he didn't want to confuse gratitude with *like*. He didn't want to like Jake. Not one little bit.

The sheriff stopped at his receptionist's desk. "I have to put a statement together for the double homicide. Give me twenty-five minutes to write it up and you can type it and print it up for me. While I'm working on it, I need everything you have on the Coleridge family. I know Mrs. Coleridge had some sort of an accident. I want everything there is."

Jeannine uh-huhed and no-problemed, and for a bright angry second Hauser wanted to drag her by her hair down to the lab so she could look at the kid who had been peeled like a piece of squirming screaming fruit to see if she could keep that same bored-to-death timbre in her voice. Instead, he walked into his office and kicked the door shut.

He went to the bar, pulled out a glass, and poured himself a caffeine-free Coke from the little stainless fridge his wife had bought him as a birthday gift last year. When he had downed the can, he popped another. Then burped.

Dr. Reagan had been very precise with her diction. *Skinned* was too blunt a term for a profession as elegant as forensic pathology so she had opted for *de-epithelialized* instead. Who used words like that? While sipping a cold coffee and standing over a kid who – at only three feet tall – still managed to make all the multibody car wrecks of the past year look like underachievers.

First he had de-epithelialized the son – they knew this because the mother's blood was all over the child, but the child's blood was absent from the mother (except the palms of her hands). Madame X had been held down while someone peeled her kid. This one took the *Best in Show* trophy. Maybe even a *Lifetime Achievement Award*. It was the saddest thing he had ever taken part in. How the fuck did you word something like that for those press assholes? He had seen other sheriffs thrust into the national spotlight. He had watched the police chief of Montgomery County, Charles Moose, examined ten times a day for three solid months. Jake had taught him how to avoid that, completely, by making it clear that the only rules were *his* rules, and that he'd throw anyone who got in the way of his investigation in jail and deal with the courts as soon as he was finished with the case. So he had followed Jake's lead and laid it out with conviction. Because when that freaky-deaky, heebie-jeebie tattoo freak opened his mouth, he seemed to be channeling from the other side. And that worried Hauser. Maybe even frightened him a little.

But what Hauser needed right now was to clear his head for this press release. He had to take his mind off of the cluster-fuck he felt brewing. Dr. Sobel had taught him to relax by focusing on something that he saw as a mini vacation. Hauser had thought of it as so much touchy-feely bullshit, but one afternoon after a particularly grueling day, he had tried it, recalling Sobel's Gins-bergian delivery. *When the going gets rough, take a little time for yourself – focus on something that makes you feel good.* And with this fruity talk ringing in his ears, Hauser had taught himself to relax by spending time with his hunting trophies.

The centerpiece of the paneled wall behind his desk was the big buck he had taken up near Albany four falls back. He was a beautiful mount, a nine-pointer, and the cleaning staff had very specific instructions on how to dust him. Flanking the buck were two shoulder-mounted black bears, both taken on a bow. Near the coat rack was the head of a Dall sheep he had bagged on his trip to Sitka, Alaska, during a sheriffs' convention last fall. And by the window, surveying the office with those two huge brown eyes, was Bernie, a big bull moose.

Hauser still felt that the space was incomplete without an elk, and he had been planning an elk trip with Martin, his brother-in-law, for some time. They were supposed to leave in two days. Now, with a double homicide on his lawn and a storm rolling in, he had to call Martin to cancel; Martin lived in Arizona and would that's-too-bad and what-a-shame him for a few minutes before calling one of his rich golf buddies to step in and pinch-hit. And Hauser'd have to wait until next year for that elk. Sonofabitch.

The sheriff reached out and stroked the fur of the big buck, concentrating on his breathing. To Hauser, this was how his wife described yoga. He stood there, staring into the lifeless glass eyeballs, thinking about hunting and feeling like a stereotype.

Five minutes later, Jeannine came in, carrying a folded banker's box that was jury-rigged with at least three kinds of tape and looked like it was stretching her arms while simultaneously clamping her breasts together. "There are two more, let me know when you want them." Her tone said she was not particularly thrilled about another trip to the archive room to carry a forty-pound box.

"Bring the other two up," he said, not quite grumbling but coming close.

Jeannine nodded, popped her gum, and dropped the heavy box down on the corner of his desk. Hauser was surprised that no dust puffed out. She shut the door when she left.

He picked up one of the yellow legal pads he liked to use for notes, and tried to come up with a statement that would in no way compromise any of the secrecy that an investigation of this type depended on. Cole had said to keep the media fed reliably so they could educate the public about what had happened and at the same time solicit information that might help advance the case. Sure. Easy. A child could write it. Suddenly Hauser regretted his football scholarship.

He had managed to get the words, *In an effort to keep the public informed*, down, then the phone lit up.

"What?" he snapped.

"There's a Mr. Ken Dennison on the line. He's with the National Hurricane Center. Says he needs to talk to you right now."

Hauser's brow knitted up. "You sure he's not media?"

"He said it was the most important call of the day."

Hauser put the cap on his pen and tossed it onto the desk even though he was unconvinced – anything was better than trying to come up with a prime-time version of what had happened at the house up the beach. "Put him through."

In three seconds Mr. Dennison was introducing himself. "Carl Dennison, Sheriff Hauser. I'm with the National Hurricane Center. Advance warning department. We have news on Dylan."

He said, "Yeah," like he could care less.

"It's headed straight for your doorstep. All our computer models say you're the landfall point."

"Shit."

"Sheriff, are you familiar with the hurricane of 1938?"

Hauser hadn't been born in 1938 but the storm had been so devastating that it was still the benchmark against which every storm in the area was judged. He had grown up knowing all the horror stories, the most frightening being how the Westhampton cinema had been washed out to sea, killing twenty cinemagoers and the projectionist. As far as natural disasters went, it was a hard one to beat. "Of course."

"When that hit the US, it had softened from a Cat Five to a Cat Three. I don't think we are going to be as lucky with this one."

Hauser squeezed the bridge of his nose. He didn't like hearing the word lucky applied to the big one of 1938. He said, "Shit," again.

"We don't see any way it is going to cool down enough to burn off any of its energy before it hits you. This is going to sound a little funny, but you are going to need walkie-talkies."

"Walkie-talkies? You're kidding, right?"

"Sheriff, the magnitude of what's heading your way is something that there are no recorded benchmarks for. Dylan generates more electricity in a minute than a Westinghouse nuclear reactor puts out in a week."

"Whoa, whoa," Hauser held up his hand, trying to stave off bad news. "Hurricanes don't have lightning."

"You need new data. Rita, Emily, and Katrina – three of the most powerful storms of 2005 – were all electrical hurricanes. The satellites are picking up flashes in the wall of Dylan's eye that are probably the largest in recorded history. Per meter he probably measures fifty percent stronger than the worst of mesoscale thunderstorms. And he's twelve thousand percent larger than any thunderstorm on record. You can expect lightning like no one's ever seen before, Sheriff."

There was something else in Dennison's voice, something behind the bad news. It wasn't huge, but it was important, because Hauser could hear it; he was used to listening to what people said between their lines of dialogue. "What are you *not* telling me?" Hauser asked.

"This is about two hours before we are past the tipping point, but everything says you are going to be asked to evacuate your county. I'd start now if I were you. Just get everyone the fuck out, excuse my frankness."

Hauser wanted to say that Montauk wasn't like New Orleans, where the poor would be left behind and nobody would be to blame. No, here the out-of-work fishermen and the old canning-factory layoffs would love to take a trip on a government bus to a week in a gymnasium in some other state where they could get free coffee and play cards all day. Maybe get new sneakers. No, it would be the rich who would refuse to go. A lot of them felt that their wealth entitled them to some sort of divine protection. "I could try. And I'd get some people out. A lot of people would refuse to leave their –" he paused, trying to find another word for stuff – "*things,*" he said.

Dennison uh-huhed, and said, "Print up flyers, distribute them by hand. Use manpower for that. Tell them you need their signatures if they are going to stay. There is no guarantee that there will be any emergency services once the storm makes land-fall. Spell it out that they are risking their lives if they stay. Let them know that the power grid will probably fail. Land telephone lines will stop like a dead heart. I don't want to sound melodra-matic, but you have to listen to me. The electromagnetic field that this storm will generate is going to fry all antennas, including cell phone towers. Forget iPhones. Forget BlackBerries. Forget the goddamned Motorola brick. No more communication. Grid-based electronics will go, everything plugged into an outlet will simply overload and die in a single flash of lightning that could be the largest in history. Even the surge-protected circuits will go. I hope we're wrong, I really do. But this is one of those times when the Boy Scout motto applies. Get all of your people together ASAP and get a working plan of defense into action. Talk to your citizens. We have a media branch that can help you get a website up to help with inquiries, otherwise you and your people will spend the next two days answering the same questions over and over and over and you need that time to get your citizenry out of there. If I had anyone I loved out on that narrow isthmus facing Dylan, I'd get them inland as fast as I could."

Hauser was still trying to absorb the walkie-talkie advice. "I appreciate the call."

"I left my number with your receptionist and we've sent full contact packages to the email address of every civil servant in your area. If you can, get another branch of the city to print the flyers and donate personnel to handing them out. The library or post office. That would be smart. Get them all orange highway vests and a flashlight; Swiss Army knife; name tag – people just fucking love name tags; and all the damned coffee they can drink. Call me directly if you need help, I'll be at the office until Dylan dies out. And please, use our media package. Get a website up fast – these days, if it's not on the web, people don't believe that it exists."

"Sure."

"Take care."

Hauser hung up, glad that Dennison hadn't said *God Bless.* Then again, *Be Prepared* was pretty close. But a lot better than trusting an invisible man in the sky. "Jeannine!" he bellowed.

He heard the click-click-click of her heels, then his door opened. "Yes, Sheriff?"

"Where do we keep the walkie-talkies?"

Her face scrunched up and she asked, "What's a walkie-talkie?"

Hauser felt the acidic surge of heartburn flare up in his stomach. He faced the nearly blank page of the press release, realizing that he was going to be doing a lot of these in the next few days. "Get me some Tums or Rolaids or some such shit and I want to see Spencer and Scopes in my office in five minutes. Get everyone in here in an hour for an emergency meeting. Pull in everyone. And call everybody you know and tell them to get inland in a hurry."

Jeannine's eyes shifted uncomfortably. "Is it going to be bad?"

"It's going to be worse than bad, Jeannine." Hauser stared at the page, his eyes unmoving. "A lot worse."

14

His father was still sleeping. Still snoring. Still looking like one of those *after* photographs that little communities put up by the side of the road to remind people to keep fresh batteries in their smoke detectors. Jake had come back here because the sheriff's department was dragging its feet with the reports. Even though eight hours was still under accepted law-enforcement standards, it was well below what a competent FBI forensics team would consider permissible. So Jake had come back to the hospital to get some more work done. With the new reports from the medical examiner, things were expanding and he needed time to correlate the new information with the old. So he sat in the corner trying to stare into the house down the beach. But all he could see was the hospital room.

The flowers had been carted down to the children's ward and the rainforest effect had almost dissipated. The room still smelled of flora and dirt but it wasn't as humid. A single tasteful arrangement of calla lilies and baby's breath in a tall wheel-cut crystal vase sat on the imitation-wood nightstand. The card was sealed in a little white envelope secured with a single staple. Jake ripped it off the foil ribbon and pried it open. On simple white stationery were the words, *Get well soon, old friend – David Finch.*

Jake shook his head, tucked the card back in the envelope, and tossed it into the wastebasket. Finch had been the first gallery owner to take a chance on Jacob. Because of this, combined with his being the shrewdest art dealer on the East Coast, Jacob had stayed with him for more than fifty years. Jake hated Finch, always had, and the thought of the obsequious little fuck tightened his stomach into a greasy knot.

"Goddamned fag flowers," a voice croaked.

Jake turned to his father. "Hello ... um, Jacob. How are you?" The doctor had guaranteed that his father would sleep for two days on the pharmaceutical cocktail they'd primed into his IV.

"What day is it? More red, Godammit! More red!"

More red? What the hell was that about? Where was the nurse? "You're Jacob Coleridge. Remember?"

"Jesus fucking Christ. What are you? Retarded? Of course I'm Jacob Coleridge. What's with the ugly flowers? White? Is it a wedding or a funeral? Who the hell buys white flowers? Only the stupid, the unimaginative, or the sycophantic send white. Must be from Dave. What the fuck do you want? Where are my clothes?" And then he saw his hands, two big gauze-wrapped stumps the size of pineapples. On his left hand, a black scab of blood was hard and cracked and the white outline of the fabric's weave shone through and he examined it. "What the hell is THIS?" he said, throwing his hands into Jake's face. "Take these off, for fuck's sake."

The doctor yesterday had warned him that the morphine could alter his father's personality. He said that many patients at the tail end of a terminal illness just drifted off into a hallucinatory dementia that robbed them of much of their identity.

The morphine, coupled with his father's Alzheimer's, could make Jacob Coleridge a very ugly man to be around. As soon as Jake had stopped laughing he told them to give the old man as much morphine as they could load into a caulking gun. But it sure didn't seem to be slowing him down at all. Suddenly he realized where his own metabolism had come from.

"Get these goddamned motherfucking things off my hands!" He looked up at Jake. Then added, without a hint of sincerity, the single word, "Please?"

Jake looked down at his father, at the better part of a century that had rolled over his features, stretching them, darkening them, aging them. Behind the furrowed brows and the clenched lips, the same man stared back at him. Angry. Mean. "I'll get the nurse," Jake said, and turned to the door.

He saw Nurse Rachael at the far end of the hallway, on the other side of the station. He signaled her and she jogged over, holding her stethoscope around her neck with one hand as she ran. As he watched her, he realized that Jacob Coleridge, the great observer, was still lucid enough to recognize that she *did* look like Mia.

When they got back to the room, Jacob was pulling at the bandaged clubs with his teeth, like a dog getting the stuffing out of an old cushion. Tufts of gauze peppered his beard and chest as he gnawed at them. He made hungry sounds as he tore at the white cloth.

"Mr. Coleridge, let me help you with that." Nurse Look-alike came forward, and produced a needle from her pocket.

"What the fuck is THAT?" Jacob asked, trying to back up in the bed, away from the syringe.

"Don't worry, it's not for you."

"The fuck it isn't! Get away from me with that. You're not sticking that in—"

Nurse Rachael jabbed the needle into the IV tube and depressed the plunger.

Jacob's eyes unfocused, his mouth closed, and it was as if someone had drawn all the frustration from his body with a magnet. His muscles went slack, he sank back into the pillow, and closed his eyes. Then his chest expanded with a single deep breath, seemed to hold it, and his head fell to one side.

Jake turned to the nurse. "Thank y—"

It was in that hang time between the two words of gratitude that Jacob Coleridge bolted upright in the bed. The metal frame jolted the nightstand, sending Finch's flowers to the floor in a high-pitched collision of lead crystal and linoleum. The vase shattered, and shards of glass and lilies bowled across the floor.

Spittle and gauze flecked Jacob's lips. He looked at his son, at the nurse, and at his hands. Then he let out a shrill scream that rattled the windows, spraying chewed bandage, saliva, and frustration across his chest. He lifted one of the torn nubs at the end of his wrist, pointed it at his son, and bellowed. "You can't keep him away! He'll find you! Run!"

Then he fell back as if someone had pulled his plug.

And was silent.

15

The preliminary press conference had gone well but the feeling that it was only the first of many quashed any momentary elation Hauser felt coming on. The storm was bad enough but somehow the specter of the double homicide was more threatening in a not so abstract way. Dennison at the NHC had done a good job of scaring him but somehow Jake Cole and his traveling road show of death had managed to eclipse even Dylan; the next few days would be an entry for the memoirs.

In his brief respite between the press release of the murders and a general meeting of his staff about the coming storm – which the sheriff had been nice enough to open up to the media in part of that give-and-take Jake had spoken of – he decided to go through the Mia Coleridge file.

The box smelled of basement and the first file was a once-bright red that had faded to pale salmon – a capital crime file. He placed the old manila folder down on the sparse top of his desk, peeled back the cover, and began reading.

The pages had become brittle and the staples had rusted, leaving dark red marks everywhere, like iron nails in a ship's hull. By nature Hauser was a patient man, and this quality had always worked for him within the framework of his occupation; he began on page one and went through the file slowly and methodically, not bothering with notes or any sort of an effort to memorize facts. He simply wanted to find out anything he could about Jake Cole so he could get a feeling for a man he was forced to work with. Hauser had learned a long time ago that it wasn't what he didn't know that could hurt him, but rather what he knew for sure that just wasn't so. It was an old logic – delivered in an almost obsolete vernacular – but it had served him well in his twenty-plus years in the department. He had very little in the way of disposable time but figured that a fifteen-minute trek into the history of the FBI consultant was worth the investment if he was going to hand over the keys to the kingdom.

He began with background notes that the officer on duty had taken the time to write out by hand – Hauser recognized the slow, careful script of someone who was bad with a pen and only took notes by hand because it was easier than using a typewriter (the not-so-distant ancestor of the keyboard), a condition he could empathize with because he shared it. A lot of the younger men on the force, the ones who had been born into the digital age, had no problem with the keyboard but Hauser wrote his reports out longhand and he recognized the fear of technology in the script before him.

It was a familiar handwriting, penciled in by his predecessor, Sheriff Jack Bishop. Hauser knew Bishop had been a good cop and a solid man when needed. Hauser also knew that three days after Bishop's retirement, he had gone out to the garage, jammed a double-barrel twelve-gauge into his mouth, and painted the rafters with his brains. No one talked about it but they all knew why. A few of the old-timers, the ones who had given everything up for the job – their families, their dreams, their lives – realized that after the badge was retired and the sidearm was put in the safe, there really wasn't much to look forward to. After all, when you had sacrificed everything for the job, what did you have when it was gone? It was a story Hauser had heard about more cops than he wanted to think about. And part of him felt smugly superior because he knew it would never happen to him. As much as he loved the job, he loved his wife more, his daughter more. And there was plenty of bird hunting and fishing still to do. Maybe even a cottage to build. Something upstate on a little lake where the musky fishing was good and the summers weren't packed with weekend assholes who had more money than brains. Maybe that place where they had vacationed that last summer before Erin had gone off to Vassar; Lake Caldasac – you could buy a cottage on the water for thirty grand. And the fish were monsters.

The file was neatly stacked, like it hadn't been rifled through as much as a murder case should be. Homicides were rare in his jurisdiction but not as rare as he would have liked. There were a few each year, usually chalked up to a drunken brawl that got out of hand or a domestic dispute that went supernova after too much yelling and not enough talking. The usual result was that someone with a surprised look on their face ended up on one of Dr. Reagan's tables.

But this was a thing of legend. He had heard that during every cop's lifetime there was a single case that eclipsed all others. Made a man want to leave the job. Maybe hang sheetrock. Even without the benefit of hindsight, Hauser knew that this would be his.

Hauser read Bishop's notes before he went to the photographs he felt sticking out of the folder with the edge of his finger. Bishop had started with the basics, first-impression kind of things. Sex: female. Age: unknown. Height: approximately five foot three. Hair color: unknown. Race: unknown. Eyes: brown.

Clothing: non-applicable. Back then, before they had started using DNA as an identification tool, they had relied on dental records – a slow and often worthless process. But Hauser checked a note that Bishop had come back and scrawled into the margin ten hours after the cover page had been time-stamped, stating that they had a positive dental match for Mia Coleridge. Hauser shook his head and snorted at that; today, when they were lucky, DNA took seventy-two hours to get sequenced, two weeks when they weren't. But back then it had been real footwork and human ingenuity – not computers – to keep the whole thing rolling forward.

Hauser went down the sheet, the details puzzling him at first. A few lines in he began to recognize words, phrases, and he started to form an ugly picture in his head. After the end of the first page he stopped, flipped through a few more sheets, and went to the photographs of the crime scene.

He had known what he was going to see before he pulled it out – Bishop had been precise in that particular way cops had. But there was no way to bolster himself against something like this. Not unless he was some kind of a monster. He picked up the photograph and felt the air lock in his chest, felt the blood stop pumping in his veins, felt his cardiac pistons seize in one massive system reset.

"Jesus Christ," he said, not meaning to. He stared at the image for a few seconds, the black-and-white doing little to stave off the nausea he felt stirring his empty stomach. Then he dropped the old photo to the desk and let out a low moan.

Staring up at him from thirty-three years ago was Mia Coleridge, body twisted in rigor mortis, teeth brittle white shards amid her bloody face. There was no expression on her visage except for the primitive animal snarl of pain. Other than that, you could barely tell you were looking at a human being, let alone a woman.

Mia Coleridge had been skinned alive.

16

Jake sat in his car under a tree in the hospital parking lot for ten minutes, trying to talk himself into heading east on 27 and not stopping until he was home with Kay and Jeremy. He listened to the radio for a few minutes, hoping that the chatter about the storm would take his mind off of what had happened in his father's room upstairs. But the radio anchor very quickly began to annoy him with his very un-Cronkite-esque fear rhetoric and pseudo-factoids. Jake shut off the radio with an angry, "Oh, fuck off!"

Jake didn't have a mountain of available time – not now, not ever – but he needed to clear his head. And he needed to get some work done. Only that had become more difficult the past little while, hadn't it? The invasive process of turning secrets of the murdered over in his mind so many times that they became worn and polished from examination had started to become common-place. Maybe he had turned into a ghoul, just like the people he hunted. After all, what did he like about the job? It was the subtle-ties, the nuances, that separated these monsters. The little signa-tory differences. The way one held a knife, the way another only bit down with the left side of his jaw. It was in these weird little psychosis-fueled details that their personalities began to shine.

Maybe he wasn't supposed to see these things. Like Hauser rushing out of Reagan's lab today, maybe Jake needed to find a little of his lost humanity. It was as if he had a keyring in his pocket, only most of the keys just opened ugly places that he had to stop visiting because they were starting to feel too much like home. Kay had been telling him to quit for a while now. A year. And she was right. Hell, she was more than right, she was justified. He had agreed. Promised. All that was left to do was to tell Carradine. Yet he somehow hadn't. Why?

Which is probably why he had come up here to deal with his father and the mausoleum of scotch and cigarettes and demented, black canvases. It was with a heavy, foul-tasting twinge that he realized that all the things that had gone on between him and his father were of no value any more. Not to him. Not to his father. And certainly not toward gaining any sort of closure. The door had slammed shut when the first threads of his father's mind had begun to unravel.

What was he going to do? He needed help. Kay would be here this afternoon. But he needed a different kind of help than she could offer, as much as she'd try. He needed someone with a little distance. Someone who wouldn't care if this was easy or tough on him. Someone pragmatic. Someone who could handle his old man. Problem was, with the exception of his gallery owner, Jacob had successfully driven everyone who had ever cared about him away. Every friend. Every publicist. Every—

Jake pulled his iPhone out and thumbed through the menu. It took a few seconds to find the number, but it was there, three months back. He sat there, the windows open, his thumb poised above the send button. Would Frank care enough to come or had Jacob burned that bridge as well?

He pressed send.

There was the sound of computer chatter, a low throaty whisper of static that sounded like the voice of the Devil played at seventy-eight RPM, followed by a series of clicks that Jake knew were satellite connections being made. It took almost half a minute until the phone at the other end began ringing, a series of double chirps that sounded strange, foreign. After fifteen or sixteen rings, a voice that belonged in a public service announcement against the dangers of smoking answered, "Frank Coleridge."

"Frank, it's Jake."

Frank didn't prod Jake with phony cheer, he simply took another drag on the cigarette that Jake knew was plugged into his face and said in that singularly unique voice, "What do you need, Jakey?"

"It's Pop."

"The –" there was a rasping sound, like someone tearing a dry leaf in half, as Frank took in a lungful of smoke – "fire?"

"You heard?"

"Yeah. Found a note on my door this morning. Neighbor left it."

Jake rolled his eyes and remembered the nine sacks of mail at the hospital; it was amazing how the fame monster affected people.

Frank continued. "I've been out –" another long pull on the cigarette – "hunting. Just got back to the cabin."

Jake scrolled through his mental filing cabinet for a second, trying to align Frank's statement with his knowledge of state regulations. "What's in season in September?"

Frank let out a dark arid laugh. "Nothin's in season, Jakey. Had a bear kill a foal. Tracked him to high country. Old sumbitch with a bad leg. Only thing he could kill would have been that foal.

Maybe a human child. Had to get him before that started happening. I was gone four days."

"What did you get him with?"

Frank responded with a low laugh. "Lead poisoning. How'd your old man set himself on fire?"

"From what they know, he had oil paint all over his hands. Maybe he was lighting a smoke, maybe he was trying to throw another log on the fire."

"He torched bad?" This was followed by another tearing leaf.

"His hands are gone. Lost three fingers and they're not sure if he'll be able to keep the rest. He was flailing around and ran through one of the plate-glass windows. Cut himself pretty bad."

Frank whistled. "Without his hands, without his painting, the best thing that could have happened to your old man would have been if a big sliver of glass would have taken his head off. Without painting, not much of Jacob Coleridge is left. And what is, is pretty broken."

"Frank, I could use your help. I need someone who's honest. Someone I can trust. Someone who's pragmatic."

There was another pause as Frank took in some smoke, coughed one short rattle, and said, "Who says you can trust me? It's not like your old man and I got along all that well."

Jake closed his eyes, and dropped his head back onto the leather seat. It was a good question. It was more than good – it was *valid*. "Frank, cut the shit. I trust you and I don't trust anyone. I need to deal with Dad's life and with what's happened to him. You wouldn't believe how he's been living."

"Worse than before?"

"I found keys, paperbacks, and sod in the fridge. The house is an ashtray. There are empty bottles all over the place. The rooms are crammed with crap. Some of them are locked and I haven't been able to get them open. The studio is bolted shut. There is a barricade in the bedroom." Then he just stopped. If that hadn't painted reason enough, nothing would. Besides, he hated feeling like he was asking for something almost as much as having no one else to ask.

"You have anyone else helping you out?"

"Kay is supposed to come up from the city but with this storm heading our way, I wouldn't be surprised if she stayed in New York."

"What kind of storm?" The question was calm, serious, and showed that Frank was obviously dragging his ass in the television-watching department.

"Category Five Cape Verde. They're advising evacuation at this point. I wouldn't be surprised if it came to a forced evacuation."

Frank whistled and even that sound was dry, brittle. "Another Express." The New England hurricane of 1938 had gone down in the books as the Long Island Express. "Stock up on water and batteries. Or better yet, get out, Jakey. Get your dad airlifted if you have to. Get him on an ambulance. Go home until this blows over."

Jake wanted to listen to Frank, but the monkey in the wrench was the woman and child skinned up the beach. He had to be here. It wasn't a question of choice. "I can't, Frank. There's other stuff I got going on."

Frank's voice grew distant, flat. "Work?"

"Yeah, work." *It happened again*, he wanted to add.

"If you stay, put a survival kit together. Something that will keep you hydrated and fed and maybe even dry for a week if things get as bad as Katrina. The one thing on your side is that you are above sea level. Put a bag together. Handgun with extra ammunition. Seal a bunch of toilet paper in Ziplocs – nothing worse than wiping your ass with a sock. Good solid knife. A Ka-Bar or dive knife. Something you can use for a tool. Antiseptic ointment. Sutures. Gum."

Jake closed his eyes, pinched the bridge of his nose, and tried not to be dismissive. Frank was a pragmatic man, which is why Jake needed his help.

Frank had never been married but had always carried on long – and more or less monogamous – relationships with very distinctive women his entire adult life. Some younger, some older, some wealthier, some not. And the relationships had all seemed solid, pleasant. But the inevitable announcement would come that she had left during the night. A brief period of a little too much booze and not enough self-control would follow, and soon another striking woman would begin appearing at his side. Not long after Mia's murder, Frank had moved away from Long Island. To hunt more. Spend more time with Nature. But Jake knew that he had moved to get away from the memories of all the good that had once been here. He had ended up in the Blue Hills of Kentucky.

Since the brothers were no longer talking, Jake had lost touch with his uncle and things had stayed broken until all those years later when Jake woke up in a quarter inch of cold shitty water on the kitchen floor. He had somehow found Frank. And asked for help.

Jake never forgot that Frank had saved his life. And he was so unused to asking anyone for help that he felt guilty about asking for it now. "This is Long Island, not Zimbabwe." There was a fondness in his voice that he didn't have for his own father. He spoke to his uncle a few times a year, mostly when the job was getting to him and he needed to get an outside perspective on the world. Jake had an enormous amount of respect for the man. "I'm a shooter, not a shootee."

Frank laughed and it sounded like a diesel engine turning over. "Still, get yourself some supplies. You're a smart boy, Jakey, always have been." His laugh rattled to a stop. "Although I guess calling a forty-five-year-old man a boy is kind of an insult but when you're as old as I am, anyone who doesn't have to tape his balls up so they don't swing into his knees is a kid."

Jake smiled, and suddenly realized that he wished he had been able to talk to his father like this. Not all the time, but once would have been good.

"And be careful. It's acting like things are the same as always when they aren't that will get you in trouble. You handling this all okay?"

"I'm good, Frank." He thought back to his father's kitchen and realized that at least *some* shopping was in order. "I just need someone who will get things done."

"And that's me."

"And that's you."

"I'll be there as soon as I can."

"I can book you a flight, I have air miles. I get free—"

"Fuck free. I'm not flying. I'm driving. I have to finish changing the fuel pump on the truck but I can get that done by supper. Be there within twenty-four hours." There was a pause as he fired up another cigarette. "He in any pain?"

Jake thought back to the tranquilizer that Nurse Look-alike had pumped into the drip. About his father's screams. And the points of white mucus in the corners of his eyes. "I can't tell, Frank. The old Jacob Coleridge is gone. Just gone. He's confused. He's scared."

"You can accuse him of being a lot of things, Jakey, but *scared* is not one of them. Never. Not when we were growing up. Not when we were in Korea together. Not in bar fights or staring down pirates. Nothing scares your old man."

An image of the barricaded bedroom door lit up for a second. "He's scared now, Frank."

Jake heard Frank pull on the smoke. "Yeah, well." The old man didn't sound convinced.

"Thanks for doing this, Frank. I appreciate it."

"That's what blood's about, Jakey. You do things for blood you don't do for anybody else."

17

The sheriff's cruiser was in the driveway when Jake got back to the house. Hauser sat inside, windows open, doing a good imitation of a man trying to sleep and being unsuccessful. As Jake's sleek Charger entered the drive, the cop got out of the car, leaving his Stetson inside. He came over to the shade of the big pine where Jake parked, his movements loose from lack of sleep, not comfort.

Hauser ran his finger along the line of the front quarter panel, feeling the metal beneath the glossy paint. Then he looked back at his own car, an updated version of the classic American muscle car, and something about the movement seemed tentative. Jake hoped the cop wasn't about to start talking cars – he hated talking about cars almost as much as talking about the stock market. More, maybe.

Jake shut off the engine, opened the door, and swung out into the afternoon. He nodded a greeting and took the bag of groceries from the baby seat in the back.

"Cole," Hauser said, trying to sound good-natured but only making it a little past tired. Jake heard something else in his voice. Embarrassment, maybe.

Jake fished his father's keychain out of his pocket. It was a flat stone with a hole drilled in the center, worn smooth from rubbing against pocket lint and scotch tops for years. "Sheriff." He figured that Hauser was here to interview him.

Jake had gone through this before – it was part of being the resident interloper with every department he visited. Hauser needed to have faith in his team. So he surrounded himself with reliable people. If Jake was part of that team, Hauser would want to know a little more about him. And if you took this equation a little further, Jake had been interviewing Hauser as well.

Jake balanced the groceries on his knee, turned the key in the lock, and pushed the big door open. "Coffee?"

"Sure …" Hauser let the word trail off as he walked into Jacob Coleridge's house. He stopped in the doorway and looked around. He saw the whiskey bottles, the cigarette butts, the paintings stacked like cordwood, and the decades of neglect covered by dust.

Hauser paused by the Nakashima console in the entry, leaned forward, put his hands on his knees, and examined the spherical sculpture that had sat there for decades. It was a wire-frame model of – what? A molecule, Hauser guessed. "Jake, what's going on?" He sounded more than tired, Jake realized. He sounded frightened.

Jake considered the question as he dumped the groceries out on the counter. He caught a can of tuna before it rolled off the edge. "I don't know. Not yet." He examined the can, then surveyed his healthy smorgasbord. Part of him was happy that Kay wasn't here to see this gastronomical crime; his foray to the Kwik Mart on 27 had yielded him two six-packs of Coke, a can of spaghetti sauce, a package of linguini, two cans of tuna, a loaf of Wonder

Bread, a squeeze bottle of mustard and another of mayonnaise, two packs of luncheon meat that resembled packaged liposuction fat, a carton of cream, some club soda, a tin of coffee, and some sugar packets stolen from the coffee counter. He had taken a little of Frank's advice; in the car were two cases of water, a flashlight, a dozen batteries, and a box of pepperoni sticks. He pulled the tab on the coffee lid and it hissed open with what sounded like a death rattle.

Hauser meandered through the detritus of Jacob Coleridge's life, unintentionally casing the place, a species-specific habit natural to cops and crooks alike – it was something that Jake both recognized and resented. Hauser stopped in front of the piano and examined a small painting that was part of a larger pile on top of the instrument, ignoring the huge expanse of ocean through the big plate-glass window. On the floor at his feet was the box the handyman had left behind, full of half-used tubes of silicone and a few cans of spray-foam insulation. "Mind if I take a look?" he asked, pointing at one of Jacob Senior's ugly little canvases.

Jake was at work on the coffee, the twelve-stepper's surrogate addiction. "Knock yourself out."

Hauser picked up one of the asymmetrical blobs that was jammed under the dusty Steinway and held it away from himself. He examined the painting for a few seconds, holding it first one way, then rotating it to look at it another, trying to decide which way it went. He flipped it around and looked at the back, as if he had missed something. After a few seconds he shoved it back under the piano. "I don't know shit about art," he said. "But if I look at a painting and don't know what the hell I'm looking at, it's not for me. I don't want a painting that represents the plight of man. How the hell can you paint that? Me? I want a field. Or a pretty girl on a swing. Hell, I'd even take dogs playing poker. But I guess I just don't understand this modern stuff." He shrugged.

"To quote my father about the only thing I'd trust him on, it's self-indulgent undisciplined crap."

"Not a fan?" Hauser sounded a little relieved.

"I like my father's early work. The stuff he did before he made it onto the college syllabuses. Maybe up until 1975 or '76. After that ..." He let the sentence trail off into a shrug.

In the ensuing silence, Hauser shifted his focus to the big window and the Atlantic beyond. "Helluva view." The wind had picked up from earlier; the high-pressure blanket that sat over the coast was being slowly pushed away by the advancing hurricane, 1,600 miles and closing.

Jake finished scooping grinds into the basket and flipped the machine on, a little stainless-steel Italian robot that had been bought before the great coffee revolution had swept America and its suburbs into believing that Starbucks knew what it was doing. It started to hiss and he came around from behind the counter. "Are you going to give me the protocols?"

Hauser looked down at the large manila envelope in his hand, as if it might be seeping pus. He held it out.

Jake tore it open, upending it over the coffee table, now clear of the forest of cigarette butts and empty bottles. Photographs, two computer disks, and a sheaf of files held together with a black office clip glided out. Jake picked up the photographs.

All of a sudden he was back in the house, walking its halls, examining its dead. Hauser, the coffee maker sputtering away, the hiss of the surf beyond the window, the slight static that every house has – faded away. He was there. In the room with her and her child. With *his* work.

The first photo – clear, color, well lit – showed her fingernails, scattered over the carpet like a handful of bloody pumpkin seeds, strands of flesh hanging off in little black tails. He flipped through the photos until he found the one he wanted, a close-up of her left eye. It stared up at him like the satellite photos of Dylan on CNN, only her eye was lifeless, the white ruptured in dark subconjunctival hemorrhages. "This guy's not fucking around," he said, and dropped the photo to the table, stepping out of the murder scene in his mind.

"You looked like you were in some sort of a trance." Hauser's eyes narrowed.

"I reconstruct things in my head. It's what I do." The smell of coffee reached him and he changed the topic. "Sugar? Cream?"

"Two sugars, no cream."

Jake wound his way through the vast expanse of the great room and the ease, the familiarity, with which he did surprised him. He had been back less than – what? Twenty hours maybe, and already the house was once again home. Except for the locked doors. The sod of lawn in the fridge. And that his father had lost his grasp on most of the tangible parts of his psyche.

Jake pulled two cups from the rack beside the sink – now full of dishes he had cleaned – and poured the coffee. He added sugar to both cups and looked up to find Hauser standing in front of the counter.

"My mother had Alzheimer's. I know how hard this can be." It sounded accusatory.

"Whatever is between my old man and me is not going to affect my performance. It took your lab –" he checked his watch – "nine hours and fifty-one minutes to process those protocols." He nodded across the room to the coffee table. "You want shortcomings, you've got all you need right there."

"I don't see how you can be objective here. I don't want some FBI ghost-hunter all hopped up on vengeance kicking the shit out of this thing. Do you have a thirty-three-year-old axe to grind?"

Jake froze, raised his eyes to Hauser. "You want me to tell you this is not personal? I don't lie, Mike, it's bad policy."

"I need to know what I have to worry about."

Jake pointed at the coffee table. "Nine hours, fifty-one minutes is a good place to start. Two full-time detectives should have had that done in five hours flat. And it would be useful, solid data. Your lack of experience in this is your biggest liability. Me? I'm the guy who's going to be doing all the heavy lifting."

Hauser stopped, swiveled his flat-top toward Jake. "Is this guy crazy?"

"Sure, he's crazy. But is that going to help you find him? Probably not. He's not crazy in his public life, at least not most of the time. It's the quiet time he has inside his own head, sitting at home in his garage, or in his study, or in the little room out behind his house, that the freak comes out to play. These guys are all fucking crazy, but they know what they do is wrong, Mike. If they didn't, they wouldn't hide it. They all know that there are consequences for their actions. Unfortunately, it's the only way most of them can fire up the money shot.

"This guy, there's something different about him, though. Most killers do it as an act to pleasure themselves. It's not about the victim, it's about enacting their own fantasies out on a stage, and that stage usually involves the victim as a bit-player. But the focus is always on themselves. This one ... he – it's about *them*. It's like he's – I don't know – punishing them. He skinned them and left. No evidence of any kind of performance or reenactment. He wanted to hurt them."

"So he knows them?"

Jake nodded, then shook his head, and the movement was unsettling. "He *thinks* he does. He's acting out against *someone*. They just take the brunt of it. His mother, probably. Maybe all women in general. I don't know. Not yet."

"You're going to stay on the case?"

"I have to. I don't want this to happen again."

Hauser looked like he had been zapped in the base of the spine by a wasp. "You think this is going to happen again?"

All of a sudden Jake realized that the thought had never crossed Hauser's mind; in his desire to see this go away, he had swept it under that vast expanse of psyche carpet used to avoid facing grating truths. And a skinned woman and child were a hard thing to deal with in any capacity. "I guarantee it."

"How do you know? Why? Are you sure? I don't—"

"What happened here?"

"A woman and her child were—" He swallowed. "Taken apart. Skinned."

Jake nodded. "What does that tell you?"

"That we're dealing with one sick sonofabitch."

Jake shook his head. "No. Think in cold, objective terms. What else does it tell you?"

"It takes someone special to do that kind of thing. To find pleasure in it."

Jake nodded. "And if he liked it, what would the next box on the flowchart say?"

Hauser froze for a second as the machinery in his head went through the process. "He'll want more." He looked up and his eyes had gone back to that sickly flat that they had possessed in Dr. Reagan's lab. "He'll want lots more."

Jake examined Hauser, wondering why he hadn't asked him if he thought it was the same killer after all this time.

18

One of the only good memories Jake had of his old man was his dog Lewis. Of course, like everything else with his father, it had been destroyed in a single act of narcissistic rage. But he occasionally allowed himself to think about the first part. The good part.

His father had brought Lewis home the morning of his son's eleventh birthday. Jake had not asked for a puppy – he would never have dreamed of asking for one – but the sight of the little German shepherd was something he thought of often. A small fawn with black hindquarters. Fourteen weeks. Jake named him Lewis.

From May on, armed with a new built-in friend, Jake began to explore the world beyond the fenced-in deck and broad patch of grass that ended at the studio, the glimmer of beach beyond. Spencer – called Spence by this point because it was so much cooler – taking his flank. Lewis was more than a mascot and companion, he was Jake's friend. A book from the library and a little help from his mother was all that was needed to turn Lewis into a relatively well-behaved dog. And Jake had his own personal bodyguard.

By November Lewis was a going concern in the Coleridge household. Jake had the dog trained like the army – he would do anything Jake asked him. Lewis sat, came, shook, high-fived, laid down, rolled over on the snap of a finger. But Jake could not teach the dog to play dead – he saw the trick on the *Dick Van Dyke Show* and wanted Lewis to figure it out. He had bribed the dog, scolded the dog, teased the dog, tried to coax the dog into understanding the command. But it had never worked out.

On mornings when Jake was tired, he'd let Lewis out the back door to do his business. The dog usually took a few minutes to go through his prebreakfast ritual, after which he'd bark and scratch at the back door. Jake would usually have a bowl of Cap'n Crunch out by now, and he'd let the dog back in and feed it a big stinky can of Alpo.

It was a late November morning and Jake was in a deep sleep. The dog had nosed him first in the hand and then in the neck. Jake had grudgingly put on his *Planet of the Apes* robe and walked the dog downstairs. It was barely morning outside and he could see the light on in his father's studio. When he opened the door a frigid breeze screamed in and the dog marched out. Jake went back upstairs, crawled into bed, and fell back asleep.

By the time he opened his eyes, it was bright in his room and he could feel that it was later. He got out of bed, put on some clothes – some *warm* clothes – and headed down to stir up some cereal, maybe make some Pop-Tarts. He was above the living room when he spotted Lewis. Just outside the back door, lying in a long rectangle of blood.

Jake had screeched out one long high-pitched wail that brought his mother running. She led him downstairs, put him on the sofa, and opened the door. Lewis's throat had been cut. A single, deep slash crossed the broad patch of white that stretched from jaw to chest. Only now it was not white.

Mia screamed. Asked Jake what had happened. Jake sat on the leather sofa, his legs sticking straight out in front of him, and stared at Lewis. "He musta been barking or something. Maybe he was making too much noise." Jake's eyes shifted to the studio at the edge of the property, the chimney stack chugging a nice hardwood smoke that the wind off the ocean swept away in a straight westward line.

His mother followed his gaze. Out to the building on the edge of the property where Jacob had been at work for the past four days. She gave Jake a kiss, a hug, and told him to stay put. She laid a big gray Hudson's Bay blanket over the dog and headed for the studio.

Jake never knew what they talked about – from the house there was just no way to hear what went on and Jake was too scared to leave the sofa. So he sat there. Staring at the lump under the blanket. Waiting to stop feeling frightened.

His mother had come back red-eyed and pale, but not crying. She told Jake that she was sorry about Lewis and then she took him out to breakfast at the yacht club. French toast – three pieces; a dozen silver-dollar pancakes; three strips of bacon; three sausages; maple syrup; and apple juice. He choked some of the breakfast down because he didn't want to waste his mother's money. They had talked very little. Then they went to a movie. That night she had slept in the guest room.

Eventually – he couldn't remember just how soon but it was less than a week – she returned to the marriage bed. But his parents' relationship had changed. Even Jake could sense it. And the change in his mother was something palpable, as if a little chunk of her had been taken away. The little boy would always be afraid of his father after that, mostly because his mother started to behave like she was running on borrowed time.

19

The pool, like the rest of the home, had surpassed disregard and was well on its way to developing its own ecosystem. The surface was skinned with algae and lily pads. A merganser circled the lip, her large, late-summer ducklings following in file. Beyond the line of birds was the sagging handrail of the deck, the beach beyond, and the Atlantic stretching out to the edge of the world.

But Jake Cole had forgotten all of this, including the sounds, because he was deep into the work. He was comfortably ensconced in the sofa, his cold coffee swirling into a loose spiral that resembled the eye of Dylan – still a day and a half away. His mind was lost in the rooms of the house up the beach. He was alone, and he moved through the lifeless house without worrying about what Hauser and his flag pin were thinking. He strolled through time, taking in the details.

His eyes were locked on his Mac as he cycled through the nearly 1,300 high-resolution shots that Conway had taken. The photographer had done a good job. Hauser's own shots were fine, but not much past adequate, and Jake had been at this long enough that he had developed his own unique way of doing things; he was glad Conway had understood what he had wanted.

Much of his work followed typical FBI protocol; the bureau had a solid forensics system that covered every base that could be imagined. Everything from the genetic evidence gathered under the CODIS umbrella to their Behavioral Science Department operated on good, solid principles. But what Jake did, the way he worked, was viewed with more than a modicum of skepticism by many of the people he helped. He understood that the sideways-glance treatment was the result of his solid – not weak – results. What they didn't understand was which set of senses he used. And as many times as he had tried to explain what he did, he ended up confusing the issue more than clarifying it.

Jake didn't believe in any of the parasciences. He didn't believe in mediums or psychics or any of the unquantifiable bullshit that the Discovery Channel was so fond of talking about. Jake didn't receive visions or see auras or summon spirits, although the people around him treated him like he did. No, the process Special Agent Jake Cole used was little more than a nineteenth-century parlor trick.

Jake knew that no quantifiable proof of tangible psychic power had ever been demonstrated. Never. Not once. People believe because they want to believe. Some are duped, others outright lied to, but the great truth is that there has never been a controlled experiment where a psychic was able to prove anything other than an extremely well-honed set of observation skills. And this was what Jake capitalized on. He didn't talk with the dead, or speak with the spirit world. He observed. Watched. Saw. And computed. The con artists who masquerade as psychics call it *cold reading*.

In simple terms, he solved riddles – it was as mundane as that.

The element of the otherworldly that his coworkers sub-scribed to was simply confusion in the face of a mental acuity they could not understand. Like a musical or mathematical savant, Jake was able to tap into something that those around him could not and the result was that they were uncomfortable around him. Some were even afraid.

Jake did not create character sketches of killers; his talent lay in creating detailed renderings of the mechanics of a murder. It was a subtle science where slight nuances equaled a vastly different image. He never changed his opinion about a case because he never made a judgment call until he was certain.

Jake looked away from the screen and rubbed his eyes. The defining factor in this case was the lack of details he was seeing. Men like Hauser would call it evidence but Jake didn't think in those terms. Jake thought of each detail as a pixel of color in a painting, and like any art, when enough pixels were present, an image took shape. But when they were absent, all the mental gymnastics in the world wouldn't be able to finish the picture. This time, though, the lack of details was a godsend. Without a lot of physical evidence to sift through he had been forced to fall back on that part of him that even he didn't understand. And through this computational process he had somehow recognized the killer's smell. After all this time. After all the anger and hate and fear and heroin and booze. He would—

The phone jolted him out of the reenactment stage lit up in his head. "Cole," he said wearily. Warily.

"This is Nurse Rachael at the hospital. You need to come down here *right now.*"

"My father—" He stopped himself. "What happened?"

"I think you should come to the hospital."

There was the cymbal-like clang of something metal bouncing on a floor. Of breaking glass. Swearing. A slap. "Please," someone said in the background. "Mr. Coleridge. Please stop. It's going to be okay."

And then the background static was buried under the wail of a single, high-pitched shriek that rattled the speaker. Jake jolted the phone away from his ear.

"*Please. He's coming. He's coming. I can't stay here! I can't! Oh, God. Please. Let me go. I won't tell him about you, I won't. But if you don't let me go, I'll have to and then …and then—*" His old man's voice was panicked, mad. "*Get away from me with that needle!*"

Nurse Rachael came back on, winded. "*Please, Mr. Cole.*"

20

Jake shoved the door open and a little old lady with an unlit cigarette clamped in her teeth and wheeling an IV stand barked a *Watch where you're going!* dodged the swinging door, and kept moving on her mission. Jake ran to the nursing station.

In the after-lunch lull, two nurses were going about various tasks at the station. A tall heavyset man in thick glasses and a thin horseshoe of gray hair looked around, smiled a public-service-announcement smile, and came to the counter. "Mr. Cole, I'm Dr. Sobel, one of your father's physicians."

Jake pulled up the name from the files he had been given – Sobel was a psychiatrist. If nothing else, Jake's profession had taught him to mistrust people who said they could understand how the mind worked.

Sobel stuck out his hand. "I've got a few minutes until an appointment – but it's important we talk. Could we have a follow-up tomorrow morning?"

"One of my father's nurses called me. She said—"

Sobel waved it away, as if Jake was being melodramatic. "Rachael Macready. Yes, her shift is over."

Jake recognized the calming tone and soothing word choice of a man trained to manipulate. "What happened?" he asked.

"Your father's okay for now. We've sedated him. Again." That last word said a little tersely, as if Jake might run out on his bills.

The psychiatrist went to a wall of cubbyholes and pulled out his father's chart, then came around from behind the counter. He pulled Jake off into a small conference room. "I have two minutes, let's make this count. Your father's very agitated. I know you were here for one of his earlier episodes so I think you know what I mean. Do you have any idea what's going on with him? What's got him so worked up?" He closed the door.

Jake perched on the edge of the conference table. "I'm the last person who could tell you about him."

Sobel made a note in the chart. "I'd like to tell you that it's full-moon fever or that the coming storm is affecting him – which it probably is – but there's something else agitating your father." Sobel kept his eyes on the chart as he flipped through the pages.

Jake resisted the urge to roll his eyes. "He burned off his hands, Dr. Sobel. He's in an unfamiliar environment. He's loaded up on morphine, which is probably not the best thing for a man of his age. You'd probably prefer an anxiolytic mixed with a muscle relaxant and a sedative. Alprazolam's your best bet. But my father's an alcoholic so his renal function comes into question along with his age. So you go with the morphine. I know what's going on."

Sobel stopped flipping through the chart and looked up at Jake. "Are you a doctor?"

Jake smiled, almost laughed. "No. But I know about managing difficult personalities and you don't have a lot of options with an old alcoholic who's been a belligerent sonofabitch most of his life. You have to keep him – and those around him – comfortable."

Sobel nodded and the planes of his face slid into a half-smile. "Your father's always been an interesting man."

"Do you know him?" Jake asked, surprised that his voice was so calm.

Sobel's head bobbed back and forth in a no-yes-nod-shake. "My wife and I knew your mother. At the yacht club. She filled in when we needed a fourth for doubles. Your mother was a wonderful tennis player."

Jake smiled. He hadn't known that. "But not my dad?"

Sobel shook his head. "We had drinks a few times. But he didn't play tennis and I know he worked a lot." Sobel was doing a good job of making Jake feel at ease. "I own one of your father's paintings. Bought it at a silent auction at the club in '67 or '68. Best investment I ever made." He realized that he was running out of time and turned back to the chart. "How was your father living?"

Jake thought about the chunk of grass in the fridge. About the eyes sliced out of the giant Chuck Close. The barricaded bedroom door. The knives. "A little obsessive."

"Any signs of paranoia?"

Not if he was worried about a boatload of Vikings landing on the beach. "What are you not telling me, Dr. Sobel?"

Sobel closed the metal clipboard. "I had to give your father four hundred milligrams – that's nearly half a gram – of Chlorpromazine and it hasn't slowed him down at all. And that's *on top of* the morphine. I can't use any more on a man his age. Hell, a man your age couldn't take that kind of dose."

For an instant Jake thought about arguing with Sobel.

"Your father has a tolerance for narcotics that I've only seen one other time in thirty years of practice. He has the metabolism of a racehorse. That, coupled with his agitation, is a formula for disaster. I am afraid that he is going to hurt himself or, God forbid, someone else. I think he needs to be restrained."

"Are you looking for permission or absolution?"

Sobel shook his head. "Neither, Jake. I just like to speak to a man before I strap his father into bed."

Jake opened his mouth to speak but was cut off by a white-hot howl that shattered the silence. He recognized the voice and bounced up off the table just as another scream rattled the molecules of the third floor. He raced out of the room.

The end of the hallway was sewn up with a throng of people, clad in muted hospital pastels, craning their necks to get a view into Jacob Coleridge's room.

Jake hit the wall of flannel-and-cotton-clad flesh and forced himself into their mass, birthing into a wide semicircle of awe-struck faces, held back from Jacob Coleridge's door by some invisible force.

Inside, kneeling before the broad wall that the shadow of his chair swung across each day, Jacob Coleridge was on his knees, his bandages chewed away, the pulpy stalks of his hands contorted and cracked, oozing pus and blood and the spider legs of torn-out sutures. His legs were splayed out on either side, like a child, and he stared up at a painting he had rendered in blobs and drips and splatters of red already drying to black.

Jake froze in the doorway, his eyes nailed to the bloody painting on the wall.

Jacob Coleridge had used his fried bone and scab-encrusted fingers to render depth and hardness to his finger-strokes, thickening or thinning a line as he applied more or less pressure, and the visage he had bled was frightening, without the slightest hint of elegance about it. It was a finger painting of madness. A three-quarter-length portrait of a man.

Jacob used forced perspective to give the figure depth and it looked like it stood in front of the wall, rather than being laid flat on it. It was the bloody image of a man, head cocked to one side as if he were examining something. But he had no expression because he had no face – just a black smear of red where his features should have been.

Jacob Coleridge had chewed off his bandages and gnawed through the gauze and tape and stitches to get at the exposed bone and flesh beneath. He had smeared blood from his sutured and cauterized veins and arteries, plunking, dabbing, stroking with the fierceness that had always marked his work. Where shadow was needed, the blood was thicker. For just a hint, a thin glaze.

Jake moved slowly forward, his eyes locked on the blood-drawn man. As he moved, it shifted with his line of sight – a masterful trick of forced perspective – and for a second Jake thought he had seen it move, twitch. It smelled like the Farmers' house last night.

Him, the voice said, and Jake felt his heart stutter in his chest.

Jake slid by his father to get closer to the painting, to take in the details. As he moved forward, the thick metallic smell of blood grew fiercer. It was something he had experienced on the job in degrees much worse – many, many times before – but he had never been bothered by it. In fact, if pressed, he would admit to having rarely noticed it – it was something he automatically blocked out. But now, staring into the black faceless portrait scribbled onto the wall, the smell brought him back to the night his mother had been taken apart.

Jake's arm came up, his fingers splayed, like a man about to push on a glass door. His hand contacted the sheetrock wall, fingers and palm pressed to the portrait, and he felt heat coming off of it. A thick, humid wave that moistened his palm. He pulled his hand away and it left no marks at all and it was only then, when he examined his skin and saw the pale white crosshatch that made up his own flesh, that he was brought back to the now.

Dr. Sobel stood frozen in the doorway.

"Close that fucking door," Jake barked.

Sobel stepped in, closed the door, and bolted it.

With the sound of the lock being driven home, Jacob looked up and the distant animal fear in his eyes softened.

"He needs help." Jake picked up the phone and held it out. "Call people. Help him. Now."

Sobel punched in an extension and barked orders. "Get Dr. Sloviak to 312, *immediately*! Operating room, now. Page Dr. Ramirez and tell him it's urgent."

And for no reason other than he thought that was what a son should do, Jake put a hand on his father's shoulder. His father rocked back and forth, his mouth bent into a low sad howl. Blood and spit and bandages splattered his face, chest, and neck. Blood from his hands dripped onto the floor. He was looking up, his face pointed at the wall. But his eyes no longer saw the portrait he had scraped with his splintered damaged bones or the room he was in. What he was staring at was beyond the wall, beyond the blood and the faceless image, beyond everything that was around him. He was staring at an image flickering madly against his gray matter, pulsing and beating and shrieking and pounding at his skull, trying to get out.

"He's coming," Jacob's voice echoed up from a metal room a thousand feet into the earth. "And I can't even barricade the door." Then he closed his eyes, buried his face into his son's chest, and for the first time Jake could remember, wept.

21

The weather had reached a neutral stasis that would be the last stretch of calm before Mother Nature let loose with her big German opera. The surf lapped calmly at the shore and the clear sky had not yet scudded over with clouds. Even off to the east, out at the edge of the horizon that framed the Atlantic, there was no cover to be seen. But the air felt different, as if it were charged by electrical particles, and Jake could feel the low voltage on his teeth. He drove with the windows open, the heavy salt air and the faint buzz of the atmosphere adding background color to the white noise fluttering through his head.

He pulled into the drive and saw a cello case tucked into the bushes beside the garage, the black fiberglass covered with *Fragile* stickers and airport luggage tags. Beside it was an old suit bag, Kay's case, and a little yellow plastic suitcase, molded into the shape of a school bus. He hadn't expected her this early and wished he had left a key. Then he thought about the mess inside and decided that it was better he hadn't. He headed around the house to find them.

Kay's motorcycle boots were on the top of the old staircase that led to the beach, its ancient rail the same color as a fossilized dinosaur bone. Beside them, like a novelty you hung from a car mirror, were Jeremy's shoes, little sneakers with wide Velcro tongues. He spotted them a hundred yards west, Jeremy holding Kay's hand and bouncing along with his little white bucket hat – the one they had bought for him in Florida last winter.

Kay was in tight jeans and a *King Khan and the Shrines* T-shirt, sleeves rolled up, bright slashes of tattoos tearing down each slender arm. As she moved, she swung her shoulders loosely, her body in that constant flow of music that came out in every little thing she did. Her purse was clamped diagonally across her chest – anti-purse-snatching style – bisecting her breasts. She was small and moved with the same compact energy as Jeremy, her hair swinging in the wind, and Jake was already imagining what she'd smell like when he buried his face in her. She looked up, saw him, and squatted to their son. She said something and his head swiveled up and down the beach, like a bird looking for food. He finally located Jake when she pointed and he took off at a run.

"Daddy!" Jeremy yelled, the high tinkle of his voice rising above the sound of the surf.

In that instant all the rust fell out of his life. Suddenly his father, Madame X and her child, Hauser and Dr. Sobel, the blond horsehairs in the evidence bag, and Dr. Reagan's subterranean office all melted away. He ran to his son, scooped the boy up, and hugged him a little too tight for a little too long. Jeremy began to squirm and Jake put him down "Hey, Moriarty," he said, plastering a kiss on his son's cheek. "How we doing?"

Jeremy laughed, threw back his head. "I found a shell! Mommy has it! We were on the bus."

"Daddy's happy you're here."

"We got MoonPies! Big MoonPies!" Jeremy sang with an enthusiasm that said that MoonPies were better than money.

"Is that so?"

Kay was almost blushing, her freckled cheeks lifting with that gentle smile she had. "Want a MoonPie?" she asked, and threw herself into him.

"Is that what you youngsters are calling it these days?"

Kay was a few months away from her thirtieth birthday – a date she was dreading and Jake found himself secretly looking forward to. Jake hoped that the fifteen-year age spread between them would feel less cavernous if her birth year was only one digit off of his. Besides, Kay looked young for her age and Jake wanted her to be in a new decade so he wouldn't feel so *old*. All he thought about now was how she smelled.

"I missed you," he said into her hair, greedily gulping in her scent. It was clean and laced with a hint of papaya.

"I missed you more."

He felt her arms tighten and the meaty presence of her breasts push into him. "You feel good."

"You *always* say that."

"Because you *always* feel good." He squeezed her a little tighter before they unclenched and headed back to the house, fingers loosely intertwined, Jeremy running circles around them like a whippet, high on MoonPies, the bus ride, and at seeing Daddy.

"I brought you some clothes. Things a little more –" she scoured her vocabulary – "corporate."

He kissed the tip of her nose, then her lips, and said, "You're not staying."

Kay stopped, looked up into his eyes. "I just schlepped my cello on a Greyhound that smelled like piss while managing to keep Jeremy entertained for the three-hour ride and you say I can't stay. You must be real tired of having sex with me, mister." She sounded only half serious.

Jake managed a small smile. He leaned over as they walked, kissed the top of her head, breathing in more papaya. "Dylan is rolling in tomorrow night. I have my hands full with Dad." He paused, hesitated. "And I have a case here that's going to take—"

"Whoa. Whoa. Back up, Mr. Not-getting-laid. Did you say you have a case?" She stopped and her grip tightened on his hand. He also stopped or he would have pulled her over.

"It just happened."

"They always *just happen*, Jake. That's the way it is. You haven't told Carradine that you're quitting?"

"This came up last night. While I was here." Jake wanted to tell her more, to fill her in on all the things that were crawling around in his skull, flipping the switches and pulling books off the shelves like an angry child. "It's important."

"Oh, Christ, don't start that with me, Jake. I know that it's important. They're *all* important. But we have plans."

"I just need to get through this thing with my father and the case and I'm done. I can deal with the Utah headhunter from home. If this thing wasn't here – right in my lap – I would have said no. Carradine wouldn't have let me pick it up in the first place. Consider it loose ends."

She listened to the timbre of his voice. "We'll leave when you leave. I think that's a fair compromise."

Jake turned his focus to the horizon. Somewhere not too far away, hell was rolling in on eighty-foot swells and 200-mile-an-hour winds. "You can stay tonight," he said softly and kissed the top of her head again. "Then I am sticking your ass on a bus and you're going back to the city." She opened her mouth to protest when he added, "I don't want you two here right now. Not with this storm. Not with my work. I don't need the vulnerability."

And something in his tone made her stop. "Okay, Jake." She brushed a strand of hair out of her face. "Whatever you need. We'll sleep wherever you slept last night."

"The sofa."

"Sleep on sofa!" Jeremy said, and threw a rock with a clumsy overhand pitch. The stone thunked into the ground at his feet and he picked it up, trying the exercise again, this time making it to the edge of the surf. He nodded appreciatively and went back to scouring the beach for appropriate stones.

Kay was quiet for a few seconds, her calm way of processing information at work. Jake knew what she was doing and appreciated it. It was one of the things that he loved about her – she listened to and believed in him. Maybe it was all they had been through together, but she trusted him to take care of himself. And her and Jeremy. Once again he felt the speed of his brain and body magically slowed by just being around her.

"We can camp on the floor if we have to. Don't worry about us, Jake, you've got your hands full here. I know you're probably overwhelmed—" She paused, smiled again. "Listen to me – you overwhelmed? When have you ever been overwhelmed?" It wasn't said cruelly, just matter-of-factly. Her grip on his hand tightened and he waited, knowing that she was in the process of asking a question. "How is your father?" The words were tentative because she knew some of what had happened.

He thought about the way a life that had seemed so ordered a few days ago, had somehow tied itself into a knot when he got the call about his old man. What could he tell her? *He's fine. Except for the terror I see in his eyes each time I talk to him. And he's painting in his own blood. And I can't forget to mention that they've given him enough morphine to tranq a Tyrannosaurus Rex and he's still making more noise than an army of hungry zombies. Or the X-Acto*

knives. Yep, shit is just fucking dandy with my old man right now.
"It could be better," he offered in the way of a healthy compromise.

Kay knew him enough to read between the lines and she simply squeezed his hand again. Jeremy threw another rock, this one actually making it to the water, and he clapped with a fervor that Jake was jealous of. He pulled Kay in closer, her hip pressed against his thigh, and their step fell into a comfortable rhythm.

"We have any food?" she asked.

"Sure. Loads. Tons. Tuna, spaghetti, bologna and mustard sandwiches. A few packets of gas-station sugar. We're set."

Kay giggled and dropped her head against his shoulder. "We'll order pizza."

A middle-aged couple walked on the beach in chinos and matching cable-knit sweaters. They ambled silently, not talking, barely lifting their heads. Their feet kicked up plumes of sand that the wind carried away. Jeremy stopped lobbing rocks and waved furiously, because on television everyone at the beach was friendly. The couple kept their heads down and continued trudging along, even though they had to have seen the boy; he was in their line of sight.

"That's rude," Kay said. "Who doesn't wave at a kid?"

Jake wasn't looking. He just shrugged and kept walking. "You two aren't local, those two people are. They don't wave to outsiders here."

"Now you're bullshitting me."

"Go ahead, wave."

So Kay waved.

No response.

A second time.

They kept walking.

"You wave," she ordered Jake.

"I'm from here. They probably know that somehow." Jake raised an arm, gave one Nixonesque wave, and put his hand back in his pocket.

Both the husband and wife raised their hands, waved, nodded, and went back to their walk.

"That's creepy." Kay sounded disgusted. "Welcome to Purgatory."

"To them," Jake offered in the way of an explanation, "You don't even exist."

"Wait until I flash the husband my boobies. Then see who doesn't exist, me or that mummy he's married to."

And with that Jake realized how glad he was that she had come. Her view of the world was going to be a big help, if only in the cheerleading department.

Up ahead, Jeremy had stopped in front of Jacob's house and was squatting down, furiously digging at something in the sand. He pulled it out, held it up to the light, and nodded in approval, his tiny CPU calculating that it was the perfect size for throwing.

For an instant, Jake saw the light hit it, saw it glimmer in his son's hand. There was a pulse, and a red flash hit his eye as if the thing in Jeremy's hand were a chunk of glass taillight, then the boy threw it. It arced nicely out over the line of weed and foam that rimmed the ocean's lip, and plopped into the waves.

"Daddy!" he chirped, thrilled with the improved pitch. He danced around the freshly excavated hole at the water's edge, kicking up sand that the wind carried toward the house.

Jake paused where the boy had pulled the object from the earth and bent down, sweeping his fingers over the sand. Just below the surface he brushed a rough object that his touch told him was a rock. He scraped the surface away and saw a piece of what looked like red glass – the same hue as the one Jeremy had launched into the Atlantic. It was not sharp, but globular, amorphous, a melted chunk of red light, dimpled with the acne texture of sand burned into the surface. Jake held it up, squinted into its depths, something about it asking to be investigated.

Inside, neatly suspended in a red translucent cloud, was a small crescent-shaped inclusion. It was light, much lighter than the material it was encased in, and for a second Jake thought he was looking at a human fingernail. Was that possible? What could—

Then Jeremy pulled it out of his hand and threw it at the water.

It arced beautifully, a red drop of light that hung over the surf for a second. Then it plunked into the ocean. "All gone, Daddy," he said, and ran up the rickety steps to the beach house.

22

While Jake went back to work on the case, Kay dug into clearing out some of the garbage so they'd at least be able to walk from the kitchen to the stairs without having to negotiate an obstacle course. She had opened the doors to the beach and fresh air funneled through the house, swirling motes of ancient dust and cigarette ashes across the floor. She wanted to hang the Persian carpets over the railing on the deck to air them out but for some reason they were nailed and stapled and screwed down to the floor in an overlapping crosshatch – more of Jacob Coleridge's handiwork.

Kay had locked the hasp on the gate to the low railing that sectioned the pool/swamp off from the rest of the deck and Jeremy was outside, swathed in a white long-sleeved shirt, sunblock, and his little bucket hat, singing one of the happy songs he had learned at daycare. He was busy repeatedly crashing a plastic fire truck into his stuffed Elmo. Sooner than Jake would like, Elmo would be replaced by Optimus Prime. And slowly his son would grow up.

Jake sifted through the autopsy protocols, layering the information into strata, each successive level building on the last. He cycled through the endless photographs; he always learned more from images than other people's notes. He examined blood spatter from different angles. Studied the macro shots of smeared fingerprints and shattered teeth. The worst was the little boy, a cracked scabbed bundle of muscle and tissue contracted into the fetal position, lidless eyes crossed, little fists tightened into bloody meatballs. At one point he looked away and sucked in a great gulp of oxygen, realizing that he had been holding his breath.

Jake had seen nearly a thousand murder scenes and for him the only common factor between them was the stench of fear. It came in various degrees, depending on what had happened, and like cigarette smoke in a room, it never really left. Spritzing a little Lysol wouldn't get it out. That stink lingered for a long time. Years. Forever. Maybe longer. Everyone moved out of a house where someone they loved had been murdered. Some people bulldozed it. Others just burned it to the ground. But they all left. Except for the hardcore narcissists; those folks put it behind them and moved on with their lives, going on as if nothing had happened. Working. Drinking. Painting.

The longer Jake stared down at the rigor-mortis contortions of the mother glued to the carpet with her own blood, the more he realized the only obvious truth in the case: this was beyond Hauser's expertise. Which meant that Jake would be working alone. Going after *him*.

Jake closed the lid of the MacBook and rubbed his palms into his sockets. Outside, Jeremy was still singing away and playing with his cars. Jake kept his eyes closed and listened to his son, the happy lyrics offset by the brittle snap of plastic cars colliding with one another. In the other part of his brain – the part occupied by murdered children and evidence bags – he was thinking about the house up the beach. The house where two suitcases were missing. Where there were no toys – no fire trucks or Elmo dolls or

Optimus Prime figures. The owners were unreachable. And there were another three hundred little things that, taken on their own, didn't yield any sort of a payback. Yet taken as part of a big picture, they looked a lot like a personal *fuck-you*. The kind that ended with a woman being skinned down to her muscles.

Jake opened his eyes and Kay was in front of him, staring down, consciously avoiding the photos spread out on the coffee table; she had made the mistake of looking at his work once before and it was not something she would do ever again.

She smiled at him, one hip cocked out, her almost Mohawk tied up with a black bandanna, and the ink on her arms splashing down, around her wrists, ending in *L-O-V-E* across the knuckles of one hand, *H-A-T-E* across the knuckles of the other. She had switched into a pair of cutoff shorts and the red-and-black mermaids that were tattooed onto her hips dipped out on both sides of the frayed denim, tails curling around her thighs below the exposed pockets that flapped below the white-cut line. The *King Khan and the Shrines* wife-beater was pulled tight across her frame, the ribbed fabric pulling taut lines between her breasts. "Can you give me a hand with something?" she asked.

Jake snapped back to the sunny room opening onto the Atlantic, to Jeremy forcing automotive destruction on the imaginary citizens of Make-believe Land, and dropped his eyes to the coffee table, to the images of death spread out like baseball cards. He began to paw the photos and papers into a pile. "Sorry about this, baby." Back in the city he had an office where he locked everything away in metal filing cabinets when he wasn't home so Kay or Jeremy wouldn't walk in and see his pornography of the dead. He put the manila folder over the protocols.

"What can I do?"

"Come help me get into the bedroom. I want to get this place a little better before I put Jeremy down."

Jake winced – he had always hated that expression, thinking it sounded ugly outside of a vet's office.

She looked around. "And these booze bottles have to go. We could probably squeeze out enough to start a really good fire, and I don't need to be around scotch right now." She chewed her bottom lip. "I can't speak for you."

That had been a nice way to ask, he thought, and pulled her into his lap. "Haven't even thought about it." He smiled, tapped the breast pocket of his café racer. "Had a few smokes though. And I think I'll have more."

"You have smokes?" Her face twisted into the mock surprise of a blow-up doll, mouth round, eyes popped.

He pulled the Marlboros out. "Don't get cancer on me. I love your playing too much."

She tapped one out, smelled it as if it were a fine cigar. "Hmmm … fresh." She patted around in his pockets, her hand finding the rigid lump of the lighter. She fired it up, taking a long haul and exhaling a clean stream straight up. "Fuck, that's astounding. Keep these things away from me. No matter what I offer you."

Jake's eyebrows joined in a single helpless peak. "Sure. No problem. But you never play fair – it's not in you. You'll pull those out," he said, nodding at her breasts, "and I lose. You have too much of an advantage. I declare unilateral neutrality."

She pulled in another lungful and laughed it out in thin jets between her teeth. "Now, are you going to go all FBI on me and open that door so I can see what we have in the way of supplies? Let's make sure we have enough bedsheets, water, and shotgun shells."

"My dad's room at the end of the hall?"

She nodded. "It's barricaded like he's Robert Neville."

Jake shrugged. "I didn't go in. Haven't had time. Maybe it should wait." There was a brittle edge to his voice, one she was unfamiliar with.

Kay pushed into him. Her flesh was warm and she smelled as good as she had on the beach, that faint whiff of papaya mingling nicely with the Mr. Clean and cigarette smoke. "For what?" she asked, and sucked on the Marlboro.

"For tomorrow. For next week. I don't know. There's plenty to do here."

Her head swiveled around the vast nave of the living room. Beneath the dust and booze bottles were the bones of a once-beautiful space, like a garden left to time; overgrown neglect that hinted at a former order. "Jake, you never told me about this place, about what it was like growing up here. I mean, look at this." She swept an arm across the room. "This is something."

Jake knew what she was talking about. It was impossible not to be in love with this place. Yet he had somehow managed it. He didn't say anything, but pulled her in closer, slid his hand over the curve of her hip, and rested it on her bum.

"You must have some good memories from here." Half declaration, half sentence.

"I guess."

"Don't dismiss me. I'm being serious."

He ran his mental fingers over the files in his memory banks. One of the dog-eared folders glimmered and he pulled it up, opened the dry cover. He felt his mouth curl with an involuntary smile and her fingers dug into the back of his neck with encouragement.

Grudgingly, he began. "One night, I guess I was about eight, it was – I don't know, two, maybe three in the morning – and someone rang the doorbell. My dad's off in the studio and my mom answers the door in one of her nightgowns – all feathers and silk, looking like a movie star. Andy Warhol's standing there with this six-foot-five Scandinavian broad and a bunch of people spilling out of the limousine like it's a clown car. After being thrown out of some club in Manhattan, they had sardined themselves into a Lincoln and headed for the one place they knew they would have a little fun. It was common knowledge that as dedicated to his work as my father was, he never said no to a drink or a good time. I crawled out of bed and my mom put me in a pair of her jeans and I spent the night painting with Warhol while his groupies smoked weed and my dad, the Grand Poobah, held court, discussing art and composition and the usual bullshit with people who couldn't even begin to understand what he was talking about.

"We painted a cake with icing, and Andy insisted that it was art because I had created it. It wasn't a matter of mechanics, it was a matter of origin.

"Andy was a soft, decent guy – at least to me. My dad called him the bitch but he made me feel pretty good for a few hours." He paused, and felt his smile turn a little brittle. "My old man called the cake tasty crap art." He shrugged. "Which was kind of a compliment coming from him."

"See, Jake? That's a fucking cool story. Remember what we learned in AA? Take the good out of a situation – not the bad." She kissed his neck, then moved around so her mouth was inches from his. "Was that so hard?"

And all at once he remembered why he loved her so much; she pulled the good out of him, helped him reach in and find the stuff he thought was lost for ever. "Stop pissing me off," he said, then laughed. "No, it wasn't. Fuck. Thanks."

Kay laughed, too, and pushed her breasts together, forming a deep crease in her wife-beater. "Here, you can stare at my cans. I know it gives you some kind of a perverse thrill. Go ahead, pay your respects."

Jake eyed Jeremy out of the corner of his eye, zooming his fire truck through the air like a red machine of destruction, and when he was sure the boy wasn't looking, kissed each of her breasts, making a loud *MWAH!* sound as he did. "Lady, if you had a dollar for all the respect I have heaped on these, you'd be a rich woman," he said.

"Um, first off, it wasn't exactly your *respect* that you were heaping on them."

"All right … all right … Mrs. Potty Mouth, there's no winning with you."

"Hey, I thought letting you heap your … um, respect, on my cans *was* letting you win. Evidently I have been using the wrong philosophy." She smiled, leaned over, and kissed him. "Are you going to help me get that rolling barricade away from the door upstairs or do I call Ready Demolition from Tucson?"

Jake thought about Dr. Sobel's questions at the hospital. *Anything out of the ordinary at your father's house, Mr. Cole?* Hell, no. Except for maybe the Alamo barricade. Oh, and the trash piled up to the rafters. Other than that, the place is as normal as a Seth Morgan novel. "Why not?" He began to push her off.

She searched his face. "Did your father always drink like this?" she asked, sweeping her hand around the room, her raised arm lifting her breast.

"Pretty much." Jake closed his eyes, dropped his head back on the sofa. "When I was a kid, it just seemed to be fuel for work. He'd booze and play music and people would always be swinging by and he'd work and the paintings just seemed to magically roll out of the studio. Sometimes he slept out there. Sometimes I'd go in at bedtime to say goodnight and he'd be starting something, just lines and maybe a background layout penciled onto a big canvas. The next day, when I went in to say good morning, it would be done, some great big sweeping allegorical tragedy, only the tragedy turned out to be him, and the paintings were just incidental."

"Don't say that." She punched his arm. "I don't know your father, Jake – you barely talk about him – but he gave me the best thing in my life." She leaned over, planted her cool lips on his forehead and kissed him. "You don't have to babysit us, you know. If you need to be at the police station, I think we can handle it. What kind of trouble could me and Jeremy get into at a beach house?"

"I only have you for one more day and I want to make it count." And with that his Spidey sense started tingling. He turned to the porch. "Where's Jeremy?"

Kay turned with him, following the concern in Jake's voice. "He's right—"

But he wasn't.

He was gone.

Jake sprang to his feet, spilling Kay in a tangle of arms and legs. "Where the fuck is he?"

Jake ran for the deck.

23

Jake's head automatically swiveled to the pool as he ran across the deck. The algae was undisturbed and still, the line of sludge that rimmed the concrete a straight demarcation around the perimeter.

Jake saw Jeremy from the top of the steps to the beach. He was at the water's edge, staring out at the ocean. His arms were crossed over his chest as if pondering some important moral question, his body unmoving.

Jake thudded down the ancient weathered planks and raced across the sand. He scooped Jeremy up. "What are you doing out here, Moriarty?" He tried not to sound angry but what he really wanted to keep buried was the panic.

Jeremy tried to squirm out of Jake's grip with the guttural grunts he reserved for times when language was just too civil for the things he needed to say.

"What is it?" Jake swung his son around. "You're not supposed to leave our sight. You know that, kiddo."

Kay came down the steps and ran over. "What the hell is he doing down here?"

Jake shrugged. "He's being pissy. You ask him."

Jeremy gave a final squirm and fell limp. When he seemed to be in control of himself, Jake lowered him to the sand.

"What's wrong?" Kay asked, squatting down on her boots.

Jeremy pointed off into the distance, to the horizon, to the edge of the world.

"What?" Kay asked.

Jake turned to the horizon, scoured the skyline. Then back to Jeremy, examining his face for clues. Then out at the ocean again. "What is it?"

"Elmo!" Jeremy screeched, a voice filled with rage.

And then Jake saw it. Rolling lazily on the deep swell, the red-orange figure of Elmo, face down, spread-eagled in the water. The tide was coming in, not going out, and Elmo was a good 150 feet from shore. Jake held up his hand and felt the steady wind that was pushing straight in at the shore.

Watching Elmo spin lazily in the swell, Kay asked, "How the hell did he—?" And she stopped, because she realized that there was no answer to the question.

The *Sesame Street* critter bobbed on the waves for a few seconds like a drowning victim. He inched closer, but it would take time for him to close the distance to shore and he'd be lucky if he wasn't pulled under by the waves breaking on the beach. It didn't take a physicist to understand that Jeremy could not have gotten him out there; Jake knew even he couldn't throw him that far, headwind or not.

"How did Elmo get out there, Moriarty?"

Jeremy pretended not to hear for a few seconds. Then he realized that his parents were smart enough to know that Elmo hadn't swum out there on his own. "He took him." The boy stood on his toes, his eyes searching for his little red friend. "Carried him into the water, Daddy."

Jake felt the skin tighten around his bones. "Who did, son?"

"The man." He looked up, smiled brightly. "Your friend."

Jake looked into his son's face, searching for … *what*? "My friend? Which friend?"

Jeremy looked like he realized that he might be in trouble. He lifted his face to Kay, searching for a cue. Kay nodded. "It's okay, son. Tell Daddy."

"He said he was your friend, Daddy. He said he played games with you and your mommy when you were little. And that now he wants to play games with me. He wants to be my friend, too."

Kay's features were white now, brittle. "What is he talking about?"

Jake was frozen in place. He tried to shrug, to shake his head – all that came out was a single sentence. "What was his name?"

Jeremy stared out at Elmo lolling on the waves like an orange patch of carpet, well beyond the heft of human strength. "The man. He lives in the floor." The boy kept his eyes locked on Elmo, waiting for him to come in from his swim. He shrugged and his little T-shirt rose up, exposing a big white tummy with a perfect dent of a bellybutton, like a well-grown albino grapefruit. "You know, the man in the floor – he's your buddy. He said so. He said he's your Buddy-Man."

Jake looked over at his wife and saw her bottom lip trembling a little. "Jeremy," she said, maybe a little too harsh.

Recognizing the tone, the boy looked up at her.

"You don't go anywhere without Mommy or Daddy, okay? We've talked about this. There are bad people out there. Mean people."

Jeremy shook his head. "Not the man in the floor. He's Daddy's buddy. He said so." He pointed at the ocean. "Like teaching Elmo to swim."

Jake turned back to the water. Out beyond the surf line, Elmo still spun facedown in the swell, a few bits of seaweed now clinging to his furry orange ass. He didn't look like he was swimming. He looked dead.

"The next time he comes to play, you tell Daddy," Kay said.

Out past the surf line, the swell capped and Elmo was driven down into the black Atlantic.

24

On the way in from a trip to the medical examiner's office, Hauser stopped at his receptionist's desk. She was busy putting office supplies into Ziploc bags – her idea of preparing for the storm.

"I need you to get on the phone to the FBI office we went through last night – the one that gave us Jake Cole. I want to speak to this witch doctor's supervisor or boss or whatever his superior is called. I want him on the phone and I want it done in the next three minutes."

The phone was buzzing by the time he sat down behind his massive slab of oak. "Hauser here."

"Sheriff, this is Field Operations Manager Matthew Carradine – Jake Cole's handler. What can I do for you?"

Handler? What kind of a word was that? Then Hauser remembered Jake's 3-D crime scene party trick and decided that maybe he was looking at a circus act.

Hauser didn't start by telling Carradine that he was glad the guy had called back – that would be too much of an aw-shucks way to start a conversation. "Who is Jake Cole?"

"I don't understand the question, Sheriff Hauser."

He could have pointed out the tattoos or the clothing or the spooky crime scene Ouija show but all of that was secondary. "Jake Cole creeps me out."

Carradine let out a low little rumble that sounded like it had weight to it. It was an irritated, bored sound that said *Go away.* Maybe it worked with people who hadn't seen de-epithelialized children, Hauser thought bitterly.

"Can you be specific, Sheriff?" Meaning, *It's none of your business.*

"Yes, Carradine, I can. What – specifically – does he do? And by that I mean beyond walking through a crime scene with that glazed expression on his face and giving me instructions on how to set up a media plan."

"The FBI is not in the habit of handing out private details pertaining to our personnel."

"Mr. Carradine, I am not some lost fuckstick local sheriff who can't find his cock with both hands. If I am going to work a double homicide with a man, I need to know a little about him."

Carradine was silent on the other end, probably thinking things through, Hauser realized.

It took him ten seconds to begin speaking. "First off, if you want to know about Jake Cole, you'll have to ask him. But I'll tell you what, Sheriff Hauser, I am going to share a little information with you because you can't afford the luxury of mistrust on this one. You don't have the time. Of all the police departments in the United States investigating a homicide right now, yours is the luckiest. If Cole's father wasn't going through what he is, I'd have Jake out of there so fast you'd think he was a dream. I am not denigrating your situation – I've read the file and you have a *real problem* on your hands – but Jake has other cases that are a lot more pressing than yours."

"What's more pressing than a mother and her baby skinned alive?" Hauser asked, reminding himself out loud what was at the center of this whole thing.

"Try nine little boys who have disappeared over the past month and whose parents have been receiving their heads in the mail a few days later – collect. With nails pounded into them. *Pre-mortem.*"

"Jesus."

"Yes. Jesus. Look, I understand that Jake Cole does not fit the bureau profile that we have set for ourselves and I'd be lying if I said that you were the first law-enforcement officer to field a call like this. It's obvious to all parties that Jake's left of center of our phenotype. He works autonomously for us and we are privileged to have him – *you* are privileged to have him." He paused again, as if he was deciding how much to open up to Hauser. "Jake has a rare ability."

"Is he some sort of a psychic?"

Hauser was surprised to hear Carradine laugh, a hearty roar that echoed for a few seconds. "Sheriff, we are good at what we do because of science. Because of protocols we have developed. Because we understand that data supports data and that the eventual outcome is a solution. Not because of some boojie-woojie evil eye. Again, I'd be lying if I told you that you were the first person who had asked me that, but as a lawman you should know better. There are no mediums. No psychics. No people who speak to the dead. That's all unsupported unscientific wishful thinking.

"In simple terms, Jake is the most pragmatic problem solver I have ever seen. First off, he has eidetic memory – I mean complete photographic recall. He walks through a room once and he can recall the tiniest detail, as if he has a digital recorder in his head. It's a little disconcerting because it's very uncommon. It's also remarkable. Jake would be the first to tell you about it if you bothered to ask."

Hauser felt himself drop the classification of Jake as some kind of circus freak to little more than a stupid human trick. "It's not some weird *I-see-dead-people* thing?"

Carradine let a little chuckle roll out again. "No, Sheriff, it's just a very keen power of observation. And if his calm gets to you, please remember that he sees the worst of humanity all the time. It takes a lot to get him flustered."

Hauser remembered Jake in the ME's subterranean room, caressing Madame X's peeled foot.

"Have I answered your questions?" The tone told Hauser that his five minutes were over.

Hauser realized that in a way he now knew less about Jake Cole than before he had made the call. "I guess so," he said, then added a tired "Thank you," and hung up.

25

Jake crouched in front of the master bedroom pocket door. He had managed to spread it a few more inches, and the opening was almost large enough for Kay to squeeze her nearly diminutive body through. She stood in front of him, her arm and shoulder already through the crack. From his vantage point, her crotch was in his face and he felt himself staring at the tight V of her jean shorts instead of concentrating on getting the door open.

"Can you get that out of my face?" he said between clenched teeth and gave the door another tug. It moved slowly in, as if the pocket were filled with tightly packed sand.

"What?"

"That," he said, nodding at her crotch.

"My vagina?"

"I can't open this door and stare at your camel toe at the same time. It's too distracting."

"Camel toe? I have a camel toe? I thought current nomenclature was *cooch*. When did we go to camel toe?"

"When you put those shorts on." Jake rolled his eyes. "Now cut it out."

"Oh, all right." She squatted down beside him, resting the part of her ass that was hanging out of her shorts on the heels of her boots again. "This better?" she craned her neck theatrically, to see if anything was popping out. "No fur."

Jake shook his head sadly. "Jesus, where did I find you?" he asked rhetorically.

"AA – us good ones all hang out at AA meetings. We get to meet the cool guys there. The guys who have no jobs, no friends, no self-esteem. Or if they do have jobs, they're like really creepy jobs that don't make them happy." That had been six-plus years now. *Before*, in the language of their relationship. *Before* they had fallen in love or had Jeremy or had found the feeling of safety neither had ever experienced but both had recognized on sight. "And in exchange these guys get hot musician babes with no jobs, no self-esteem, and big juicy camel toes." She leaned forward and kissed him. "Now open this fucking door, Houdini, we need a place to sleep and if we have to crash in the living room, you won't get to put anything in my warm parts tonight." Her freckled face scrunched up. "Clear?"

Jake nodded. "I'm working on it, okay?"

Another good tug and it opened enough for Kay to squeeze through.

"Lucky you," she said. "You're gonna get some lovin' later."

Jake stood up without brushing the dust bunnies off of his jeans. His peripheral vision stayed on Jeremy engineering the death of more imaginary two-inch motorists. "I'm glad he doesn't pay attention to your mouth."

Kay managed to squeeze through the crack by putting her hands over her head and sliding sideways. Her breasts made a scraping sound on the wood when they popped through. She flipped a switch and a single table lamp on the floor in the corner sputtered to yellow, feeble life.

"Oh, hey. Here's why you couldn't budge the door."

There was a soft clack and she slid the door back, a two-foot screwdriver in her hand. "Your dad drove this through the wall, into the door."

Jake rolled the door closed again, and saw the crude hole whittled into it.

"How did he get out, though?"

Kay looked at the doorway, the hole in the wall, the screwdriver, and did some rough calculating. "He could have reached through and locked it from the outside. You'd have to know where this was to get to it but if you've got long arms …"

A heavy chest of drawers blocked the opening and Jake slid over the top. The room, like the rest of the house, was cluttered, although this one felt more like a lair. The bed didn't look filthy but the sheets were crumpled and knotted on top of the mattress in the shape of a human nest. Clothes – mostly his father's standard work outfit of jeans and white T-shirts – were strewn about. There were empty scotch bottles, cracker boxes, and anchovy tins in the way of garbage. And, of course, a few dozen yellow plastic utility knives.

"This isn't good," Kay said in a long, low whisper.

"Let's jimmy the locks on my old room and my mother's office."

His mother's office was a static photo of what it had been all those years ago – exactly as it had been when Jake left – exactly as it had been for the five years previous to that. More than thirty years of closed air and dust and sadness. His own room was sparse and bare, as if no one had ever lived there at all.

Kay brushed her hands off on her thighs. "I'll get some garbage bags. We'll be sleeping in your father's room."

Jake watched her walk down the hall and head for the stairs. As she passed Jeremy he watched her gingerly lift her foot above the invisible crowd he was plowing his car through. When she was out of sight he turned his head back toward the bedroom at the end of the hallway. A single question looped through his head: *Why would he barricade the door?*

26

Hauser sat on a stool by the counter dividing the kitchen from the open room that made up most of the ground floor and the exposed hallway that ran overhead. He sat back, his Stetson on his knee, stoically fingering the rim of his coffee cup. He felt better about Jake, more at ease, after talking to Carradine. They had a case to get to. But first Hauser felt like he needed to apologize.

Jake stood behind the counter, leaning against the bank of drawers that hid more of the creepy little paintings. Kay and Jeremy were upstairs in the bath, cleaning off. The sound of the water running was almost overpowered by a radio belting out *Sesame Street* tunes, Jake's attempt at making up for Elmo's mysterious drowning.

"I called Carradine." Hauser's finger stopped tracing the rim of the hand-thrown mug and his eyes lifted.

Jake took a sip of his own coffee, pausing the lip of the cup below his chin. "What did he tell you that you think I wouldn't have?"

Hauser loosened up a little. "I'm sorry, Jake. I am not used to working with outsiders. It was a mistake."

Jake shrugged. "I have a predictable effect on people. I'm sure Carradine told you this is more than some sort of Freudian fantasy to find my mother's killer."

Hauser shifted uncomfortably in his seat, lifted his hand. "I didn't say—"

"I did," Jake said very calmly. "This is not some subconscious quest to make things right in the universe so I can put the little frightened boy that still lives inside me at ease."

"That sounds like therapist speak."

"It is. I've spent a lot of my time in the offices of people who spend their time listening to other people's problems. I had to. I wasted too much of my life being angry and self-medicating."

"The booze?"

Jake laughed. "When I was roaring, the booze was the least of my vices." Something in Jake's eyes turned off and the light coming in through the big windows was no longer reflected in his pupils. "The booze was how I pressurized, how I medicated in public. Problem with me is that I inherited my old man's metabolism. I have an LR that's in the basement – meaning little reaction to alcohol – and that goes for *anything* I put in my body." Jake shook his head. "And I put everything you can imagine into the machine. I have a pacemaker in my chest, Mike. I did so much heroin they're not sure my heart will beat without a mechanical aid. I used to do speedballs for breakfast."

The sheriff shifted in his seat; he was a man who was used to people trying to hide their secrets from him.

"Whenever my heart rate rises above – or drops below – a certain point, I get zapped by the little plastic juice-box they wired into my sternum." He shrugged, like it really didn't matter one way or the other. "In a lot of ways, it is a drug of its own – the lets-me-know-I'm-not-yet-dead drug."

Hauser finished his coffee in a big gulp and slid the mug across the counter, declining a refill with the shake of his head. "I thought you were some sort of a paranormal freak."

Jake's mouth flattened a little. "There are no psychics. It's called *cold reading*. Remember the Sherlock Holmes story, *The Sign of Four*?"

"I'm more of a movie guy."

Jake smiled. "Watson hands Holmes a watch and asks what can be deduced by observation. Watson feels that as a mass-produced item, it reveals nothing of the owner. Holmes examines the piece, hands it back, and rattles off a litany of details about the previous owner – who he says is Watson's brother. The man was a drunkard, he was often broke, and so on and so forth à la the smug bastard everyone knows Holmes to be. Watson gets pissed and accuses Holmes of contacting his family to learn the history of his poor brother." Jake took a sip of coffee. "The deductions were simple. Holmes saw the initials and knew that it had belonged to Watson's father, after which it was handed down to the eldest son – as was customary. There were pawn numbers scratched into the case that pointed at the brother falling in and out of debt – otherwise he would neither have pawned the watch, nor been able to pick it up. The keyhole was scratched and Holmes figured that no sober man would miss the hole as consistently as was evident. To Holmes it was obvious. Watson thought it was witch-doctory.

"There is no contacting the *other side*. It's bullshit like tarot card reading and palmistry and tea leaves and faith healing. Like Sagan was kind enough to point out, there is *zero data*. There are no psychics, Hauser. And anyone who believes in them is ill-informed or stupid." He had given the monologue enough times that it was stage-honed.

"I'll go with ill-informed on this one," Hauser said slowly and Jake could see the wheels in his head turning.

Jake smiled. "A vast segment of the population out there believe in stupidity. John Edward, that guy who dupes people into thinking he's talking to their dead loved ones, should have his fucking head cut off on live TV."

"A little harsh."

"Just truth. There is no afterlife. There are no leprechauns, or religious visions, or extraterrestrial visitors. There are only psychotic breaks from reality, chemical-induced hallucinations, and good old-fashioned fucking lying which is the one that I see employed more than anything else."

Jake went to the big doors that opened up onto the beach. He pulled the latches and accordioned them open. The air in the house changed with one big pulse and all of a sudden everything smelled fresher, newer.

Hauser was still leaning against the counter. "You believe in the Devil?"

Jake put his hands on his hips and eyed Hauser for a minute. "Every culture has a name for the bogeyman and when you look at shit like that," he said, pointing at the files on the coffee table, "I understand why."

"You didn't answer the question."

Jake locked him in another stare. "Guys like Francis Collins think that God had to have a hand in our design because morality exists. I look around at our species and I can't for the life of me figure out what the fuck he's talking about. The history of this world – especially the religious history – is one big disgusting bloodbath." Jake shook his head. "So no, I don't believe in the Devil. I don't need to, man has done enough horrible things to impress me. You give human beings the opportunity to be monstrous and you will never be disappointed." His point made, he turned to the horizon. "What's the news on the storm?"

Hauser swiveled, keeping his butt in the seat. "Landfall is right here."

"Fuck."

"Yeah, well, that's one way to put it." Hauser lifted his mass out of the modern stool and came over to the window, put his hands on his hips – the right automatically resting on the grip of his sidearm, the leather holster creaking with the contact. "I spoke to the Weather Service and the National Hurricane Center this morning. Dylan's a strong Category Five and there's a good chance that it stays a five. I don't know shit about hurricanes and even less about categories in particular, but I looked it up and five is bad, worse than 1938 and that thing wiped out the highway, the railroad, destroyed half the houses here, washed buildings out to sea, snapped our power poles like they were straw, and killed seventy people in the area. The shoreline was rearranged like a shovel going at a carton of eggs." Hauser's lips pursed for a minute, and he shook his head. "And it's electric."

"No such thing," Jake said.

"You need new data," he said, mimicking Dennison from the NHC. "This thing will be pounding lightning around like some kind of science fiction film. We could be the last people to be standing on this spot, Jake. A few days from now, this could be in the ocean."

"In a few days from now we could be dead," Jake said, taking the existential statement one step further. "Or the planet could be gone."

Hauser shifted his gun hand. "You are one grim sonofabitch, you know that."

Jake shook his head sadly. "Every time I see some broken, discarded person left in a field, or washed up on a riverbank, I think to myself, *This is it – this is the last one. Tomorrow I will wake up and people will no longer do this to one another.* Yet they do."

"Is that it? The work? I mean, have you gotten so used to seeing –" he paused, his mind taken back to the skinnings up the beach – "things like last night that you just think all people are bad?"

"It's like we're just filling out time until the whole anthill bursts into flames."

"What about your kid?" As a father, he knew that children could bring a lot of good to their immediate surroundings. He also knew they could bring a lot of sadness to the world. Hauser's son had been killed by a drunk driver.

Jake walked through the open doors, onto the stained, salt-eaten deck. "Jeremy's the best. But he's three and there's a lot of road between now and the end of his life. He's never going to grow up into one of the monsters I hunt – I know that for a fact." At the back of his mind, hidden behind a few crates of bad memories, he felt something twitch in the darkness. "But I can't guarantee that he's going to be happy. Or have good self-esteem. Or marry someone who loves him as much as I do. Sure, right now – I mean *right now* – things are all shiny and bright." He thought back to Jeremy on the beach that morning, still giddy from riding on the bus, thinking that Moon Pies were better than anything in the world. It would be great if things stayed like that. But what about thirty years from now?

Hauser's head shifted a few degrees, like a dog listening for a noise it thought it had heard. "One of those glass-is-half-full kind of people."

Jake shook his head. "Not at all. The glass is what the glass is."

"You have a unique way of looking at things."

On the horizon the clouds had thickened. They were not yet ominous, but something about them suggested that they were recon scouts for an approaching army. "Landfall's not until tomorrow night but the NHC guy said we'll see the front come in later this evening. The wind'll pick up and the rain is going to start. It'll be uncomfortable by tomorrow afternoon. By nightfall hell will be rolling through town."

Jake thought back to the woman and child up the beach. *Skinned.* He thought about his father, ramped up on sedatives and scraping portraits onto hospital room walls with fried bones and charred flesh. He thought about the old man's screams. About how his mother had been murdered. About all the poisonous water that had gone under the bridge in this place. "Hell's already here," he said, and walked back into the house.

27

Hauser was gone, and Kay and Jeremy were finishing up lunch, Jeremy's face bisected by a line of raspberry jam that made him look like the Joker. The clouds on the horizon had grown fatter, and the pregnant belly of the ocean was hazing over. The wind had picked up but it was still little more than a fall breeze, a light little hiss that would soon begin to change into a malevolent beast. Jake stood in front of the studio, another member of the quarter-century club, and wondered what he would find inside Pandora's building. He felt like he was using his father to avoid the case even though there was very little he could do right now. He had seen the crime scene, talked to the ME, and received Hauser's protocols. There wasn't much for him to do now but sift through what he had – and give Hauser all the information he could put together. So he occupied himself with trying to find a way into his father's studio.

He walked around it a few times, searching for an entry. There wasn't much in the way of security; the windows were all single-pane, glazed with brittle old putty; the door had a decent lock on it but the top half was glass – all he'd have to do is smash it and reach inside. The weird part – if he could even consider it weird after everything else he had found – was that all the windows had been painted over from the inside. Wherever he tried to see into the building, all he saw was a black mirror reflecting his own image.

"Fuck it," he said aloud, and pulled his elbow back to punch out one of the mullioned panes. Then the voice – the one with the perfect memory – reminded him of the ring of keys back in the fridge.

He ran inside, grabbed them, and came back out – all in a quick jog. He tried a few keys until he found one that worked, then opened the door and stepped inside.

Jake closed the door behind himself, flipped the lock, and slowly moved into the dark.

He cracked the lighting to life and looked around. Like the house, the space had a large main floor and a mezzanine overhead. About a quarter of the downstairs was the garage, and had a single door centered in the wall as access. The rest of the space had been Jacob Coleridge's studio, but unlike the stasis of the house, the studio had changed. A lot. Jake looked around and sucked in a long, low breath that actually scraped his windpipe as it went down.

Jacob had painted every available surface – including the floor and ceiling – a flat black. He had then decorated this negative space with dozens of portraits of the same bloody man from the hospital wall, filling the dark expanse with anatomical studies out of a Hieronymus Bosch-inspired hell. They were deftly executed and hyperdetailed – anatomically perfect. Except they were faceless. The sense of menace they conveyed could not be ignored.

Jake walked to the center of the studio and spun in place, trying to take in the work. Each figure was frighteningly executed, the flesh breathing, the blood pumping. No matter which figure Jake looked at, it seemed to be watching him back with faceless malevolence.

The ceiling was twenty feet above the painted concrete floor of the studio, hidden in a seamless cloud of shadow and black paint. As he moved beneath the beams the figures painted on the ceiling looked like they were crawling around in the darkness, following him. When he stopped moving, the illusion ceased, and the bloody figures froze in place.

But the strange part – the part that somehow eclipsed Jacob's garage/studio Sistine Chapel of demented demons – were the canvases piled up everywhere; the same senseless pieces that were scattered all over the house. There were hundreds of them – maybe even thousands – filling every available scrap of space, stacked like valueless cargo. Jake looked around in awe, thinking of the old adage about the manic woodchuck. *How many crazy paintings would a crazy painter paint if a crazy painter could paint crazy paintings?*

The answer was, of course, *a shitload.*

Jake picked one up and examined the composition. It was like the ones in the kitchen drawer, or in the upstairs hallway, or under the piano – a lifeless shape of near-color. He flipped through a few. Some were gray, others black, some the color of rotting tumors. More paintings of nothing. Negative space. Dead blobs. But the quantity gave them a communal voice that let him know that there was a point to them. How long had these taken? A year? Two? Ten? He put the canvas back and looked around the studio.

The faceless figures up in the rafters were still following him. His father had never considered himself a classicist, but the three-dimensional representations of whatever the fuck he was looking at were beyond lifelike. They were astounding. Tormented, horrid effigies, that represented ... that represented ... he swung his head across the black skyline of the ceiling, pulling in the details of the same man Jacob had painted on the wall of his hospital room – just what *did* they represent?

Skinned, they whispered in unison.

These were a message. A signal. There was a reason behind them. Jake could sense its signal but he couldn't isolate the meaning. And this bothered him. These lifeless little canvases said something. Like the faceless man of blood on the hospital wall. Like the Chuck Close portrait with the missing eyes. Like the stacks of paintings. Could it be nothing more than madness? Alzheimer's? Paranoia? All of the above?

Somewhere in the decaying apple of his father's mind was a worm of a thought that the old man listened to. It had wriggled through his skull, sending him diseased instructions that he deciphered in his own way. How much of that had bled into what he had tried to say here? This couldn't all be random – there was too much in the way of long-term planning and execution. Someone with Alzheimer's would have gone off the rails a long time ago. So what was he trying to say?

Jake spun on the floor, his eyes digging into the walls, trying to see around the pillars of canvases stacked like pizza boxes. From a *trompe l'oeil* perspective, it was an engineering feat. Wherever he stood, the faceless watched him.

They were trying to tell him something.

Like the speech of the dead that he deciphered, he needed the code. The common language. That secret way his old man's mind worked. Which might as well have been written in Easter Island glyphs.

What he did – what he was good at – was figuring out how killers thought. And the killers he hunted were artists. From a societal perspective it was demented, sadistic art, but that was missing the obvious; to *them* it was art. And it was always expressed with a unique voice; the language of the worm firing bursts of code into the rotting apple. Jake's gift had always been figuring out the artist-specific language of the murderers he hunted, figuring out their own personal symbolism and its subtext. If he could look at a murder scene through the eyes of the psychotic, how much harder would it be to look at this space through the eyes of a man he shared some common ground with? It was a different language – the language of the mad – but it was still *language*. Which meant it was decipherable. What was—?

—And there was a jolt of electricity that came at him out of nowhere, shaking the engine room beneath his ribs. He had time to grab his chest before there was another crackle in the circuitry. Fell to his knees.

Then his stomach.

The floor stretched away into the dark at a right angle to his line of sight, and dust bunnies danced in front of his face with his breath.

How many crazy paintings would a crazy painter paint? echoed somewhere off in the distance.

Then everything faded away, even the canopy of faceless stares.

28

For a second there was the black-hot pain of a fist clenching inside his skull and as quickly as it took hold, it faded to a distant hammer against the membrane of his mind. Kay was in a rectangle of light, her hair outlined in a phosphorescent glow, rushing forward, mouth flying open. A filling twinkled amid her molars.

"Jesus! Fuck! Jake!"

He pushed himself up onto his knees, holding his chest.

"I prefer *See Spot run*, but if it turns you on …" He let the sentence trail off.

Kay helped him to his feet.

"Sorry, baby. The jukebox took a hit. I guess I got too excited." He stood up shakily, massaging his chest.

She punched him in the arm. "Thanks for scaring the piss out of me. Usually you just twinge a bit and you're good." Kay wondered what could have set his heart rate through the roof.

Jake turned away from her, back to the images on the walls and ceiling. "Whacha think?" he asked, nodding up into the darkness.

She followed his nod and her mouth twitched into an uncomfortable grin, all teeth and no lips. "This is Gustave Doré on psychotropic leave."

Jake nodded. "Apt comparison."

Kay walked slowly around the room.

Like Jake, she was more impressed with the endless stacks of little paintings than the bleeding men in the black sky overhead, although it was obvious that she felt they were following her as well by the way she kept glancing up at them. She threaded between the pillars of paintings, trying to make sense of it all. "There has to be three thousand of these things."

Jake did a rough and dirty calculation. "Closer to five."

"There's a bunch in the house, too." Kay stopped, picked one up. "Are they all a different shape?"

Jake shrugged. "Looks like. Just in framing it would take a year to stretch all of these. Then to gesso the canvases and paint them ..." He let the sentence die. "Mad as a –" he looked around the place and a wave of sadness sunk into his flesh – "painter. You sure you want to spend the rest of your life with a guy like me? This," he said, sweeping his arm over the piles of canvases, "is hereditary. Except with me, it will be pictures of dead people." Jake sat down on the edge of the framing table, one of the only uncluttered surfaces in the studio.

Kay pointed at the door to the garage. "What's in there?"

Jake, brought away from the dark ride he was taking through the demon-haunted universe painted by his father, looked over. "Garage."

"Can I?"

He shrugged. "Knock yourself out."

She turned the knob and to both their surprise it swung open on greased hinges. Kay flicked a switch beside the door and the lights in the garage hummed to life. The room, in direct contrast to the studio, was painted in a bright blue-white. A car sat in the middle of the space and Jake eased forward, not realizing that he had stopped breathing again.

He got closer to the door and the image of the automobile began to widen. The skin was obscured by a thick layer of dust that hadn't been disturbed in years. The windshield was opaque and the whole car looked like it had been sitting in here unnoticed forever. Jake knew this car, knew what it looked like under the neglect, and it reminded him of the night that everything had fallen apart. His life. His father's. Everything turned to bloody black dirt in one big swing of fate.

It had been his mother's – a 1966 Mercedes W113 in factory cream with a red leather interior. Jake remembered the morning they had brought it back on a flatbed after her murder. Jacob was drunk and had stayed in the house. Jake had helped them back up the truck and when they had rolled the Benz off, it had grazed the paneling under the window. They had closed the door and that seemed to be the end of it all. The sealing of the tomb of the queen.

At the front of the garage sat a cracked leather Eames lounge chair. It was dust free and surrounded by a forest of whiskey bottles, the floor at its feet worn smooth. He saw the chair, the bottles, and a quick flowchart sparked to life in his head. How often had his father come in here? Once a year? A month? A week? Looking at the forest of bottles and the smooth ring worn around the base of the chair, Jake guessed that he had come in here often. Maybe every night. Perched in his Captain Kirk chair, bottle of anger fuel in his hand, thinking about his dead wife. Probably never driven the car. It had stayed right here for how long? Thirty-three years now.

Jake moved slowly down the wall and peered at the back bumper. It was still touching the panel where it had rolled to a stop all those years ago, a fibrous tear in the grain of the wood, still splintered but now covered in dust and cobwebs.

It was obvious that it had not been moved since the morning after his mother's murder.

The last people to touch it had probably been the flat-bed guys. Before that, the police. And before that, his mother's killer.

"Don't touch anything," Jake said, holding his own hands up as an example.

"Why?"

Jake ignored her and took out his cell phone. Dialed. "Yeah, Smolcheck, Jake Cole. You have time to do a car for me? Sure. Yeah. No. 1966 Mercedes convertible. Two-seater."

Pause.

"It was part of a murder scene thirty-three years ago."

Pause.

"I think so. Local police went through it."

Pause.

"Returned to the family within twenty hours of the crime."

Pause.

"Bare storage. Unheated but safe from the elements."

Pause.

"No, no traffic. No one has touched it. Yeah. Yeah. I think so. Yeah."

Longer pause.

"Okay, I'll book storage from here. I'll do the best I can. Poly-ethylene and duct tape. Got it. Sure."

Pause.

"Thanks, Smolcheck. I appreciate it. It's cold but it's going to help me with a lateral case. I'll make sure I go through Carradine. Don't worry, it will be okayed by the time it gets there."

Jake hung up and focused on a note taped to one of the scotch bottles: *YOUR NAME IS JACOB COLERIDGE. KEEP PAINTING.*

Oh, you kept painting, you mad old motherfucker, Jake thought. *And what were you trying to say?*

He looked up and Kay was gone, back in the house with Jeremy. How long had he been in one of his trances?

He put his hand to his chest and felt his heartbeat. Everything was fine. Fit as a fucking fiddle. When he thought about it, it was amazing what you could live through. Nietzsche had been right. After killing yourself three times with a high-octane mix of China White and Columbian, there was pretty much nothing else on the planet you were afraid of.

Except maybe the past.

29

Jake sat atop an old dented mechanic's chest filled with brushes, palette knives, and the assorted implements of his father's trade. It was an old Snap-on model, covered in painted fingerprints, brush-strokes, and random cuts of color. An open but untouched bottle of Coke sat on the concrete floor, bleeding condensation in a wet ring that seeped into the dust. He had one boot up on the edge of the tool chest and he hugged his knee, staring off into darkness decorated like Breughel's *The Triumph of Death*. There was no exterior light, and bright bulbs lighted the room.

At first he thought it was the wind. Just an oblong sound that the ocean had somehow kicked up. Then he heard it a second time, the distinct cadence of human speech in its vowels. Someone was yelling. It was a tentative yell, but a yell nonetheless.

"Hello? Hello?"

Jake recognized the voice, the accent. He unfolded himself from atop the tool chest, stood up, and walked outside.

A man in a suit was on the balcony, bent over and peering into the living room. The posture, the hair, the soft pink hands clasped behind his back, the well-tailored suit – hadn't changed in twenty-eight years. Jake walked quietly up behind him, leaned in, and very softly said, "Hello, David."

David Finch jumped, banged his head on the mullion, and converted the startled jerk into a quickly extended hand. "Hello."

Jake stood there for a second, appraising the man. "It's me. Jake."

Finch's eyes narrowed, and he took in Jake with an exaggerated up-and-down. "Jakey?" He examined his face, his big polished smile opening up. "You still look like Charles Bronson."

David Finch was one of the top gallery owners in New York and Jacob Coleridge had been one of his first discoveries. The two events were not mutually exclusive.

"And you look like a parasite coming to feed on a not-yet-dead cash cow."

"I didn't know you and your father were that close, Jakey."

"Fuck you."

"Still making money with that mouth?" Finch asked.

Jake took a step closer to the man and opened his teeth in an ugly smile. "What do you want?"

"I sent flowers. Did your father get them?"

Jake remembered the broken vase on the floor. "My father isn't getting anything anymore."

Finch looked around the deck. What for? Help, maybe. "Jakey, can we talk?"

Jake thought about the last time he had seen the man. About how he had asked for thirty-one dollars. About how he had been turned down. About the things he had done to feed himself because of that. "No, David, I don't think we can." Besides, Kay and Jeremy were inside and Jake didn't want them to get contaminated by any more of his old life than they already had.

"I need to talk to you about your father's work."

Jake thought about the bloody portrait splattered onto the hospital wall. "Dad's not making a lot of sense on any level, David. The old Jacob Coleridge is on a permanent vacation."

Finch pointed at the Chuck Close through the window, the eyes gone. "Jacob Coleridge would never do this to a Close. Cy Twombly maybe – *maybe*. But a Close? Rome could be burning and he'd be the guy defending the museum with an axe."

"It's Alzheimer's, David – not a German opera. Jacob Coleridge is not coming back."

Finch's head swiveled in an angry jerk. "I know you and your father haven't exactly been simpatico, Jake, but *I* know your old man; we've been friends for almost fifty years. We've stuck by one another when the going was tough and both of us had plenty of opportunities when we should have taken up other offers in the interest of our careers. But we didn't because we were a good team. And that only happens when you know someone. Know them intimately. And Jacob Coleridge could be drunk off his ass with his cock falling off from a bout of syphilis and be using someone else's liver because his was out being dry-cleaned and he'd never lay a finger on a Chuck Close. Too much respect. Too much professional admiration. Never. Ever. No way." Finch turned back to the painting.

Jake followed his gaze, then looked beyond the painting into the kitchen. Kay and Jeremy were gone. Maybe down on the beach for a walk. He saw his own reflection staring back at him. "If you say so."

"Did your father have any work in the studio?" The gallery owner asked, the unmistakable lilt of greed in his voice.

"It's empty. It was filled with crap and most of it's gone." It was a lie but Jake didn't feel like having an argument with Finch. If the sycophantic little fuck had his way, he'd be peeling up the paint-splattered floor in the studio and selling it by the square foot at Sotheby's in their spring sale of important American art.

Finch stared into Jake's face for a second. "Jake, you do know that I am your father's sole representative. We have a *lifetime and beyond* contract."

"What the fuck does that mean?" Jake's patience was running out. His old man had fried his hands off and this parasite was here to sniff out a commission.

"That means that I have proprietary rights on his paintings in reference to sales. No one – and that means you, too – can sell a Jacob Coleridge."

Jake crossed the space that had developed between them in a long-legged stride that would have made Hauser proud. "David, you and my father may have been friends but as far as I'm concerned, you're a smarmy little bloodsucker who would do anything for his wallet. Do you remember the night I showed up at your house when I left here?"

Finch sunk into himself, brought his head down. Said nothing.

"I was seventeen years old, David, and I was alone on the streets of New York. I came to you because you were the only person I knew in the city. *The only one.* And do you remember what I asked for?"

Finch shook his head but it was clear from his expression that he did.

"I asked for some food, David. I asked for a meal and thirty-one bucks. I didn't ask for too much because I didn't want to jeopardize your relationship with my father – I knew he'd get rid of you if you helped me. So I asked for very little." Jake's hands hung loosely at his sides and Finch's eyes kept looking at them, something about the way they hung limply more threatening than if they had been rolled into tattooed fists. "You said no. Do you know what I had to do to eat? Do you, David?"

Finch shook his head slowly, keeping his eyes on Jake's hands.

"I had to blow some guy, Dave. I know that's your kind of thing, but it's not mine. I was seventeen and alone and I had to suck some stranger's cock so I could get something to eat. Nice, huh? So if you're thinking about threatening someone, you're picking on the wrong guy. Not only will you never see another of my father's paintings, but I may just burn them."

Finch gasped like he had been kicked in the pills.

"I can use them for fucking target practice." He pulled out the big stainless revolver and placed it to Finch's head. "You know what I do for a living, David?" Finch would have looked into it before coming out here – he was the kind of man who liked to cover all his bases.

Finch nodded. It was a frightened, skittish action.

"Then you know I don't have a squeamish bone in my body." Jake cocked the hammer on the pistol and pressed the heavy barrel into Finch's temple, denting the skin. "I could empty your head all over this deck for trespassing and no one would think twice about pressing charges. So don't you fucking threaten me, you little sack of shit, because I passed *don't-give-a-shit* about ten years back and have become comfortably ensconced in *don't-give-a-fuck*. Are we clear?"

"What about your wife? Your child?" Finch asked, his voice half an octave from hysteria.

"Was that a threat, David?" Jake's other hand came up and locked on Finch's larynx in a Ranger chokehold. "Because if it is, you are a dead man."

Finch shook his head, coughed, brought his hands up to the tattooed vise fastened to his throat. "No. No. I didn't—. I—. I—. Let go—!"

Jake pulled his hand away and Finch fell back against the railing. It creaked in protest.

"I think you better leave, David. Before I start getting angry."

Finch opened his mouth to protest but his jaw froze. There was an instant of indecision as he made whatever calculations he thought necessary, then he turned and walked away.

Jake followed him off the deck, around the house, and watched him open the door to the big silver Bentley GT Continental. He stopped again, turned to face Jake, and said, "Not that it makes a bit of difference, Jakey, but I'm sorry. I always was. About everything. Your father's drinking. Your mother's murder. All of it."

"Don't ever contact me again, David. You're dead as far as I'm concerned."

Finch got into the big sedan, closed the door, and slipped out of the drive onto the Montauk Highway. Jake watched the Bentley until it was out of sight, then turned and walked back to the studio.

30

The wind had picked up considerably over the past few hours and the ocean was hazed over with low-slung blue clouds and the jagged dance of whitecaps kicking up. For a few minutes he stood leaning against the railing, knowing that something was off but not being able to localize it. Something felt odd, eerie – then he realized that the ever-present shorebirds had disappeared; there were no plovers, sandpipers, or gulls milling about the beach or riding the stiff wind coming in off the water. What do they know that I don't? Jake wondered.

He stood on the deck, sipping what felt like the hundredth coffee of the day, watching the truck pull to a stop in front of the garage, beeping like a gargantuan alarm clock. One of the carriers stood at the truck's flank, directing the driver with the lazy movements of a man who trusts the guy behind the wheel. He was dressed in gray workman's Dickies with the telltale bulge of a sidearm pressing the fabric each time he raised his arm.

Jake stepped off the weathered wood planking and walked over to the big Hino. The twenty-four-foot covered flatbed was one of the bureau's "clean" trucks, a boxed-in van that shielded evidence vehicles from the elements as well as peripheral con-tamination. The driver was simply that but the second man, the one who had directed the truck with the airfield hand gestures, was a technician, here to make sure that as little evidence as pos-sible was disturbed.

The technician in the Dickies met Jake at the edge of the gravel drive. True to his kind, he was all business. "Special Agent Cole?" he said, extending a hand.

Jake nodded, shook.

"Miles Rafferty." With the exception of the firearm pressing against the fabric of his coveralls, Rafferty looked like a guy con-tracted to paint the garage/studio. "I was told that the evidence you are looking for in the vehicle is twenty-eight years old."

Jake nodded. "Thirty-three, actually."

Rafferty's face didn't change. "The wind's a little strong here so what I'd like to do is bag the car before we pull it onto the bed."

"The tires are flat and I'm not sure—"

Rafferty waved it away. "I have a set of wheel dollies that'll take care of that. Can I see the vehicle?"

Jake asked him to wait outside while he went through the studio; he didn't want anyone getting a look at the crazy shit his father had painted all over the room. He went into the garage and lifted the old door about three feet and Rafferty crawled under.

Rafferty walked around the car, examining it with profes-sional scrutiny. He scoured the vehicle with a flashlight, occasion-ally leaning in close to examine something that caught his eye, getting down on the floor, balanced on his gloved palms and the tips of his booted toes, to peer at the undercarriage. It took him five minutes to go around the car. When he was done he stood up, went back outside under the half-closed door, and came back in with a sealed bag the size of a large pillow.

He pulled two static-free plastic jumpsuits out of the bag and handed one to Jake. "Pull this on over your clothes – it won't pick up any dirt or contaminate the car. Use the hood, it's not too hot in here so we won't sweat too much."

Rafferty pulled on his own, standing on one foot at a time, balancing as the other went through a leg hole that seemed designed for someone a lot shorter and heavier. Jake stepped into his and when he closed his eyes it smelled like he was putting on a new shower curtain.

Rafferty pulled the rest of the contents out of the bag, a folded sheet of polyethylene. They stretched it over the Mercedes and Rafferty taped the corners. When the car was encased in the plastic, he ran a second piece beneath it, protecting the undercarriage.

Jake knew that the plastic would protect it from contamination and losing evidence on the way into the truck.

Jake's phone rang.

Without being asked, Rafferty said, "I can take care of myself." And with that he opened the garage door.

"Jake Cole."

"Jake, it's Hauser. Two things, I wasn't able to reach the Farmers, but I spoke to their daughter – she lives in Portland – said her folks rented the house to 'some nice people' they met through an online real-estate rental service. There was no computer in the house and the Farmers live in Boston. I've asked for a warrant to access their email accounts but that will take until the morning to clear since we've only got the daughter's word on this and it doesn't look like the Farmers are in any way involved in the murder. I have, however, been able to get to their banking records.

"They're renting the place out for four grand a month. Not very much money for a place like that. Funds were in the form of postal money orders. They were bought with cash. I've put a trace on them and when they come back we can check with the actual branch that sold them; unfortunately no one keeps track of postal money orders. You're not allowed to purchase them with a credit card and if you're paying cash, no one really asks questions unless you buy ten grand. It will take three days and it's probably a dead end." Hauser sounded frustrated. "So each step takes us further and further away."

"*Nice people* implies more than a mother and child, doesn't it?" Jake went back into the studio, closing and locking the door behind him. In here, in the womblike dark, there was a soft silence.

"One of the neighbors – she wasn't home the night of the murders – walked by the Farmer house on Tuesday afternoon and thinks she saw a woman and child walking on the beach. She couldn't give any sort of a description other than she looked thin and the child had a lot of energy. They were too far for her to get any solid details. Saw them twice. But no husband. No boyfriend."

"Could be the man works a lot. Could be she has a girlfriend," Jake offered. "If she saw the child on the beach with a woman more than once – and she couldn't identify the woman – maybe there were two women."

There was a pause as Hauser digested this little bit of possibility. "Hadn't thought of that."

"How long have they been renting the place?"

"Two weeks back. Looks like an end-of-season rental. Daughter said her folks were happy that they had found someone who wanted the place for the fall. It was short notice."

"Why come here in the fall on short notice?" Jake paced the studio, painting the pixels of data into the 3-D model he had assembled in his mind the night before when he had walked onto the set. "When did the first money order get deposited?"

"August thirtieth."

"September first lease. They've been here more than two weeks. Someone has seen them. Guaranteed."

Hauser let out a sigh. "Problem is, most of the neighbors have packed up and left."

Jake remembered the advancing storm. "How long until it's too late to leave?"

"The wind will get bad tonight. Rain, too. Serious rain by the morning. By supper things will be intense. I'd say leaving at two p.m. tomorrow is cutting it short. Just in case something goes wrong – and something *always* goes wrong." There was a pause. "You thinking about your wife and child?"

"I'm thinking about all of us."

"When are you getting on the road?"

Jake thought about lying but it wasn't something he felt good at. "I'm staying."

"Jake, the Southampton hospital is a solid building that is going to resist the storm surge and winds. It was designed to withstand a hurricane. Hell, any municipal building erected after the big one of '38 was designed to withstand a missile attack." There was a pause. "I will personally look in on your old man. You don't need to worry about him."

What could he say to that? *I really don't give a flying fuck? Because when it comes down to it, it's everything else that has me on edge. It's the woman and her child up the beach. It's the studio with the bloody men in the flat-black sky. It's these canvases that my old man spent years painting – these lousy dead meanderings of a diseased subconscious. It's my mother's car, sitting out there for the past quarter-century like some pop art shrine, my father perched in his* Star Trek *chair, guzzling back scotch and doing what –? Weeping? Laughing? Screaming his fucking lungs out? Too many loose threads for me to walk away from.* All he said was, "It's not just my old man. It's everything else. The case. All of it. What was the second thing you wanted to tell me?"

"The ME's people just finished going over the house. If you want to take another walk through, now's the time. We can go up there together before things get too bogged down with this storm. And after the storm there may not be a crime scene to visit."

Jake pulled his eyes away from the ocean, then swiveled back to the house and headed inside. "When can you pick me up?"

"I'll be there in fifteen minutes."

31

Hauser's new Charger sounded like a German Panzer from half a mile off, the supercharged Hemi growling as it tore up 27. It made a statement but Jake saw the car in the same light as he viewed a lot of American industry – yet another rehash in a once innovative field that had been reduced to copying its glory days. He had to step back when the sheriff swerved off the road onto the gravel shoulder. The taste of electricity in Jake's mouth was replaced with dust and exhaust. He climbed in.

"Ever lose anyone to this car?" Jake asked as he strapped himself in.

"Sort of."

"Sort of?"

Jake realized that this was the first time he had seen Hauser look even remotely comfortable around him; it was probably a home-court advantage. "City asshole tried to outrun me with his Ferrari and hit the corner at Reese's dairy doing one-eighty. Went straight off the point and disintegrated. By the time we picked up all the pieces from the rocks, it was a different season."

Jake shook his head. "In this line of work you get to see people at their best, no doubt about it."

Hauser's eyes slid over to Jake for a second. He swallowed and the comfortable body language of a few seconds ago was lost. "How'd you end up doing what you do?"

Jake reached into his pocket for a cigarette, then realized that Hauser wouldn't want that new cop-car smell to get fucked up by his Marlboro. He let the smokes fall from his fingers and put his hand on his thigh. "Bad luck, I guess."

Hauser shot another sideways glance at him and said, "You and those rose-colored glasses. You need yoga or tai chi. You ever try any of that?"

"Smoking relaxes me."

They lapsed into a silence that lasted until Hauser's cell phone pinged the national anthem. "Yeah?" the sheriff said into his hands-free earpiece.

Hauser listened for a few seconds, then glanced in the mirror, flipped the siren and cherries to life, and pounded down on the brakes. He spun the wheel and hit the gas and the big rear end of the Charger swung in an arc of squealing tires. The car fishtailed in a 180-degree high-pitched scream on the faded asphalt and pulsed forward in a smoking cloud of rubber, heading back the way they had just come.

He snapped. "Yep. Yep. Yep. Six minutes." And threw his earpiece violently into the dashboard.

Hauser turned to Jake, his mouth curved down like the edge of a hunting knife. He punched the gas and the big Hemi pulled the car into the future. "Your skinner just hit a woman in Southampton," he said.

32

It was a neat neighborhood of postwar cottages with single-car garages, predictably pruned yards, and lawn chairs set up on small concrete porches. Cars were being loaded for the evacuation, some on the grass in front of the concrete steps, some in the driveway, trunks and doors open, pet carriers and prized televisions waiting to be loaded. Some houses were already empty, shutters fastened over windows – some neatly done in plywood and cut to size, others haphazard patches of scrap lumber. One home had duct tape over the windows in a sloppy silver weave. Jake watched the hurried, nervous movements of the people leaving their homes, and wondered when, exactly, the American motto had changed to, *I'll give you my television when you take it from my cold, dead hands.*

From the end of the block Jake saw the police cruiser parked at the curb, lights blinking, yellow lines of tape strung out in the web of a giant 1950s science fiction film spider. A police officer stood on the lawn, just back from the perimeter, his back to a bunch of kids that were milling about. Jake recognized the posturing gestures of a man trying to look like he is in charge. It was a few hundred feet before he recognized the officer as Spencer.

Hauser rolled to the curb and both men rose from the interior, Hauser in his crisp khakis, Jake in a pair of jeans and a black T-shirt. As they moved toward the police line, the children's attention focused briefly on Hauser but quickly shifted to Jake, eyes going wide at the ink covering his arms and creeping out of the collar of his T-shirt. Many of them backed up from their positions near the tape. Spencer held up the yellow line of defense as Hauser and Jake crossed under.

The cloud cover had lost a little of its translucency and the lawn had grown dark. The house shifted in hue with the overlay of clouds, and Hauser and Jake led Spencer away from the line of children waiting at the yellow tape like a contingent of the world's tiniest paparazzi.

Hauser faced the house, locked his jaw, and spoke through clenched teeth. "Please tell me what's going on."

Spencer had the same eerie complexion he had had last night at the house up the beach, his pale skin pulsing blue and red in the lights of the cruiser parked at the curb. This afternoon it was mixed with shock and a good dose of revulsion. He took a few deep breaths and began, his eyes locked on the toe of a boot that he used to pick at the grass. "Neighbor called in, said she knocked and there wasn't any answer which she found weird because the car was in the driveway." Spencer jerked a thumb over his shoulder at the Prius. "The victim was supposed to be home. Neighbor thought maybe she was in the shower and came back an hour later. Still no answer. She peeked in the window and saw some blood on the kitchen floor. Called us. I did a walk around. Peeked in a few windows. Went in the back door."

"And?"

Spencer swallowed hard. "And she was right."

"You found some blood on the floor?"

Spencer looked up, his eyes two pinholes in the fabric of his face. "Some? No, Mike, there ain't *some*. There's a *lot*."

"You call the ME?" Hauser asked in a thousand-yard voice.

"Right after you." Spencer was running his tongue over his teeth and Jake knew it was the coppery taste of blood he was trying to make sense of.

Jake took a step toward Spencer. "What's inside, Billy?"

"Another one," he said, his eyes dancing nervously away.

"Another one what?"

Spencer's blue-and-white skin seemed to tighten on his body and he pursed his mouth. "Skinned like a hunting trophy, Jake. Fucking bucketloads of blood everywhere." He turned away, spit into the grass.

"Don't do that. If you have to spit or puke or contaminate the crime scene in any way, do it across the street. Don't embarrass yourself and don't fuck up the crime scene."

Spencer's complexion pulsed red. "Embarrass myself? It's a horror movie in there, Jake, and you tell me not to embarrass myself? What the fuck is wrong with you? You have any emotions?"

Jake pointed over his shoulder. "You want to look like some hick cop on national news?"

A news van came down the street. It picked up speed when it saw the yellow bull's-eye of police tape.

Jake pursed his lips and grumbled, "Try to look professional," just above a whisper.

Hauser turned to him. "I thought the media was our friend. *Let them help us* and all that." Hauser's voice carried a thin veil of sarcasm. The distant wail of a police siren was getting closer.

The van rolled to a stop at the curb and the crew rushed out. "Every single news team in the country is going to be here if they think we have a serial killer." He turned to Spencer. "Don't let them past the tape."

"And if they try?" Spencer asked, tapping his sidearm like he had last night at the gate to the Farmers'.

"Warn them twice real loud. Then fire a round into the air. Then warn them one final time. Warn that you will fire if they do not cease and desist. Then shoot someone in the leg." Hauser eyed the news crew heading over. "Those are specific orders."

Spencer smiled and a little of the color returned to his face with the prospect of being able to deal with a situation that was familiar.

As the news team marched over, lugging lighting, cameras, and microphones, Jake leaned over and whispered in Hauser's ear. "Tell them it's an unrelated crime that as of yet is uncategorized. If they ask if it's a murder say you cannot make comments that might jeopardize the investigation."

He turned back to Spencer, wishing he was working with a proper bureau team right now. "Spencer, you make sure they don't talk to the neighbor who found the victim. Tell her that if she talks to the media she could face prosecution for tampering with a murder investigation. Tell her it might make her look like a suspect. Scare her but shut her up. Assign a cop to her to make sure she doesn't get bullied."

He turned back to Hauser who was already breathing like a cornered animal and trying to smile for the cameras. "Tell them you'll make a statement as soon as you can and you'd appreciate it if they'd stay across the street to leave the scene clear for emergency vehicles."

A Southampton cruiser drifted around the corner and Jake recognized the big form of Scopes behind the wheel. Hauser seemed to be a little more in control with the sight of Scopes pulling up. He walked up to the line of tape and into the bright glare of the camera crew.

"I have no comment at this time. If you'll wait across the street I promise to give you a statement just as soon as information becomes both available and pertinent."

Across the street Danny Scopes climbed out of the cruiser.

"Officer Scopes will escort you across the street where you will wait for me." Hauser turned away from the now disgruntled news team and nodded at Jake. "Geronimo," he said.

They left Spencer standing by the line of tape.

Around back and out of sight of the news team, they both slipped their hands into nonpowdered latex gloves.

The screen door creaked open on a hydraulic closer and Hauser held it with the tip of his boot. The inner door was slightly ajar and the sheriff reached up and pushed it open from the top. It swung silently in and the warm smell of blood, feces, and burned food boiled out.

33

The kitchen looked like hell had crawled out of the walls and emptied onto the floor. Blood was splattered in great gusts that had pooled in the low troughs of the linoleum, etching a pattern of symmetrical death in the space. The floor wasn't level, and a bucket of blood had gathered in one corner under the cabinets in a dark cracked triangle, the top skinned over like wrinkled pudding. It had run in from the hallway, a thick sloppy soup the color of the Ganges in spring, mud and silt and garbage and iron oxide. From somewhere beyond the kitchen door came the hum of an electric appliance left on, its motor whining noisily.

Hauser eased along the counters, carefully minefielding his way over the caked black topography of the linoleum. Jake stood at the door, taking in the space, committing details to the memory banks of his reconstructive CPU. He focused on the long isosceles triangle of blood, followed its inflow over the once-yellow fake tile, out to the hallway. Hauser poked his head through the door, into the hallway, stiffened, and lurched back to the sink and was sick.

He retched out one violent cable of vomit, coughed, spit, and looked over at Jake. "Sorry," he said, yellow spittle hanging from his bottom lip.

Jake looked down at the sink, usually the primary source of evidence in any messy murder, and once again wished that he was here with some of the hardened bureau boys. He had seen lifers throw up down their own shirts in order not to contaminate murder scenes.

Jake moved past Hauser, like a slow spider. He got to the door to the hallway and saw why Hauser had chucked his doughnuts.

A woman lay on the floor. Or, rather, what *used to be* a woman. Like Madame and Little X, she was skinless, lifeless. She lay like Da Vinci's *Vitruvian Man* on the rug, arms and legs splayed, scabbed to the floor with lines of glop and fluid that had hardened. There was no small electrical appliance humming away – Jake had been mistaken – the sound came from the black writhing mass of flies that swarmed over her body like an insect exoskeleton. Where the hell had they come from?

Jake stepped over the threshold into the hallway. Keeping clear of the bloodspatter with fluid movements born of experience. Hauser was still clearing his throat at the sink. Jake skirted the area rug where the woman lay, now thick and heavy with her blood. Back in the kitchen, he could hear Hauser at the sink, spitting like he had a down feather stuck to the back of his throat. Jake moved by the woman, past a fan-shaped arc of blood on the cracked wallpaper in the hallway, and into the body of the home.

The house was typical of its kind and Jake knew the layout without having to be told: kitchen at the back, living room and dining room in front, two small bedrooms and a bathroom – all with sloped walls – on the second floor. Basement. Detached garage.

He headed into the living room to be sure that there were no more victims even though the little voice was telling him that she was the sum total of occupants; the unmistakable flavor of a single inhabitant filled the place, even thicker than the smell of blood and the buzz of flies.

There was an old upright piano, a long low sofa in tufted velour, a pair of Barcaloungers, a glass coffee table piled high with copies of *People* and *Us*, and a small television with a paperback on top. There was a plug-in fireplace with a few photos perched on the plastic mantel; bright happy splashes of color that smiled from across the room. Other than the few pieces of furniture and sparse reading, the room was sparse, and Jake knew that the woman who lived here worked a lot.

Jake moved toward the photos, stepping high to avoid creating static that might pick up errant trace evidence. He had not been aware that his heart had been pounding until he took the first step and felt the woozy flush of lightheadedness that told him his fuel pump was racing. He took one of the deep belly-breaths that Kay had taught him to use when he had to oxygenate his blood, and the vitriolic smell of death pierced his head like a flechette. He stood still for a second, concentrating on his breathing. When his chest stopped vibrating like it had a live animal in it, he moved forward, taking full breaths, smelling the skinless woman sprawled on the carpet behind him. The photographs had grown from indistinct flashes of color to fuzzy face shapes bisected by white smiles. Another step and the fuzziness hardened, became clear.

He reached for one of the framed photos, and the movement pulled all the blood from his system, as if his arm were a pump handle. His fingers touched the frame and he stared into the face grinning out at him. A woman – and he knew that it was the same woman back on the floor, splayed like a sideshow knife-thrower's assistant on a spinning plywood wheel – sat on the gunwale of a sailboat somewhere off Montauk Point, the lighthouse behind her by an easy mile. Jake brought the photograph up, his gloved fingers holding it carefully by the corners.

He looked at the face smiling out of the frame, unaware that his breath squeezed though his teeth in ragged birthing pants.

Skinned.

She smiled up at him. Bright white teeth. She looked so alive. So happy.

Now fly-covered on the hallway carpet.

He felt his chest tighten and his heart hammered as he was hit with a bucket of adrenaline. His chest went numb, cold.

The frame slid from his fingers and thudded to the carpet.

There are no coincidences, Spencer's tinny voice echoed through his head.

Then everything slipped off the edge of the world and went cold as he hit the floor.

Jake knew her.

34

"Jake? Jake?" Hauser's voice cut through the static brazing his circuitry and the sheriff's face materialized above him. His breath smelled of vomit and his thousand-yard death stare had been pushed aside with concern. "Jake?"

Jake lifted himself onto his elbows and groaned. "Sorry about that."

Hauser was eying him suspiciously. "Did you faint?"

Jake shook his head. "It's not drugs or booze or anything you'd understand." He stood up, consciously avoiding touching anything.

"Try me."

Jake stood in place, staring down at the photograph he had dropped. "I have an appliance – a CRT-D."

"You were right, I *don't* understand."

Jake didn't move his eyes from the photograph on the floor. "It's a cardiac resynchronization defibrillator. A pacemaker."

"Bad heart?"

No, my heart's fucking perfect, that's why I have an appliance to make sure it keeps pumping. "I didn't take as good care of myself as I should have and it translated into cardiomyopathy." He kept his eyes locked on the photograph. "Whenever my heart rate stumbles, my appliance is supposed to regulate things." She was smiling up at him, unaware that in a year – two? three? – she would become a nightmare for people in the neighborhood. "I assume that it's this electrical storm moving in. Any strong magnetic field can affect it." He lifted his head. "But this is not supposed to happen."

"We'll get you to a cardiologist."

Jake shook his head. "It does this sometimes." Which was a lie.

"This isn't the best kind of work for someone with a bad heart, Jake."

Jake shook his head. "My pulse isn't affected by work. Not usually." He bent and picked up the photograph. "I know her." He replaced the photograph to its perch atop the faux-wood plug-in fireplace.

"Know ... her?" the sheriff asked, jerking a thumb at the body on the floor, over his shoulder at roughly the same angle as the Montauk lighthouse in the photograph, now back in its place until relatives came to pack everything up.

"She's my father's nurse at the hospital. Rachael Something." He looked at the photo, at the smiling, live face grinning out at him. Even in the photo it was hard to miss that she looked like his mother.

The sound of cars pulling over outside was punctuated by the thudding of doors.

Hauser's jaw took on a new shape and his eyes went cop again. "I'm starting to get the feeling that somebody's fucking with you." He turned, looked out the window. The medical examiner's people were outside in their white cube-van convoy along with another Southampton cruiser. Across the street, craning their necks and standing on their toes, the line of journalists looked like alpacas at a petting zoo.

"Let's go talk to these assholes," Hauser grumbled, and headed for the door.

But Jake's eyes were on the woman laid out on the floor. She had looked like his mother. Maybe even more so now.

35

Jake took an hour to go through the home of Rachel Macready, age forty-four, 2134 Whistler Road, Southampton, NY. This time Conway didn't ask any questions, he just listened and did as he was told. The ME's people had a newfound respect for Jake; whereas last night he was viewed as an alien interloper, today he was an outside professional. A few phone calls to Hauser's receptionist had loosened details about Jake's behavior in the morgue that morning and the chattering classes had spun up their own version of the truth about him. Last night the tattoos and clothing had been *otherness*; today they had been elevated to some sort of spiritual armor.

Jake was leaning against Hauser's cruiser, smoking a Marlboro, when the sheriff came out the front door. His complexion had reverted to the same waxy apple-green as last night in Madame X's presence. He came over, leaned back on the car with Jake, and held out his hand. "Mind if I bum a smoke?"

Across the street, the media were doing a good job of entertaining themselves – a flashing light-show of rictus grins and shoe-polished hair, the dance of entertainment by people lacking real marketable skills. Jake and Hauser ignored them.

"You smoke?"

"I do when I have the taste of puke in my nostrils," Hauser said, sounding embarrassed. "That was mighty professional," he added.

Jake held out the pack and Hauser clumsily took one, firing it to life on Jake's sterling Zippo, tooled with dancing Day of the Dead skeletons. Jake blew a light stream of smoke from his nostrils, dragon-style. "Anyone who sees something like that and isn't affected is a monster."

Hauser sucked in a lungful, picked a bit of tobacco off of his tongue, and turned to Jake. "Doesn't seem to affect you." The words came out in a puff of smoke.

Jake pulled on his cigarette again. "I just lock it all away. I have to or I'd lose it. But I think I've reached the point where something's gotta give. I'm retiring. I've had enough of the dead to last me—" He stopped, looking for the right words.

"The rest of your life?"

Jake nodded a thank-you. "*The rest of my life.* Yes. Perfect. Thank you. Apparently I'm running low on clichés. The first sign of tension rot."

Hauser spat on the ground. "Your heart, how bad is it?"

Jake shrugged. It was an academic question. "Bad enough that they wired in a computer-run defibrillator to keep it from shitting the bed." Jake was staring at his motorcycle boots. "Back in my Death Valley days I'd do heroin for breakfast followed by some coke, then keep going until I ran out, usually after rolling through three days of headaches, dry mouth, diarrhea, and the occasional cardiac failure. Died three times." Jake took a long haul on the cigarette between his index and middle fingers. "I started to feel like a parody of myself."

"You find God?" Hauser asked earnestly.

It wasn't the first time he had been asked the question, but it was inapplicable. He never understood why junkies and losers seemed to find God. "I woke up one morning and decided that I'd had enough of hating myself. Somehow I had the resolve to stay straight long enough to hunt down my uncle and ask for help. He checked me into a psychiatric hospital. Three days in hell bleeding poison followed by months of having a candle put to my head. Then years of NA and AA meetings. No matter how bad I think the shit in my life is, at AA there's always some poor fucker who makes me realize that I've hit the lottery of good times."

"We're motivated by the good and the bad."

"You sound like Yoda."

"I can butt out if you want."

Jake shook his head. "Cops don't usually like talking to me."

Hauser remembered his earlier mistrust of the man and he felt the blush of embarrassment. "Why is that?"

"You tell me," Jake said, shrugging and pulling another cigarette out of the pack.

Hauser dropped his to the ground, heeled it into the asphalt. Just a few hours ago he hadn't trusted Jake but the collapse in the house had turned him from an aloof adversary into a regular guy with problems. "You look like the other side."

Jake held up a hand, dark lines of script running across the metacarpals.

"Don't you find life challenging enough without inking your whole body with an Italian horror story?"

Jake was surprised that Hauser had even noticed what his ink said. "It wasn't a conscious decision. I woke up with this one morning after a four-month bender I don't remember." He turned his hand over and the script wrapped around onto the palm. "The font is courier, halfway between a fifteen and sixteen point. I had the lab at work go through it, hoping that maybe they could help me put those four months back." Jake fired up another cigarette. "A job like this is roughly five hundred hours of work. Letters are complicated. And in the thousands of words there isn't a single spelling mistake or typo. All the letters are perfect. And there isn't a tattoo shop in the city that did the work. Some guy spent a good five hundred hours marking my flesh and I don't know why. I don't know his name. And I don't know how I paid for it."

Hauser looked at the script that wound up Jake's neck from his collar. His expression said that he didn't understand how that was possible. "Jake, what you do scares people." He paused, reorganized his thoughts. "It's just … I don't know … incomprehension. Cops train their whole lives to be able to read a crime scene properly. You waltz in with that crash-test-dummy expression on your face, and it's like you don't have any of the emotions we associate with the good guys."

Jake took a drag on the cigarette. "You of all fucking people should understand that it's part of this job. Every time you tell some parent that their kid had his brains scattered over the shoulder by a drunk driver, or that their kid was DUI and killed someone, you go into combat mode. It's a defensive thing. Self-protection. Otherwise we'd be walking around weeping."

For a second Hauser remembered his son, Aaron, killed by the swerve of an Econoline when he was ten. "Or throwing up all over the crime scene," he added.

Jake smiled around the new cigarette. "There is that, yes."

Hauser leaned back, crossed his arms over his chest. "What's going on here, Jake? I don't know what to do. I have crime in my jurisdiction. Hell, some of the wealthiest people in America live here – you have no idea how much crime that attracts. But three people skinned?"

Jake's eyes went back to the pavement and his words were slow, deliberate. "She opened the front door for him. She probably just got home. It was after her shift – Dr. Sobel sent her home early and the ME will put the time of death within half an hour of her knocking off. She asked him in. Maybe a neighbor saw, but I wouldn't count on it."

A few sentences in, Hauser realized that Jake's words were coming from somewhere else. Maybe Jake didn't see himself as a psychic. Maybe Carradine didn't believe in channeling. But Hauser knew what he was hearing, and it was most certainly *not* Jake Cole talking.

The cigarette smoldered away in Jake's fingers, the blue smoke taken away by the wind that had started up, full of electricity with the coming storm. "She turned her back on him and headed for the kitchen. I think she would have offered a drink. Tea, not coffee. He followed her down the hall, and as he did, the knife came out. Same one – big-bladed hunting knife – recurve edge. She turned. He kicked her hard in the stomach. A few of her ribs are broken.

"He came at her head with the knife when she doubled over. She was trying to breathe and he yanked her head back. Swept the knife across her forehead – there's blood spatter across the wallpaper beside the stairs from this. Threw her to the carpet. Put a foot on her back and yanked her head back by her hair, scalping her. She couldn't scream because she couldn't even breathe. No one would have heard a thing."

Hauser held up a hand. He was almost successful at keeping it from trembling. "How do you know this?"

What could Jake say? That he had taken a mental snapshot of the body and the blood spatter and position of the corpse and it painted a perfect picture for him? That there was no other way for this to have happened? That he could do a blind walk-through and get everything – including the length of time it had taken the monster to skin her – 100 percent right? Hauser wouldn't understand. All he said was, "I know." The cigarette, still forgotten, continued to smoke, the ash long and curved. "Her scalp was off before she could even begin to understand what was happening to her. He flipped her over again and belted her in the stomach with a knee, a little higher this time, breaking at least two ribs. Bounced on her to drive the air from her lungs. Then went to work on her in earnest."

Hauser's complexion had reverted to the pale green that Jake now associated with him. "He did this to her while she was alive?"

Jake shrugged, as if the answer was self-evident.

"Guys like this, where do they come from? I mean, they can't come from good loving parents who care about them, can they? Someone who understands love couldn't do this."

Jake looked up at the house, getting dark in the pewter light that was slowly seeping into everything. "Some families run on love, some run on anger and madness, some run on worse things." He dropped his cigarette to the ground.

"I never thought I'd have a serial killer in my town."

Jake crushed out the smoking butt on the asphalt. "He's more than that."

"What are you talking about?" Hauser's voice fluttered with the question.

Repeating the definition from the bureau's literature, Jake said, "A serial killer is defined as someone who kills three or more people with a cooling-down period between the murders. The time between Madame and Little X and the Macready woman was his cool-down. And the years since my mother's death certainly constitutes a cool-down." He thought about the night she went to the Kwik Mart for cigarettes and Mallomars. "He's not going after random targets – he's going after specific ones. Targets that are connected to my father, and by extension to—" He stopped and stood up. "—Me."

"You okay?"

He shook his head. "My wife and son are at home alone."

36

Hauser's Charger ate up the road at 120 miles an hour and the car vibrated so badly that it felt like they were about to crack the sound barrier. Hauser had the gas punched to the carpet as he slalomed through traffic, taking the nearly two-ton mass of Hemi-powered Detroit iron onto the shoulder when cars ahead didn't get out of the way fast enough. From inside the Dodge the siren was barely audible above the scream of the engine.

Hauser had called ahead but there were no cruisers anywhere near Sumter Point. Jake had Hauser's BlackBerry suction-cupped to his ear as he tried to hear Kay's phone ringing over the roar of the angry V-8. It was his third call and there was no answer. "Fuck," he snarled, and pitched the cell phone against the dashboard. It bounced off and flew out the window. "*Motherfucker!*"

Hauser kept his attention on the road and his hands on the wheel. "About two minutes," he said flatly.

Jake squirmed with the horrors splattering across the canvas in his head. He wished he was in his own car instead of Hauser's beast – Hauser had the disadvantage of caution; Jake would have had it to the floor. He had to get home *now*. If that monster got to Kay and Jeremy—

He pushed the thought away and tried to snap his mental armor into place but the pieces wouldn't click home; his mind kept going back to Kay, to the thought of someone tearing her scalp off with a piece of honed steel.

The adrenaline stab of fear had flooded his system and his heart was throbbing like a venomous snake in his rib cage. There were a couple of jolts from the CRT-D sewn into his chest but none of the bright pyrotechnics that had fried his circuitry twice today.

She's fine.

Skinned.

Jeremy's fine.

Skinned.

Why did he go after the nurse?

Revenge.

For what?

You're just not looking hard enough.

It's a coincidence.

There are no coincidences, you naïve motherfucker!

They rounded the gentle wide arc that was the last bend in the road before Sumter Point and at almost 120 miles an hour it was neither gentle nor wide. Hauser counter-spun the steering wheel and drifted the heavy car through in a blast of noise and gravel.

After the corner, Jake had his seat belt off and his hand on the grip of his pistol. Hauser punched up the last quarter-mile of asphalt with a final burst of power from the big-block V-8 and floored the brake at the last second, pulling into the driveway in a power slide that spewed rocks and dust in a wide arc. Jake was out of the car and through the front door before Hauser had turned off the engine.

Hauser stormed out of the car and ran around back, his Sig out of the holster, safety off, one in the chamber, his finger on the curved sport trigger. He didn't know how to deal with the aftermath of human skinnings but he was pragmatic with a good old-fashioned meat-and-bones adversary. It had made him a brief success on the football field.

He reached the deck as one of the big glass doors slid open. He raised his Sig, locked on the opening, and centered on the chest of the man coming out.

The figure materialized into Jake holding up a square of notepaper. "They're in Montauk."

Jake came out onto the deck and dropped onto the steps that grinned down at the beach like the gray wooden teeth of a funhouse dummy. "Shopping." He looked at the note for a second, then balled it up and stuffed it into his pocket. He still had the gun in his hand and after Hauser slid the safety home on his own sidearm and returned it to the holster, Jake tucked his away.

With the threat gone, Hauser's adrenaline dissipated and he collapsed to the steps, resting his elbows on his knees. "Maybe they shouldn't be here, Jake."

Jake let out a long breath, leaned back, and stretched. "They're going home. I don't want them here for the storm. I don't want them here for the skinner. I don't want them near me or in harm's way."

Hauser thought back to the house of death back in Southampton where Rachael Macready had been reduced to past tense. "Jake, what do I do about this guy?"

Jake pulled his cigarettes from his pocket, offered one to Hauser who passed, and fired one up with the sterling Zippo. He watched the ocean get darker as the sun began its descent behind them, over the western flange of the island. He wondered how different the ocean would look tomorrow morning, with the storm five hundred miles closer. And how bad would it get tomorrow night? Would it just rip everything out of the ground and set it down in Kansas? "There were two killings last night. Another this afternoon. That's close. Even for an extreme maniac. Working that fast you make mistakes, bad decisions. It's as if there's a time limit."

"Storm's coming," Hauser said, pointing at the ocean.

Jake shook his head and pulled on his smoke. "That's not it. There's purpose to what he's doing. He's working hard because he has to. We – I – have to figure out why. With the *why* we will have a lot better chance at figuring out the *who*." He sucked on the filter and the paper cracked and sizzled.

"Back at that house, you said it looked like revenge. Why?"

"These guys like what they do. They take pleasure in the act. They cherish it and hold it and drag it out. Not this one. He's in and out. Or at least he was with the Macready woman. He shows up angry, doles out his punishment, and leaves. Why?"

"Why would he cart off thirty pounds of skin and hair? Is he making jumpsuits in his basement? Lampshades? Wallets? Jesus, listen to me."

Jake shook his head and let out a cloud of smoke that the wind coming off the water smacked away. "I don't get that feeling. If he's punishing them for something, it's payment. That means a personal motive."

Hauser held up his hands. "Are you saying that he knows the victims?"

"I don't know."

"If I was the guy running this investigation—"

Jake pointed at Hauser. "You *are* the guy running this investigation."

"You know what I mean. The only thing I can say for sure is that this sonofabitch scares me – *deep-down* scares me."

Jake's face stayed flat, calm. "Me, too," he said.

"Is it true that these guys want to get caught?"

Jake smiled, shook his head. "Not that I've noticed."

"Then why the fuck would a killer write letters to the police or keep dumping bodies in the same place? It's counterproductive."

"It's not that they want to get caught – they don't think they *can* get caught. You have to remember that these people – if you can call them people – all have *severe* personality disorders. There is no such thing as a repeat killer who is a well-adjusted human being. It's all about them. Getting away with a killing builds confidence. Getting away with a second one builds more. All of a sudden the guy thinks that he's a criminal mastermind. It's cockiness. Serial killers generally follow the same intelligence guidelines as the population – running the gambit from barely functional to high acuity. But the rule of thumb is that they are maladjusted losers."

Hauser examined Jake's face for a few seconds, trying to see behind the skin. "I'm glad you said that."

"Why?"

"The way you talk about these guys – the way you seem to understand them – makes it look like you have some kind of deep-down respect for them."

For the first time Jake could remember, something caught him off guard. "This is not big-game hunting where I relate to the animal. I don't have any respect for these monsters – and believe me, that's all they are. Social misfits and broken people. The people who romanticize them as anything else are losers of a lesser degree, but losers still. Christ, I fucking hate these guys." He looked back at the ocean and saw that the weather was building up to go with what was happening here. Maybe he had been right, maybe this was some sort of a German opera.

"Me, too." Hauser stood up, brushed sand off his seat. "I'll be back at the Macready house. Get me through the station since I don't have a cell phone right now."

Jake's mouth moved into an embarrassed smile. "Sorry about that."

"I thought someone was going after my family ..." Hauser let the sentence die and he paused at the top of the steps, his eyes locked out on the ocean. "I'll get a cruiser out here to keep an eye on things."

"You can't afford the manpower right now."

"And you can't afford to let something happen to your family. Get them out of here in the morning, Jake. You should leave, too."

"Can't." He shrugged again. "Won't – it amounts to the same thing. My dad. The killer." He wanted to add the weird paintings over in the studio, the studies of the faceless men of blood. "I have to be here." He nodded out at the frothing Atlantic where the clouds had woven into a gray blanket that rose from the ocean. The waves were sloshing up on shore and foam and bits of flotsam were kicked around at the water's edge. "Where'd the birds go?"

Hauser looked into the sky. "If I had a choice, you think I'd still be here?" He turned and walked away.

37

Jake was still sitting on the steps watching the ocean build up its courage for the next day's big show when Kay walked out onto the deck with Jeremy bouncing along beside her. He was watching the surface of the ocean chop in on gray swells topped with white that slid halfway up the beach, hissing and bubbling, as Jeremy came over and sat down in his lap.

"Daddy, there's a policeman in the driveway."

"He's going to be watching over the house when Daddy's not here." The fatigue of the world melted away and for an instant he felt like everything was all right with the universe.

Kay plopped down beside him and gave him a smooch. "How was your afternoon?" she asked.

How could he even think of answering that? Groovy. Except maybe for the poor woman who was scalped and skinned. Probably for no other reason than she had the misfortune to be my father's nurse. Oh, and the skinned woman and child in the morgue – can't forget them. "Fine," he said, keeping what he did from her yet again – another reason he had decided to stop doing this.

She was in a pair of Levi's and a tight T-shirt that had the smiling face of David Hasselhoff beaming back with the words *Don't Hassel The Hoff!* scripted across the curve of her bust.

"Where did you get that shirt?" Jake asked, laughing.

"Nice, huh?" She pointed her breasts at him like gun turrets. "Kind of gets your attention, doesn't it? Nobody messes with *The Hoff!*"

"The man in the store said Mommy looked smoking," Jeremy offered cheerily.

Jake's laugh blossomed and it felt good. "Smart man."

Kay smiled over at him. "He was about fifteen. I don't think he had ever seen boobies this close." She looked down at the shirt. "He said he thought my tattoos were cool."

"Cool, huh?"

"When you're semipubescent and staring at a chick's cans, you have to say something."

"Smoking," Jeremy repeated. "Is Mommy burned?"

Jake hugged his son closer. "No, she's beautiful."

Kay's eyes misted over and she said, "Why are you the only man who has ever called me beautiful?"

Jake shrugged, something he felt he had been doing a lot lately. "Because you are. And because you used to spend your time with assholes." Kay had come to her first NA meeting with her arm in a cast. Her last boyfriend had smacked her around while she had been asleep. He broke her wrist – her *playing* wrist.

"Now I got me a shiny happy nice guy!"

"And I got me a delusional woman."

She punched him in the arm. "I'm hungry."

"So go make some food."

Kay's talent in the kitchen was an old faded joke between them. When Jake wasn't working, he did the cooking; otherwise a good chunk of their income went toward restaurants. Jeremy was fond of pizza with anchovies, Reuben sandwiches, and sweet-and-sour matzo-ball soup from the Chinese kosher restaurant down the block from their apartment.

Jake stood up with his son and flipped him around to a piggyback position like a chimp handling its baby. "How about pizza, Moriarty?"

Jeremy's arms went around his neck. "And apple juice?"

Jake remembered the Angelo's Pizza Palace flyer mixed in with the pile of mail by the front door. "I think we can do apple juice."

Supper came half an hour later. The first thing that struck Jake was the single box in the delivery kid's hand.

"What do I owe you?"

The kid seemed about twelve, his half-beard cropped into a chinstrap that looked like it held down his Yankees cap. "That's twelve thirty, sir." He added the last word with a little hesitation.

"For three pizzas, two Cokes, and an apple juice?" Jake reached into his pocket, his hand coming out with a few crumpled damp bills.

Chinstrap's face went from bored to worried and he examined the bill. "Um, no, there's just a single pizza and a Coke on the bill."

Jake just felt the end of a bad day get a whole lot worse. "No, man, I ordered three small pizzas, two Cokes, and an apple juice."

The kid shrugged. "If I had two extra pizzas in the car I'd give them to you. All they gave me was this." Chinstrap held up the single box and for a second it went dark in the doorframe like one of Jacob Coleridge's weird little canvases.

Jake stood with the bills in his hands, trying to decide who had fucked up. Then that little light in his head went off. "One pizza, sure. You mind coming in while I call the restaurant?"

The kid shook his head, stepped over the threshold. Jake closed the door and went to the phone as the boy stood in the entryway, taking in the time capsule to the polymer era. "Cool," he said, nodding in approval as he looked around.

At the phone, Jake wondered if one of his friends had sold Kay the T-shirt. He hit redial and a girl answered. "Angelo's Pizza." There was a distant tinny quality to her voice that hadn't been there when he called earlier.

"Yeah, hi, I'm on Sumter Point and I just got my order."

"Oh, yeah, sure. Everything all right?" Her tone said that she didn't expect any problems with the meal. After all, how could a place called Angelo's fuck up a pizza?

"It looks like we're missing two-thirds of the order."

"I … don't … see … how … that's … possible," she said as she flipped through some papers at the other end. "Here we go. One small pepperoni pizza with anchovies and a Coke. Twelve dollars thirty. What didn't you get?"

"No. I ordered *three* pizzas, *two* Cokes, *and an apple juice.*"

"One pizza and one Coke. Thirty-two minutes ago."

Jake thought about Jeremy, upstairs putting on his PJs, looking forward to pizza before bed. And Kay probably hadn't eaten all day. Did he want to spend his time arguing with a teenage girl on the phone? He pushed it aside and focused on the single bulb glowing brightly in the middle of his mind. "You keep the addresses of everyone who places orders with you?"

"Yes, sir, we keep copies of all orders. That usually includes phone number and address. I'm telling you, I'm looking at *your order*, sir."

But Jake wasn't thinking about his order. He was thinking about Madame and Little X up the road. Maybe they had ordered a pizza. "Thank you." He hung up.

He went back to the door, gave the kid twenty dollars, asked for two back, and let him out. On the way back to the table with the pizza box he hollered up to Kay and Jeremy. "You guys will have to share this."

His wife and son appeared at the top of the stairs. Jake smiled when he saw them and realized that he wasn't that hungry after the day he had had. "No apple juice, Moriarty. They were out. How about a nice glass of milk?"

Jeremy nodded approvingly as he came down the steps in footed felt pajamas. "I like milk. We got 'chovies on the pizza, Daddy?"

Jake thanked the powers that be for reining in his supper fuck-up. "Yeah, we got 'chovies. Lots of 'em."

"Then everything is groovy," the little boy said.

Kay and Jeremy went to the kitchen table to start on the pizza and Jake went to call Hauser. Maybe Madame and Little X had received Angelo's flyer in the mail. Maybe they had ordered a pizza in the past two weeks. Or cheeseburgers. Steamers. Chinese.

Someone had to know their names.

38

Jake was past tired and well into the static-caked fuzz of exhaustion. The last twenty-four hours had been an emotional shock-treatment session and sleep was the only thing that would regenerate his singed nerve endings. But he had experience with this particular type of combat fatigue and knew that needing sleep wasn't the same as being able to get it. After supper he had gone back to the Macready woman's house for another walk-through. But unlike other law-enforcement professionals, Jake did the bulk of his work in his head, not a lab, office, squad car, or crime scene. From the Macready woman's house he had stopped back at the hospital. Now he stood at the foot of his father's bed, breathing in the smell of sweat and cleaning fluids.

The room was dark, the only light a thin wedge that the hallway fluorescents grudgingly threw across the floor. The hospital lights were dimmed to half power like an airliner cabin at night and Jake had to fight the temptation to snap on the overheads. He kept glancing back over his shoulder, searching for the blank suction of the painting behind him. No blood-painted eyeless face loomed out of the dark; his father had been moved to a new room.

When he had walked in, one of the nurses – Rachael Macready's replacement – had pulled out his father's file, clucking her tongue and nodding over the pages clamped to the dented steel clipboard. She handed him Dr. Sobel's card with a seven a.m. appointment scrawled across the back in sloppy script. Jake had folded the card into his pocket and resisted the urge to tell her that her perfume smelled like vodka.

Tomorrow Sobel would pose the big question: *What do we do with Dad?* All they really wanted was the bill paid and a chronic-care patient out so that they could hand the bed over to a person who would actually benefit from a stay in the hospital. In reality, it had a little to do with economics and a lot to do with common sense – after all, Jacob couldn't stay in the hospital indefinitely.

But Jake didn't see there being all that much to discuss. He'd humor Sobel, pretend to be interested. Sobel would say, *We could use the bed. And there's really nothing further we can do for your father. With the accident, he will need constant supervision.* Jake would listen, take a few pamphlets on places Sobel promised would take good care of him. Jake didn't know how much – if any – money his father had salted away. If necessary, Jake would sell the house and the money could go to his father's new jailer; Jake didn't want anything from the estate. He had walked out on all claims at being a Coleridge twenty-eight years ago and as far as he was concerned, they could send the money and all those grim paintings up in one big mushroom cloud of beach house and canvas. There was always the veterans' hospital; Jacob had served his country in Korea and he was entitled to that much.

Only he couldn't do that – it wasn't what his mother would have wanted. Regardless of the man Jacob Coleridge had become, she would have wanted him taken care of. And she would have expected Jake to do the right thing. So here he was, standing

at the foot of a $2,700-a-night hospital bed, wondering why he
didn't feel a shred of love for the old man. It wasn't that he hated
him – what had once been an actual emotion had burned down
to the cinders of disregard.

He thought that maybe, after all this time, he should feel
something. Real emotions like anger or regret or disappointment
– anything but the vacuum of apathy that couldn't even swirl itself
into any sort of caring one way or the other. Jake had done a stellar job of dragging his emotions out behind the figurative garage
and executing them – the same garage where he hid his collection of pornographic holograms of the dead from his regular life.
There were images, now numbering in the tens of thousands, of
every lost mutilated soul he had ever seen; his sick little fetish that
he kept locked away. Along with anything he had ever felt for the
man he was staring down at now.

Jake took a sip of coffee from the vending-machine cup. It
was cold now and he wondered how long he had been standing
there, lost in his head with the *what-ifs* and the dead.

He turned away from the bed and walked out into the hall.
His father's old room was three doors down and he went to see if
they had finished the final coat on the wall. For some reason, he
needed to see that bloody portrait erased from history.

It was well past visiting hours but with Jake firmly entrenched
in a homicide investigation, drop-in privileges had been approved.
It was the hang time after the patients had taken their meds but
before the first rounds of the nighttime staff, and the floor felt
empty. There were no old ladies shuffling along in their robes,
wheeling IV stands like divining rods to the smoking section. The
only noise other than the sound of his boots on the battleship
linoleum was the distant chant of classical music and the more
immediate sound of a thin, reedy snore. An ice machine hummed

off in a small corridor that led to the utility elevator. Other than that, it was quiet.

Jake pushed the door to the room open, worried that they had already filled the space with another patient. The single wedge of light from the hallway exposed an empty bed. He expected to be greeted by the smell of fresh paint and disinfectant but recognized the metallic scent of blood as soon as he was inside. He closed the door, locked the deadbolt, and flipped the light switch.

The bloody portrait still clung to the wall, the pigment baked to black.

Jake stared for a second, wondering why it hadn't been painted over. He looked at the featureless face, mesmerized. But something had changed – a one-inch line of masking tape ran around the portrait. He stepped closer and saw notations on the tape. There were pencil-marked arrows around the masking-tape frame, pointing outward, with the words *CUT OUTSIDE TAPE* printed in handwriting that Jake recognized from somewhere.

Before he had backed up a full step, he realized that the handwriting was David Finch's and he was having the painting removed.

He thought about the mercenary little fuck paying the hospital for the portrait. Then his mind's eye focused on Finch, in his tailored suit, standing self-importantly under a spotlight on the salvaged floor in his Soho gallery. He'd stand poised just right while the final work by the great Jacob Coleridge was hoisted into place by two workmen using a lift. He thought of the way he would market the piece, leaving a few raw nubs of stud extending beyond the skin of sheetrock like denuded bone. *It's so raw*, he would say. *So primal.* The best work Coleridge had ever done. *His last, too.*

Price?

He'd shake his head sadly, eyes downcast as if embarrassed at having to discuss something as crass as money.

But you must have an idea of a price!

He'd look insulted, as if the potential client hadn't understood what he had said. Then he'd slowly let a pensive look bleed into his features, as if the thought of parting with the piece had never crossed his mind but he was beginning to give it some thought. Sure, he was a gallery owner – but he was also an *art lover.* And some pieces you simply couldn't put a dollar sign to. But the sincerest thing he'd say, while placing his hand conspiratorially on the potential client's arm, is that there just isn't a price on friendship. And Jacob Coleridge was – *had been* – his friend.

Forget Damien Hirst, Jasper Johns, and Willem de Kooning (hand placed reverently over his heart). Did they ever paint in their own blood? I don't think so. They were/are great. But they were/are *not* Jacob Coleridge. Coleridge's work was known for its *truth.* And after all, what could be more truthful than sacrificing yourself for your art. *Bleeding* for your art.

Then he'd look back at the painting and say maybe it *should* go out into the world with someone who would *appreciate* it. Maybe it *deserved* to have a loving home. Then he would raise his hand, twitter on the precipice of indecision for a second, then put it back in his pocket, shaking his head and saying, *No, I couldn't. He was a friend.*

How much?

A friend! Finch would repeat, fraternal pride in his voice. Wipe a single tear from the corner of his eye.

And after a perfectly measured pause, he'd say, *Fifty million dollars.*

After all, you didn't rise to the top of a field so full of navel-gazing as modern art without possessing consummate skills in both theatrics and bullshit. A PhD in ass-kissing didn't hurt.

The toe of Jake's boot dented the sheetrock and stopped at the stud behind, puffing out a white cloud of dust. The wall shuddered and a suspended acoustic tile spun to the floor. The second kick, a little higher and to the right, went through the sheetrock, punching out a neat square hole. Another ceiling tile fell like a dry leaf.

By his third kick there were footsteps in the hall. They passed by, searching for the noise.

On his fourth they doubled back.

He reached down into his boot and pulled out the knife he had carried there since he was a teenager. Instead of the clumsy Mexican-made switchblade of his youth, his hand came up with a Gerber titanium airframe knife; standard issue for FBI personnel.

Someone tried the door. Rattled the knob.

"Fuck off!" Jake roared, and thunked the blade a quarter inch into the wall at the top corner of Finch's indicated cut-lines. He slashed down, the carbon steel sliding through the yellow topcoat, and the wall hemorrhaged white dust. He drew the knife down, then across the bottom, and up the other side.

"I'm getting the key," a voice said from the other side of two inches of maple.

Jake hauled the bed over to the door, jammed it up against the frame, and locked the wheels; it wouldn't stop a determined man but it would slow down a single nurse. Then he went back to his father's blood, pulled the knife out of the wall, and slid it back into his boot.

He kicked out the bottom corners, wrapped his fingers around the ragged dusty skin that hung in shreds around the holes, and flayed a massive strip off the wall in one clean yank that uncoiled him from a crouch to an overhead reach. He took the painting off in five irregular patches, bits of blood and white dust floating in a small weather system above the floor. A few small scabs of paint and blood remained and he kicked and punched these in.

He folded the five latex-and-blood-covered parchments into a quick ball, kicked the bed away from in front of the door, and snapped the big stainless thumb bolt open.

Out in the unsure light of the corridor, a nurse was bounding toward him, jailer's keys jingling in her hand. She slowed to a shuffle and barked, "What were you doing in there?" She stopped a few paces away, looking like she'd just realized that she was alone in a dark corridor with a six-foot-two madman who tore up hospital rooms in the middle of the night.

Jake held up the folded skins of the painting. "I was told this was going to be painted over. Not sold. Not salvaged. *Painted over.*"

"That's medical waste. The hospital can do whatever they want with it. I was told—"

Jake took a step toward her and she stopped, backed quickly up.

His long arm came up, his finger aimed at her head. "I don't give a fuck what you've been told or what you think you have the right to do, lady. This is going to be destroyed. You grok me, sweetheart?"

Her face shifted emotions for a few seconds before the elasticity gave way to a rigid stare. She stepped aside and Jake walked on down the hall, his boots leaving a dusty trail, the portrait of one of his father's demons tucked under his arm.

Behind him, the patients who had been jarred awake began chattering like insects.

39

Jake swung into the circular drive and his headlamps lit up the police cruiser sitting on the shoulder, facing west on 27. The cop behind the wheel had a big silhouette and he covered his eyes in the glare of the old muscle car's lamps. Jake pulled up under the tree, got out, and walked over to the cruiser. When he was a few feet away he saw Scopes grimace and try to wave.

As Jake came up to the cruiser, Scopes rolled down his window. "Special Agent Cole." He sounded sincere.

"You draw the shitty end of the stick?"

Scopes nodded. "Short straw." He paused for a minute, looked up at Jake, his face a series of shadows in the moonless night. "I'm sorry about last night. I'm not usually an asshole. I was trying to make everyone feel a little less – I don't know. Unhappy, I guess."

Jake waved it away, looked up at the house. "Anything happen?"

"Light's on in the northeast corner of the house." He nodded up at the master bedroom. "But nothing's been turned on or off since I got here."

"I appreciate it."

Scopes rolled his eyes. "Making amends."

Jake turned away.

He walked back to his car and pulled the balled-up blood painting from the passenger seat. It was damp and heavy, like human skin; it was amazing how the salt air out here got into everything, filling the pores with molecules of water that weighed it down.

The lights were off on the main floor and he knew Kay and Jeremy were asleep upstairs, both of them wearing tiny T-shirts and smelling like a life so beautiful he wondered how he had managed to earn it. The painting under his arm somehow felt immediately lighter. And infinitely less important.

He had started asking himself just why he had come back here. His feelings for his old man did not come into play at all and he realized that he really didn't give a fuck what happened to him one way or another. So what was he doing here? Why had he even talked to the doctor who had phoned him at home in New York? At the first mention of his father he should have said thank you, but we're not buying, and slammed the phone down. But he hadn't. And the only reason he could come up with was that his mother would have wanted someone to look after his old man and since there was no one else around to do the job, it had fallen to Jake – the taker of jobs that no one else wants. Like deciphering the last moments of people's lives.

The part that was getting under his skin – *skinned*, the voice whispered and he shrugged it off – was that the hatred he had felt for his father, that turpentine-tinted taste of disgust and anger, was long gone. Without the anger, he felt a lot lighter, a lot more flexible, which, when he thought about it, boiled down to better. And wasn't *better* the American dream? Everyone wanted to forgive their parents, move on, and build their own fucked-up lives on their own steam. That's just the way things were done.

Amen and pass the doughnuts. So what was the blackness he felt skittering around in the shadows? Why wasn't he walking around giddy and happy and glad that this was all behind him? The short answer was because something still felt *wrong*.

The geometry of the studio rose out of the terrain above the beach and in silhouette it looked like the boxes Kay had stacked at the curb that afternoon – asymmetrical, canted to one side, and filled with old booze bottles. Beyond the building, past the horizon at the edge of the world, there was a small break in the clouds and the moon shone through in a single dim spear.

Jake walked past the studio and stood at the edge of the grass where the landscape gave way to a fifteen-foot drop to the beach. The wind was a solid beat now and the ocean was rolling in on ten-foot swells that had finally broken into waves. The swells dropped onto the beach like wet hands, pounding up sand and debris in noisy slaps. Jake absentmindedly scoured the surf to see if Elmo's corpse had washed up. From the ledge of grass above the water all he saw was black.

Up and down the beach there were no signs of life. From his vantage point on the shelf of grass he could see an easy three or four dozen houses and there wasn't a light on in the bunch. For a second he felt his chest tighten with the thought that he was the only man left alive, like a character in an end-of-the-world novel, everything around him just wishful thinking. There were no boats out on the water, no planes blinking hopefully in the night sky, no visible signs of life anywhere except for the strobe of the lighthouse to the east. He headed for the studio.

The sight of the three-dimensional bloody featureless men on the walls and ceiling of the studio looked like a backdrop for a magic act and there was something more menacing about them now that it was night. When he dropped the balled-up painting onto his father's framing table it hit the masonite and tufts of dust mushroomed out. He stared at it, wondering what it was, what it meant, and how the hell he was supposed to deal with his father with the specter of all this extra drama dragging at his heels like some drunken horror-riddled shadow. The ancient Kenmore fridge where his father used to keep enough food and booze to keep the pigment flowing without having to go back to the house was humming like a robot working over a complicated math calculation. Jake pulled it open to get a drink. His eyes swept past the Coke to three big paper bags that contained chunks of lead pigment; his father was old school – the environment on his list of concerns right after a manned mission to the surface of the sun.

He cracked a Coke open on the lip of the tool box and the cap hit the floor and bounced into a corner. He sat down on top of the paint-splattered surface and put half the bottle away in two furious gulps. It was bright and sweet and it brought tears to his eyes and a burp to his throat that he ripped out in one explosive report. He looked around the room to see if he had attracted the attention of any of the bloody men splattered on the space above him.

Jake polished off the rest of the Coke, dropped the bottle into a dust-covered cardboard box, and pushed himself off the steel cabinet. The crumpled ball of the portrait sat on the table, folded in patches of hospital yellow, plaster-dust white, and drips of Jacob Coleridge's most valuable pigment. Jake circled the table a few times, his arms crossed over his chest, his eyes never leaving the bundle sitting under the task lighting like a car bomb waiting to fulfill its destiny.

With the taste of Coke still fresh in his mouth, he began unfolding the portrait like a cabbage, layer by layer, some pieces tucked into others. He slid them around, laying them out in sequence, and for one minor second he knew that in some twisted way Finch had been right; this *was* art.

When the painting was assembled he took a step back to get perspective and he thought he heard the figures on the walls and ceiling gasp in approval. Even they had to admit that it was beautiful.

Jake stared down at it. He may not have had the talent of his father when it came to mechanics, but Jake understood composition, perspective, and technique. He had always paid attention and the least one could say was that he was fifty percent his father. What he was looking at now was astounding.

Part of that came from it being painted in blood by a half-crazed man. Another part came from his having chewed off his bandages and used his charred, nerveless fingers as palette knives, the split bone and half-broiled cartilage of each finger lending a different edge to the lines in his diminished arsenal. He had lost three fingers – would probably lose more – and Jake saw at least seven distinct lines in the painting. He knew that his father's natural ability had come out without thought, or premonition – it had come out in the rawest of ways, in *instinct*.

The portrait was not sloppy or haphazard like a child's finger painting but controlled, directed. You didn't need a degree in art history to see the consummate skill in the rendering. It had a raw and honest power that was impossible to ignore. But the skill was incidental; the import was in the meaning.

He went back to the old Kenmore for another Coke and thought about it.

There was no doubt that his father was trying to say *something*, even if it was from behind the foggy curtain of dementia. Little bits of almost-signal were getting through from the other side and what was coming out was … was …

What?

The big *what*, of course, was, *What difference – if any – would figuring out what the old man was trying to say, make?* Like deciphering *Finnegan's Wake*, at some point the detective has to ask himself, *What's the point?*

Was this man – this faceless man – the manifestation of a psychotic episode? Schizophrenics often had religious visions, so why not his father? Because the old man had never believed in God. He had never believed in any sort of higher power other than random chance and pure accident. These renderings had nothing to do with the idea of church or God or Satan. This drawing of the bogeyman was something more immediate, more menacing, than some made-up bullshit – Jake couldn't explain how he knew, only that he did.

Jake was an expert in examining evidence from someone else's point of view. But throwing the entire Freudian history of the Coleridge men into the mix pushed him back from any sort of objectivity and he knew that objectivity was where unbiased, untainted, unpremeditated observation was able to function. You throw in the father–son dynamic, especially one as poisoned as theirs, and the results were guaranteed to be skewed.

What did the painting of the man in blood mean? What did the repeated studies of him on the walls mean? Why did he have no face?

And what about the canvases piled around the studio in skewed columns? The highest one looked to be about eight feet and there wasn't one under six. He walked through the pillars of canvas, shuffling some around, picking some up, examining them, putting them down. Jake knew if his father had painted them, they had a purpose. He wouldn't – couldn't – believe that they were just the byproduct of a lifetime spent at the easel, with no greater objective other than to take up time. No hell. No way. If Jacob Coleridge had believed enough to pick up a brush and put it to canvas, it was because it meant something.

No shit, genius.

He rifled the Coke bottle across the room and it hit the wall, bounced back, and smashed on the concrete, skittering shards across the floor. He hated this. The being here, the dealing with his father, the man with the hunting knife and his nightmare skill set.

And they were all connected. Somehow sewn together with a thread so fine that the light wasn't even hitting it.

Finding it was impossible, unless you ran into it. And when you did, chances were it was at neck height, and maybe you'd feel a slight pinch, then you'd hear your head hit the floor and get a last-second glimpse of your body stumbling forward, then bumping into something and going over in a clumsy crash of arms and legs that would twitch because they no longer had the software to tell them to stop and then the lights would go out and—

"STOP IT!" Jake roared, the words coming up like black hot vomit from his heroin days. He forced a few deep breaths down into his belly where they would do the most good.

It's there.

Look for it.

I am.

No, you're not.

Would you fucking stop it!

Sure. As soon as you figure it out. Witch doctor, my ass.

I've always said that.

That was when you were good at seeing things.

I can do this. It will take a little time.

You don't have time. He's coming.

Who?

Him.

Him, who?

Him.

Jake pinched the bridge of his nose and decided that it was time to get to bed. It was almost two a.m. He wasn't much of a sleeper, in fact he never had been, but today, with the defibrillator misfiring like a gremlin-inhabited fuel pump, he needed to give the old corpus a little downtime. Mostly because tomorrow promised to be another rock-'em-sock-'em robots day. He turned off the lights and closed the door.

Outside, the wind was stronger and the swells were breaking before they hit the shore now, ugly white slashes against the black ocean, like blisters rupturing. The moon was squelched somewhere behind the bank of clouds and for the first time he realized how fast the weather was changing now, like watching time-lapse photography.

Jake came in the front door and flipped on a few lights. The Nakashima console lit up, the bright pin spot illuminating the sculpture of the sphere – a polyhedron, his father had once yelled at him – in stark relief. His old man had built it – no, *built* was the wrong word – engineered was more accurate. Out in the studio one night with a hundred-plus stainless-steel speargun shafts and a determination to learn how to TIG weld. Thousands of tiny transepts that terminated in triangles that connected into a perfect sphere. It looked like a NASA engineering model, sitting forgotten under the lone spotlight, a shrine to his father's only experiment in three-dimensional art. He ran his finger over the frame and pulled up a line of fuzzy, greasy dust. The piece almost vibrated at his touch, it had lived alone for so long.

Kay had done a nice job with the place, even going so far as to lay some coasters out on the coffee table. Jake laughed at the gesture; the surface of the table was pitted with cigarette burns and drink circles that stared up like empty sockets. The big Chuck Close portrait with the cut-out eyes leaned against his mother's Steinway like some Oedipal warning.

Something about the painting needled Jake, and he hated that he couldn't nail it down with any sort of precision. He wanted to write it off as stress but the inability to put things together was becoming much too familiar to him lately and he was worried that it was some sort of permanent handicap. He hated not being able to see. The only event he could equate to it would be Kay blowing out her hearing and having to stare at her cello afterward. He stood above the sunken living room and took in the vandalized canvas.

Chuck Close was forced to reinvent his approach to painting after an unlucky roll of the genetic dice left him with diminished motor skills. His earlier photorealistic technique was replaced by pixilated portraits he painted with small blocks of color; Close had literally reinvented himself by writing new code.

Jacob Coleridge considered Chuck Close one of the truest American painters in history. And that meant something coming from a man known for hating everything. Even his own family.

Yet he had sliced the eyes out of the painting.

Hardly defending the museum with an axe.

Jake turned off the lights and headed upstairs into the quiet dark.

40

Jake padded softly down the hallway, tiptoeing past his old room – Jeremy's for now – to the master bedroom. The door was open and Kay was sitting cross-legged on the bed, a massive atlas open on her lap.

"Hey, baby," she said as she looked up from the tome.

"You're supposed to be sleeping." Jake pulled the door half closed.

She snickered. "Yeah. Sure. A cop parked out front and a hurricane coming like some kind of judgment and you expect me to be dead to the world."

He smiled. "Yeah, I do."

She closed up the book and eased it over the side of the bed, quietly lowering it to the floor. "If what the radio is saying is true, you wouldn't believe how big Dylan is." She pointed at the atlas. "Three whole inches. That's bigger than most countries, pal." Kay turned off the light and the room went quickly gray.

The nightlight in the hallway threw a soft glow into the room and his eyes quickly adjusted to the near-dark. He sat down on the mattress to pull off his boots.

It was then that he realized that she had cleared the barricade and made a path to the bed. Even in the gloom he could see that she had cleaned out the old clothes and food wrappers. The sheets were tight over the bed, unwrinkled, and smelled like fabric softener. The room smelled like Pledge. She had done a lot without him and a tinge of guilt made him wish he had never let her come here. "Sorry I'm so late."

"Did the day end all right?"

What could he say to that? Sure, until I kicked in a wall. At the very least I'll get billed four grand to repair it, at the worst charged with vandalism and destruction of private property. "No glitches. Not really." His boot thudded into the carpet. "What did you guys do?"

Kay giggled. "Tonight was a hoot. I had to explain where the bread went when you put it in the toaster and where the toast came from. Jeremy couldn't figure it out. It was wonderful."

Jake laughed, and his other boot hit the floor. "Man, I know how he feels."

"Jake?"

He knew what she wanted to talk to him about. "The man in the floor?"

"I don't like it."

Jake wanted to agree with her, to tell her that it made him uneasy, too, like some sort of a bad meal rumbling around in the plumbing. But he didn't. "He come back?"

"Tonight, when I put him down—"

Jake rolled his eyes. Why did she have to put it like that?

"—he asked if the man in the floor was going to visit him when he was sleeping."

Jake felt his skin tighten and steadied himself in preparation for a jolt in the engine room. All of the moisture had leeched out of him in one great gust, and his bones were rasping against the suede underbelly of his hide. He turned toward her shadow, now visible in the dark.

"He said that the man in the floor – who he keeps calling Bud – was disappointed in us." She swallowed. "He swears that the man in the floor is not an imaginary friend. I'm afraid that he's nuts."

Jake heard an unvoiced accusation in her tone. After all, the mental illness seemed to be firmly entrenched in his side of the DNA. He stood up and went to the window. The weak glow of the moon was completely gone now and the ocean was putting on its war paint in earnest. The waves were well past small-craft-warning status. "*Disappointed*? That's not the word of a three-year-old. He's trying it out. He's not nuts. Maybe it's some kind of coping mechanism."

"Coping mechanism for what? What's wrong in Jeremy's life? You work a lot but so what? So do other fathers. My hours are weird. But he gets time with both of us. *Quality time*. He's well behaved and even if the other parents down at the daycare think we're freaks, we're loving decent people who do a pretty fucking good job of raising our son." The accusatory tone was gone, and had been replaced by a defensive one. "We've built something great here."

The windows rattled a little – soft, almost inaudible, squeaks. "I don't know, baby. Maybe he needs more friends."

"More friends? I had to cancel three play dates and a birthday party to come out here for two days. He doesn't need more friends."

"Maybe he's tired. I know how I get when I'm tired." Jake let something that he had never shared with Kay come out. "After my mother was murdered, she used to visit me. You know I don't believe in ghosts or the afterlife or any of that other religious bullshit. So I know it wasn't one of those things – I knew it wasn't *really* her – but she would come visit me. We would walk on the beach, sometimes sit in my bedroom, and she'd talk to me, listen to what I had to say. She'd answer me, help me with problems. She was there when I went through what I did with my dad. She's the reason I'm here, pretending to care where he ends up. But it's not really her. It's my mind putting her together. Constructing her out of the parts she left behind." Jake turned back to the bed and he felt his skin shift against his muscles and the frame of bones beneath. "But she seemed so real that it looked like I could reach out and touch her. Her dress rustled, she smelled of cigarettes, I could see eyeliner."

Kay lifted herself up on her elbows. "You build things with your head. With your memory. That's why you do what you do." She paused, weighed her words. "I don't want you here. You're going backwards. I can see it in the way you move, the way you talk, the way you are reacting to all of this. It's like circuits are blowing with all the shit you have to deal with."

Another point he couldn't argue with. "You and Jeremy go back to the city and I'll be back as soon as I can. Maybe I can finish up tomorrow morning, maybe not. But I'm tired. I'm so fucking tired of doing this that I just don't want to any more. But I have to close this case."

Kay's voice came out of the dark. "I don't want you out here when the hurricane hits, Jake. Your appliance is going apeshit as it is. What happens if you get a bad jolt?"

I die, he wanted to say. "Cockroaches and Keith Richards and Jake Cole." It was an old joke between them. "Before you can say 'invisible friend' we'll be back in our flat listening to the MC5 and Jeremy will be sleeping in his own bed."

He could see her clearly now, sitting up in bed, cross-legged in the dim of the half-light, *Don't Hassel The Hoff!* riding up her tummy and bunched up under her breasts. Her hair was tied in pigtails and she was grinning.

"What are you grinning about?"

"You always make me feel safe." She fell back and tugged her little white panties off, rolling them into a knot. She curved her tattooed leg down, yanked the underwear off her pointed toes, and pitched them at Jake. They bounced off as she opened her legs.

A pair of ink pistols crossed over her vagina with the words *Tough Love* underneath – Jake's second-favorite tattoo on her body. "Now come here, because you make me horny."

Jake pulled off his T-shirt, and the ink added to the deep shadow etched into his lean body. As he moved, part of him disappeared, became the background. Kay propped herself up on her elbows, folded herself forward like a cat, and undid the big sterling-and-turquoise buckle on his belt. It snaked through the loops of his Levi's and he undid his jeans. Then he was naked in front of her and she smiled up at him.

Kay reached up between the heavy oak spokes of the headboard and Jake slipped the worn police handcuffs over her wrists. He snapped them closed – a shining pair of silver eyes – and began.

She rose up into him, her eyes locked on his. He reached down beside the bed and found his belt. He picked it up and her eyes twitched when she heard the buckle clink. She tried to turn her head, to see it coming, but he held her jaw and kept his eyes locked on hers in the almost-dark. The deep shadow of her sockets yawned up at him as he slipped the belt around her neck.

The black leather fell between her breasts, its tail curling up against the crossed pistols. She clenched her teeth and kept her eyes locked on his.

Her breaths rasped out in those little birthing whistles she made before the sex circuits in her head went supernova. The belt around her neck thrashed and writhed as she threw her hips into his weight, and he felt her hard pelvic bone beneath the flesh, knocking into his.

Kay was sliding back and forth beneath him. She snarled.

Jake reached down, looped the snapping tail of the belt around his hand, and began to tighten. The black noose circled in around her flesh and the buckle rose up against her chin, dimpling a small fold of skin with its floral edge.

She moaned the word, "Now," only it came out in four fuck-jarred syllables.

He pulled the loop tight and Kay's face jolted pale. Then red. Her mouth opened, to breathe, to scream, but she was unable to get air.

He tightened the belt one more turn of his fist and his fingers went numb.

Her mouth broadened, then opened like a beached fish sucking air. Her eyes snapped wide, gleaming out of the deep shadow of her sockets. Then bulged. The veins in her neck rose to the skin like fingers trying to claw through and there was a startling deep-space second when their eyes connected, then she arched her back violently and shuddered.

She lay there afterward, completely still, her unfocused eyes pointed into the dark.

41

Mike Hauser was only going to be home for a few minutes – very likely his last visit until the storm was gone. Very possibly his last visit to this house. This wasn't melodrama speaking, just honest analysis of a situation that had so many outcomes that the possibilities could keep a supercomputer busy for a year. The hand of God was coming, advancing on a roiling storm that might obliterate Hauser's community from the earth – and that's precisely how he thought of this little patch of land – *his* community. And unfortunately that included the invisible motherfucker with the hunting knife. Along with Jake Cole – a man who attracted death like some kind of magnet for the broken. Right now Hauser's kingdom had more than a few ugly shadows circling overhead. The trick would be in surviving them.

It was 2:12 a.m. and the sheriff walked into the kitchen in full gear, including the web belt with his Sig and the various accoutrements of his trade. He poured himself a ginger ale from a torpedo-sized plastic bottle in the fridge. He took a sip, got disgusted that it was flat, and poured it down the drain. Of all the things progress had bulldozed under in the name of improvement, he lamented the loss of glass bottles the most. He settled on water from the tap, put it away in three loud gulps, and placed the glass in the dishwasher.

Stephanie was out of town and he suddenly wished that she were here to give him one of her talks, maybe a smooch and a punch in the arm. But he had flown her inland, to her brother's house where she'd be safe. Only Hauser's concept of safe had changed a lot in the past few days. Irrevocably so.

Of all the images that this case brought with it, the one that kept popping up from behind the bushes was the woman and child up the beach, still known as Madame and Little X. More than two full turns of the hour hand later and all their forensic and digital know-how couldn't answer the simple question as to who they were. It was like investigating the murder of two people who had never really been there at all.

He moved down the basement steps by feel, listening to the new voice of his house in the approaching hurricane. When he was at the bottom he flipped the two middle switches and the floor-to-ceiling display cases flickered to life, humming yellow like a bank of supermarket freezers.

One wall was taken up by his shotgun collection, the second by his deer rifles and handguns, the third by his reference library, and the last by his knives.

Hauser stared at his reflection in the glass. He had organized what had happened to the point where images of Madame X and her son no longer popped up randomly, but they were never far from the viewfinder in his head and he continually turned his mind's eye away from them whenever one fired to life. Things like this were not supposed to happen here. But he knew that wasn't how it worked; if he put a little horsepower into the thought process the next deduction was that things like this weren't supposed to happen *anywhere*.

Only they did. All the time. All you had to do was look in the bedroom of the house up the road. After all, why should this place be special?

The one break they were getting in the investigation – the single little let-up – was with the media; with Hurricane Dylan ripping in, reporters were having a hard time nailing down interviews. Usually, Hauser would worry about one of his men getting cornered over beers at the Scrimshaw Lounge after work, or one of the Macready woman's neighbors ending up on Fox. But with the storm advancing, no one had time to talk to these people – they were too busy saving their iMacs and Franklin Mint collectibles. The very definite side benefit to this was that the news was now more interested in the weather than in the three dead bodies. Of course, Jake had assured him that this wouldn't last for long. Not once those parasites attached the word *serial* to the killings.

Then everyone from the greengrocer to the gas station attendant would be popping up on Channel 7, analyzing the evidence, waxing poetic about DNA, CSI, and the rest of the acronyms they had picked up from prime-time television. The worst, Jake had assured him, would be watching the talking heads – the self-professed experts – yakking away, coming up with motivational or personality profiles of the killer when they were missing very important pieces of evidence – most notably facts.

Hauser had come home to pick up a few personal things, the first being his great-grandfather's 1918 trench knife. If the house and everything else was torn from the earth, this was the only thing he wanted to save besides his wedding band and that one trophy his son, Aaron, had won in little league. The rest of the shit could go and he wouldn't care. Not in any real sort of way.

He opened the case and removed the weapon. He had no memories of his great-grandfather, but this knife had meant a lot to his grandfather, and then to his father so, by extension, it meant a lot to him. He had hoped that it would mean something to Aaron some day – a little piece of honor handed down from man to man in the family – but all that had been taken away by a drunk in a van. But that didn't mean that Hauser was going to let it sit here and maybe get taken away by the storm.

The waxy feel of the metal gave way to a greasy one as the protective oil on the knife warmed to his touch. He examined it for a few minutes, hoping that it would give up some of its secrets. What did Jake see when he looked at a knife? Something told Hauser that a man like that didn't see just another tool in the history of human evolution – for a man like Jake, a knife was a potential opera of horror.

The sheriff looked around the room, examining the display cases full of his hunting gear. Suddenly he understood why to a man like Jake Cole, the world looked like an accident waiting to happen.

Hauser slid the knife into its worn leather case, snapped the stay, and strung it onto his tactical belt. Then he shut off the lights and headed out to his cruiser.

42

Kay lay still, cuffed to the headboard, Jake resting solidly on top of her. The belt around her neck hung in a loose loop now, the tight lines of pressure bruised into her throat. She had popped a blood vessel in her left eye, and it had ruptured into a beautiful red flower.

Jake watched her face for a few minutes, a series of unmoving geometric shadows in the dark. She lay still, barely breathing. He stared at her, willing himself to be here and now, not there and then. He wondered how he had learned to compartmentalize his life so completely, so utterly, that he could visit horror all day yet come home to such happiness. And in this swirl of thoughts came the realization that it really was time for him to quit the job. To leave. To move on with his life and become a whole man – a man without fractures.

"How did I find you?" she asked.

Kay was beautiful lying there, but Jake knew that behind her, deep in the pockets of her mind, things were not bright or happy or safe. Her eyes were riveting, mesmerizing, but something was missing in the way they moved, as if a little of the happiness had been knocked out along the way. Once, after they had begun to suspect that what they had might be something special, she told him that she had always loved bad men. There was something about the danger – about the not knowing what was next – that was as addictive as the booze had ever been. She said she still hated herself for it.

Jake suspected that sometimes he did, too.

Her mouth started a smile, the blistered vein in her left eye tinting it with weirdness. "I love getting fucked by you," she said.

"That's because you're a hopeless romantic."

The tinkle of laughter turned into a wide-mouthed roar that wracked her body and the buckle clinked in the dark, a scratchy metallic note that sounded like Hauser pushing the Macready woman's door open.

Jake stiffened. "I want you two on the noon bus."

Her laugh stopped cold and he felt her stiffen beneath him. "No way, Poppy. I didn't haul this hot little ass out here for a fast fuck and the bum's rush. I'm not leaving without my man."

"We'll talk about it." But he knew she'd be off Long Island at noon no matter how much she bitched, even if he had to shoot her and Jeremy in the ass with tranq darts and send them home in a pair of FedEx boxes.

He tilted his head and looked into her eyes. Her face held a loose peaceful edge that he knew he was lucky to see. He kissed her.

"Another one?" she asked.

The day ran through his head on fast-forward, from the bloody portrait to Rachael Macready bled out and abandoned on the sopping carpet. He thought about the lighthouse over her shoulder, about Hauser pacing the morgue, about the departmental Charger pushing 120 miles an hour and the sound the Coke bottle made when it hit the floor in the studio. He wanted to say he was too tired, that he needed some sleep, but it would have been a lie.

He opened his mouth and fastened it on hers.

She moaned, slid her legs wider apart, and shimmied further under him. The buckle clinked.

Then he wrapped the belt around his fist.

And began to squeeze off her oxygen.

43

Day Three
Sumter Point

"Jake!"

The single word was filled with such panic, such wrongness, that he was down the hall with the pistol in his hand before he was fully awake.

He stopped at the top of the stairs and looked out at the nave. Jeremy stood in the living room, his back to the staircase, his head canted over at an odd angle as if some of the hydraulic hoses that powered his neck had ruptured. Jake couldn't see his face but the boy's body language was foreign, unfamiliar, and with that realization came a little more of the fear he had heard in Kay's voice.

Kay was on her knees in front of the boy, holding him at arm's length, her face sculpted tight with shock.

Jake walked down the stairs with the pistol still clamped in his fingers. He was naked.

Kay didn't look up. Didn't acknowledge his existence. She was staring at Jeremy with the same eyes she had last night during climax – bulging and glassy. Both of them had hemorrhages now, and the second had burst into a bloody storm that raged around her pupil. She was holding Jeremy and shaking, the tremors traveling down her arms and transferring to his little body, which was vibrating like more hydraulic hoses were about to pop.

Jake moved slowly. "Baby?"

Kay just stared at the boy's face, and a bright rim of tears formed on her lashes below the hemorrhaged reds and it made her eyes look like they were bleeding.

Jake's foot hit the bottom stair and this nearness flipped a switch in Jeremy's head because he shrugged off his mother's grip and turned around.

His sockets, cheekbones, and the curved line of his jaw were outlined in sloppy red finger strokes. The stitching of the mouth was broad, and went across his face in thick vertical lines that were crooked and unequal. The boy's face was painted like a skull. The whole thing had the lilt of madness about it, as if his face was a funhouse prop. Jake didn't need to be told that it was blood – he could smell it.

Jeremy's bottom lip trembled and he was crying red streaks. Tears dripped down his cheeks and ran to the collar of his T-shirt, slowly turning pink. Jake could see that he was one breath away from flying into hysterics.

Jake scooped him up, covering the back of his head with his hand, and hugged him. "Moriarty, what happened?"

He looked at Kay over the top of the boy's head. She stood there shaking her head, her red eyes leaking clear tears. The big door to the deck was open a few inches. "We were in here alone, Jake. I opened the door to get some fresh air because it smells so … bad. I turned my back on him for a minute. Maybe less." She shook her head. "I was making coffee … just making coffee when Jeremy barked – literally barked – like a dog and I rushed over and he was … he was … like that … I … don't … um … I—" She shuddered and for a second it looked like she would throw up.

Jake looked at the open door. "Moriarty?"

Jeremy squeezed him, his little body quivering.

"What happened?" His voice climbed up a little, and he had to add the words, "It's okay, son," to let Jeremy know he wasn't angry – the natural assumption of someone without fully developed emotions.

"It was him, Daddy."

Jake pried his son's head out of the nook in his collar. Jeremy's little tear-streaked blood-skull leered up at him, teeth outlined, eye sockets darkened, the logo for an album cover. "He said he wants to play with you, Daddy."

Jake felt his chest tighten again and he sat down on the sofa, his skull-painted boy clinging to him like a lemur.

"Then he touched me," the little boy said. "He touched my face. And now it smells icky. He said he started a game with you when you were a little boy and he likes playing with you very much. He said you don't get scared. Is that true, Daddy? You don't get scared? Because I'm scared. I'm very scared and I want to go home and I don't want to play with him any more. He's not nice. He's mean and ugly and he smells bad and—" The words stopped and he looked around, as if the room were bugged.

"It's okay, son," Jake said again.

Jeremy's eyes widened, two contrasting orbs in black-red sockets. "Remember the time in the park when I found that bird, Daddy? Remember that? I said it smelled yucky and you said that's because it was dead. Do you remember? And you 'splained that sometimes birds and animals have accidents or get sick and then they are made dead and that makes them smell bad. Do you remember, Daddy? Do you?" There was a fevered, crazed quality to the boy's voice.

Jake looked over at Kay. She had her back to the window and she was hugging herself and crying, bright streaks streaming down her cheeks. She didn't see him. Or Jeremy. She was off in the theater behind her eyes watching a test pattern.

"I remember, son."

"The man in the floor smelled just like that bird in the park, all bad and sick and dead. And he's not nice any more. Don't play the game with him. Please promise me that you won't play the game with him."

Jake pulled Jeremy in close, cradling his head in his collarbone. He stepped forward and grabbed Kay and the touch of another human seemed to snap her out of the place she had retreated to. She sniffled, looked up, and locked her eyes on him.

"You okay?" he asked.

Kay shook her head. "Do I look okay?" She wiped her nose on the hem of her T-shirt. "I don't want you staying here. I don't care what this job is about. I don't care if this whole fucking place gets washed into the ocean. You are coming home with us."

Jake nodded.

"They won't let him on the bus with no pants, Mommy."

Jake and Kay looked down at his naked body. "You, my friend, may have a point," Jake said, and reached for the phone to call Hauser.

44

Jake was relieved that the medical examiner was at one of the Olympus microscopes in the corner of the lab instead of headed west in the Long Island Hurricane Exodus. It was obvious that she had been here all night. She was hunched over, her face squinched up with the expression common to microscope-gazers everywhere. He dropped a Ziploc containing Jeremy's bloody T-shirt onto the table beside her and the noise jarred her from her scientific myopia.

"Special Agent Cole," she tried as a greeting.

Jake was glad people were laying off the Charles Bronson thing – he hated it. "Dr. Reagan."

She offered her version of a smile – the same tight line she had shown at Madame and Little X's the other night. "To what do I owe the pleasure?" There was something about the last word that sounded insincere.

Jake put on his be-nice face, as Kay called it. "Could you please analyze the blood on that?"

She picked up the bag and examined it. It squished against the polyethylene, red like a battlefield dressing. "What is it?"

"T-shirt. There may be some contaminants like mucus and saline from another source but it's the blood I want analyzed."

"DNA?"

"First check the typing against all three bodies. Madame and Little X and the Macready woman."

"Where did you get this?" she asked.

"Something smeared it on my son's face."

"You mean someone."

"No." Jake's voice sounded a million miles away, even to him. "I don't."

45

The doctor's waiting room looked like every one he had ever been in, the chairs just a little past being presentable and the walls adorned with the unimaginative combination of public health posters and ugly hotel-room art.

Jake sat with his head in his hands, feeling like his brain was filled with ants. He was going over Jeremy's Misfits makeup, trying to figure out where it had come from. The cop in the driveway hadn't seen a thing; no one had come via the road, and with the way the house was situated on the property, he would have seen someone approach from three of the sides. Which left the beach as the only viable route.

But by looking at things this way, he was forgetting to ask the most important questions of all: *Who was the man in the floor and what did he want?*

Jake lifted his head and eased back in the vinyl seat, letting his focus drift to the thought of pulling up stakes and heading back to the city. But he knew that he couldn't leave – even the thought of it in the abstract felt treasonous; he would stay in Montauk until everything was tied up and nailed shut. And like the old saying about how to eat an elephant, Jake knew that the next step in the process began here, in psychiatrist's office.

Sobel's receptionist, a woman of twenty-five with the unhappy face of a burgeoning depressive, busied herself behind the desk. A mother and daughter sat at the other corner of the office. The girl was about twelve, and had the look of someone plugged into a different sensory universe. Jake guessed that she was autistic. She played with a bowl of colored candies. Her mother sat reading a thick paperback that had a beautiful man with beautiful hair embracing a beautiful woman with beautiful hair, and they were wearing beautiful clothes, and back, in the distance over their shoulders—

— *like that goddamned lighthouse over Rachael Macready's shoulder—*

—*skinned—*

—was a beautiful estate filled with their beautiful life. The book was titled *The Bluebloods of Connecticut* and Jake knew there were horses in the story. Horses with long, well-groomed tails. Probably a private jet. Kisses and muscular embraces. Unadulterated crap.

The girl stared off into the distance, as if watching a movie behind her eyes. She slid the large glass bowl of candies from the center to the side of the coffee table and had cleared all the magazines into a neat pile. As her mother read of the steamy sexploits visited upon the handsome characters of the Connecticut estate, Jake watched the girl mechanically remove candies from the bowl one at a time, then lay them out on the table. She was sitting on the floor and her hand would dip into the bowl, then place the candy on the table. Then she would repeat the process. The table was strewn with candies in no apparent order, most not touching. Her mother was too engrossed with the heavy breathing between the pages of her paperback to notice that her daughter was making a mess.

"Mr. Cole," the receptionist said, her mouth turned down at the corners. "Please go on in."

Jake stood up and stepped around the coffee table. Neither the woman nor her daughter seemed to notice.

Dr. Sobel got up from behind his desk and shook Jake's hand. "I'm sorry about yesterday, Jake. If I thought that your father was a danger to himself, I would have had him restrained before."

Jake eased into the mail-order-catalog chair and examined Sobel for anything that he could make use of. The psychiatrist's face was a blank sheet of meat and Jake recognized the clinical training of a man trying to study him for, well, anything *he* could make use of. Jake put his hands on the knuckles of the chair arms, crossed one booted foot over his knee, and waited. After Sobel's eyes finished taking him apart, he took a deep breath and opened his hands as if he were trying to sell Jake pet insurance.

"I know how tough this can be." Sobel did a pretty good job of sounding sincere.

"I'm not having this conversation – I'm not here to have a candle put to my head."

Sobel seemed to mull this over for a few seconds.

"What's going on with my father? How do I best take care of his needs right now, in the immediate future, and in the long-term?"

Sobel opened a large file on his desk and Jake recognized the same colored pages and Post-Its from the metal clipboard the day before. "For a man of eighty, your father's vitals and blood work are spectacular. He's obviously taken care of himself."

Jake snorted. "Not that I know of."

Sobel's mouth turned down at being contradicted.

How to say this without sounding like a prick? No clean route. "My father has been a raging alcoholic ever since he could raise his arm. He ate for shit. Never exercised. Ran himself ragged. Sometimes he'd stay up for a week solid, fueled on booze and anger. No, I don't think that your tests have painted an entirely accurate picture."

Sobel penciled a note onto the page. "What is his domestic life like?"

Jake felt the cold flash of wasted time burst in his head. "Dr. Sobel, I thought you had done an evaluation on my father. You should know all of these things. If you don't even know who he *was*, how can you compare that to who he *is*?"

Sobel stopped nodding and folded his arms across his chest. "I am also trying to get a feel for you, and what you are willing to do for him, Mr. Cole. This is not solely about him. I need to see how much you're willing to handle. How much you *can* handle. Your impressions of your father also give me a lot of insight into you."

"You're kidding."

Sobel shook his head.

Jake reached into his jacket and took out a black leather bill-fold. He opened it to the badge and the ID card, leaned over, and slid it across the desk to the psychiatrist. "Dr. Sobel, I am not open for analysis. I am not interested in analysis. I have more dark secrets locked away in my head than you are ever going to know. But since you ask, I will provide you with a little insight into this classic Freudian situation.

"My father and I have not spoken for nearly thirty years. I do not like the man and, if you really want to get to the bottom of it, for a long time I hated him. No surprise there. Good old Sigmund handled this in his self-justifying twenty-first lecture in *A General*

Introduction to Psycho-Analysis. I'm sure you've read it, even if it is complete horseshit.

"I may think that how he raised me – or didn't raise me – was shitty, but his work is something else entirely. I don't think that money is any sort of a problem but I haven't spoken to his lawyer. Worst-case scenario, I sell the house and that should buy him ten years wherever he needs. What I want out of you is where those ten years should be."

Sobel closed Jake's badge and slid it back across the desk. "Do you want to be involved?"

"I think we are getting a little ahead of ourselves here but the short answer is no. I need to know exactly what is wrong with my father so I can start making the proper arrangements for his future. A future that I have no intention of being involved in." Jake knew he sounded like a prick but he didn't care.

Sobel turned his thoughtful nod back on. "Right now your father is still suffering the effects of shock, a little post-traumatic stress disorder, and he's been taking painkillers. These things combined don't give me a very stable subject to begin with and when you throw in the classic signs of Alzheimer's, things get exponentially complicated. He's confused, he's irritable, and he's aggressive."

Jake held up his hand. "Dr. Sobel, my father has been irritable and aggressive as long as I can remember."

Sobel signaled that he expected to be allowed to finish. "That painting on the wall of his room –" he paused, and his voice softened, as if he were speaking to himself –"showed no degeneration in his motor skill, which is something I should see in a man at this stage of AD. That piece shows that he is more than capable of abstract thinking – the mere fact that he was able to make a connection between his blood and paint is abstract enough but when we add in the kind of picture he painted, I feel he can clearly think in abstract terms." The psychiatrist turned back to his notes, flipped through a few pages. "His vocabulary shows no degeneration as far as I can tell. Like I said, I don't have an evaluation from before his accident, but your father is very well spoken, if somewhat opinionated." Sobel looked up from the folder and leaned back in his chair. He clasped his hands on top of his head and continued, "Symptomatically speaking, he lies somewhere between early and moderate dementia, stages two and three respectively. There are signs of moderate dementia and yet certain telltale signs of early dementia are missing, and vice versa. This disease is different in each individual but there are certain symptoms that are – or should be – a given." There was a shift in his voice that told Jake there was something he wasn't being told.

"Are you saying that he might *not* have Alzheimer's?"

"I know you talked this through with his GP but I'm working in a vacuum here." Sobel shrugged and with his hands knit together on top of his head, it looked like an exercise. "I don't have a lot of collateral history from relatives or friends, and that is one of the cornerstones of diagnosing Alzheimer's. Your father spent a lot of time alone and that doesn't help me. He's also an artist and artists are eccentric to begin with. I need to know certain things that, at this point, I don't."

"What are we not talking about, Dr. Sobel?"

"Excuse me?"

Jake smiled. "I can tell when I'm being left in the dark."

"Jake, I don't know exactly what is going on with your father. What I do know is that his neural pathways are not translating the real world into terms that he can always understand. I usually get to see a patient long before they begin to have even minor accidents. Your father set himself on fire and crashed through a plate-glass window. I am having a hard time believing that he managed to get to this point and still be living alone. He should have been here long before this. A year, maybe. Possibly before that."

"I found sod and keys and paperbacks in his fridge. I don't know how the hell he managed to live like that. I am not going to sit here and make excuses that you don't really care about anyway, but I've been off the Christmas card list for a very long time."

Sobel nodded again. "He's not malnourished. He's not suffering any deficiencies. And his hygiene, although not perfect, was much better than I expected." He paused. "I don't like his nightmares – combined with that painting that he did on his wall—" Did Sobel know that he had taken half the wall down last night? "That portrait came from somewhere deep in his mind. He's frightened of something and it's manifesting itself in his dreams and his rantings and he's bringing it to the surface and trying to show it to the world. All this talk about this *man of blood* living in the floor has me con—"

Jake stood up. "What?"

Sobel froze, as if he had said something wrong. "This happens a lot. That painting is a manifestation of whatever he fears, and by bringing it out, he's trying to tell us—"

"Forget the clinical diagnosis. I want to know what he said – *exactly*." Jake reached across the desk and tore the file folder from Sobel's grasp.

The doctor pushed his chair back and stood up. "Jake, I do not—"

"Sit down or call security," Jake said flatly, and scanned the page of notes. "Here," he said, pointing to Sobel's notes. "Read this." He spun the folder on the desk and held his finger to the page, like a drill instructor showing a drop zone to a cadet.

Sobel leaned over and focused on the writing. "*For about fifteen minutes this morning the patient appeared lucid and was aware that he was in the hospital. Blood pressure and heart rate were stable and commensurate with a man of his age and general health. Only signs of the onset of dementia were several comments patient made regarding someone he called the blood man. When asked to explain, patient grew agitated, apologized. Heart rate and blood pressure began to climb and breathing became shallow, panicked. Patient asked the nurse to check the bathroom and the closet. Particularly the floor.*" Sobel looked up. "Do you know what he's talking about?"

Jake felt his heart hitch a beat. Then a second time. Jeremy had his ex-friend who lived in the floor. The floor back at his old man's house. Jeremy had called him Bud. Jake thought about laying it all out on the table, but there was no way a psychiatrist was going to help solve this. Not now. Not in a day. This was going to take a strong stomach and federal resources. What he needed from Sobel was information. "Does he know what happened to the nurse who looked like my mother?" It was a valid question. Maybe he had heard the other nurses talking.

Sobel raised an eyebrow. "She did look like your mother, didn't she?"

Jake nodded. "A little."

Sobel shrugged. "I know none of the staff would tell him. And I haven't heard anyone gossiping. We had two reporters come by this morning but security escorted them from the building pretty fast. So I don't think he knows. How could he?"

Jake was thankful for that, at least. "Yesterday he didn't recognize me once during the three times I was here. He's come apart a little. Maybe this man of blood is just the rantings of a scared old man who made a lot of mistakes in his life. The man of blood could be—" He stopped and triangulated the past few days. Blood man. Blood. Man. Bloodman. Only a three-year-old would say it differently, wouldn't he? He wasn't saying *Bud, man.* He was saying *Budman. Bludman. Bloodman.*

Bloodman.

Sonofabitch.

Sobel's face shifted. "Something's going on inside your father, Jake. Something one part of him wants to verbalize and another desperately wants to keep suppressed. He has opposing emotions about this man of blood – whatever that is."

Jake thought about the text that covered his skin, about the Canto, about the men of blood that Dante had described. The violent, the viscous, the dangerous. Kept in a lake of fire and blood where their screams echoed and their souls were tortured. Was his old man talking about them? "All you seem to be telling me is that my father may or may not be in the early-to-mid stages of Alzheimer's—"

Sobel shook his head, held up his hand. "If this talk about the blood man is just a misnomer for something – or someone – that he's afraid of, it could be that he's just over-compartmentalized his life in order not to have to face whatever it is that's scaring him. And he *is* scared, Jake. The man inside is hiding from something."

"He's been doing that since my mother died." *Skinned*, the little voice hissed.

"That was the summer of '78, right?"

Jake nodded. "June sixth."

Sobel made a note on the chart. "Jesus, how time flies. I'm sorry about your mother, Jake. Besides having a killer backhand, she was a lot of fun. Elegant. Every woman at the club was jealous of her."

"I remember that. Living with her was like living with Jackie Kennedy. She could make an egg-salad sandwich and a Coke look refined."

"Could this have anything to do with your mother? Her ... accident was never solved, was it?"

Jake shook his head.

"So could it?"

Jake shook his head and shrugged at the same time. "I don't know. Maybe. Yes. No. All of the above. I'll figure it out."

"If all of this is tied in somehow, maybe your father is afraid of something out of his past. Maybe it's just a flashback to her death. Bad memories coming back."

"I don't think so. After my mother's death, Dad never talked about it. Never seemed to react." *Liar.* He sat in front of her car every night with a bottle of booze and wept until he fell asleep.

"The memory is a peculiar place, Jake. It functions under different basic tenets than the rest of the mind. Maybe he is being plagued by ghosts you don't know about."

Jake thought about the blank bloody face that he had splattered on the hospital room wall and realized that Sobel had to be partially right. "Maybe he's had a real struggle," the psychiatrist added. "Maybe his accident wasn't an accident at all."

"Are you saying that he burned off his hands on purpose?"

Sobel's head clicked from side to side but the grimace refused to be shaken loose. "*On purpose* is a little strong. Sometimes we do things for reasons we're not aware of. Maybe your father wanted to leave the house. Maybe a part of him knew that it wasn't safe for him because of exactly the same reasons you cited – he opened the fridge and saw sod and keys and he couldn't understand why they were there. The rational part of his brain realized that the environment wasn't good for him. Maybe he had an accident so he could leave. And maybe the blood man is just his way of lumping his feeling of insecurity into a neat package. I think that something has your father very frightened. Something he's calling the blood man."

The receptionist was jammed into her office chair, scowling over the Day-Timer, crossing out appointments with a red marker, the phone pressed to her ear. "Yes, that's right, Mr. O'Shaunnesy, we have to recalibrate with the storm. I don't know when we'll be back but you will be at the head of the line. Of course. Of course. At least four days …"

Jake nodded a thank-you as he walked past her desk.

The little girl was still folded into the lotus position under the coffee table and by now the two-foot-by-five-foot surface was armored with a layer of candies, laid out in a brightly colored mosaic. From beside the receptionist's desk, Jake saw the wrappers at an angle, a shelf of color. The girl was staring straight ahead, her hand dipping into the bowl like a metronome counting time, not missing a beat. As before, one candy would be placed in an empty slot at the far upper-left-hand corner of the table, the next somewhere in the middle, as if she had a pattern laid out in her head and was merely illustrating it for her mother – but the woman was still engrossed in her shitty book.

Jake's head swiveled as he passed the girl, scanning the pattern on the table. The mother didn't lift her eyes from the novel and the little girl kept dipping her hand into the bowl and laying out the candies as single pixels in a digital image.

Jake was almost on top of her when he stopped.

She had laid out a copy – a nearly *exact* copy, limited by the size of the surface she had to work on and the colors at her disposal – of the cover of her mother's book. Jake froze in midstep.

Two beautiful candy people embraced, a cubist mansion in the background, a tree line behind. *The Bluebloods of Connecticut* spelled out in cursive sweets.

Each candy was a component.

A speck of color.

A single pixel.

Like Chuck Close's work.

"She does that all the time," her mother said in a thick Long Island accent.

Jake looked up, saw the book folded in her lap. "It's beautiful," he said.

The mother shrugged. "I s'pose. I try not to get annoyed but it's hard sometimes. She'll do this with anything. Playing cards. Scraps of paper. Dead leaves. Thumbtacks – but I try to keep her away from them. She even does it with bits of food. Can't give her no Froot Loops or nothin' with color or she's makin' pictures of faces and stuff. When you scrape dried raisins off the car seat for the fifth time in a week it gets old real quick."

Jake was trying to listen but the image of the Chuck Close painting back at the beach house wouldn't leave him. He saw the sliced-out eyes, the pixilated image of his father's face staring out of the huge canvas. He thought about the dreary little paintings stacked up in the studio, random nothings that seemed meaningless and incomplete. He thought about the whole often being greater than the sum of its parts.

And suddenly he knew what the canvases stacked in the studio were.

46

He tried to get Jeremy to explain the man in the floor, to describe him in some concrete way, maybe even to summon him. But when he had pressed – really pushed the boy – he had run to the middle of the living room, jumped up and down, and screamed, "Bud! Bud! Bud!" over and over until Jake had finally picked him up and told him to forget it. And for some reason this made Jeremy even more frustrated, more angry, as if jumping up and down in the middle of the living room *was* the answer.

Jake and Kay spent the morning photographing the paintings in the studio. Kay held the digital recorder and Jake flipped through the paintings, holding them up one at a time – just long enough for the camera to capture it – then he moved onto the next. Jake knew that when the video was finally viewed, it would look like a meth addict's homage to Dylan's "Subterranean Homesick Blues." But he had spoken to the lab back at Quantico and they had software that could isolate each individual canvas and apply it to its place in an overall pattern.

They worked fast, some minutes capturing up to forty canvases, others barely getting ten. By the end of the first hour they had cataloged 1,106 canvases. By the end of the second hour, another 897 – a sizeable dent in the process.

"I need a sandwich," Kay said, her arm up on the camera, bent at the wrist, the word *L-O-V-E* inked across her knuckles.

"And a Coke," Jake added.

Jake didn't want Jeremy in the studio proper where the studies of the faceless men of blood looked down from everywhere, so he had been relegated to the studio's small entryway, doing a pretty good job of entertaining himself with more Hot Wheels mayhem. Kay had found a Patti Smith album in one of the milk crates under the ancient freezer-sized oak stereo and Jeremy was using the soundtrack to his full advantage, little imaginary car-accident victims meeting their maker to "Redondo Beach."

"You want a coffee, Moriarty?" Jake asked above the music, and walked over to the entryway. He stepped in. "A big coffee?"

Jeremy laughed. "I don't like no coffee, Daddy. I like milk and apple juice."

Looking at his son now, sprawled out on the tiled floor of the entryway with his cars shining like metallic insects, he could see the machinations the boy's mind was going through to forget what had happened that morning. The part that frightened Jake was that his son refused to talk about it. What was he afraid of? Was it the same man in the floor that had his father spooked? Was it a communal hallucination or was it something more tangible? The answer was easy in coming: hallucinations couldn't finger-paint a skull over your son's face in blood.

"So let's get some lunch," Jake said, to Jeremy and Kay's applause. "You guys are easy to please."

"That's us, *easy-peasy*!"

"Well, *Mrs. Easy* –" he said, winking at Kay – "and *Mr. Peasy*, how about some tuna sandwiches?"

Jake looked at his watch and saw that they had about an hour before Kay and Jeremy headed back to the city, and he wanted to catalog as many of the paintings as possible. They headed inside, Jake carrying Jeremy in his arms, Kay with the camera and tripod over her shoulder like a spear-bearer. Kay flipped off the lights.

The outer edge of the storm had made landfall and the sky was gone in a mass of gray and white that misted the coast with a solid shower. The grass was already saturated and the falling water pushed by the wind that had fired up etched shifting patterns in the rolling chop of the ocean. Jeremy laughed as Jake ran through the rain, swearing in Moriarty-friendly language that made him sound like a crazed Yosemite Sam.

Jake held the door for Kay, his hand protectively covering the back of Jeremy's head. Wind ripped into the house and dust devils and papers swirled in mini funnels. The wind slammed the door for him as he jumped inside after her.

"I don't want to be here when Dylan rolls in, Jake." Kay took the camera off the tripod.

Jake put Jeremy down in the kitchen and dried his hair with a fistful of paper towels. "I say we have some sandwiches, then hit the road. Who's with me?"

Jeremy shot his arm into the air in a Fascist vote and Kay nodded, grinning brightly. "What about the case?" she asked.

"F-U-C-K the case," he said. "We are *leaving*."

Kay's T-shirt was wet and clung to her body and her nipples earned her a happy stare from Jake. "After a quick nap, that is," he added.

"All right, coffee, Moriarty?"

Jeremy shouted, "I said I don't drink no coffee!"

"Oh, yeah. Forgot. Sorry. I must be thinking about some other little boy I know." He bent down, kissed his son, and sent him out of the kitchen with an affectionate pat on the bum. "You go play with your cars and I'll make us some lunch."

Jeremy ran to the living room and plopped himself down on the multicolored tapestry of intertwined rugs. He fished in his pockets, then threw his cars down like a handful of Yahtzee dice. Within seconds the casualties were piling up amid three-year-old dinosaur roars.

Jake washed his hands and pulled out the loaf of Wonder Bread from the Kwik Mart. He thought about Mallomars. And about what had happened to his mother three-quarters of his life ago. About his old man, terrified to the point of hysteria, screaming about the blood man, fastened to the bed frame so he wouldn't open up his painter's tool box and do any more portraits in the medium of dementia. Sobel, sounding a little too much like Vincent Price when he spoke of his father's terrors, the academic nod of his head somehow giving his old man's fears more weight than Jake wanted to allow. There was Madame and Little X, Nurse Macready, Hauser and his impromptu hurricane task force. His mother's Benz, already in the science lab in Quantico, having her honor compromised by the best of modern forensic investigative techniques – being forced to give up her cherry after a third of a century. He thought about the goddamned lighthouse over Nurse Macready's shoulder in the photo and about the isosceles puddle of black blood in the corner of her kitchen. About the beautiful people of Connecticut, laid out in candy by an autistic girl in a psychiatrist's office. He thought about the approaching hurricane and about Jeremy's creepy new friend, the man in the floor, who he wouldn't discuss. There were the five thousand or so canvases – an obsessive-compulsive's jackpot – stacked up in the studio. He thought about his wife's cello and about Jeremy's Hot Wheels.

And he knew that he wanted to get away from here. To go as far and as fast as he could and not look back, not come back, not ever think about the stinking place for as long as he lived.

But he had a son to feed and he concentrated on that, the simple act of mixing a little tuna with mayo and adding a smidge of salt and pepper. He would have liked to add onions and some celery but like his old man had often said, you can only eat what you kill. So it was going to be boring tuna, a glass of milk, two Cokes, a quick nap, and it was off to the city in an ancient car with—

"Kay?" he said, simultaneously glopping a scoop of tuna salad onto a square of cancer bread. "We don't have room for your cello. It won't fit in the car and if we lash it to the roof rack, it'll get soaked."

"F-U-C-K the cello, Jake," she said. "I just want us to get out of here." She stood on the other side of the counter, the T-shirt clinging to her little frame. Beneath the white cotton the calligraphy of her skin moved as if it were a separate living creature. Jake knew how she felt about the instrument – it was the only material item she cared for – and if she was dismissing it so easily, he knew that she wanted to get out of here.

"It's supposed to be airtight, right? I'll duct-tape the seams – maybe that'll help. It's one for all—"

"And all for one!" Jeremy hollered from the living room.

"That's right, Moriarty. Lunchtime. Come wash your hands."

Half an hour later, Jeremy was down for a nap and Kay and Jake had packed up everything they were taking. They had a bit of downtime before they woke Jeremy for the trip home.

Kay had changed into a dry shirt with *Motorhead* spray-painted across the front. She wore no bra and her breasts were sliding around under the fabric with her movements. She looked at Jake and asked, "Would it be insensitive of me to ask for a round before we hit the road?" Then began peeling off her clothes.

Twenty minutes later they were knitted into a knot of limbs on the damp sheets. The pheromone smell of sex was thick and the air was electric with the rattle of rain on the window.

Kay had popped another blood vessel in her left eye and Jake knew she'd be wearing sunglasses to rehearsal for the next few days – it had become an accepted side effect of their sex life and with the people who knew them well, she passed it off as an ocular condition. She usually dealt with the occasional bruise or ligature mark on her neck with high collars or big necklaces. The fact was, the sex set off the endorphins in her brain like nothing else she had felt since her drug and booze days. She realized – they *both* realized – that with their determination to leave their mutual addictions behind, they had stumbled across a new one. One that didn't involve needles or pills or alcohol or chemicals; a natural high from the ancient blood-powered sex machine between their ears. Their sex life had simply become a replacement for their old addictions.

She was facedown, stretched out like Supergirl, her hands cuffed up through the oak spokes of the bed. "Thank you, baby, I needed that." Her handcuffs clinked and as Jake kissed the back of her head she pushed up and into him with her bum. "Now uncuff me so we can get the fuck out of here."

There was a crash somewhere off in the house.

"Daddy!" Jeremy's voice screeched in the bright shatter of panic.

Jake jumped off of Kay, grabbed his pistol from the nightstand, and pounded down the hallway.

He threw the door to Jeremy's room open.

Jeremy was gone.

There was a brief instant of complete and absolute silence in his head, as if the circuitry had just frozen in place. He stared down at Jeremy's empty bed, trying to will his son into it. There was a thick surge in the atmosphere as if the house had been zinged by a bolt of lightning and Jake felt the electric hammer of fear slam into his chest. There was an audible pop as the hot wallop of his resynchronization appliance overloaded his heart. Then silence covered him like a blanket of wet sand.

47

Hauser had garaged the Charger and was now using the department Bronco. With the weather setting in, the four-by-four offered a lot more in the way of practicality. The vehicle's traction was a welcome relief from the Hemi-driven muscle car that he recognized as one of the substitutes in the war on his fading youth – the others being his boat, his bird gun collection, and his wife's new plastic titties – all of which he liked to pull out and play with as often as possible.

Hauser's speed was down and he negotiated the road slowly, continually correcting for the loose traction he felt with every gust of wind that got under the truck. Night was hours off but Dylan had painted the sky with a tone of metal that was somewhere between gray and black. A long line of headlights stretched out behind him, the bright eyeballs of the evacuating populace, and for a tiny fraction of time he thought about not turning around. About not stopping. About no longer being here. But he took a deep breath and when he blew it out the thought was gone from his mind. Temptation – a cop's worst nightmare.

The ocean had begun its descent into madness and was throwing the Atlantic at the highway all along the drive. Water sloshed over his windshield and the wipers droned on. The outer rain bands of the hurricane had landed a few hours ago and for the next twenty-four hours, Hauser knew that he would be living in his rain gear except for the brief passing of the eye – a few hours of silence before the whole circus started up again.

Hauser saw the car up ahead hit the brakes for a second too long, fishtail, and barely regain a westbound azimuth. He shook his head and hoped the guy would make it west before paramedics were picking windshield glass out of his eye sockets with tweezers. Hauser was no stranger to what bad driving could do to the human body – professionally or personally. Like any resort-town law-enforcement officer, he had cleaned up his share of asphalt casualties. On a more personal level, he had lost his son to a drunken driver fifteen years back, halfway through the boy's tenth year. It wasn't one of those spectacular accidents that had everyone shaking their heads, wondering what the guy behind the wheel had been thinking – just a slight swerve onto the shoulder and the mirror on his Econoline had clipped Aaron (who had been riding his bike into town) on the back of the head. DOA. The driver, to the credit – and benefit – of all drunk drivers that Hauser would pull over from then on, had stopped, gotten out, and called it in.

He no longer carried around that squirming coal of misery he had lived with for so long. Somewhere around the six-year mark it had started to fade and the agony of loss had dulled to a heartburn lump that occasionally gave him a respite when he was doing something he enjoyed, or had to concentrate on. Miraculously, he and Stephanie had managed to use the twelve years they had already chalked up on the fuselage as some kind of a raft when the floodwaters of grief and finger-pointing could have done irreparable damage, and they had somehow stayed married. Concentrated on bringing up their daughter. Moved on.

Hauser missed his son every single day, and an estranged relationship like the one that Jake Cole and his old man shared was something he simply couldn't wrap his brain around. Families worked it out, they talked it out, even fought it out. But they stuck together. End of discussion.

The red eyes of the brake-happy driver ahead lit up and the car took a dangerous jog to the right, skimmed the shoulder, then regained the water-shrouded asphalt in a sloppy lurch. Hauser shifted his bulk on the seat and the wet slicker let out a fartlike squeal against the leather. He could light up the cherries, pull the idiot over, and give him a talking to, but what good would that do? If the guy didn't know how to drive, a three-minute course by an angry cop in a storm certainly wouldn't change things. And with the heavy gypsy-caravan exodus behind him, Hauser didn't want to risk getting hit by one of the other cars. The turnoff for Mann's Beach made his mind up for him. Hauser hit the index and the cherries and swung off the highway.

Hell was moving in, something straight out of the Old Testament if the guy at the NHC was even half right – and Hauser believed that he was. After all, those guys were wired up with more satellites and science and shit than you could imagine. He pulled up to the gate that locked the peninsula off from tourists – it was open.

Mann's Beach was one of the few places usually only frequented by locals – the gate generally kept tourists out (except the striped-bass fishermen that swarmed in every spring and fall – those assholes would swim through lava for the shot at a big striper). Scopes had called and told him to get his ass out to

Mann's ASAP. He had asked him to bring Cole but Hauser had come alone – he wanted to see this with his own eyes, feel it with his own instincts, without Cole's letter-to-the-editor diction turning the whole thing into an academic exercise.

Besides, the next two days would be a marathon of one major emergency after another, the least of which would be car wrecks, drownings, collapsed houses, and downed power lines. Hauser was aware of these things – as the sheriff he had reserved a large part of his energy for battling whatever the storm was going to throw at him – but they took up a lot less real estate in his psyche than he would have previously believed possible. It was the guy with the knife that really had his attention.

Hauser lit up the overheads and the beach road in front of his car went white. He moved slowly in the rain, both glad and pissed off at himself for sending Scopes out here. The nose of the Bronco swung around a low mass of scrub and a luxury sedan lit up in the glare of the overheads. Scopes stood outside, staring at the vehicle.

Hauser got out of the still-running car and the thump of the wipers was lost in the wind. He pulled his four-cell Maglite from the center console and fired it up. Scopes didn't turn away from the car or acknowledge Hauser in any way. He stood stock-still with the rain clattering against his police poncho like a swarm of angry termites, his Maglite throwing a tight but now-dim oval of yellow on the bloody sand at his feet. The bulb flickered intermittently, as if the water was shorting it out.

Hauser moved past Scopes, and lit up the car in the beam of his flashlight. It was a Bentley, one of the newer GT Continentals, in a silver or tan – it was hard to discern in the yellow beam of the light. The interior was dark and there was no driver silhouetted behind the wheel. The windows were closed and as Hauser got closer to the vehicle, he saw his own reflection shining back at him, shimmering with the rain cascading over the glass. The beam lit up flashes of the interior. Some sort of rich red. But the windows were splattered with something, like a thin coating of dirt, and the effect reminded Hauser of a terrarium. A micro-ecosystem different from the world in which it sat.

The beam of the Maglite grew brighter when he pushed the lens against the wet glass. That was not dirt on the inside of the windows. It was blood. Black dried blood. Hauser pressed his face to the wet glass, shielded his brow with a gloved hand. He swung the beam over the interior and the terrarium comparison came back to him; a closed-in space where monsters lived.

When he turned back to Scopes, he saw that the man's expression had gone blank, and it reminded him of the way Jake Cole looked around the dead. *Disconnected* was the expression that came to mind. Only this wasn't Jake Cole, this was Danny Scopes, and Scopes was still supposed to give a shit. "You call anyone else?"

Scopes nodded. It was a slow nod that took a lot of effort. "Murphy's coming with the truck. I already photographed the sand here but the rain's washed all tracks and everything else away."

Hauser looked down into the red dirt. "Except the blood."

Scopes nodded again, this time more slowly. "Except that, yeah."

"You run the car?"

Scopes's line of sight swung back to the Bentley, rippling with the rain that bounced off its surface. "Yeah."

"And?"

"And I think Jake might be bad luck." He turned away, spit into the wet sand.

Hauser nodded and flicked his Maglite off. He looked down. Scopes's flashlight had died completely, but still hung loosely in his grip. "Someone he knew?"

Scopes nodded again. "The guy sold his father's art. Name's David Finch."

"We can't leave this here – it'll be washed away. Get as many photos of the inside as you can – open the lee side front door – then get Murphy to take it to the garage. Use the one that's up Jarvis. Make sure he covers it up. When you're done, come to Cole's. And bring the photos."

Scopes nodded solemnly. "Photos. Sure. Great." He reached into his pocket for the camera. "Who would do something like this, Mike?"

Hauser looked out at the angry ocean pounding the beach, then back to the car still lit up red in the spearing eye of his flashlight. He switched it off and all the red went black. "Just some guy," he said.

And with that he realized that he was getting used to it.

48

Jake was—

    —unconscious—

Then he—

    —wasn't—

There was no fighting back through the turgid layers of in-betweenism associated with sleep and awake. He had been out. Now he was back.

He stood up, naked and sweating, the pistol still knotted into his fingers. There was one single second of gratitude for being awake before the fear came back like ten tons of truck that nearly knocked him out of his skin.

"Moriarty?"

How long had he been out? He glanced at the window and took a mental snapshot of the sky, now dark and flat. Rain washed over the window, and the gray clouds shimmered.

"Moriarty?"

He raced out, down the steps. He flipped lights on. Tore through the living room.

"Moriarty!"

Where is he?

"Moriarty!"

And that ugly old whisper started up.

Skinned, it said.

Jake ran through the house naked, knocking over chairs, lamps, screaming his son's name.

Where was he?

He stopped at the front door, beside the Nakashima console. Where was his son? What had happened to Jeremy?

Then he remembered Kay handcuffed to the bed upstairs.

He covered the steps three at a time and ran down the hall.

The door was half closed and he slammed it into the pocket where it clattered off its track. He flipped on the light and the crisp white sheets on the bed fired to life.

The handcuffs hung from the headboard, dead still and empty.

49

Jake stood at the foot of the bed with a knot of snakes writhing in his head, the sound of their scales scraping against his skull overpowering the voice of the storm outside. The pistol hung from his hand and he stared at the empty bed, the black stabs of ink that covered most of his body gleaming with the sweat of panic that had replaced the earlier sweat of sex.

Not them.

Anything but them.

Please.

He ran down the steps, jumping almost all of them.

"Kay!" he roared.

Sand and rain clattered against the window and the sheet of plywood. Outside, something was banging against the side of the house. Jake raced down the hallway to the front door.

He ripped it open, slamming it into the wall. The handle punched through the sheetrock and a white cloud of dust puffed out and showered to the floor.

Out on the driveway. "Kay!"

He ran to the road, snapped his eyes up and down the empty highway. Rain came down in waves, shimmering on the asphalt like live insects.

The cruiser was still parked on the shoulder. Jake stepped toward it, saw a figure in the front seat, head back, mouth open. It wasn't Scopes – it wasn't anyone Jake recognized. He yanked the door open and pulled the man out into the wind and the rain.

"Where the fuck is my wife? My son?"

The cop looked confused. "I … I … don't—" His eyes dropped to Jake's naked body and his expression flattened out like he understood what was going on. "Have you been—?"

"I'm not drunk or stoned, you fucking moron!" He shook the man. "My wife and son are gone."

The cop tried to wriggle free. "I didn't see—"

"You were out here sleeping." Jake pushed him away and stared at him for a few seconds. "Do you know what's happened?"

The cop stared back for a few seconds. "I'm sure—"

Jake lashed out with the pistol and the butt of the revolver caught the cop across the bridge of the nose. There was a crack loud enough to be heard above the wind and rain and the man's legs gave out with a grunt and he crashed to the ground in front of his car.

Jake ran around the house, through the garden, to the building at the edge of the property.

He burst in and snapped the lighting to life, illuminating the army of faceless men that climbed out of the walls. He tore through the studio, the garage, even the small cabinets where he knew Jeremy could hide.

Nothing.

Empty.

Gone.

Where?

Skinned, the voice hissed sweetly.

Not my family. *Anything but my family.*

Please.

PLEASE!

Then where are they? the ancient voice in his head asked.

He ran out onto the grass, jumped down the drop-off to the beach. Waves rolled up past the surf line of a few hours ago, sloshing his legs with foam and stinging sand and bits of weed. He snapped his head around like a dog searching a scent. First up the beach, then down.

The beach was alive with the ocean and the black tangled masses of seaweed thrown up looked like bodies washed up at the water's edge. Small ones, Jeremy. Slightly bigger ones, Kay. Some moved in the wind. Others were pushed by the waves. He ran to one, ripped at it with his hands. Cold, wet, lifeless. Then another. Hopeful. More nothing.

They were gone, he could feel it.

Knowing. Was. The. Worst. Part.

Where?

Skinned, the ugly little voice crooned again, letting the Ns roll out, and Jake screamed at it to *shut the fuck up!*

No. No. No no no no no.

Jake stood in the surf, rain and sand and spray stinging his skin. He stared up at the house, windows lit up like an angry drunk. Big planes of white amid the dark modern architecture.

Something inside moved.

Movement.

Movement meant life.

Jeremy?

Kay?

But even through the rain, Jake could see that it was a man. Someone else. Him.

Him who?

HIM.

Jake raced up the steps to the house, across the deck. He tore the patio door open and jumped inside. The door clacked against the frame, stuttering with the buffeting force of the wind. A man stood in the middle of the living room. He started to turn.

Jake raised the pistol. Cocked the hammer. Went running forward, blood and horror and rage in his mind.

The man turned to face him.

Jake lowered the pistol.

And stared into his father's eyes.

50

Hauser came down the stairs with his mouth sealed in a tight line. He hit the overlapped Persian carpets and turned to Jake, shook his head. Another cop – the one Jake had punched out at the road – hung back in the kitchen, with a broken nose that was quickly turning from pink to purple. Soon it would crawl under his eyes in bruised black scythes. Blood was caked over his lip in a gruesome Chaplin mustache. It turned out that his name was Whittaker. He'd probably press charges but Jake was past caring.

Jake leaned against the piano, his arms folded over his chest, wearing nothing but a pair of Levi's, the barrel of the big stainless revolver sticking out of the coils of his arm like the head of a steel snake. Another man stood on the deck, on the other side of the swimming pool, framed by the black ocean beyond the beach. He had a rain jacket on and his back to the wind and every time he pulled in a lungful of smoke the glow of the ash lit up his face in a creepy, orange light. He made no movements and if it weren't for the intermittent jack-o'-lantern glow of his cigarette, no one would have noticed him there.

Hauser walked slowly to Jake and reached out to touch him. For the first time he saw the extent of Jake's ink, the endless black text that enshrouded his body, from neck to ankles, emphasizing the contours of his musculature. He put a hand on Jake's shoulder and felt the cold clammy skin twitch at his touch.

Hauser spoke loudly – not out of anger but out of necessity; the storm had grown vocal cords a little while ago and the constant humming of the wind brought the new element of white noise to the world. "We can't find a thing, Jake. There's no sign of struggle. No forced entry. No footprints or tire prints or any physical evidence. It's like they just—"

"Evaporated," Jake finished, his eyes now black marbles that didn't seem to move at all.

Jake had torn through the house three times while Frank – his father's twin brother – called Hauser. Jake had ripped all the closet doors open, taking three off their hinges; overturned the beds; dug through piles of clothing; emptied cupboards. He had flipped the sofa and torn down the shower curtain in the bathroom, scattering the teardrop-shaped rings. He had only put pants on when his uncle had forced a pair of jeans into his hands.

Jake had gone somewhere deep into himself, someplace far away. It was an evil little place filed with rage and violence that he had locked years ago. But the door had been kicked open and the ugly things that had lived in the dark for so long had begun to scamper out. He didn't know if he would be able to control them. "I am going to find him, Mike." Jake's eyes were locked on the breakers beyond the deck but Hauser could see that his mind was someplace else. "I am going to find him and I am going to take him apart."

The front door opened and someone came in.

He felt Jake's skin twitch again. "Jake," he began, then stopped, remembering how he had felt when Aaron had died. His hand stayed on Jake's shoulder, a man trying to calm a spooked horse through energy transmission – a horse with a coat of smooth, cold porcelain.

"We were leaving in a few minutes – a few hundred seconds," Jake said with that weird tone that Hauser had heard in front of Nurse Macready's house.

Out of the corner of his vision, Hauser saw Spencer come in, pause at the edge of the patchwork of Persian rugs, and shake his head – no sign of Kay or Jeremy in the studio, either. Like Hauser, he had a Maglite in one hand and his sidearm in the other.

"I put Jake's Charger in the garage. Just in case."

On the porch, Frank finished up his cigarette and came inside. When he walked in, Hauser was amazed at the likeness to Jake's father – a man he had never met but who held enough points in the local celebrity bank to be recognizable. Frank was still famous from the yacht club all those years ago – Frank Coleridge with his young intelligent women. Frank was a digital copy of his brother, right down to the mean look in his eyes. When he shook off his coat and hung it on a chair Hauser saw that he wore battered chinos, engineer boots, and a flannel shirt with a Remington patch over the breast. Even naked, Hauser would have recognized that Frank Coleridge was an outdoorsman; the sheriff heard a silent language in his movements that spoke louder than the patch on his shirt – everything about him, from the calm gaze to the sure movements of his hands, said that Frank Coleridge was a man who spent time hunting.

When they arrived, Hauser saw Frank's Hummer parked in the driveway, listing on the slope of the gravel like a sleeping rhinoceros. It was monstrous and no doubt army surplus – Hauser had seen enough of the spoiled city folks drive into town seated behind the wheel of one of the beasts to know a utilitarian one when he saw one; besides, while checking the premises for Kay and Jeremy he had shone his Maglite inside and recognized the sparse metal interior as a working truck that you cleaned out with a hose, not an expensive shampoo job. It had Tennessee plates and the sheriff wondered how many white-tailed deer had been strapped to the hood of the beast, tongue out, throat cut, gutted, a single round from a medium-bore hunting rifle – a .223 or a .277 most likely – mushroomed into the discarded heart.

Frank tapped another cigarette out of his pack and screwed it into Jake's mouth – Jake took it mechanically, eyes still locked on the breakers slamming the beach – and flamed it to life for him with an old USMC Zippo. There was the unsaid love of family in the action and Hauser was glad that Frank was here.

"Jake, I need photographs of your wife and son." He dropped his eyes to his feet, then said, "We'll get them on the missing persons registry. With the storm coming, and the traffic heading down 27, we can't put up a roadblock. It would slow things down too much." Meaning: *It could cost more lives.*

Jake stood up, uncoiling to his full height, and Hauser expected him to say that he didn't care, that he wanted his wife and son found.

All he did was shrug. Then he went to his wallet and pulled out a photograph. Kay and Jeremy smiling up, Alice and the Mad Hatter behind them, taken in Central Park back before time had stopped.

For the first time since he had known Jake Cole, Hauser realized that he was afraid of him. Initially it had been the clothes and the tattoos and that creepy way he shrugged everything off, as if horror was an inevitable part of life. But now, watching him face the disappearance of his family with the same grim lack of hope he attached to everything else, he saw that Jake was one of those men who went through life with nothing to lose because it had all been taken from them long ago.

Hauser had read the reports on his mother's murder, and knew that the impact from an event like that was immeasurable. It surpassed Freud and went straight into Hitchcock country. Besides being afraid of him, Hauser had come to respect and like Jake, and that was odd because Hauser consciously kept a professional distance from the people he worked with – it helped to keep his judgment clear. But behind this atypical fondness was a silent specter of fear, bunched up like an ink-covered creature with cold, dead pupils and a flat voice.

Jake's eyes had melted into furious black tunnels that bore straight back into his skull. He raised an arm, pointed at the officer with the broken nose and embarrassed posture. "That fucker was asleep on the job." He turned his head from Hauser to the cop who now looked a little frightened. "I find out that you could have stopped this, and you are going to have to hide on the bottom of the ocean. That's not a threat, it's just the way things are." Jake spat on the floor. "Now get the fuck out of my sight."

Hauser held up his hand. "Jake, you're angry. You're upset. You're not thinking clearly. I need you to be calm."

Jake's head swiveled around and he laid his eyes into Hauser. "Do I sound calm?"

Hauser realized that he did. He turned back to Whittaker and nodded at the door. "See one of the EMT people at the station about your nose."

The cop opened his mouth to say something but Jake nailed him with another angry look. He closed his mouth and slipped outside.

Jake put his revolver down on the piano. "This all has something to do with my father."

Spencer looked at Hauser, his eyebrows going up in a quick question mark. Hauser shifted his gaze so Jake wouldn't catch on to their silent dialogue. It was a subtle, furtive movement but one that Jake's radar instantly picked up.

"What?" Jake asked.

Spencer looked at his feet.

Hauser looked at Jake. "You know a man named David Finch?"

"My father sells through his gallery. He came by yesterday. Piece of shit."

"You don't like many people, do you?"

Jake shrugged. "What does that have to do with David?"

Hauser sat down on the piano stool. "We found him out on Mann's Beach."

"Found?"

"In his car. Same as the Macready woman."

Jake's eyes narrowed. "When were you going to tell me this?"

Hauser waved his arm through the air. "Like I said, you have your hands full. The car couldn't stay where it was with the hurricane coming in so I had it moved to a garage. We photographed the interior as best we could—"

"You get Conway to do it?" Jake asked.

"No. Scopes did it with his camera."

"Scopes?" Jake shook his head. "That car needed to be filmed in place. A trip on a flatbed will rattle it like a cocktail shaker."

"I couldn't leave it out on the beach," Hauser said defensively.

"No, but you could have recorded the crime accurately. Is Scopes some kind of hotshot photographer that I don't know about?"

Hauser stayed silent.

"When was David killed?" Jake asked.

"I don't know. Dr. Reagan is with the body right now."

"Did you take a temperature reading on site?"

Spencer asked, "A temperature reading?"

Jake shook his head like he was monitoring a village idiots' convention. "A body loses heat at a calculable rate. By measuring the temperature, you can fix a TOD."

Spencer's face went a little white. "How do you take a temperature?"

Jake rolled his eyes. "What is this – kindergarten? You use a rectal thermometer. Of course, without an epidural layer the rate of cooling would be different, but you need that reading. If nothing else, you need a timeline for this guy." Jake looked at Hauser. "Who found him?"

"Scopes," Hauser said.

Jake and Spencer used to hang out at Mann's Beach after work sometimes. It was a great place to take girls because no one ever went out there. It was fenced off on a little isthmus of rock that might as well have been the dark side of the moon. "What was Scopes doing out at Mann's Beach?"

Hauser eyed Jake. "With this coming down," he said, indicating the storm outside with a jab of his thumb, "I had all the beaches checked. I didn't want any of those storm-chaser dimwits to get killed while camping out in a pup tent and shooting the storm with a Sony Handicam."

Finch's death had no effect on Jake; he was too busy trying to connect dots. "And now Finch. Why is this guy so pissed at my father?"

Frank cocked his head to one side, and if Jake would have been paying more attention he would have seen one of his father's movements reflected in the genes. "Why do you think this has something to do with your dad, Jakey?" he asked, his voice a near-yell like Hauser's.

Jake let the shrug roll off his shoulders again. "I've been look-ing for this guy for thirty-three years, Frank. I didn't know it, but I was. He killed my mother. He killed a woman and her child up the beach. He killed my father's nurse. He killed David. And now …" He let the sentence fade out.

Jake swiveled his head and locked the black rivets that used to be his eyes on Hauser. "I'd like to say that Madame and Little X were practice. I'd like to believe that. But I can't. It's not the way this one would work." Even talking loud, his voice had that long-distance sound to it again. "My father had something to do with Madame and Little X. This is all about him somehow." Behind the shock smoldering away in the greasy loops of his guts, Jake felt something else squirming around. He thought about Sobel and the blood man and about Jeremy and the man in the floor.

Hauser nodded fatalistically. "We have someone at the hos-pital." With the storm coming in, it was an expensive sacrifice in resources. "We'll take care of your old man. Don't worry."

Jake looked up. "Do I look worried about him?"

"I need to know what's going on inside your head right now. What are you seeing or not seeing that might help me with all of this? Where are the soft spots? The weaknesses?"

"Weaknesses, Mike?" He handed the photo of his wife and child to Hauser. "There are the weaknesses."

Hauser took the photo, stared down at Kay, Jeremy grinning goofily along with Alice and her demented friends in the back-ground. "What are you going to do?"

Jake took a T-shirt off the piano and slipped it on, then he snapped the pressure holster onto his belt. The big-bore handgun with the black combat grip was nearly invisible against the black fabric, the stainless frame winking intermittently. He put his bare feet into his boots, and he pointed at Spencer. "I need him for three hours. Pull the guy off my dad at the hospital if you need manpower."

"What do you need him for?"

Jake thought of Sobel and the blood man again. "I think my father knows who is doing this. I think he's too scared to say it in words but not with paint. He spent years filling that studio out there with about 5,000 weird little canvases. It's a puzzle. And it means something. I think it's a portrait of who is doing this. The Bloodman. I need to photograph those paintings and I need to have them analyzed by pattern-recognition software. If they fit together in a certain way, the computer will see it."

Hauser looked at Jake for a few seconds. "Then what?"

"Then I know who to kill."

51

Frank parked the massive Humvee at the edge of the lot where he'd be able to four-by-four it over the fence and onto the street if the area flooded. The sky was coming down in a steady stream and the parking lot was covered in dancing rain, a foot deep in some places. A Starbucks coffee cup skittered across the lot, followed by an armada of trash. Frank stepped out of the truck and a plastic Walmart bag floated by like a contestant in a corporate-sponsored jellyfish race. He headed into the hospital, moving steadily through the lot, the water sloshing up the sides of his boots.

Frank Coleridge didn't recognize the destroyed shadow of a man that used to be his brother, asleep under the yellow rectangle of fluorescent light that hung over the headboard like a grave marker. His face came through like the reflection in a distorted, fire-ravaged mirror. He and his brother had been born identical twins but a lifetime of individual road-wear had left each with different battle scars. Now, after the fire and accident, the resemblance was peripheral at best. Frank was astounded that two bodies constructed from the same molecular building blocks could have turned out so differently.

The destruction to his brother's earthly vessel had been extensive – his beard and eyebrows had been burned off and an eight-inch scar where a ragged sliver of plate glass had bisected his left brow and cheek gleamed with stitches and opaque antiseptic ointment. Jake told Frank about his hands, but seeing the bandaged batons at the ends of his wrists had hammered home that Jacob's painting days were – the one creepy blood portrait notwithstanding – over. And whatever physical problems he had been prepared for were negligible when compared to the decay of his mind.

The brilliant Jacob Coleridge was losing the core reactor in his head was the hardest thing for Frank to fathom. Jacob had been a fixture in his life since the day their cell had divided, before he had become a husband or a father or a painter, and the one continuous fiber that ran through all the stages of their lives had been Jacob's genius. Technically, Frank knew that cell for cell they possessed the same gray matter, but he had lived long enough to know that technicalities didn't count for shit in the practical world; a show on the Discovery Channel had NASA engineers mathematically prove that technically speaking, bumblebees couldn't fly. So in a genetic sleight of hand, Jacob had ended up with more than a fair share of that indefinable quality called talent. But Frank had never been jealous of his brother's gifts in anything except Mia.

Mia.

Her name was still a dull ache in his chest. He had never told Jacob. Or Mia. He had, in fact, believed that it had been his only secret from his brother. But one night a few years after she had been murdered, Jacob, in one of his highball-fueled diatribes, had spat it out, like some poisonous tumor rotting in his stomach, and Frank had been forced to confront his brother. He had lied, shaken his head, denied, denied, denied. But Jacob had been relentless and had lost his temper, smashing his knuckles into the table, then into the wall, then into Frank's face. That had been the end for them.

Frank looked down at his twin brother, strapped into the bed, medicated, small, asleep, and wondered why this opera was being carried out. "What do I tell them?" The only sound was the soft rasp of Jacob's breathing and the hum of the fluorescent bulb.

His voice sounded serious in here, solemn, and he reached out and touched his brother's foot through the blanket. For a brief second, he hoped that good wishes and the best of intentions could be transmitted through the waffled cloth. He squeezed Jacob's foot, warm and stiff under the yellow shroud, then withdrew his touch. Jacob's head moved on the pillow and he tried to lift one of his arms. The buckle clinked. And his eyes popped open, gleaming sickly in the yellow light that dropped down from the fixture hanging over the bed.

Jacob licked his lips and his eyes swung halfway across the room, from the window he had been facing, to his brother standing at the foot of the bed. Their eyes met and Frank realized that their lives had gone by, that most of the sand had dropped to the lower bout of the hourglass.

"Frank?" Jacob said tentatively, as if he didn't trust his own judgment.

"Yes, Jacob, it's me."

Jacob looked around the room like a drunk waking up in an alley, not sure how he got there. "Frank," he said again, and tried to move his arm. The belts and buckles holding him in tightened and he swiveled his head and glared at the straps. Then he looked at the spiderweb of nylon harnessing him in. "Frank, what the fuck is going on?"

Frank's face split into a broad grin because he knew his brother was lucid. "Hospital, pal."

"You here to spring me?" His eyes focused on the big clubs at the ends of his wrists. His face grew puzzled, then angry, like a character in a science fiction movie who wakes in a lab to find that his hands have been replaced with giant lobster claws. "And what the fu—" The sentence stopped short and he sucked in a long breath. "Oh, God. The fire. The window." He tried to move his leg, his other arm. "Frank, can you undo some of these buckles?"

"The last time you were free you chewed off your bandages and painted a picture on the wall in your own blood. If I unleash you, you gotta stay put."

Jacob's face went red, only under the yellow light it came through as a sickly pink. "Jesus fucking goddamned Christ, Frank. Unbuckle me or cut these fucking straps or get the fuck out of here."

Any other time, any other place, without having heard everything that Jake had laid out back at the house, he would have taken the old Ka-Bar out of its sheath and cut his brother free. But with everything he knew, everything he had been warned about, it took him a few seconds to make up his mind. "Fine. But keep it together."

"Or?"

"Or the nurse is going to come back in here and shoot enough tranquilizers into your ass that they'll be able to remove your brain with a vacuum cleaner and you won't even notice. We clear?"

Jacob glared with the two pieces of flint he was using for eyes.

Frank undid the restraints at his brother's feet and wrists, leaving the loop that shackled his waist fastened so that he wouldn't be able to get out of the bed; the pineapple-sized knobs at the ends of his arms made undoing any buckles impossible.

Jacob stretched, brought one of his former hands up to his face, and rubbed his eyebrow and cheek like a bear scratching against a tree. The stitches sticking out of the antibiotic ointment made a soft rasping sound against the fabric. "How bad are my hands?" His voice was clear, but there was a slight slur to it, no doubt from the painkillers going into him one dull drop at a time.

"You want me to get the doctor?"

Jacob let out a long irritated sigh. "If I wanted you to get me a doctor, I'd have asked you to. What I want is for you to tell me how my fucking hands are."

"Not good, Jacob. You burned most of the flesh away and the musculature and mechanics are gone. You'll need prosthetics but chances are you won't get them because you're barely lucid and you've been violent."

Jacob's eyes drilled into Frank and his jaw clenched up, the cables under the skin tightening like a fist. "You're certainly cheery."

Frank thought about the bloody portrait and the screaming and panic and fear. "The doctor's think that it's Alzheimer's," he said flatly.

For a second there was flicker of black electricity in the dark behind Jacob's eyes. "Yeah? Well, even the eggheads with the diplomas get it wrong, Little Brother." The current hit the corners of his mouth and they twitched a few times, then went dead.

"Jacob, look, I don't know how long you're going to be –" he paused, searched his head for the right word, and settled on – "yourself. And we've got some problems. I need some answers."

His eyes narrowed. "We? We, who?"

Frank knew the story of the two Jacobs from the beginning. He had been a spectator in the great Coleridge saga until he had packed up and left Montauk. He had gone missing, not letting anyone know where he was, and hadn't heard from a soul until years later when his nephew had called and said he needed help kicking drugs. He was still having trouble equating the child he had known with the hard, armored man he had seen tonight. "Jakey's back."

Jacob's face played around with various expressions of sadness before the life fell out of it. "He should have stayed away."

"You're his father. He couldn't just leave you to the vultures."

Jacob's lips tightened up. "I don't want him here. Make him leave. Make him go away. He can't stay, Frank. He can't stay in Montauk." There was a tremor in his voice, a little flutter that was so subtle that it might have been imagined.

"Why not, Jacob?"

"Because it'll come looking for him."

Frank took a step toward his brother, put his hand on his leg. "Are you talking about the storm?"

Jacob's voice came out a high-pitched screech, as if someone had taken a fishhook to his eardrums. "No, you idiot. I'm talking about *him*. If Jakey's back, *he'll* know."

Frank tightened his grip on Jacob's foot, trying to soothe him. "It's okay, I'm here. I'll look after Jakey."

Jacob laughed – actually snorted with derision – and turned his face away. "You're already dead. You're just too stupid to know it."

52

In a little over two hours they had captured nearly 1,800 more canvases. Jake held up a painting, Spencer snapped a photo, and Jake pitched it aside. The studio was piled up with a mountain of canvases that looked like preparations for an insurance fire. The building was not as solid as the house and the walls buffeted with the wind. Every now and then some part of the flashing or roof would be torn away in an angry bark.

Spencer stepped back from the camera. "I need two minutes to take a piss and have a drink." He had to yell to be heard over the wind.

Jake looked at Spencer's sweat-soaked shirt and tired expression. "We're out of Coke in here. Let's go to the house. I need a smoke."

They left the camera and ran for the house, hammered by the gauntlet of rain and wind tearing in from the ocean. They jumped in through the door to the deck.

Any other time, there would have been swearing. As things stood, Jake went to the fridge and Spencer stretched his shoulders.

The world was a deep gray that pulsed with white stabs of lightning, and the ocean was slobbering in on great rolling swells that were close to being the worst Jake had ever seen. He stopped on the way to the kitchen for a second and tried to see the dim outline of the beach through the rain. The pool shuddered and thrashed with the storm and the lily pads had bunched up against the wall closest to the house, many of them sloshed over the side and thrown up against the window. And this was just the beginning.

"Jake, can I ask you something?" Spencer leaned against the piano, below the Marilyn. Off to his left, blocking the big slate fireplace that stretched up into the rafters like a fossilized tree, was the Oedipal Chuck Close, eyes slashed. Spencer looked at the painting for a second, blinked like an owl, and tried to focus on the damaged canvas.

Jake opened the fridge and pulled out two glass bottles of Coke. The lending library was gone; all that was left was the cold pizza from last night's dinner, half a loaf of Wonder Bread, and an untouched bowl of tuna salad.

Spencer turned away from the painting. "What happened to you out there?"

Jake popped the caps with a stag-handled bottle opener and held one out to Spencer. "Out where?"

"Wherever you were."

Jake took a long swallow off the bottle, and for some reason, it tasted good and he was surprised.

"We hung out at the yacht club, smoking weed and chasing city girls on the weekend." Spencer's voice changed as he went back in time. "I mean, it all seemed okay to me. One day you're my best friend, the next you're gone. There were rumors in town that your dad murdered you and buried you out in that fucking garage, man. Thirty years later you come back some kind of paranormal expert on the John Wayne Gacys of the world looking like Rob Zombie's stylist."

Jake paused in the middle of a second swallow and pulled the bottle away from his lips. He felt a headache coming on and thought about a few Tylenol. "I was going for the Tom Ford look." And then it hit him. Again. Riding in on an image of his wife and son came a jolt in his chest that signaled piston failure. He put his hands on the counter's edge, wrists turned out, fingers clamped around the worn formica that at any other time he would have noted as cold. Now it vibrated with a low-frequency hum that rattled his teeth and throbbed through his bones. Buried in all of this was the sound of Kay's voice, laughing. And just below that, Jeremy was making dinosaur roars. There was radio interference and then his antenna lost the signal and their voices stuttered into squelch. Then hissing. And finally silence.

He looked up to see Spencer staring at him with a good dose of *What-the-fuck?* in his eyes. "Jake, what?"

Jake shook his head with a finality that said he wasn't going to talk about it; if he did, he'd come apart. He couldn't even think of her, and up until now he had done a pretty good job of it. Sort of. The trick was not to reach out to her in any way. And that was the hardest part.

Jake turned back to the conversation. "Where were we? Oh, yeah. The big *Why?* If I could do it over, I would make different decisions, but leaving's not one of them." He rummaged around the kitchen and found the Tylenol in one of the bags from the pharmacy that held essentials. He opened the childproof top, poured three of the pills into his hand, and chased them down with a mouthful of Coke. "Coming home?" He just let the question hang in the air. What else could be said?

The rain outside came straight in off the ocean and hammered the windows, rattling the plywood that filled in for the broken thermo pane. Water leaked through invisible gaps and was gathering on the floor in a slowly expanding puddle.

Jake finished his Coke and walked down into the living room. He looked around for something to sop up the water – or at least put down on the floor to stop it from spreading. He kicked some of the bundled newspapers into the puddle, newsprint sandbags to hold back the flood. They quickly turned gray. On the way back to the kitchen he stopped in the middle of the spot he had just cleared of litter, and froze.

Spencer saw the switches flip in his head. "What?"

Jake stood still, his eyes locked on the floor, taking mental snapshots of the pattern he saw in the mess. "Sonofabitch," he said, only the sound was lost in the noise of the storm. He began clearing the room.

He shoveled newspapers aside with his foot, swept chairs into corners, upended the coffee table and flung it aside. Jake grabbed the end of the steel-and-leather sofa, lifted it, and dragged it across the floor. The carpets didn't bunch up because they had been nailed, screwed, and stapled down by his old man. "Come on," he ordered Spencer.

Spencer, still stuck on confused, picked up the dragging end. "Where are we taking it?"

Jake nodded at the door and barked, "Outside," like it was obvious.

Jake swung his end of the sofa around, balanced it on his knee, gripped the knob and pulled the door open. He hadn't been prepared for the wind and it slammed the door in, nearly tearing it off its hinges. They squeezed the sofa through and Jake dropped his end onto the deck. Spencer lost his grip and the sofa banged down and fell over onto its back. They ran back into the house.

"Come on!" Jake threw a footstool into a bronze bust by Rodin, knocking it over. He dug like a dog, flinging things off the carpet. A vase exploded in sharp colored shards when it hit a bookcase. Paintings toppled.

Jake jammed the piano aside and it brayed like a wounded elephant. Within minutes they had cleared the center of the living room, exposing the dull, paint-splattered quilt-work of carpets.

Jake ran up the stairs and turned back to the living room to take it in. His eyes locked on the clear area excavated amid the garbage and furniture. He sat down.

Spencer stumbled up, turned around, and flopped down beside Jake. "Holy fuck," he said.

Up close it was just a jumble of color, of overlapped carpets and splatters of paint. But from the staircase, with the benefit of distance and perspective, an unmistakable image was visible in the center of the room, like an X-ray of a coffin. It was a portrait of the same eyeless face Jacob Coleridge had painted on the wall of his hospital room.

"What the fuck is that?" Spencer asked.

Jake thought about Jeremy jumping up and down in the middle of the living room when asked to describe his friend Bud. "The man in the floor."

53

Frank now understood what Jake had been talking about on the phone yesterday: Jacob *was* frightened. "What are you talking about?"

Jacob rubbed his face with one of the cocooned insect pincers that had been sewn on. The movement was unselfconscious, feral. "August 1969, Frank."

Frank pulled a chair over from the window and the plastic on the bottom of its feet sounded like fingernails against the linoleum. He sat down, just beyond Jacob's reach, and laced his fingers together behind his head. Not that his brother could do much damage with those soft clubs, but Frank was a cautious man, a quality that years of hunting big game had honed to a second-nature status in his library of life skills. "Jacob, whatever you are going to say, whatever has you scared, is not true. Okay? This is me you're talking to. Whatever you want me to deal with, I will. Okay? I don't know how much time you have – *we have* – and I don't want to piss it away on stupidity. I have things I want to say to you and—"

"Shut up!" The buckles hanging against the bed frame rattled loudly.

Frank recoiled, looked into the fierce black holes of his brother's eyes. Is this what Jake had been talking about? This background chatter of fear, some sort of subliminal message hidden in the signal of his voice? "Jacob, what are you talking about?"

Jacob was rocking side to side in his bed, something about it disturbing.

"You were there. You know what happened. Mia saw it first. And then she died. And then Jake … began sliding away. I lost him, too, Frank. I promised not to tell anyone. I promised and I kept my word. But I can't keep a secret like this forever. Not forever. No matter how hard I want to." His words spilled out like dirty motor oil, flecked with charred bits of his broken brain, and Frank wondered if Jacob had left the room.

"He's here, Frank." The black specks of Jacob's pupils no longer looked focused, or even human; the planes of his eyes had dropped away and he was looking at images inside his head.

"Who is?"

"Him!"

"Jacob, this has nothing to do with the boat. Be rational. How could it?"

Jacob's eyes came back on like someone had put new batteries into the compartment in the back of his head. "You never went aboard. You didn't see what happened." Old ghosts were coming out of the dark now, firing up the fear machine.

"Jacob, what are you talking about?"

The beams of his brother's eyes crawled across the room and stopped on his face.

Frank wanted to believe that it was Alzheimer's talking, not a rational human being, but his brother's voice was calm and even. "Jacob, listen to me. You have to stop talking this shit. Okay? We both know what you're talking about. We didn't do anything wrong – you didn't do anything wrong. There was nothing you could have done differently."

"We could have left him there."

Behind the burn marks and stitches and antibiotic ointment Jacob Coleridge looked scared.

Frank shook his head. "He was just a little kid, Jacob. If we would have left him there, he would have died."

"Better him than all of us."

54

It was easy to see that the main event was only a few hours off; the world outside looked like it had been scripted for a Hollywood disaster film. By the time Frank pulled into the driveway, Spencer's cruiser was gone. He ran from the big H1 to the house and the rain clattered against his hood like ball bearings. When he turned the knob the wind ripped the door away from him and slammed it open, sending a pile of mail flapping off into the house like frightened birds.

Jake was suiting up inside the entryway. Beside him, on the Nakashima console – a broad slab of undressed walnut – the weird spherical sculpture of welded steel shafts hummed with the electricity the storm carried, like a static tuning fork. On the floor a little to the left sat Kay's airline-tag-covered cello case.

"Jake, I gotta talk to you."

Jake nodded at the door. Or the world beyond. Or maybe at nothing at all – it was hard to tell. "I have to get to Hauser's. We can talk in the truck."

Frank pulled the big brass zipper on the Filson rain slicker up to his chin. "Let's roll, kiddo."

They ducked out into the storm.

The only sign that life existed anywhere other than the interior of the big metal beast that carried them west was the steady stream of man-made debris that blew over the empty highway and the intermittent flicker of lights in roadside homes. If Jake had been paying attention to these things he would have been surprised that anyone had stayed behind. As things stood, he couldn't muster up enough interest to notice. The smart ones had left. The rest stayed. That was as far as he got in the equation.

The wind and rain hammered in on a horizontal trajectory and Frank had to continually fight the massive vehicle to keep it on the road. The interior smelled of diesel fuel, shell casings, blood, and wet pencils. Jake unconsciously gripped the handle by the windshield, his mind turning the events of the past few days slowly over.

"This is important, Jake." Frank had to yell to be heard over the combined noise of the storm and the big diesel engine.

Jake came back to the present, to the world outside the car pulsing with the dark storm, and blinked like a man who was trying out a new pair of eyes for the first time. "What are you talking about?"

"You know I don't believe in astrology or God or any of the other stupid shit people lie to themselves about because it makes living in fear a little more bearable. Maybe I'm the wrong guy for this. Maybe you need someone who believes in that stuff."

A plastic patio table scrambled across the road like a spider. When it hit the gravel shoulder it upended and spun off into the dark. Frank reached under the instrument cluster and turned on the LED light bar bolted to the roof rack and the road lit up in underwater hues of blue.

A gust of wind slammed into the side of the Hummer and Frank wrenched the wheel to the left, fighting the vehicle away from the shoulder and the ditch beyond.

In the blue-green light of the basic instrument cluster, Frank's face drained of a little more color. "I'm an old man, Jake. I've seen the world go from astounding to shitty in the course of my insignificant life. And I've been part of some of it." Frank's face tightened up a little more and he pulled out his smokes – unfiltered Camels – and tapped one out for his nephew. After giving the cigarette to Jake, he took one himself, returned the pack to his pocket, and fired his up with his faithful Zippo. He pulled the tip of the cigarette through the flame, then passed it across the cabin. The flame left a white trail in Jake's vision and the heavy taste of lighter fluid made the cigarette taste foul and better at the same time. He took in a deep lungful of the tobacco and held it for a second.

Jake ignored the screaming rain outside, the squeak of the big wipers across the two flat front panes, the rattle of the big diesel, and the smell of gunpowder and cedar. He simply watched his uncle, hoping that images of Kay and Jeremy would leave him alone for a little while – long enough for him to figure all of this out.

Frank nodded at the computer sitting in Jake's lap. "I asked him about the paintings, Jake – about those puzzle pieces." Jake, the eternal student of behavior, recognized that background static of fear in Frank's voice. Or was that just the residual taste of the first call he had received from the hospital two nights and a handful of lifetimes ago?

Jake stopped thrumming the top of the laptop case.

"He said that you'd figure it out. That you'd know what to do." Frank sucked on the smoke and the tip went bright orange for a second. "He was letting go of old baggage, Jakey. I think those paintings are some sort of gift to you. Some sort of –" he paused and the click of the wipers filled a few seconds – "apology."

"I don't think Jacob Coleridge knows what an apology is."

Frank cleared his throat and two jets of smoke spewed out of his nostrils. It was the action of a man trying to build up his nerve. "Part of this story is true, Jakey – I know because I was there for it." He stopped again, like his clockworks had jammed. "Jesus, if there's something in here that will help find your wife and little boy, then I don't mind breaking a promise."

"Drop the melodrama."

"I swore I'd never tell you."

"Swore to who?" Jake almost yelled to be heard over the jet-engine sounds of the world. "My father's way past caring, Frank."

"I promised your mother, Jakey. I mean, *really* promised. Swore–on–my-life kind of promised. And I don't know how well you remember your mom—"

"Perfectly," Jake said, cutting him off.

"Then you'd know that she'd be pretty pissed with me if I told you. She didn't think you should know about this. No one did."

"Frank, this fucker has my wife. My son. If you know something that might help me find him, I better not find out after the fact." An image of Kay and Jeremy walking on the beach, Jeremy waving to the passers-by, blinded him for a second. "I'm not the forgiving type."

"I noticed." Frank sucked on the cigarette again and nodded, smoke hissing out from between his perfect white teeth. "What the hell, we all die sometime, right?"

And he began to break forty-two-year-old promises to the dead.

55

August, 1969

121 Nautical Miles Due East of the British
Virgin Islands

They were heading north, lazily making their way back to US
waters after a summer spent island hopping. The trip had lasted
a little over twelve weeks and the sybaritic retreat had done them
good. Jacob had immersed himself in his work, trying his hand at
watercolors and doing some good studies of lush island vegetation
and crystal waters; Mia had learned to scuba and fish and perfected
her skills with a barbecue; Frank had nursed yet another broken
heart back from the dead. They were all browned by the sun and
running on that late-August glow that comes from a summer well
spent.

This was the third vacation they had taken as a threesome but
twelve weeks penned up in a boat with his brother and wife was
making Jacob squirrely; at least, that's what he had thought at the
time. It wouldn't be until later, with the clarity of hindsight, that
he'd understand that wrong had indeed been waiting for them at
the edge of the horizon.

Mia was on the foredeck, stretched out in the sun, reading
a paperback. Jacob was at the wheel wearing nothing but a pair

of worn Bermudas, eyeing the compass and working his way through a bottle of Johnnie Walker – his make-do alternative to the Laphroaig he couldn't find anywhere in the islands except Bermuda. Frank was below deck in one of the staterooms, sleeping off another failed attempt to keep up with his older brother, the resident champion, the night before.

Jacob watched Mia stretched out, the bikini hiding very little of her body. He loved her skin, its smoothness, and he took great pleasure painting her whenever she felt like sitting still long enough for him to commit his impression of her to canvas. He took a swig of the bottle and ran his eyes over her form, taking in her proportions, her musculature. They had been together for a few years now, and he could see small signs of aging starting to creep in. She was younger than him – they had met in a New York tavern when her date had been late and Jacob's was back at the table. He had barreled up to the bar, demanded a bottle of scotch for his table, and insisted the beautiful woman to his left try a nip of Laphroaig before he carted it away. It had been an instant given that they were meant for one another. Within a week he was painting her. Within two she had moved in.

The weather was right and they were making good time. They had a southern wind pushing them home like an invisible hand and with the exception of a few small patches of sargasso weed that they had managed to steer around, there was nothing to slow their progress. Mia kept glancing starboard, following a pair of bottlenose dolphins that seemed to be finding pleasure in their company. She was adjusting the strap on her bikini when something to the east caught her eye. It wasn't much, little more than a glimmer of light, but it was enough to make her reach for the binoculars.

"Jacob." In the language of married people that single word was a whole sentence.

He lifted his eyes and followed her arm to the east. It was a little after one in the afternoon and the sun was at its peak overhead. Jacob squinted in the direction she was pointing, then took off his sunglasses. It was a small triangle of white in the ocean, two miles off, maybe more. He didn't know how Mia had seen it; it was the kind of thing that if you didn't know was there, you could easily miss.

"Give me the binoculars."

Mia came down into the cockpit, handed the binoculars to Jake, and climbed back up on the deck and around to the pushpit. She steadied herself on the backstay, raised her hand to her brow. "It's a boat," she said.

Jacob brought the binoculars up and swept his field of vision across the water to the east. Mia was right, it was a boat – a good-sized monohull – sticking out of the water at a bad angle. Jacob had nothing as a reference point but by looking at the pulpit, then following her line back and seeing the top third of the mainmast sticking out of the water a good distance back, he guessed that the boat was at least a forty-five-footer, maybe more, with three-quarters of her length under water.

"Get Frank," he said, loosened the main halyard, and spun the wheel. The boat leaned heavily to port and came around in a tight arc.

A minute later Frank came topside, bleary-eyed and wet from the cold water he had splashed in his face. "What is it?" he asked.

Jacob handed the binoculars over. "There's a boat in trouble out there. Dead ahead. Mile – mile and a half."

Frank climbed up on the cabin, put his foot up on the mast step, and peered through the field glasses. The craft was white and blue and had the sleek lines of one of the new Dutch fiberglass yachts. The bow stuck up at an odd angle, like a missile aimed at the horizon. Thirty feet back the mainmast stuck out of the water and from the angle Frank knew that the boat hung in the water at a good forty-five degrees. Debris floated around her but at this distance it was impossible to tell just what it was. The boat wasn't in trouble – it was sinking.

"Jesus," Frank said and lowered the glasses.

"Get the Thompson," Jacob said.

Anyone else would have argued but Frank and Jacob operated on that frequency that many siblings share, twins more than most. Besides, Frank knew that these waters were dangerous, which was why they had brought the machine gun in the first place.

"And a mask."

While Frank was below, Jacob kept his eyes locked on the white triangle of the sinking boat. Mia had moved to the bow and was standing in the pulpit, staring ahead. Jacob couldn't explain it, and would always wonder about it afterward, but as they approached he consciously wished that Mia had never spotted the faltering craft. Years later, when he had finally wrapped his brain around the incident, he would attach the word *Fate* to the sighting – sometimes upgrading it to *Destiny*. But at the time the only feeling he had was that it was a mistake and if they were lucky it would sink before they got there.

He reached under his seat and pulled out his service revolver, an old blued Colt 1911 wrapped in oilcloth and secured with twine fastened in a tight shoelace knot. He pulled one of the tag ends, dropped the frayed fabric to the deck, and slipped the pistol into his pocket.

It took them nine minutes to reach the boat. By the time they were one hundred yards out it looked like it had fallen from the sky – clothing, plastic bottles, a single life vest, and a library's worth of books floated around her in the debris field. A single shark – a twelve-foot tiger – swam through the litter, nosing larger chunks out of curiosity.

They watched the shark for a few seconds, swimming through the scattered flotsam, her triangular dorsal slicing the blue water. She bumped the life jacket, gave a piece of decking an exploratory bite, then sank out of sight.

"What happened?" Mia asked. She put Jacob's shirt on over her bikini and it covered her to mid-thigh.

"Something bad," Frank said softly.

"I'm going aboard," Jacob said. "You see any other boats on the horizon, fire a round into the air."

They pulled their boat – a sixty-two-foot Werf Gusto that Jacob had named *The Forger* – alongside the sinking monohull. Bubbles rose from below the waterline and there was a soft gurgling that seemed to come from everywhere. They lashed a line to a cleat on the other boat and Jacob went over the side. When he set foot on the sinking vessel, he turned back to Frank. "This thing starts going down, wait until the line is tight to cut it."

"What if you're still aboard?"

Jacob looked past Frank to Mia and smiled. "If I have to swim free, keep the Thompson ready and shoot that bastard shark if he comes back."

"Go through the front hatch," Mia said.

Jacob shook his head. "Can't. That's where the air is trapped. I open that and the ocean will rush in and this thing will head straight to the bottom. I want to see if there's anyone on board."

Mia gave him a look that said, *Be careful.*

Jacob stood on the steep angle of the deck, his foot against the cabin front for balance. He dipped the mask into the water, emptied it, then rubbed some spit around the glass to keep it from fogging up. He still had on the Bermudas and the bulge of the gun in his pocket made him look like his leg was bolted on with massive fasteners. With the trench knife on his belt, the mask on his head, standing on the prow of the derelict sailboat, he looked like a shipwreck survivor. He slid down the deck into the water.

The deck of the boat slid by as he moved down to the cabin hatch, using whatever was available as a handhold. He focused on where he was going but paid attention to details in his peripheral vision in case the shark came back. The entrance to the cabin was under the water and he'd have to climb at a forty-five-degree upward angle to get inside her. Jacob made a mental note of this so that he wouldn't get disoriented when he was inside and drown before he could find a pocket of air. He moved down, through a tangle of lines, and dipped under the lip of the cabin doorway.

The door had been ripped off the frame. More debris floated around the portal. He ducked inside.

Maps, clothing, and bits of wood floated in the zero gravity of the cabin. Jacob headed up into the prow of the boat, toward the air pocket that was keeping her afloat.

He clawed his way up the ladder, which felt awkward and wrong. At the top he found a small reserve of air and he took a few shallow breaths, then filled his lungs and moved farther into the belly of the boat.

From inside, the gurgling sound was louder, more intimate.

Papers, books, bottles, ropes, and clothing floated by, blocking his vision, disorienting him. He moved up, through the kitchen and past two staterooms – both were empty except for the debris that floated everywhere in the flooded craft. He reached the final stateroom and the door was closed. He pulled on it and it was locked.

Jacob put the blade of his old army knife to the crack and hit the pommel with the heel of his hand, driving the blade in between the jamb and the door. He wrenched the heavy blade to one side and the door opened with a loud crack that seemed to shake the whole boat. He swam through the door, up into the main stateroom, and his head broke through the surface, into the air bubble keeping the boat afloat.

A body lay in one of the bunks – bloody and dead. It had been a woman. Now, mouth stretched into a last scream, eyes rolled up, fingers clenched into bloody fists, she was a sculpture of horror. Her throat had been opened up in a violent seesaw slash that ran from one clavicle to the other. Jacob had spent twenty-one months in Korea and was no stranger to death but something about this reached inside of him and opened up a little piece of hell. He turned his head away.

Then saw the second body, this one a man.

He was up against the wall, hanging like a winter coat, held in place by a stainless-steel speargun bolt that fastened him in place. It was buried in his chest, and if it wasn't through his heart, it was damn close. Blood leaked out and down and the water swirling around him was black and dense. He hung there, head down, the light crowning his head casting a long shadow that almost covered his body. A bloody knife stuck out of the wall beside him. Probably the same knife that had sawed through the dead woman's throat.

"Jesus," Jacob whispered.

And that's when the little piece of hell that was inside him ruptured and a portal to somewhere else – somewhere evil and wrong – opened up and a little noise came scrambling out.

At first Jacob thought that the sinking boat was creaking, some part of its structure giving way, but he was only able to lie to himself for a second before he admitted that it was a human sound. Or an *almost* human sound. A moan. Soft and fueled by pain.

The man nailed to the wall lifted his head and the light filled his features with detail. His tongue came out, licked his lips. He coughed once and blood drooled out of his nose. He tried to speak but all that came was the sound of air escaping his body, as if it had somewhere else it had to be.

Jacob grabbed the bunk and pulled himself up, toward the man. His feet slipped and he splashed sideways. Fell. Grabbed a railing for balance. Fought his way forward.

The man's skin was an ethereal blue and the water around him was getting darker with the blood that he had lost.

No wonder that shark was hanging around.

He got to the man, reached up, touched his face. Eyes fluttered open. There was no white to them, only a deep scarlet with single black nails of fear in their centers. "*M ... m ... mio ...*"

Jacob recognized Italian from his year spent in Florence. "*Si?*" he said softly and in the cabin it sounded like a hiss.

The man coughed more blood and winced with pain. "*Mi ... mi ... mio figlio,*" he said softly, barely above a whisper. *My son.*

And Jacob went back through his Italian lexicon. "*Che cosa?*" *What?*

The man stiffened and his chest heaved once, violently, and he vomited out a rope of blood that spattered into the water. Then his head fell over.

Jacob knew that he was dead. What the hell had he been talking about? His son? What—?

And then he understood. But there was a great groan from somewhere far below the waterline and the boat shuddered and listed a few more degrees. The water in the stateroom boiled up, past Jacob's nipples, and the dead woman slid off her bunk with a red splash.

Jacob threw open hatches, pulled out drawers. Most of the stateroom was underwater so he didn't have many options. He hoped he was right – that he had understood the man. The water rose quickly and blood swirled around him, making it greasy. He searched frantically as water filled the compartment in a big gurgling thrust of pressure. He pulled open doors, drawers, and hatches.

The boat was going under. He had a few seconds, thirty at most, before the vessel slid below the waterline and began its descent to the trench, nearly 28,000 feet below.

There was a small box above the main bunk, a closet for pillows and bedding – there was a similar one on *The Forger* – and Jacob grabbed the handle and yanked it open. It came off in his grip and he flung it aside.

A small child was curled up inside. A boy, no more than three, splattered with blood. Jacob didn't think – didn't have time to formulate any thoughts at all – he grabbed the child by the arm and yanked him out of his hiding place.

The boat lurched sideways again and Jacob slipped, fell below the water. He splashed up. The child screamed. Slapped his face. Kicked and bit him. Fear coming out in the only way he knew how to express it.

From somewhere far away Jacob heard Frank yell at him to get out.

Water billowed into the stateroom. Jacob clambered up onto the bunk where the woman had been murdered, the child clamped to his chest like a football. He reached out and tried the hatch. It was locked. He tried the handle. Twisting it violently. It broke, came off in his hands.

And the sea filled up the last pocket of air and the boat slipped under the calm surface of the Caribbean.

There was nothing but black and the greasy feel of blood and the heartbeat of the child held to his chest. Jacob pulled out the Colt, pointed at the porthole, and squeezed off a round.

He kicked up through the jagged hole he had chopped with the slug, child in one arm, the pistol clamped in his free hand. He moved toward the blue sky over the ocean, toward the world above. The suction of the sinking vessel was all around him, an invisible force pulling debris – and him – down with it. He kicked hard, pushing for the surface. He moved a few feet. Then a few more, putting distance between himself and death.

Then something grabbed his foot, tightened, and began to pull him down into the black water along with the boat.

Jacob let go of the pistol, grabbed the knife from his belt, and slashed down in one desperate swing. He had no more oxygen in his lungs, no more fuel in the tank to take him any farther, and he was lucky that the blade arced through whatever had snarled his foot. A vibration thrummed up through his leg, then he was free, kicking for the surface. Up. Toward the light above.

He broke into the sunny Caribbean afternoon and sucked in a great lungful of air. He coughed and hacked and spit but managed to lift the child and swim for the boat. All around him the water churned and bubbled with air escaping the sinking boat.

Frank yelled.

Mia screamed.

He held the boy up, splashed clumsily for *The Forger*.

His wife screamed again, this time a high-pitched shriek that almost froze him in midstroke. It was a single horrific word.

Shark!

Jacob spun and his hand came up with the knife. He saw the fish, bearing down on him, the single dorsal rising out of the water as it came in to feed.

Jacob lowered the knife to get under the shark if it came in on the surface; if it came up from below, there wouldn't be much he could do. The fish homed in on him and the child he cradled to his chest like a football. He felt the boy in his arms and had no idea if he was conscious or even alive, but he wasn't going to let him go, not even if it meant going to the bottom of the planet in the belly of a fish. He held the boy protectively, head over his shoulder, and watched the shark coming.

It was ten feet away when the clatter of Frank's Thompson split the sky open and the water at the base of the fish's dorsal exploded. There was a flash of white belly followed by blood. A violent roll in the water. Then the shark banked to one side and disappeared in a widening pool of red.

Jacob paddled to the boat, keeping the child's head above water. He passed the boy up to Frank, then clambered aboard. While Mia and Frank tended to the little lone survivor, Jacob found the bottle of Johnnie Walker under the wheel. He dropped down into the cockpit, cracked the bottle, and took a long slug, his old army knife still clamped in his fist.

Mia had the boy on his side and pumped his ribs to drive the water from his lungs. He coughed, gagged, vomited up a stream of water, and began to cry. She lifted him up, wrapped him in a towel, and held him close.

Frank turned to his brother. "What happened in there, Jacob?"

Jacob took another swallow of the scotch. "Something bad." He turned back to where only a few minutes before the boat had hung suspended in the water. Debris floated in a wide patch, bobbing lazily on the gentle swell. "Something very bad."

56

A jagged crystal of lightning slammed into a telephone pole up ahead, shattering it like a mortar round. The beach was supposed to be one hundred yards to their left but the storm had crawled nearly to the highway and threw up great sweeping swells that smashed at the road. When the waves hit the embankment, a fifty-foot wall of water shot into the air, then crashed down and washed over the pavement in a four-foot drift. Jake couldn't understand how the road was still there. Or how Frank's truck made it through.

A wave slammed into the big diesel beast and it lurched sideways, braying like a dinosaur. Frank hammered down on the gas and the sudden traction pulled it forward; the Hummer was designed for harsh conditions but it wasn't a submarine. Frank's knuckles were white.

Jake was trying to absorb the story his uncle had just told him. He was trying to put it into some sort of context, some sort of focus. But he had too much rattling around under the dome to deal with this now.

"Jakey?" Frank yelled above the noise.

Jake moved a little, shifting in the seat. He pried his eyes away from the eerie reflection in the windshield. "Yeah."

Frank's teeth were clamped tightly around his cigarette and he kept his attention on the underwater world crawling under the hood of the Hummer. The tires threw thick reams of water up against the armored undercarriage and it sounded like Roman cavalry. "You okay?"

Jake's shoulders shifted with a shrug. After everything else, after his mother and Madame and Little X, Nurse Rachael Macready, David Finch, what did this really change? Of course he wasn't thinking about Kay and Jeremy – he couldn't or he'd just stop breathing – so he decided on, "Fucking fantastic."

57

August 1977
Sumter Point

Jacob had spent the morning in the studio, working with the torch. He wore his standard-issue uniform of jeans, a T-shirt, and paint-crusted canvas sneakers that had once been a shade of white. Patti Smith's *Horses* was spinning on an ancient Telefunken console stereo salvaged from the garbage up the highway – the same stereo and album Jake and Kay would listen to over thirty years later.

He had been up for two days now, but had taken a break at six a.m. and gone for an hour-long walk on the beach before a breakfast of some hard-boiled eggs and a piece of cheese dug up from the fridge. Now, four hours later, he was in a different day, a different place, and the piece was finished.

Somewhere around ten he cracked open the bottle of whiskey and poured himself two solid fingers worth into one of the many stained china teacups he bought at garage sales for his brushes. The great thing about them was their disposability. Of course, sometimes he confused the spirits in the cup and a painting ended up smelling like good scotch. More often, though, he found himself retching up half a swallow of turpentine.

There had been a lot of work, and to work he needed fuel. So he had fed the furnace with a good supply of booze. Of course he knew he was drinking too much, but wasn't that the point? What was the point of not having a boss if you couldn't do what you wanted to, when you wanted to?

At forty-six, Jacob Coleridge was at his professional apex. He had been making a living as a painter for almost two decades, had been a growing force in American art for his whole working life, and was well past the point where he never had to worry about where the next meal (or drink, hallelujah!) was coming from. And this should have given him some sense of peace. Maybe even a little sense of pride. But it hadn't. All it had really done was make him a little less at home in his skin, like he was wearing someone else's body, one that had been tailored with a smaller man in mind.

He thought about Mia and Jakey and raised his china cup. "All for one, and one for all," he said aloud. And why not? He had toasted to lesser causes – acquaintances just met in bars being the most common – so he hoisted one to the musketeers. Swallowed. Filled it again. Grabbed another from atop the fridge and spun the cap off. Took a slug. Went outside.

Back in the studio, sitting in the center of his framing table, sat his single experiment in three-dimensional art – a model of a sphere, perfectly assembled from chunks cut from stainless-steel speargun darts. It was a polyhedron, perfectly executed in nearly 2,200 precision cuts from the chop saw and twice as many hits from the torch. It was precise, complicated, and signed on one of the transepts, *Jacob G. Coleridge.*

58

The sheriff's office was the kind of place where the ragtag survivors in a zombie film would make their last stand. The building was an Edwardian no-nonsense brick-and-limestone box with wedge-shaped keystones over the windows and an arched double front door. One side of the structure housed the holding cells and county jail, the other a joint office shared by the administration and the Southampton Sheriff's Department proper. The parking lot was empty and the building looked like it might be deserted. A few lights were on inside but the parking lot was conspicuously bare except for two departmental four-by-fours and a heavy EMT cube-van; the news trucks of yesterday were no doubt out filming the damage being wrought by the Long Island Express Redux.

Frank parked on the grass, applying the logic that an extra six inches of high ground could make the difference between life and death if a storm surge rolled in. Of course, the higher profile made it an easy target for the vengeful temper of the hurricane. They stepped out into the howling wind and staccato clatter of rain and ran across the road and up the steps to the entrance.

The lifeless impression of outside was erased as soon as they were through the doors; the station hummed like a beehive, uniformed policemen running back and forth, absorbed in their tasks. Phones rang, radios squawked, coffee brewed. In one corner, an ancient Zenith was tuned to the Weather Network, the sound turned off – a young reporter in a blue rubber raincoat with the network's logo on the left breast reported from a second-story motel balcony somewhere along the coast. The picture was heavily pixilated – the digital-age version of static. Behind him, huge swells were pounding the beach and his expression transmitted the realization that he was here because he was expendable; the true talent was back in New York, where they would lament his loss on camera if he were unfortunately washed out to sea.

Jake grabbed Scopes as he ran by. "Hauser?" he said, knowing that need-to-know was the order of business.

Scopes jerked a thumb at an open doorway halfway down the hall. "If he's not in there, try the radio room, two doors past."

They found Hauser behind his desk, barking into the phone. "Jesus Christ, Larry, listen to your son. You can grow more tomato plants next year. Get in the car and head inland—" He saw Jake and stopped. "I gotta go, Larry. Forget the plants, they're not worth your fucking life." He slammed the phone down and stood up. He wore rain bibs but his Stetson, encased in a plastic protector, hung on the back of his chair. His rain poncho was spread out on Bernie's antlers, dripping onto the floor.

"Jake, Frank," he said. "Get the paintings photographed?"

Jake held up the laptop. "I need your satellite connection. 337 gigs of data. Where's your comm. room?"

"Beside the—" There was a terrific crack and the world outside went white for an instant. The lights fluttered, and for a brief instant Jake's chest tightened up with the electrical pulse of the building. Then the lights died and there was a communal groan from the hive. A half second later the generator kicked in and the offices lit up in bright halogen emergency lighting. "—radio room. Follow me."

Jake felt the tingle of electricity in his system. His put his fingers to his chest, and his heart was banging against his ribs as if it wanted to get out.

"You okay, Jake?" the sheriff asked.

Jake nodded, took a deep breath, and followed Hauser.

"Our communication is down," Officer Nick Crawley said cheerily, as if he were enjoying the adventure.

"Down? What do you mean down? I need a satellite link, not a telegraph cable. How can they be down?"

Hauser held a cup of coffee out to Jake and one to Frank.

Jake took the cup absentmindedly, absorbing the warmth through the pads of his fingers. Frank took a noisy slurp off the top of his.

Hauser explained. "The atmosphere is filled with the hurricane. There's no line of sight to the sky. We might get a few seconds here and there but until the rain band has passed over it's like trying to use a radio from a submarine on the bottom of the ocean – water offers a lot of resistance. And there's a lot of electricity out there. We still have phone lines but our Internet connection is satellite-based."

"Why is it satellite-based?"

Hauser glanced sideways. "In case of an emergency, we don't have to depend on phone service."

Jake threw his cup of coffee at the trash basket. It hit the lip and sprayed over the floor. He turned and headed for the door. There was another mortar blast of thunder and the emergency lights fluttered nervously.

"Jake!" Hauser ran after him.

Jake stopped in the doorway, turned.

"I'm spread a little thin right now. I don't have a solution. There's no other way to figure out what that painting is?"

Jake shook his head. "Not without an airplane hangar and a month of time. I have 337 gigs of data that I need to get to Quantico. There are five thousand-plus pieces in this puzzle," he said, tapping the laptop. "And I need the right software and minds to do it—" He stopped cold and that thing he did – that magical process of connecting the dots – kicked in.

Hauser saw his expression change. "What?" he asked.

"That girl at the hospital," he said slowly, deliberately.

"What girl?"

Jake told Hauser about the girl in Dr. Sobel's office; about the candy portrait laid out on the teak coffee table beside the sailing magazines; about how she was able to create entire portraits with single pixels of information. Maybe she could decipher it. Recreate it. Draw it.

Hauser waved one of his deputies – a short barrel-chested man who was consuming the last half of an egg-salad sandwich while swearing at his useless cell phone – over. "Wohl, get a Dr. Sobel on the phone – Southampton Hospital staff psychiatrist. We need the name and number of one of his patients – a child that he saw this morning. She may be helpful in the homicide investigation. He is not allowed to mention his involvement to the media."

Wohl ducked away, his jaw mashing the last bit of sandwich in great swirling bites.

A burst of rain shrieked against the entrance and the ten-foot arched oak doors swung in a few inches. A wedge of water spilled through the temporary weakness and fanned out over the marble floor, sprinkled with leaves and another of the ubiquitous Starbucks cups.

"And tighten up that door," Hauser barked to the workers of the weather-battered hive.

Outside, Dylan was in character, and his ugly, offensive nature was shining. He was four hours away from hitting his earsplitting apex, and until then there was weaponry to suck into his belly, monstrous columns of condensation that he slurped off the ocean in million-gallon gulps. He gave a little of this back to the earth as rain. But the rest – the lion's share of his spoils – was stored in the armory.

It was obvious that he had no intention of calming down any time soon.

59

Frank bounced the clunky Hummer over the curb and up onto a lawn to avoid a tree across the road. He sucked on his cigarette and the end glowed bright orange, then faded to a dull red that was lost in the ash. "You really think that this little girl can help you?"

Jake shrugged, his signature move now. "It's a long shot. Christ, it's more than a long shot, it's a winning-the-Powerball-two-weeks-in-a-row kind of shot."

Frank wrenched the wheel and the truck spun to the right, kicking up water and great gulps of wet lawn. "This kid retarded?"

Jake shook his head. Frank was old school – *real* old school – and didn't have the disadvantage of political correctness to shut down his thought process. "No, Frank. She's autistic. And she's got a form of savantism." Jake had a strong understanding of psychology. He read academic papers, sat in on classes at George Washington University under an auditing waiver, and had picked the brains of hundreds of psychiatrists and psychologists over the years. He could have taught a second-year psychology course at college.

"What's that?"

Jake half resented, half appreciated having his thoughts drawn away from Kay and Jeremy and he decided to thank Frank with dialogue instead of silence. "Don't you watch TV?"

Frank shook his head and snickered derisively. "Why the hell would I do *that*?"

"It's a hypertalent. Half of savants are autistic, the other fifty percent have some form of neural abnormality. They can do things no one can figure out."

"Example?"

"Eidetic memory is common. Some can add numbers together faster than a computer – a column of three dozen six-digit numbers instantly. Many have a thing with dates. My birthday, for exam—" His chest tightened up and he just stopped. Stopped talking. Stopped thinking. Stopped trying to be part of the world. Because he realized that he actually had no idea what his real birthday was.

He thought about the father who wasn't his father, strapped into a hospital bed ten miles from here, and about the clues left behind like Brothers Grimm breadcrumbs – clues that so far pointed to a faceless killer: the bloody portrait on the hospital-room wall; the carpet optical illusion; and the eyeless studies climbing out of the walls of the studio. He thought about the mother who hadn't been his mother, and how she ended her time on the planet in an abandoned lot down the highway, stripped of her skin and robbed of her future. He thought about his uncle Frank, who wasn't his uncle at all. And he realized he was connected to these people not because he shared their genes but because he shared their tragedy. "—um, you tell certain savants a date – ten years ago or a century and a half – they'll tell you what weekday it was, what the weather was like, and what time the sun rose. They're *never* wrong."

Frank whistled. "Idiot savants. Read something a long time ago, can't tell you the date, and certainly don't know what day of the week it was."

"They're called savants now. *Idiot* is not politically correct. Neither is *retard*, *moron*, and anything else that can be misconstrued as derogatory." Wow, Frank really *was* old school.

Frank shook his head disgustedly. "Fucking politically correct assholes. They're changing *Huckleberry Finn* because of these small-minded people. You know who else did shit like this? The Nazis!" Almost on cue, the headlights caught a BMW X6 half submerged in water and jammed up against a tree, abandoned. "Goddamned Nazi pansy mobile! Buy American!" he hollered, and slapped the wheel of the Humvee. "Where was I? Oh, yeah – everybody's so goddamned worried about offending the wrong goddamned people all the time. Sorry, the world isn't fair. Some people will be made fun of. I don't care if they're fat or stupid or from Latvia, someone's going to call them a name. You don't see me lobbying to stop old-man jokes, do you? Fucking country has gone to shit. Everyone wants to be more equal than the next guy." Frank was talking loud – not quite yelling, but close – to be heard above the engine and the wind and the rain. "What does this girl do?" he asked.

Jake was grateful that Frank was keeping his mind off the places it wanted to go. Tortured, dark, foul places. "She puts pictures together. I'm hoping that she can see something in the photo stream of –" he paused, weighed the next word – "Jacob's paintings. I'm probably wasting time I don't have."

Frank shook his head. "But he's already left paintings of this guy."

Jake thought about the faceless men on the studio walls. The hospital portrait rendered in his own blood. Jacob wanted his son to see those so he would get used to looking. Then the carpet mosaic – a portrait with a blank face constructed of pieces – fragments – like the Chuck Close. Like those canvas puzzle fragments. "He left faceless portraits, Frank. Those were to get me started. The portrait of the killer – if that's what this is – is for my eyes only. I don't think he trusted anyone else with this." It was starting to look like his father had sent him away on purpose. "This is something he wants *me* to figure out."

60

Judging by the lighted windows on the block, one in ten residents had opted to stay, probably figuring that if the hurricane got bad, and a storm surge rose up, they'd be safe this far inland. Everyone had been talking about how lucky they were that the storm had made landfall at low tide. Of course, no one thought that they were only nineteen feet above sea level and a good surge would scrub the town from Long Island. Or that the tide was destined to rise again.

Frank pulled the truck into the driveway of a small two-story postwar bungalow that was not dissimilar to Rachael Macready's. They ran for the door, Frank zipped up in the oilskin jacket, Jake wrapped in one of Hauser's rain ponchos. Mrs. Mitchell opened the door before they were up the steps and ushered them inside with the standard small talk that a change in weather generates. When they were inside she pulled the screen door shut, then the white-painted main door with the diamond window centered in it.

Jake could see her playing in the living room. Sobel had given Hauser her mother's name and number and the sheriff had called ahead asking her mother's permission for Jake to speak to her. Her name was Emily Mitchell. She was twelve.

Jake knew that there was no way to guarantee any sort of result. Maybe she was behind a linguistic wall that he wouldn't be able to penetrate. Maybe he'd just burn up more time. But he didn't have much in the way of options and even less in leads.

Jesus, he thought. *Listen to me. Grasping at straws.* If it hadn't been so goddamned sad, he'd have laughed at it.

Mrs. Mitchell was bundled in an old cable-knit sweater that had splotches of paint on one arm and a patch on the other. Jake guessed that it was her version of a security blanket. "Mrs. Mitchell, thank you for this." Jake pulled the hood off of the poncho. "This is important."

Frank receded into a corner of the small entryway. "M'am," he said stiffly.

Jake pulled out his badge and held it up. She dismissed it after a cursory glance – it was amazing how many people did that. "I talked to you at Dr. Sobel's office this morning, I wasn't sure you'd remember …"

On the table inside the entry were a kerosene lantern, a box of candles, and two flashlights that looked like Cold War relics. Jake wondered if she had tested them or simply pulled them out of whatever junk drawer they had been relegated to. Beside the hurricane essentials was another crappy novel, this one featuring a velvet-clad pirate in the midst of foreplay with a buxom countess whose expression belied lust more than rape.

"I remember you," she said slowly, and something about the way she spoke told him a lot wasn't being said. "I never thought you were an FBI agent, though." She smiled awkwardly.

"I get that a lot." But not as much as he had since he had come back to Montauk, he realized. "This is Frank." Jake knew that the woman had to be a little skittery at having two strange men in her house during a hurricane asking her daughter questions as part of a murder investigation – regardless of what Hauser had said over the phone.

"Come in," she said.

Jake pulled off his boots and Frank sat down on a small bench near the door to undo his old lace-ups. Mrs. Mitchell disappeared into the kitchen and he saw that the layout was identical to Rachael Macready's house. "I made some coffee," Mrs. Mitchell offered from the other room.

"That would be great."

She came back with two steaming mugs just as Frank finished taking off his boots and Jake – the eternal student of human behavior – was surprised how flexible the old man was.

"Mrs. Mitchell – like Sheriff Hauser said on the phone, you don't have to help me. Your daughter's not a witness or anything like that. I am not even sure that she can help. I am here because I have nowhere else to go and, to be honest, I'm probably wasting your time as well as my own." He was able to say it with conviction because it was the truth. "You've heard about the people who were killed in Montauk?"

She stiffened, and a little of the coordination seemed to leave her. "Everyone has."

"I think the same man who killed those people also took my family." He thought about Kay standing on her tiptoes so she could kiss him, about the way her hair smelled of papaya. And he thought about Jeremy and MoonPies. "My wife and three-year-old son."

Mrs. Mitchell said, "I'm sorry," barely above a whisper.

"I think I have an image of him but it's in pieces."

She held out the mugs. "Like a puzzle?"

"Yes."

Frank took a sip of his coffee and said, "You're an angel."

She led them into the living room. "She either pays attention or she doesn't. There are no in-betweens. Yelling doesn't help. Shaking her doesn't help. Slapping her doesn't help. It can be frustrating. If she moves something, or touches something, don't interfere, even if it's yours – it makes her mad and you don't want her to get mad." She looked Jake over with an expression he hadn't seen in a long time. "You have things to do, so you best be started."

The living room was identical to the Macready victim's, including the placement of the furniture. The only difference was a small bookcase crammed with candy-colored paperbacks with saccharine titles on their spines, denoting more romantic embraces between oversexed people with good hair and trust funds.

Emily was on the floor, putting a puzzle together. She had upended the box on the carpet and had flipped all the pieces over so they were upside down and all she had to work with now was a fragmented cardboard pallet of like shapes. She worked fast, snapping pieces home with the precision of an assembly-line robot. The scene looked like a film played in reverse.

"Emily," Mrs. Mitchell said softly. "This man wants to show you something. It's a puzzle. A picture puzzle."

Emily kept locking the colorless cardboard shapes into place and the puzzle was growing rapidly. If she had heard her mother, Jake had seen no sign of it.

"She does these all the time. Won't do a puzzle twice. I've tried to fool her by putting a puzzle she's already done into a new box and laying it out upside down for her and she knows instantly. Just slaps it aside." She brushed the hair out of Emily's eyes and readjusted a big yellow barrette. "Don't you, sweetheart." She leaned over and kissed her daughter on the head. The girl hadn't reacted to the introduction, the caress, or the kiss. She just kept firing the pieces of the puzzle home with the same blank expression Jake had seen on her face in Sobel's office that morning. Back when he still had a family.

Mrs. Mitchell nodded at Jake and he put his laptop down on the floor in front of the girl. He opened it up.

The image frozen in the video frame was him, holding up one of his father's weird little paintings. He looked half asleep in one of those typical poses taken between the ending of one movement and the beginning of another, like an alternative version of himself. Jake hit play on the trackpad and the miniature himself-but-not-himself version put the canvas in his hands down, picked up another. Then put it down and picked up another. And another. Again. And again.

Emily paid no attention to the computer. Her eyes were locked on the puzzle in front of her, her hands mechanically assembling the pieces as if each were invisibly numbered and she was wearing special glasses. Frank watched from a chair near the window, sipping his coffee and observing the girl with focused attention.

A few seconds in, Jake realized that he hadn't started the film at the beginning. He reached over and hit the rewind button and the picture ratcheted back.

And that's when Emily froze, a single brown puzzle piece held above its place in the big picture she was assembling.

Jake looked at Mrs. Mitchell. She shrugged.

Emily dropped the puzzle piece. Reached out. Put her finger down on the trackpad, and swung it across the black frame. The video began sliding by at high speed.

"No, Emily, that's—" and Mrs. Mitchell grabbed his arm as he reached for the child. Jake froze.

The girl was watching the screen with rapt attention as the video sped by at sixty times its recorded speed.

Emily's eyelids fluttered as the sped-up version of Jake went through the process of holding one painting up after another – in an endless loop. Her eyes didn't seem to be looking at the screen, but beyond it, and Jake wondered if she was seeing anything in the random shapes that were snapping by too fast for him to catch. Every now and then he would get a glimpse of a canvas, an image that flashed by slowly enough for his brain to register its shape, but by the time he saw it, it was gone.

Emily sat photo-still as she watched the video, her only movement being that slight twitch in her eyelids. The wind and rain bombarded the house and the images of the canvases flicked by in jagged splashes of color against Jake's almost unmoving form in the frame.

As he watched the girl, Jake forgot the mug of coffee cradled in his hands. Frank drank his absentmindedly and his attention was divided between the girl and the storm tearing through the neighborhood outside. The sea was funneling down the street in a two-foot-thick surge. A big wheeled garbage can somersaulted down the middle of the saltwater river, lid flapping like the jaw of a basking shark straining for plankton.

Emily watched the blue-glow screen, enrapt. By the second minute, she was whistling through her nose, a rhythmic hiss that was almost musical.

The video came to an end and Emily gasped. Without pausing, she drew her finger back across the touchpad, and the video began to crawl backward. The jerky, puppetlike movements that

Jake's alternate self had just danced through began to run in reverse, and it had the same unreal quality to it as Emily's upside-down puzzle making.

The girl was humming now, a thick, deep-throated buzz like a power transformer heating up. Jake understood how ignorant thirteenth-century peasants could see autistics as being possessed; their world was so distant, so impenetrable, that there was no way to equate it with the nuts and bolts of the average mind. He watched her stare at the video – even if you ignored that almost complete upside down puzzle on the floor – and realized there was no way to label this girl as average. Not even in the abstract. Which said something.

The video ended.

Emily's eyes stayed locked beyond the screen, her eyes focused on the pixilated universe inside the laptop.

"Did you see anything, Emily?" Jake asked, trying to keep the edge of hope – or was that hysteria? – out of his voice. Without her, they were at a dead end.

Dead.

End.

Skinned.

The little girl stared ahead, unmoving.

"Sweetie?" Mrs. Mitchell asked. "Did you see anything? Was there anything there?"

No movement.

Jake felt the adrenaline of expectation fizzle into the dull ache of despair. He began to stand.

Emily clicked to life.

She stood up and her expression changed from blank disregard to intense concentration. She stomped out of the room and Jake continued to rise but Mrs. Mitchell put her hand on his shoulder and shook her head. "She's on a mission now. Maybe it has something to do with you, maybe she's just off to stack the soaps in the bathroom, but she's going to do *something*."

Frank had stopped sipping his coffee and waited for the girl to return, absorbed by the whole weird process. Jake sat stone-still on the sofa beside Mrs. Mitchell, waiting for – what?

Off in another room there was the sound of a drawer being emptied, of utensils being gone through, then it stopped. More heavy footsteps as the girl moved to another part of the house. A door opened. Closed.

Emily came back into the living room carrying a beach ball under one arm and a pair of scissors and a few felt markers in her hand. She walked over to the stereo, snapped the power on, and pressed play on the CD player. The high-octane music of Johnny Puleo and the Harmonica Rascals came on in full volume.

Mrs. Mitchell leaned over and spoke into Jake's ear. "She loves that CD. It's all I'm allowed to play." Something in her tone suggested that she wasn't all that fond of the music.

Jake watched the girl, mesmerized.

Emily sat down on the floor and locked the beach ball between her legs. She turned it over like a gemologist looking for a flaw, and when she found whatever she was looking for, stabbed the scissors into the thick rubber surface. The ball sighed, then let its life out in a long protracted fart.

Then the little girl with the expressionless face went to work with her scissors and magic markers.

61

It took Emily Mitchell eleven minutes to finish her scissor surgery on the beach ball as Johnny Puleo and his Harmonica Gang belted out musical mayhem as accompaniment. She worked quickly, without time for reflection, her fingers deftly manipulating the skin of the ball like an Old World tailor going at a pattern. To most people it would have looked like there was no thought or deliberation behind her actions – just raw industry. Jake recognized the innate ability of someone born with a gift and for one of the few times in his life he understood why the people he worked with couldn't understand how he did something – it was a simple lack of language.

Emily slashed at the rubber with her scissors, turning the wrinkled skin this way and that as she made precise cuts in the material. When she was done, her thick black bangs were plastered to her forehead with sweat and the bright yellow barrette that secured them hung lopsided by her temple.

She laid the ball out on the floor, colored side down, and the hundreds of cuts had reduced it to a flat plane, myriad small irregularly shaped shards barely connected by thin strands of rubber. Jake recognized these shards as a miniature model of the weird little canvases piled up at the beach house. The pieces were not independent of one another, and the gestalt was roughly the shape of a lopsided lobster with odd, clubbed feet and a deformed body, formed by thousands of small interconnecting scales – each denoting one of Jacob Coleridge's blobs of madness.

She made her last snip in the ball and lay the scissors gently down on the floor. Then she picked up the markers and began coloring in her handiwork. At one point she stopped and stood up and Jake wondered what was wrong. But she just walked over to the CD player and hit Repeat.

"She only likes the first four songs," Mrs. Mitchell offered as explanation.

Emily returned to the carpet by the sofa and went back to work like a high-speed robot programmed to color.

It took her another nine minutes of coloring in the loosely connected bits of rubber ball until she was finished. She stopped, placed the markers on the floor beside the scissors, and went back to work on her upside down puzzle.

Mrs. Mitchell looked over at Jake and shrugged. "I guess that's it."

Jake looked at the ball, laid out like a dissection in a biology class.

Mrs. Mitchell shrugged. "Looks kind of like some of the pieces on your video."

Jake stared into the swirling rubber puzzle, trying to pick out details that made some sort of sense.

It was Frank who said, "It's upside down."

Jake stood up and walked around to the other side of Emily's artwork. In the middle of the spider's body, sprawled out like a gerrymander map, four irregularly shaped pieces of rubber came together and formed the image of a human eye.

"You sonofabitch," Jake said through his teeth.

"What?" Frank came over and stood beside him.

"It's a sphere. Jacob meant for this to be assembled into a sphere."

"What would be the point?"

Jake squatted down and lifted one of the legs of the rubber skin; it was cold in his hand. "So you could only see the painting from the inside." He looked up into Frank's eyes.

Frank looked at the model that Emily Mitchell had constructed from her vantage point, way out beyond comprehension. "He really has lost his mind."

Jake shook his head and tried not to sound too reverent. "This is brilliant." He thought of the stainless polyhedron model on the console by the door, the one his father had welded thirty-plus years ago. It was about the same size as the beach ball. In fact, if he thought about it, it was worth betting that it was *exactly* the same size as the beach ball. Somehow the old man had broadcast on a frequency that Emily Mitchell had received. The idea that the panels back in the studio were actually the mock-up for the real piece of art, which was right here in his fucking hands, was too far-reaching to consider. How could he know that we'd be able to do this? Jake wondered.

And the answer was, *he hadn't*. This was a fluke, a one-in-a-trillion-squared shot that had panned out. The girl had deciphered the panels, and she had somehow stumbled upon – or been magically instructed by the video to find – a beach ball of the right size. Jacob Coleridge's wire-frame sculpture was just that – a frame. And this piece in his hand, this cold piece of rubber that felt a little too much like human skin, was the tailor-made canvas. This was what the old bastard had wanted. A spherical painting to be viewed from the inside – the perfect way to hide his work. And Jake had somehow stumbled on a solution. It had been an accident, one of those things that you read about every now and then.

The thought of anything else was simply ridiculous.

The cold, almost epidermal rubber felt perverse, wrong in his hands. But he had his mug shot.

Skinned.

Jake turned to Mrs. Mitchell. "Thank you for your help."

62

Jake and Frank headed for the hospital, fighting into the wind this time, their progress handicapped by the lousy aerodynamics of the big metal beast. With the new lead, Jake had come out of his angry grief enough to be amazed at the force Mother Nature was throwing around. He wondered if the house back at the point was still standing or if it had been snatched from the shoreline in one violent grab of the ocean.

"You think that's a portrait of the killer?" Frank jerked his thumb at the mutilated beach-ball skin that lay in Jake's lap, wrapped in two garbage bags.

Jake caressed the plastic beneath his fingers, wondering what was in there. "I don't know." He thought about the mind it had taken to put this together – a three-dimensional painting that was supposed to be viewed from the inside. How many men were capable of something like that? A handful on the planet at most. Maybe less.

And he thought about the other part, the part that was a little too freaky-deaky to really examine, because there was no way to put it into any sort of context.

"Jacob wanted this to be seen from the inside? I don't understand, Jakey."

Jake wasn't sure he did, either. "All those little canvases at the house – all those little irregular shapes piled all over the place, are parts of a whole – of a bigger piece. Alone, they are nothing. It's like a digital photograph. Up close – too close – all you see are little squares of color, like tiles in a mosaic. I knew they meant *something*, I just couldn't figure out what."

"How'd he design it? Did you look at the way that kid chopped up that beach ball? Something like that takes a shitload of smarts." Frank shook his head and fired up a cigarette.

"You can fault Jacob Coleridge on a lot of things but you can't accuse him of being dumb. And I think that this thing was designed to be stretched over that sculpture in the—"

Frank slapped the steering wheel. "—hallway! Sonofabitch, that's smart, I mean—" And he stopped, realizing that meant that this had been Jacob's plan for three-plus decades. "Oh, boy."

Up ahead there was a dip in the road that had filled in with water. Jake shifted in his seat. "That looks deep, Frank."

"Don't worry. Got a snorkel," he said, and tapped the windshield, pointing to a pipe that stuck out of the hood in front of Jake. "Besides, this thing won't float – it's designed to fill up with water so we don't lose traction. Might get your pants wet but do you really give a shit?"

Jake's fingers wrapped tighter around the support bar mounted on the dashboard in front of his seat, keeping one hand on Emily Mitchell's artwork in his lap. He looked to the east, to the waves detonating against the newly gouged shoreline, and tried to ignore that if the storm wanted them to drown, a snorkel wasn't going to do shit.

63

His father stared at the ceiling, making scared little sounds that belonged in a children's ghost story. "Who is this, Jacob?"

Jake laid the skin of the beach ball out on a bulletin board he had rolled in from the doctor's lounge. It was held up with pins, like a prized specimen on a dissection table.

Jake had other things in the back of his mind. He wanted to ask his father about where he had come from, where he had been found. About who he really was. But he had no time. The storm was raging against the world around him and the Bloodman was raging against the world within. And his entire focus had been reduced to finding his wife and child. "Who, Jacob?"

Jacob Coleridge stared at the piece, fascinated, something like pride shining in his eyes. Then he shifted his gaze to his son's eyes, and for a second they were the eyes of a rational, sane man. Maybe even a man who loved him. His mouth twitched in one weak little smile, the kind Jacob had never given his son; *I love you*, it said.

Then someone threw the big breaker in his head, his mind shorted out for good, and he fell back onto the pillow, mumbling beneath his breath.

Jake spent another ten minutes – ten minutes he didn't have and couldn't spare – trying to coax his father's mind out of wherever it had retreated to and all he had to show for it were a few mumbled pleas and some crying. Jake finally gave up and steered Frank out into the hallway by the elbow.

"Give me the keys to the Humvee."

Frank fished into his slicker and pulled out his keychain, an old .3030 cartridge with a single car key attached. He tossed it to Jake. "Where you going?" He had an unlit cigarette tucked into his teeth and it bobbed up and down as he spoke.

"You stay with Dad. See if he says anything else. See if he comes back. Ask him what this is about. Ask him who is doing this. And why." Jake thought about his father, a frightened figure out of a Gothic horror story, and felt a little part of him inside go cold. "You got a weapon?"

Frank pulled back the waxed raincoat and an old blued .45 winked out at Jake. "Also got the Ka-Bar," he said, tapping the hilt of the big trench knife he had carried since Korea.

They didn't make men like Uncle Frank anymore.

Frank was grinning and in the dim emergency lighting he looked like Jacob.

"Stay with Pop."

Frank smiled, his hand still on the hilt of the knife. "Not even the Devil is getting by me, Jakey."

Jake stared at him for a few seconds. "He's going to come, Frank. After you or after me or after Dad. We're all that's left, unless Kay and … and …" He let the sentence get drowned out by the wind. Or was that his own scream?

Frank put his hand out, laid it on Jake's arm. He felt the muscles under the fabric shift like bunched steel cables. "Jake, you don't fucking worry about anything. You don't worry about your dad and you don't worry about me. I might be old but I ain't rusty. I've killed just about everything out there – including men – in my time, son. I can still kick ass. So go do whatever you have to do to find your wife and your son."

Jake wanted to say something, to maybe thank the old man, but he knew that if he opened his mouth he'd only cry. And maybe not stop.

He took the keys and ducked into the black stairwell.

64

It took Jake twenty minutes to negotiate the terrain between the hospital and the sheriff's office, a trip that under normal circumstances – even in the midst of long-weekend tourist traffic – should have taken five. The big military vehicle handled the deep trenches of water that sloshed over the roads with ease but the wind was an entirely different matter. The Hummer had been designed for slow going over bad terrain – it could climb rocks, riverbanks, and other cars with ease – but heading straight into the 150-mile-an-hour winds that were screaming over Long Island was an effort for the big clumsy truck. A few times he felt the wind get under the front end and try to flip the vehicle. Like Frank, he found himself talking to the Hummer, calling her all kinds of sweet names as she made it from one endurance test to the next.

It was night now, and the hurricane had blocked out the sky in a roiling canopy of black water that screamed at the earth. The tall cement curbs that kept the lawns free of rain during the big summer rainstorms were funneling water down the streets and it raged and boiled like a river. The entire town was flooded and half the trees were uprooted. Houses were collapsed and there was debris everywhere.

He saw no one on the roads and wondered how the coast was doing. Was all this water from the rain that belted down or had the ocean made it up onto land? At the intersection of Front and Lang he had to climb over the lawn of the Presbyterian church. The windows were dark, absent even of the flicker of candlelight, and Jake knew that it was empty, with no one inside praying. He found this strange since the holy rollers always like to ask God for protection and help through times like this. To Jake, swearing at the old motherfucker made more sense since wasn't it the Almighty visiting this shit on them in the first place?

The parking lot of the sheriff's office was still empty of official vehicles and he parked near the side door, in the lee side of the wind howling by.

The cop with the egg sandwich, Wohl, was inside the door, barking at his walkie-talkie with demented enthusiasm. He stopped when he saw Jake, rain-soaked and one hundred years older than two hours ago.

"Where's Hauser?" Jake barked.

Wohl nodded at the two big slabs of arched oak that did duty as front doors, hastily secured with duct tape and two pieces of iron pipe. They flexed and rattled with the wind trying to blow its way in to get to the little piggies. "Trying to help the EMT guys over at the mall. Propane tank at the Denny's blew up. Custodian got a red-hot doorknob launched through his head."

Jake lifted the MacBook. "You got communications up yet?"

Wohl held the walkie-talkie up with his index and thumb like it was a turd on fire. "You think I'd be screaming at this thing if we had satellites?"

Jake stopped, took a few seconds to gather his thoughts. "I need a garbage can. Maybe two foot across. Size of a beach ball. And something to eat. You got a vending machine?"

Wohl smiled, glad that there was something he could do. "How about egg salad with plenty of onions on rye with a little mustard? And coffee. I got coffee. Lots of coffee."

"Sounds good."

"How you take it? We got no sugar."

"In a cup."

On his way he passed Scopes, leaning against the wall by the door digging mud out of his boot treads with a big tactical knife. He looked up, saw Jake, and waved with the knife.

Kay's face popped up in his head, smiling, freckled, beautiful and alive. Behind her, not far away, Jeremy was there with Elmo, dancing around with a Moon Pie in his hand. Jake blinked and willed the images to stop, to crawl back into the dark.

Kay blew him a kiss. Then fell away into the shadows.

Jake shoveled two of Wohl's sandwiches down followed by two cups of coffee. Then he went to work on the dissected beach-ball skin.

He didn't have the time to go back to the beach house to get the stainless-steel frame that sat on the console by the door; right now he needed to jerry-rig something so he lined a large garbage can with paper towels, balled up to make a rough bowl, and set the skin of the beach ball into it. He padded it out, and was surprised that it was a pretty good fit for a half-assed mock-up.

As he tried to align the parts, which slipped by one another like a handful of guitar picks, he got glimpses of features here and there. Almost a nose. A bit of an eye. A cheekbone. Finally he had it laid out in the bottom of the can enough that all he had to do was push a little more of it together. He fiddled it into shape, held it into place, and looked down at the image that Emily Mitchell had drawn for him.

It was a portrait.

A good portrait.

The girl had done an unbelievable job.

But Jake knew that it wasn't what his father had painted on the canvases back at the beach house.

No hell. No way.

And for the second time that night, he felt the warm fist of defeat heat up in his stomach. This was it – his last shot at figuring out what his old man was trying to tell him. And behind all the static of grief and anger and frustration, he knew that his father was trying to tell him who had taken Kay and Jeremy.

Now he would never get them back. Not Kay. Not Jeremy.

Skinned.

They were gone.

Skinned.

For good.

Scopes burst into the room. "Special Agent Cole, the medical examiner is on the phone."

Without lifting his head, Jake said into his hands, "I thought the phones were down."

"Actually, they're the only thing that's held up. Push line three."

Jake wobbled to the old oak table, the top stained with countless coffee-mug rings and cigarette burns. He picked up the receiver and pressed line three.

"Cole, here."

"Special Agent Cole, Dr. Reagan. Two things. First of all, the blood on the child's T-shirt you brought in this morning is the same type as the boy from the Farmer house. It hasn't been sequenced, but it's AB negative."

Jake remembered Jeremy standing at the bottom of the stairs, his head tilted to one side, pink tears streaking his face. "And?"

"And the second thing is that whoever killed Rachael Macready cut out her tongue. At first I thought she had bitten it off like Madame X but it wasn't in the house."

"Did you check her stomach?" Jake asked.

There was silence on the other end of the line while Dr. Reagan swallowed once, loudly. "It wasn't there, although I hadn't thought that it might be." She had that mistrust in her voice now, the one they all got around him sooner or later when they began to understand how well he knew these monsters. "You've got more experience than I do in homicides of this type – what do you make of that?"

Jake ran through the endless parade of murders he had seen in his years hunting down killers. It was usually standard Freudian backlash reasoned out by a psychologically fractured mind. Edmund Kemper was the poster boy for this kind of thinking; he had killed six women before building up the courage to go after the one he really wanted to take out. To understand these men, all you needed was the key. And it was usually pretty simple. He said the first thing that came to mind. "He saw her as a traitor."

"Why?"

His conversation with Hauser that afternoon popped into his head. "She helped me. She helped my fath—" The words clanked to a halt in his throat as an image of Emily Mitchell and her bright yellow barrette flashed in his head. "Oh, God."

Jake slammed the phone down and threw his borrowed police poncho on. He ran through the corridor for the back exit, hollering at Scopes. "Get in touch with Hauser. Tell him to meet me at the Mitchell house. Now!"

He slammed through the back door, out into the gyrating screech of the storm that was taking everything he had left apart, a little at a time.

65

The truck threw up thick plumes of water as it barreled down the empty streets of Southampton, enough that the Israelites could have followed in its wake. Since leaving the Sheriff's Department, Jake had forded two newly-formed storm-fueled rivers that had sprung up in town and both times the water had actually climbed up over the hood – somehow Frank's snorkel contraption seemed to be doing its job because the engine had not so much as coughed. When he wasn't resorting to naval tactics, Jake kept his foot down as he ripped through the empty town. After a few blocks he realized that he had to ease off or he'd flip Frank's gas-guzzling bitch and end up drowning alone in the middle of one of the abandoned streets.

Gunning it through the dark neighborhoods had a creepy, postapocalyptic quality to it. The farther he got from the sheriff's office – the deeper into Southampton – the more visceral this feeling became. The whole time he barreled toward the Mitchell home, his brain was working on his father's fragmented portrait. Was it just a symbol of his fractured mind or had he meant for it to be a portrait of the Bloodman? Jake was sure he had left all those faceless portraits for Jake to see, to pique his curiosity, to get him used to thinking. To get him used to looking.

Why hadn't he just told Jake who the killer was? Left a note? A letter? Why the babushka-doll approach? A riddle hidden inside a riddle hidden inside a riddle hidden inside a … Jesus fucking Christ, it was endless!

Jake ran his mental fingers over the years, trying to find anything in the dust-caked pages that would help make sense of why his father had done this.

Jake knew that he was the one who was supposed to see it; that's what he did – even his old man would know that. Bury a needle in a haystack, hide the haystack in a field of haystacks, and unleash Jakey with that divining-rod head of his and he'd find it, figure it out, solve the mystery.

Only it wasn't just a mystery. Not any more. Not a job or a game or even an obsession. It was a need.

Something told him that Kay and Jeremy were alive. Why? Because they hadn't found any bodies. And this fucker – the Bloodman – liked to leave a little something behind for his fans.

And if Jake didn't drown or get crushed by a falling tree or get jolted by an electromagnetic pulse, he knew that he would find who he was looking for. He would find *him*.

At least now Jake would have something to call him when he put the barrel of the revolver to his head and opened it as wide as the sky.

66

Jake pulled up on the Mitchells' lawn and the 9,000-pound truck settled to the rims in the wet earth. He kicked the heavy door open with his foot and jumped out into shin-deep water. The street was flooding, the neighborhood was flooding, the lawn was flooding. In another hour it could all be washed away. He wondered if Wohl had reached Hauser and if the sheriff was on the way. He wished that Hauser were here, or Scopes, or anyone else, because if that fucker showed up ...

He raced across thirty feet of lawn, moving through the current that mired him down like a foot of wet cement. Candles now flickered in a few rooms and it looked like Mrs. Mitchell had fired up the old kerosene Coleman that had been sitting on the hall table. There was movement inside. A shadow passed by the big front window, stopped to look out. Jake recognized the shape of Mrs. Mitchell. His heart leveled out a little.

His foot hit the precast concrete step and he grabbed the iron railing. Mrs. Mitchell opened the door. She smiled for an instant.

And then Jake saw him. Behind her, standing in the kitchen doorway. For an instant he thought that it was his own reflection, but then he moved.

There was a knife hanging from his hand, the gleam of death in the dark.

He was just a dim outline but Jake knew the shape; it was the faceless man that Jacob had splattered on the wall in his blood. The man from the portrait. The man of blood. The Bloodman.

Jake's hand went under the poncho, into his jacket, and he felt the rubber combat grip of his revolver, warm and dry against his hand.

The thing behind her moved. Twitched.

Jake got his index through the trigger guard and began to draw the weapon. He opened his mouth to scream, to warn her. There was a shift on Mrs. Mitchell's face as she saw his expression, saw him go under the poncho for his pistol, and she began to turn, to look behind her.

Jake saw the faceless form move in the darkness.

There was deep *whump* followed by a resonant crack that lit up the sky like a billion-watt generator blowing its magnets. The earth rang as the bolt of lightning impregnated the ground and the soil went supernova, killing every earthworm in a quarter-mile radius.

Jake saw the world overload for a millisecond before the power went out. Then it was just as if nothing existed at all.

He fell back.

Away.

Away from the world.

Away from the steps.

Away from Mrs. Mitchell and Emily and everything else he had promised he would not leave to the Bloodman.

67

Jake stood in the entry with the fractured sounds of the storm battering the house a distant drone that barely penetrated the static swirling around his skull. He stared at the top of Emily Mitchell's scalp sitting on the newel post, a skullcap of thick black bangs held back with a bright yellow barrette. The bridge of her nose and one eyebrow were visible beneath. The rest lay in the living room in the middle of a cheap imitation Persian carpet sopping with blood and flecked with puzzle pieces. The thing that used to be her mother lay beside her, stretched out and butchered.

Hauser was outside throwing up and Jake hoped he was pointed downwind. It was one of those back-of-the-mind things that came to him while he examined the top of the girl's head, thrown carelessly onto the newel post like a winter cap, a little lopsided.

Hauser and his deputy had found Jake floating near the road. The drag of the heavy water-filled poncho had acted like a sea-anchor and saved him from being washed away in the surge that sloshed across the lawn. He had been unconscious and Hauser had slapped him, yelled, shook him. His eyes had fluttered open, and that first big breath hit him in the chest like an atom bomb. He sat up, screamed Emily Mitchell's name. Hauser had run for the house. Taken the screen door off the hinges. Stumbled out fifteen seconds later and barfed in the swamp that used to be a garden.

Jake lifted himself from the water, his brain actually making a cartoon spring sound as he tried to keep the world from spinning. He fought to his feet and lurched across the lawn and fell up the steps like a drunk trying to make it to the toilet in time.

Mother and daughter were in the living room. Mostly.

68

Jake shuffled up the emergency-lit stairs of the hospital on autopilot, his feet taking him from one dim pool of light to the next. He was soaked through now, and the wet leather of his boots rubbed against his shins and every time he took a step the storm squished between his toes to remind him just how unfinished all of this was. He had very little left in him and the only thing that kept his heart beating and his legs pumping was the chance that he could somehow save Kay and Jeremy. He wondered if there was anything remotely rational in this line of thinking or if it was just blind hope. After all, there were no bodies. That was something, wasn't it? Because this guy liked to leave behind— Jake stopped the image from welling up in his head. He couldn't – refused to – think like that. Not with his wife and son.

He opened the steel door and stepped out into the hallway.

The third floor of the Southampton Hospital throbbed with the collective voice of the bedridden, the frightened, the infirm. The lights had been reduced to thirty percent power, an engineering decision made to cut strain on the generator. In the dim half-light, the hallway linoleum looked like a cancerous supermarket pizza that couldn't be identified by the age-old question of *Ani-*

mal, vegetable, or mineral? All the patients who could travel had been moved after a mountain of releases had been signed and those who remained were mostly palliative care and ICU trauma cases. Accompanying the murmur of the patients was the sound of windows shifting in their frames and the unmistakable krang of metal flashing being tortured by the wind somewhere outside.

Frank was at the nurses' station, trying to get a Tylenol to combat the headache that the incessant wail of the storm and the patients had brought on.

Jake moved by him, the dim light morphing his shadows into a long spiderlike animation that headed down the hall.

The passage was darker than it had been two hours ago and the sounds coming from the rooms were more like the animal grunts at some midnight petting zoo than a place where human beings were sent to mend. The taste in the atmosphere was unmistakable and every breath he took in stunk of fear.

The door to his father's room was the only one closed. He opened it and Jacob Coleridge was harnessed in, the nylon straps and bright chrome buckles gleaming dementia in the dark room. With the sound of his footsteps, his father's head turned on the pillow like a lifeless dime-store mannequin being run on rudimentary mechanics. His hair scraped the pillow as his face rotated, his eyes deep screws of terror. The soft shimmer of a noise began at the back of his throat, a low, bubbling sound.

Out of the corner of his eye, at the edge of his peripheral vision, Jake saw the spattered nightstand, something dull and dead on top and the bright gleam of steel. He didn't deflect his vision, didn't take his eyes from the old man's face, although every fiber in his brain was screaming for him to look at the thing at the edge of his sight.

Jacob Coleridge's face, barely visible in the dim light of the room, was smeared with the same bloody graffiti that had decorated Jeremy that morning. His sockets and cheeks smeared in red-black lines that outlined the skull beneath his flesh. The bloody teeth finger-painted over his mouth unzipped, and his lips formed into a black O, a sightless eye socket. The soft rasp simmering in his throat grew into a howl, like the distant call of an injured animal, and blood bubbled out and down his chin, splattering his chest.

Jake took a step toward his father and the mournful howl rose to a bright scream of panic that was supposed to be the word *No*, but only came out as a long tortured vowel. Without having to look, Jake knew that Jacob Coleridge's tongue lay on the nightstand, lines of blood and mucus gleaming on the surface of the safety razor lying in the slop beside it.

69

After they rushed his father off to emergency surgery, Jake grabbed Frank's arm and led him into the stairwell.

"Where the fuck were you?" It was anger again, not real language.

Frank had the shell-shocked expression of a plane-crash survivor. "I ... I was there the whole time, Jakey." The old man bit his bottom lip and his teeth made a soft, scraping sound against his whiskers. "I didn't even go out for a smoke." To illustrate his point, he held up a cigarette. The filter was chewed and the shaft bent. Then he paused, and the mechanics of his face jittered. "Wait a minute! Just wait a fucking minute!" He pointed at Jake. "You don't think—!"

Jake's eyes were dead black points nailed to his head. In the weak light and dark shadows, he was expressionless. He thought about the question for a second. "No, I don't."

"So what's going on, Jakey?" Frank rolled up on the balls of his feet.

Jake shook his head. It was a defeated movement powered by a long string of failures on his part. "Someone wants to keep something from me." He paced the small landing.

Frank finally fired up the cigarette he had been chewing for the past two hours. The snap of the lighter sounded like a gunshot in the small confines of the stairwell and the flame was brighter than the dull bulb illuminating the space. "Jakey, I wasn't away from that room more than five minutes before you showed up. No one went in." He wrapped his face around the cigarette and pulled in a deep chestful of smoke. "No one, Jakey." The old man's eyes narrowed and his face tightened up. Jake saw a little fear in there and he wondered what Frank wasn't telling him.

Jake paced the welded boilerplate floor. Thunder shook the building and drowned out the clunk of his boots on the painted steel. He did jail-cell laps while Frank smoked his cigarette, his hand cupped around the butt, like a kid smoking in school. "What did that little girl draw? Did you have time to look at it?"

Jake stopped, lifted his head. "She used my father's concept but her drawing had nothing to do with what he painted. She got the shapes right."

Frank dropped the cigarette and crushed it out with the heel of his boot.

"She's dead, Frank."

Frank winced. "Dead? Who—" And then he got it. "Jesus. How?"

Jake took a cigarette from Frank's pocket and fired it up. "The same way, Frank. Her mother, too. It's what this guy does."

Frank lost a little of his height and a lot of his presence in one great sigh. "Where is the portrait?"

"Sitting in the bottom of a garbage can at Hauser's." Jake suddenly realized that he was very tired and very cold. His fingers felt like they had been salvaged from someone else's hands and he was storing a frozen roast in his chest. "I need a hot shower, some dry clothes, and about a thousand years of sleep."

"Go bed down in one of the empty rooms. This is America, Jakey. You can do shit like that."

"Can't. Kay, Jeremy. I won't stop until I know …" The words dropped off for a few seconds. Then he came back with things he could do. "I need to talk to Hauser. I need to get back to the station."

"And your father?" Frank said.

Jake headed down the steps. "They'll get him through surgery. There's sweet fuck-all I can do here. Let's go."

Frank stood in place, his foot poised a few inches over the next step down. "What if he – *it* – comes back?"

An image in grainy brilliance flashed on the TV tube behind Jake's eyes, an image of the figure standing in the corridor behind Mrs. Mitchell. "If he wanted Dad dead, he wouldn't have cut out his tongue. He'd have cut his fucking head off, Frank. He's gone from here." What else could he say? That he really didn't give a fuck about his old man, not if forced to make a choice between the old bastard and his wife and son? No, he couldn't say that. Not out loud.

Frank pulled out another cigarette and started down the steps. "If he's done with everyone else, Jakey, he's coming after you next."

Jake felt the frozen roast shift in his chest. "I'm counting on that."

Jake had to put his shoulder into the steel emergency door to force it open. He held it for Frank and it bucked and pulled against his fingers and he pushed it closed with both arms.

They kept low, hunched into the wind, and moved as fast as they could for the Hummer parked around the corner of the hospital, up on the grass. Jake climbed over a mailbox that the storm had thrown across the parking lot and jammed up against the side of the vehicle. The roof of a house sat in the lot on Frank's side of the truck, shingles ripped up, joists sticking through like broken bones.

He got in, snapped the seat belt on, slid the key into the ignition, and froze.

A T-shirt was slung over the steering wheel like a towel left to dry. It was hacked through with dozens of slash marks, the once baby-blue cotton now stained black. David Hasselhoff grinned up obscenely from the bloody fabric, the line *Don't Hassel The Hoff!* blaring out in bright script streaked with blood.

It was a gift – a postcard – a note to let him know that someone was thinking about him. *Having a grand time. Wish you were here.*

Jake screamed.

70

Jake had his hands wrapped around a cup of warm coffee and his fingers almost felt like his own again. Hauser had scrounged up a pair of jeans and a T-shirt and the dry clothes combined with the warm mug had almost stopped the shivering. He sat in a wooden chair in the same interrogation room where he had hastily put together Emily Mitchell's portrait. Hauser sat on the edge of the table, cradling his own cup of coffee and looking just as tired as Jake. Frank stood in the corner, working on a sandwich and another cigarette that Hauser had grudgingly allowed him to smoke inside. Kay's bloody T-shirt sat on the table in a clear evidence bag.

Jake and Frank showed up at Hauser's office just after the sheriff had returned from the Mitchell house – in these conditions the crime scene investigation would have to wait, and Hauser had left his most inexperienced (i.e., expendable during the storm) deputy to make sure that no one contaminated the scene. The ex-quarterback's usually calm demeanor was showing signs of tension rot from watching the community he was sworn to serve and protect get ravaged by forces far beyond his control. After Jake filled him in on what had happened at the hospital, he had run through an extensive – and impressive – litany of curses. Now, after the initial rush of adrenaline, the three men sat in an exhausted silence.

It was Frank who spoke. "This sandwich tastes like ass. And not the good kind."

Hauser shook his head. "It might taste better if you didn't smoke while chewing on it."

Frank snorted in derision and went back to work on the cigarette break/snack.

Hauser crossed his arms on his chest. He looked at Jake, his bloodshot eyes narrowing. "What do we do to stop this guy? Wait until he runs out of people to kill?"

"I have to stop him. There is a way. He has a purpose here, I'm just not seeing it."

"How the fuck can you sit there so goddamned calm and analytical? Your wife –" he picked up the evidence bag with the wet T-shirt inside – "your son – are missing! This guy has your goddamned family and you sit there like the fucking Rock of Gibraltar. Jesus Christ, where do you come from?"

Jake sprung up and threw his cup at the two-way window. It hit dead center and detonated in an explosion of ceramic and coffee that sprayed the room. "You think I'm calm? I'm one inch away from going out and executing everyone I see on the off chance that it's him! I'm real sorry about Madame X and Little X and Rachael Macready and David Finch and Mrs. Mitchell and her daughter and my father and the rest of the people who have been hit by this – I *really* am. I'd like to be benevolent. I'd like to believe in sacrifice. But I don't. Not now and not ever. I'd trade all of them for my wife and son. And if I can't get them back, I can go forward until this burning in my guts turns to despair and I give up." Jake pointed at Hauser and his eyes filled with tears.

"The only way I can do this – the only way I keep from eating a round from this –" he yelled, slapping the pistol in the holster on his belt – "is by remembering that this monster is going to keep doing what he does until I stop him. And you, with your *I'm only a poor country cop* soliloquy, certainly aren't going to do it! Not with your whole fucking troop of inexperienced egg-salad-eating morons out there! The one chance we have at this – the one guy that can find this fucker – is *me*. He's here for me. And you want a little fact, Mike? I hope he finds me. I pray to whatever roll of the dice put him onto me all those years ago that he finds me, because he and I are going to have a little talk." Jake's eyes went a deeper shade of not there. "And only one of us is walking away."

Hauser pursed his lips. "So what's next?"

"I go home. That's where this started, that's where it's going to end. I don't know how I know, but I do. He's going to come looking for me. He *has* to."

The door flew open and Wohl burst in. "Special Agent Cole, we got a satellite link. I don't know why – the storm's not getting any better – but it's up. I don't know for how long."

Jake reached for his laptop on the table beside Hasselhoff's bloody face grinning up from the evidence bag. "I need a few minutes for this."

Wohl shrugged. "You can have all the time you want but when it comes to the satellite, that's up to Mother Nature."

Jake followed Wohl and Hauser closed up the rear. Frank opted to stay in the interrogation room now that he had someplace to smoke.

The communications room was pretty much what Jake expected: a pair of dispatch transmitters – a hot unit and a backup – blinking like pachinko machines; three computer terminals equipped with enormous monitors for tracking cell phone and handheld calls; and an assortment of server towers and network hubs, all running off the backup generator.

Jake sat down and the communications officer, Mary Skillen, nodded a hello. "We've had a connection for one minute, thirty-one … thirty-two … thirty-three seconds. It ain't gonna be here forever." There was a FireWire cable and a computer printout in her hand. "Here's the system access code. Get your mail out as fast as you can."

Like theatrical punctuation in a high school play, the lights dimmed and Jake heard the three officers hold their communal breath. Jake ignored the brown-out, connected the MacBook, and hooked up to the server. He was past hoping for anything and running on autopilot at this point.

Skillen's eyes were glued to the network monitor. "You're on, Special Agent Cole."

Jake brought up the FBI mail service and uploaded the video he had taken – half with Kay, half with Spencer. The status bar began an agonizingly slow crawl across the bottom of the screen.

"You really think that this is a portrait of the killer, Jake?" Hauser asked from the doorway.

Jake shrugged. "I don't know. Maybe it's another dead end. But Dad went through a lot of trouble – a lot of mental gymnastics – to do this. And I can't believe it was simply the artist in him talking. He was trying to tell me *something*. With that portrait he arranged in the carpets, with the painting he did in his own blood, with the Chuck Close he chopped the eyes out of. They were all messages – hints – that I had to look at things from a different perspective. From *his* perspective."

"Your dad gave you a lot of credit," Hauser said slowly.

Jake hadn't thought about it in those terms but when Hauser laid it out like that, he realized that the man was right; this was not the kind of Easter-egg hunt that most people would be able to follow. The old man *had* put a lot of trust into him.

He sat watching the status bar, feeling like time was running in reverse. Then it hit 3 percent ... 3.5 percent.

The only noise was the rage of the storm outside, now at its zenith, and Hauser was waiting for the eye to pass over, giving them a few hours of much-needed time to recharge their batteries. Then the weather would descend back into biblical tragedy and Act II would rip over Long Island, tying up loose ends, finishing any manmade buildings that had had the audacity to remain standing. If they were lucky, they'd all be here when this was over.

But the word *lucky* was slowly being purged from Hauser's lexicon. He had seen a string of bad luck before – the time his knee had been crushed on the football field had been a study in the butterfly effect gone wrong – but this thing with Jake and the Bloodman had crossed bad luck the moment his mother had been killed all those years ago. As far as the sheriff was concerned, this was more of a curse.

And he knew that curses have a way of finishing things off on their own terms.

71

Frank and Jake headed east on 27, toward the point, sticking to the empty oncoming lane because it was farther from the shore, if only by a few feet. Off to their right the ocean was boiling up fifty-foot swells that slammed into the beach and snow-plowed the hundred yards to the highway where they detonated against the embankment, launching tons of water into the air. A three-foot surge pulsed over the asphalt, and Frank held the wheel to the right to keep the heavy truck out of the ditch. Every now and then the wash would lift the Hummer just a little, drifting it sideways; Frank would wrench the wheel and hit the gas, hollering for more purchase. So far this had happened three times in four miles and both of them knew that if they kept at this long enough, the law of diminishing returns guaranteed that they'd get washed off the highway. But maybe – just maybe – with the storm past its worst, they'd make it. So they kept going. For Jeremy and Kay and for the simple reason that there was nothing else they *could* do. It was that old Destiny thing again.

The bottom foot of the truck was filled with water – a design detail that ensured the Hummer didn't lose traction in flash floods or swampy conditions. Jake's feet had been wet for hours now and he wondered if they'd ever be dry again.

Hauser had asked them to remain at the station but Jake had insisted on leaving. He knew that the chances of the highway still existing were as slim as the house still standing but something told him that he had to go there. At least he'd be findable at the beach house. Not that that had made much of a difference up until this point. Still, it was all he could think to do.

The Old Testament wall of water that shot up over the road made Jake understand how primitive man had seen storms as God's wrath. A thick blanket of seawater hit the rock-strewn ditch beside the road, shot straight up in the air, and came down into the pavement with a muffled smack. Frank steered into the surge and the tires managed to stay connected to the road; a smaller vehicle would have been washed off the highway and it was only Hauser's call that had got them past the roadblock that cut off access to the tip of Long Island.

Frank negotiated the truck over enough debris to build a small city. It looked like ground zero for a nuclear test; at least a dozen homes were sprawled across the asphalt like smashed shoe boxes. Everything from crushed lampshades to a thirty-foot section of cedar deck blew across the road and Frank kept petting the dashboard and telling the truck she was a good girl. And when that didn't work, he called her other things.

Jake worked on a cigarette and decided that when this was all over he was going to crawl into a bottle until he stopped knowing who he was. He had had enough. And without Kay and Jeremy, none of it mattered anyway.

Jake felt they were moving at the speed of plate tectonics but when he looked outside at the black world illuminated by the bright glow of the LEDs and found a landmark, he realized that they were actually making good progress. At this clip they'd be back at the beach house in another ten minutes.

Then the real waiting would begin.

Jake put the data through his head, crunched the numbers, and he knew he was missing something – something that would make sense of why things had happened the way they had.

"I want to know why," he said out loud, not meaning to.

"What?" Frank steered the Hummer around a twenty-five-foot cabin cruiser lying on its side in the wash, each slam of the waves coming in off the Atlantic nudging it a little further toward the opposite side of the road.

A wave reached out of the dark and rose up beside the truck like the wall of a cliff. Jake flinched as it came down and Frank steered into it. The front of the truck bucked as it took the impact, then bounced back up. Frank hammered down on the gas to gain a little more purchase and the truck miraculously stayed on the road.

When he caught his breath, Jake said, "This guy took my mother. Now he's taken everything else. Why?"

"The same guy? After all this time? He'd be old – I mean, she was killed thirty-three years ago." Frank's cigarette glowed orange as he sucked on it. "Christ, where did the time go? I remember the day she was killed like it was yesterday. Your father had a big show in New York and he had nailed it. Sold out. He wanted to stay in town and get ripped and talk with his painter buddies and his good-time party friends. Your mom wanted to get back here to you. She worried about you, you know."

A small smile creased the corners of Jake's mouth.

"She left the city. I put her in her car and we drove back together. We ran out of smokes but she didn't even want to stop at the Kwik Mart because she wanted to check on you. Wouldn't even drive me down my street, I had to get off at the corner and walk." Frank smiled.

"It sounds like you miss her, too, Frank."

Frank nodded and smoke came out of his nose and teeth. "I do, Jakey. You know, I never told anyone this, but I envied him Mia. He thought I was in love with her but that wasn't it. Your mother was just something special. Whoever took her from your old man effectively killed him, too."

"Why didn't you ever get married?"

Frank laughed. "Isn't it obvious? I'm not exactly what you'd call husband material."

"Neither was my father."

Frank nodded and stubbed his cigarette out on the metal dashboard. "You got me there. But your dad didn't find a typical woman – he found Mia. You know how many women can live with guys like us?" he asked, his thumb twitching back and forth, indicating Jake and himself.

"Guys like us?" Then he thought of Kay, and realized that the old man was right.

"Come on, Jakey. Me? I spent half my life on safari or in the mountains, hunting down just about everything that runs, walks, or crawls on the planet. Even now, I fuck off into the mountains for three-week stretches. You think that your average woman wants a man who does that? As much as they talk about being liberated, as much as they talk about wanting an equal share, I have yet to find a woman who lets me be *me*. And you?" He laughed, but it was a kind, loving laugh. "You're the same. I don't care who your genetic parents were, you're a Coleridge. Only you hunt *people* for fun."

"I don't do this for fun, Frank."

"I'm not big on advice, Jakey, but you get into trouble when you start believing your own bullshit." Frank's voice nearly disappeared in the noisy cab. "I watched you today – you *like* what you do."

Jake shook his head. "You're wrong. I'm quitting. I made up my mind. This case and one more to tie up. At least I was."

Frank nodded. "Sure. And one more, then one more, then one more. Always one more. It's like a bad relationship that you can't get out of. Because we love the things that destroy us, Jakey. In that destruction we feel alive."

They reached Sumter Point and Frank swung into the driveway. In the bright lights of the truck the house looked like it had been abandoned for years. Most of the flashing was torn away, chunks of the roof were gone. The shrubs had been washed away along with the gravel drive – now just a muddy track. Behind the house, close to the ocean, the studio was leaning back, toward the sea, as if it had lost its grip on the earth and was thinking about diving into the ocean.

Jake knew that the Bloodman was going to come here. He had to – there was no one left now but him and Frank. He thought about telling the old man about his plan, about what they were doing here. But Frank wouldn't like it. Not one little bit. Because no one – not even a tough old sonofabitch like Frank Coleridge – liked to be used as bait.

"Home sweet home," Jake said.

72

Hauser had swallowed so much coffee in the past two days that he figured it would take a week to leach from his system. He hadn't looked in the mirror in some time but the taste in his mouth suggested that even his teeth were brown. He walked down the hall, his left hand holding a mug, his right resting on the hilt of his great-granddad's trench knife, taking a lull in the action to survey the station.

It was still on the move but the directed frenzy of a few hours ago had given way to an exhausted hum. Most of the officers were on their fourth set of dry clothes and Hauser saw a few nonissue T-shirts and boots among his people. He watched the dulled movements and the thousand-yard stares – good people who had spent the last sixteen hours at the business end of the storm, helping a citizenry who should have listened to them and evacuated.

He had wanted to put all his attention and resources into the homicides that were multiplying as fast as cells dividing but truth be told, he had limited resources. Of course, come tomorrow morning, the National Guard would roll in and he'd be able to put his men where he thought they'd be the most effective. But he doubted they'd be much good in hunting down this murderer – for that he'd need people who had experience with this kind of thing coupled with a personality that rested somewhere beneath the frost layer of human emotions. In short, he needed a cold analytical man like Jake Cole. Crazy fucking Jake, ripping around town in a tan Humvee hunting down sinners. Jesus, how could a life get so fucked up? he wondered. Then he realized that he was part of the same caravan. Well, *almost* the same caravan.

Hauser had passed most of the night out in the hurricane, where the physical world had been thrown around. He was no stranger to what Mother Nature could do – being the sheriff of a seaside community came with its own broad set of experiences – but he had never imagined that Long Island itself could feel like it was being filed off the bedrock. Tonight, when he had been out there in the worst of it, he had been humbled, frightened even.

A good chunk of the town had been taken apart – he couldn't begin to estimate how many houses had been ripped out of the ground by the wind or pushed off their foundations by the mountainous swells that had come down like God's own hand. Roofs were gone. Cars totaled. Land swept away in great mouthfuls. And this was only the first round.

In another few hours, the first part of Dylan would be finished, and they would find respite in the eye of the hurricane. But for how long? An hour? Two? Then it would start up again and finish whatever business it had left undone, whatever damage it still felt like doling out.

Hauser had spent half the night saving people from their own stupidity; why couldn't they have listened? He felt sure that he had done his due diligence, that he had made an effort to get his citizens to abandon their … their… what? Crap, was what it amounted to. Sure, some of it cost a lot of money, but it was all just stuff. Stuff could be replaced. Or done without. But Hauser knew they wouldn't be selling lives down at the Montauk Hardware store come Monday morning.

As much as he tried to focus on the storm, to believe that it was the worst thing to ever hit his community, images of the Bloodman's work kept coming back to him. Compared to this guy, Dylan was a minor inconvenience – and when you called the hand of God a minor inconvenience, you had some serious shit on your doorstep.

Wohl came running up to him, a pink phone-sheet in his hand. "Sheriff, window on Myrtle Avenue blew in, blinded a lady. Her seven-year-old called it in. EMT's dealing with two heart attacks and a guy who lost his leg so all three units are out. Want me to take it?"

Hauser shook his head; Wohl had good organizational skills and he was needed at the station to keep the calls prioritized. "Send Scopes."

Wohl shook his head. "Scopes is out on a call. He shoulda been back half an hour ago but he ain't." The look in Wohl's eyes was hopeful – he wanted to do some hands-on in the community, not spend the night safely inside eating egg-salad sandwiches and fielding messages.

"Spencer?"

Wohl shrugged. "Spencer's out, too."

Hauser's mouth turned down. "Shit." He took a sip of coffee, then put the mug into Wohl's hands. "Give me the address," he said, and went to get his poncho. Better to deal with God than the Devil any time, he figured.

73

Jake held the door and Frank rushed inside. As he swung by, Jake saw that the past few hours had taken their toll on the man. He was a tough old bastard, but the night had chipped a lot of him away and the years showed through the fissures. Jake closed the door.

Frank shook himself off and stopped at the Nakashima console. Sitting on top, looking a little like Sputnik, was the wireframe sphere that Jacob had welded all those years ago. Jake stared at it, seeing it with new eyes, new history. Frank did, too.

They walked into the house and it was like the driveway; what had been a neglected filthy place was now taken over by the storm. The big front windows had caved in and the floor was a swamp of sand and water and glass. Outside, the pool was canted down, toward the ocean, the ground holding it up chewed away by the waves that had battered it for hours. It was obvious that physics would eventually beat out determination and it would fall into the water – it was only a matter of time.

Jake flipped a few light switches but of course there was no power. It was in that hang time between expecting power and not getting it that his mind did that magical thing that no one understood and all of the pieces fell into place. Not iffy tentative places, but form-fitted and sure.

He put his pistol to Frank's head. "Where's my family?" he asked calmly.

74

It was as if Wohl had grown extra hands over the life of the storm; for most of the night he had at least five calls going at any particular moment and scribbled down messages faster than he thought possible. The landlines had taken quite a beating but were somehow still going. The cell phone towers had been fried hours ago – failing one after another as the storm rolled in, lightning from the Book of Revelation firing down. He had passed the night inside, with the windows boarded up, but every now and then the world outside would light up white-hot and the cracks around the shutters and paneling would shine sunlight for a second, then blink out. The power grid had been taken out with one monster motherfucking whump that had pretty much fried anything connected to it, including residential appliances. But somehow, magically, the phone lines were golden. When this hurricane was over, Wohl was going to invest in some Bell Atlantic stock – and the cell phone folks could go suck his love pole; he was going analog after this.

He hung up one line and another blinked to life. "Sheriff's" – the full greeting had been abandoned hours ago.

"This is Matthew Carradine, Field Operations Manager, FBI. Is Sheriff Hauser in the building?"

"Who did you say you were?" Wohl asked.

"Jake Cole's boss. Can you tell me if Sheriff Hauser is available?" There was urgency in his voice.

The world outside overloaded again and the cracks flashed white. "Hauser's out. I can try to bring him up on the radio but with the lightning nothing's working. We're lucky we still have phones."

"Who's next in charge?"

Wohl looked around the station and all he saw were junior officers. Scopes and Spencer were still gone. "I guess I am," he said.

"Then you better listen to me."

75

Frank was secured to one of the kitchen stools, ankles duct-taped to the legs, waist fastened with a length of curtain cord, hands cuffed behind his back. Frank didn't struggle, wasn't angry or shocked – he simply sat in grim silence, staring at Jake.

"Where's my wife? My son?" Jake asked, yelling to be heard above what was left of the storm.

"You're the guy who thinks like a murderer, Jake. *You* do the math."

Jake leveled his pistol at Frank's face. "I'm not going to kill you, Frank, but I am going to make you beg me to."

Frank shook his head sadly. "Jake, this is me – Frank. The guy who's been here for you whenever you asked. Like I am now. You're distraught, Jakey."

"Do I look distraught?" His voice was even, calm, and his eyes had reverted to those two black spots that looked like they were on loan from a snake. "I passed distraught when my son went missing, Frank. By the time you took Kay, I was well into angry. When I found the top of Emily Mitchell's head sitting on the newel post in her entryway, I entered murderous. And I think you know me enough to understand that I can be dangerous – but I will do this as my last act as a compassionate human being: if you tell me where my wife and son are – even if they are dead – I will shoot you in the heart. It will be quick." Jake leaned forward, his hands on his knees, the pistol gleaming bright in the weird dark. "But if you don't, Frank – if you fuck around and try to plead the fifth and try to step by this, I am going to take that Ka-Bar –" he jerked his head at Frank's big knife, sticking out of the top of a table a few feet away beside the box of spray-foam insulation and caulking the handyman had left behind – "and I am going to drive it into your eardrum. Just one, because I need you to hear me on the other side while I ask you questions and pry parts of your body off. I have learned from the masters, and it is going to hurt." He stood up and backed away a little. Outside, the rain was still coming in and he stopped at the edge of its spray. "You won't believe the toolbox of torture I have in my head." He tapped his temple with the pistol.

Frank's eyes were now frightened. "Jakey, Jakey, it's me. Okay? Why would I want to hurt you or your family?"

"It wasn't me, Frank. I thought it was, but it wasn't. I didn't figure it out until a few minutes ago and I should have. You were in love with my mother, Frank."

Frank nodded. "Sure I loved your mother, Jakey. Sure I was a little jealous of your old man. So what? Everybody's jealous of something."

"Where is my wife? Where is my son?"

Frank shuddered in the chair, testing the restraints. "That's your territory, Jake. You know all this shit better than any of us – you're the guy who speaks the language, who reads the signs, who understands the dead. Aren't they talking to you?"

"Are they dead, Frank?"

Frank shrugged. "Would we be having this conversation if they weren't?"

There was a crash and the screech of wind as the front door erupted and for a second Jake thought the wind had forced it open. Then it closed and a voice called, "Jake, you here?"

Jake went to the entry. Spencer stood there, beside the welded-steel polyhedron. He was soaked through and had a flashlight in his hand. "What the fuck are you doing here, Jake?" he asked.

"Waiting. You?"

"I wanted to make sure you were all right, that you got the tape out, that the storm didn't take this place away."

"I'm busy, Bil—"

The front door kicked in with a massive gust of wind that tore a painting off its hook by the door. There was a bright burst of light as a billion volts rattled out of the sky and hit the Hummer in the driveway. The house rocked on its foundation.

Jake's CRT-D shorted and he grabbed his chest. He felt his heart stop and he went to his knees.

Spencer lunged, caught Jake before he hit the ground.

Jake wanted to tell him to leave Frank in the chair.

Maybe even to run.

All he managed was a dry croak.

Then passed out.

76

To Hauser, Southampton looked like a junkyard. He hadn't realized that there was this much plastic lawn furniture in the world. He was finished with the call on Myrtle Avenue – had taken the woman and her little girl to the ER. They had rushed her in and the doctor said that her vision would probably bounce back – most of the blindness had been from blood in her eyes. *Score one for the good guys*, Hauser thought as he headed back to the station.

He swerved the Bronco around a sailboat jammed into an intersection, sails snapping like cannon fire, when the walkie-talkie on the dash bracket flared to life.

"Unit twenty-two, Emergency. Please respond." Twenty-two had been Hauser's number during his four-game career with the Steelers. The voice was garbled by the storm, but discernible.

Hauser picked up the unit and keyed the mic. "Yeah, Wohl. Hauser here."

"Sheriff," the voice crackled. "… need … ou …back here … gency." Even in the static, Hauser could hear that there was something wrong.

"On my way," he said as the brush guard on the front of the Bronco took out a lawn umbrella that skittered across the road.

Why the hell would they need me at the station? he wondered. If there was an emergency, Wohl should have told him where it was and sent him on his way.

What was going on?

77

The first thing to hit him was the silence. The blare of the storm had gone and all he could hear was a soft wind and the distant sound of waves breaking somewhere nearby. A few seconds later his sense of touch returned. And with it the realization that he was lying in a puddle of water and shivering.

He opened his eyes to black and wondered if his pacemaker had survived the surge – his fingers were still tingly and the unmistakable stench of fried circuits accompanied the dull ache in the middle of his chest. Without moving any of his other muscles he blinked a few times and realized that there was something in front of his face. The shape clarified into the sole of a shoe. No, not shoe – boot. Heavy-treaded. Size thirteen. He pushed himself up onto his elbows and he saw that the boot was on a foot. Attached to a leg. He pushed himself higher, fought to his knees. And saw that the leg belonged to Spencer.

Jake tried to stand up and slipped on the stone floor of the entryway. Then he saw that he hadn't been lying in a puddle of water at all.

Spencer's throat had been cut, one neat slightly diagonal line that angled up from his right clavicle to just below the lobe of his left ear. The cut was deep and Jake had seen enough knife wounds to know that it had been done in one quick slash with a very sharp blade; the academic in him noted that it was a right-handed attack, blade facing up. The weapon? Easy-peasy – Frank's Ka-Bar was sticking out of Spencer's chest, sunk up to the handle just slightly left of center – a perfect kill. Jake wiped his hands on his pants, sticky with the already coagulating blood, and knew that he had been unconscious for a while. How long? An hour? Two?

Spencer's arterial spray had pissed on the wall in a wide, graceful arc that had hit two paintings and the Nakashima console where the stainless sphere sat.

Then Jake remembered Frank.

He ran to the living room because of course, Frank was gone. Spencer had untied him and Frank had cut his throat. Why hadn't he killed Jake? Why hadn't—

Jake's flowchart froze.

Frank was still in the chair.

Opaque yellow foam mushroomed from his nostrils and burst from his mouth like the thick roots of a cancerous tree. Beside him, on the floor, lay a can of spray insulation, the handy dispensing straw covered with blood from being forced into Frank's nose. The thrust of the expanding foam had distorted his head, twisted his sinuses apart, pushed his eyes out, and his jaw hung wide like a python trying to swallow a dachshund. Frank's neck and throat were distended – puffed out from the expanding death that had choked off his air, clung to his throat and nasal cavity like glue. His skin was white, highlighted with blue veins that shone through like circuit wiring.

The foam was still expanding and it popped and ticked like a cooling car engine as it continued to push his skull apart by degrees.

Jake looked out at the beach. It was still night but the winds and rain and hell of before were on leave as the eye passed overhead. The sky was clear and the bright orb of the moon hung over the water like a camera lens. Stars twinkled. The waves lapped at the shore in a steady rhythm. The beach looked like a barricade had been thrown up to keep the water at bay; everything from fifty-foot trees to upside down boats were woven together in a line of garbage that stretched down the coast as far as he could see.

Jake turned back to Frank. The expanding foam had filled his lungs, stomach, and esophagus, forcing his body tall and straight in the chair, an unnatural position for the dead.

And a sudden sickening realization lit up in his skull – he had been wrong. Wrong about Frank. Wrong about the clues his father had left. Wrong in his interpretation of his father's fears. Most importantly, wrong about the man who had been doing this. Wrong about everything.

He thought about his father's Sistine Chapel at the edge of the property, decorated not with an image of God infusing Adam with life, but tattooed with demons – men of blood – put there to give the Coleridge boy a message – a message he had missed. Jake instinctively turned, tried to focus on the building at the edge of the grass. The concrete slab where it used to sit was still there but the building itself was gone.

Jake heard the front door open.

Close.

Footsteps.

Pause (at Spencer's body).

More footsteps.

Then the beam of a flashlight swung through the doorway, crept over the room, and stopped on Jake.

"Hello, Special Agent Cole," a voice said from behind the light.

78

Jacob Coleridge woke up in the recovery room, alone; the nurse assigned to him had left to answer a call in surgical ICU, two doors down the hall. Jacob, of course, had no way of knowing this – he just knew that he was alone.

He was not restrained and other than the sharp thud of a mouthful of fishhooks he felt relatively level-headed and strong. He sat up. Beside the IV plugged into his arm he had a tube feeding oxygen down into his lungs through his nostrils. He was lucid enough to realize that this was probably because his mouth was wadded up with cotton and sutures. He had no idea why.

Jacob shimmied down to the end of the bed, managed to get a skinny naked leg between the side rail and the footboard, and pushed the release with his toe. The side rail clunked noisily down and he swung his other leg over the side and stepped onto the cold linoleum.

With one of the batons that did duty as his hands he managed to paw off one side of the tube feeding him oxygen, then he backed up and the tube sluiced out of his nostril with a wet pop. He turned and walked away from his bed and the elastic IV hose stretched, the needle pulled out of his arm with a zing and flew back, flecking the sheets with a spit of blood. There was nothing clandestine or furtive about his movements, he was simply a man with someplace to go, a mission to accomplish.

He shuffled out into the empty hallway, dim and dark and still, found the door to the emergency stairwell, and pushed it open.

The Southampton Hospital, built with hurricanes and storm surges in mind, was designed to be evacuated not merely through the ground floor, but also through the roof – all government buildings built near the ocean have this feature. But Jacob was not following this knowledge, he was just following his logic, and his logic was telling him to climb. So he began.

He made it to the top of the stairwell in a little over two minutes. He stood, breath whistling through his nostrils, the lump of cotton and stitches in his mouth feeling like a sour cactus, until he caught his breath. Then he put his weight against the door.

The alarm for this door was hardwired to sirens and as soon as he pushed on the panic bar, the gloom began to howl.

The storm was on temporary hiatus but the wind up here almost knocked the old man down and he stumbled over the backwash threshold and into the water that had built up. Rain was flushing off the roof in great torrents through the downspouts but the old painter had a foot to wade through and the sharp gravel sliced the soles of his feet.

He thought about his son, about how he had driven the boy away. It had been the only thing to do. And now, clambering through the shin-high water on the roof, he wondered if he had saved the boy at all. He was back here in harm's way and it hit Jacob that all he had done was prolong the consequences for both of them. A deep thud of despair welled up in his chest as he realized that none of it mattered. Not anymore. The damage had been done.

At least it had been spectacular damage.

David Finch had once told him to *Go big or go home* and in his fractured and terrified mind, Jacob Coleridge felt pride that he had carried that philosophy through to the end.

Even in the lull of the eye, the wind ripped at him, chewed at his robe like an angry dog. He raised his arms and it was gone, pulled off into the night by the hands of the storm. He stumbled on, naked.

Jacob moved cautiously, the good part of his mind knowing that if he fell he would not get up. His feet were bleeding badly and he could feel the warmth seeping from his body.

He was ten feet from the edge of the roof when he heard the door clang open behind him. Flashlight beams shot around. Locked on him. Shouts. He saw his shadow stretch out before him, to the edge of the building, off into the empty darkness beyond.

More shouting.

His name.

He didn't look back.

Didn't stop.

His shadow danced. Footsteps sloshed behind. Voices implored him to stop.

Couldn't they see that he had no choice? That this was what had to be done?

He never doubted his mission, never doubted the reason for this; he knew this was the only way to get away from what was coming. He had lived in fear for too long. No one could save him. Not even Jake. Not anymore.

His progress took all of his strength, all of his concentration, but his mind allowed him one brief image, a picture of Mia sitting on the deck of the sailboat all those years ago. Young, beautiful, when life had been full of potential.

He reached the edge of the roof.

Lifted one bloody foot from the water.

And stepped out into the sky.

79

Jake moved away from Frank's corpse with slow but fluid movements, as if his bones were not connected to one another. "You want to tell me what's going on?" he asked.

Hauser stepped down into the sunken living room. "I thought that's what you did, Mr. Witch-doctor. Figure shit out." He said it softly, almost kindly, but there was something else, something angry, behind the words. He had his pistol in his hand.

"Where is my wife? My child?"

Hauser moved against the fireplace. The remaining curtains danced like ghosts, tattered and torn. The sheriff looked over at Frank's misshapen head, disconnected jaw. "I ask the questions, Jake," he said, bringing up the Sig, and that's when Jake saw the big trench knife hanging off his belt – a killer's knife, not a cop's.

Jake now understood that part of him, the part that knew this was all going to be over relatively soon, had stopped caring. He also realized that back there, in the static of disbelief over how this had unfolded, Kay and Jeremy's voices had stopped. Along with this came a great weariness. He nodded at the kitchen. "I need a drink." It was a statement, not a request. He had stopped asking anyone for permission when he had walked out of this place all those years ago and he wasn't going to start now, not even when he was staring down a nine-millimeter Parabellum.

There was a foot of sand in the kitchen and he had to wrench the door to the cupboard under the sink open. He pulled out a bottle of scotch that had been hiding at the back and poured two fingers into a teacup. His head was buzzing like a shorted bulb and he heard the harsh chirp of electrical circuits simmering. He knew that after the blue-white jolt his heart had taken, he'd need a few minutes to get his think box back on line. Spencer was dead. Frank was dead. While he had been out on the floor, some-one had killed them both. No, not *someone* – the man his father had been terrified of. Jeremy's man in the floor – Bud man. His father's faceless portrait. The killer. The Bloodman. All of them. "You want a drink?" he asked Hauser.

Hauser nodded wearily, and came forward, the pistol still up. "Why not?"

"You're on duty," Jake said, and poured one for Hauser.

"And you're a recovering alcoholic."

"Just a drunk between drinks." He slid the cup across the counter, then raised his own in a toast. He looked at Frank, dead in the chair over Hauser's shoulder like the lighthouse behind Rachael Macready in that goddamned photograph in the house of the dead. His eyes filled with clear, bright tears.

All he could wonder was, *Why?*

He downed the booze and the fire was sweet and familiar. He closed his eyes, took in the heat and the beauty of the flames in his stomach. How long had it been since he had had a drink? But he knew, down to the minute if he really wanted to think about it – a gift from his perfect memory. Except for those four months he had never been able to buy back – those were gone for good.

He opened his eyes and Hauser was still standing there with that unhappy look welded onto his skull, eyes distant, mouth turned down. He looked like the stickers that Kay put on the chemicals under the sink so Jeremy wouldn't pour himself an afternoon cocktail of bleach and stainless-steel cleaner.

Kay. Jeremy. Where were they?

The living room was full of sand and debris. The portrait of the man in the floor was gone, covered over. Jake swiveled his line of sight to the pool. The storm had emptied the algae and lily pads and the foundation had all but been swept out to sea. It still hung off the deck, tilted into the ocean, the waterline at odds with the angle of the rim. The water was a dirty brown now. Murky. Lifeless.

And he remembered what Frank had said. *You're the guy who thinks like a murderer. You do the math.*

And his head lit up like the lightning that had been coming down all night. He knew where the bastard had put them. Somewhere no one would check, not even the cops when they had combed the property. Someplace so fucking close no one would think of looking there.

Jake came out from behind the counter. Fast.

Hauser flinched but Jake was so fast he was past the sheriff before he understood what was happening.

Jake barreled by, jumped through one of the blown-out windows, and dove into the pool.

The underwater world tasted of salt and mud, not chlorine. Jake kicked for the bottom and felt his hand sink into the muck and garbage that had settled after the storm. He palmed through the silt and his fingers brushed aside pebbles and stones and empty beer cans and scotch bottles.

His pulse throbbed in his ears. He slid his hands back and forth over the bottom, searching the debris. The air in his lungs tried to pull him to the surface, back to the world, but he kicked to keep himself down. He felt a hubcap, a broken plate, more empty cans and bottles. Then the rough form of a cinder block. And below it, something soft and rubbery that could only be skin.

Jake ran his hands over it and it rippled, coiled back onto his knuckles like it wanted to touch him, to let him know that it knew he was there. His index finger slid into a slimy depression – like Braille, it was familiar to his touch – a small, perfect belly button. And beneath that he felt the crescent-shaped ridges created by a single-edged knife. Beneath that, the rough concrete bottom of the pool.

A human skin. Weighed down with a cinder block.

Jake screamed and lost the air from his lungs in one violent roar. He breathed in, sucked in silt and saltwater and despair. Vomited under the water. Instinctively pushed for the surface.

Broke through.

Screamed a long, horror-wracked vowel. Then dove back into the muck.

He found the cinder block, lifted it up, and wrapped his fingers around the oily skin below.

Foraged on the bottom.

Found a second cinder block.

And a second skin.

He wrenched it free, pushed for the surface, and came up in the shallow end.

They were as thick and as heavy as lead-shielded X-ray bibs. Jake stood there, his heart pounding against his ribs, unwilling to look down.

What was left of Kay in one hand.

What was left of Jeremy in the other.

Hauser stood on the deck above him, his mouth still turned down at the corners in such a way that it looked like his face had taken on a permanent set. He turned on his Maglite, flashed it on Jake. On the things in Jake's hands. Then snapped it off.

Jake went to the steps, stumbled up, and collapsed on the deck.

Kay's skin unrolled with a meaty slap. Her eyeless, toothless, lifeless face pointed up into the sky and Jake saw that a knife had opened her mouth from ear to ear. The pool had scrubbed her clean and every bruise, every laceration, leered up at him in madness.

"No," he said so softly that it may not have been spoken aloud at all.

Jake turned to the skin that had covered his son. It was ragged around the edges and scrubbed clean from its time in the pool. There were no ears.

Hauser came over but kept the light off. "Inside, Jake." The pistol hung loosely in his hand, glimmering like a prosthetic attachment.

Jake picked what was left of his little boy up, and something about it felt sickening. He got an arm under Kay's torso, and her tattoo of the crossed pistols flashed in front of his eyes. *Tough Love.*

He looked down at her torn, chopped-up hands. *Love. Hate.*

Back at the pistols.

Tough Love, with a jagged line through it.

He remembered the T-shirt she had just purchased with *Don't Hassel The Hoff!* across the front.

All that was left – slogans.

Jake picked up his family and they sluiced around his thighs, caressing him with long tendrils of skin. Kay's hair made a rasping noise against his jeans.

He brought them to the living room, laid them out at Uncle Frank's feet, and sat down on the floor. For a second he just stared.

"Are you here to kill me?" he asked without lifting his eyes from the horror on the floor.

Hauser took a step forward and lifted the pistol. "I guess you've figured it out by now."

80

Scopes slalomed through the debris that littered 27, lights flashing, siren blaring. The world around him looked like the old black-and-white footage of Hiroshima he had seen on the History Channel. But without the frame to hold it in, to cut it down, it was so much larger than anything he could imagine by orders of magnitude. He felt like he was driving through a madman's dream. Everywhere he looked – for as far as he could see – the world had been kicked apart.

This was the eye of the storm. There was still more to come. Looking around, he wondered why it would even bother coming back? What was left to take?

As of nine minutes ago when he had left the station, the death toll was at fourteen. Of course they would probably find more bodies. Buried in the debris. Hanging in trees. Washed up on the beach. And then there'd be the bodies they would never find. The ones that the storm had dragged out to sea to be swallowed by the Atlantic.

While the other officers back at the station regrouped – catching up on sleep and writing out their wills – Scopes headed to Jacob Coleridge's beach house. He wanted to talk to Special Agent Jake Cole about a few things. He wanted a little perspective on what was happening. And maybe to hand back a little perspective.

Scopes was not a naturally inquisitive man, but the chewing-out Cole had handed him had been rattling around in his head the past two days and it got him thinking. Thinking about the six murders. About the disappearance of Cole's wife and son. About the way Hauser was handling the investigation. What Scopes realized no one had clued in to was that this had to be coming from somewhere inside – somewhere close. But close was a matter of perspective, wasn't it?

Scopes had been on the job for four years, which translated into more than a few shifts hosing chunks of bone and brain off the side of the road after some summer asshole had loaded up on too many Bombay Sapphires and missed a turn on the way back to the beach house; four years of dealing with hysteric widows after their husbands painted the ceiling with gray matter because their stockbroker had pissed their fortune into the pocket of some corrupt CEO; four years of responding to domestic calls where he had to read the Miranda rights to some crying drunk who had just finished his wife off with a tire iron because she had bought the wrong kind of beer. So Scopes was no stranger to punishment and he had always been able to hold his cookies.

But Jake Cole had a tolerance that couldn't be measured in human terms. At least up until now. Scopes wondered how the Iron Man was holding up now that his family had gone up in a puff of smoke. He had seen him at the station last night, doing his dead man's walk, trying to act like he was still alive when his guts had to be on fire. Scopes wondered how that felt for him.

He didn't find any pleasure in these thoughts, but as he threaded his way through the obstacle course that used to be the town he had grown up in, he needed to occupy his mind with something. And Jake Cole and his missing family were a helluva lot more interesting than some fucking storm. He couldn't do anything about Dylan. But Cole? That was something else entirely.

81

Hauser sat down on the edge of the hearth and rested the hand with the Sig on his knee. He watched Jake for a few minutes. "Wohl got a call from Carradine – you were right to send your mother's Benz to the lab."

Jake looked up at Hauser, his bloodshot eyes filled with tears. "What are you talking about?"

Hauser smiled and shook his head. "This is over, Jake. It stops with you and me." He raised his eyes to the beach out beyond the windows. "The lab found two prints on your mother's car. Index and middle finger of a left hand. Under the armrest on the console. Fingerprints in your mother's blood. They had been wiped off but one of your magicians was able to raise them. Modern science – it's a hoot, isn't it?"

Jake felt his stomach tighten on its axis and the room suddenly felt a thousand times too small. Then his guts clenched and he bent over and vomited on the floor, beside his wife's skin. He retched until he was burping up nothing in convulsive spasms.

"You want to know why the recent murders are so polished in comparison?" Hauser's eyes slid back onto Jake. "You've evolved."

82

He got Lewis for his eleventh birthday. His father had bought the ugly dog because it was a gift that required little imagination and even less common sense. Jake had tried to like it – actually sat staring at the stupid awkward thing and *willing* himself to like it – but it was another in a long line of lost causes.

The part that infuriated him the most was how stupid it was. Tell it to sit, and it just stared at Jake as if he had asked it to tell him his telephone number. Shake or high-five was akin to a grammar question. Lie down or roll over was like asking that fucking dog to solve the Riddle of the Sphinx. The dog became neglected very quickly.

Then one evening Jake saw a dog play dead on the *Dick Van Dyke Show* – one of those boring old black-and-white programs that his mother made him watch because she thought humor was good for him. He saw the trick – performed with a German shepherd no less – and he became determined to teach it to Lewis.

By the fifth minute he realized that wonder dog was not going to be playing dead anytime soon. The only thing this dog was good for was smelling bad and pooping.

"Play dead!" the boy snapped, pointing at the ground.

Lewis stood there, eyes vacant, tongue lolling out of his mouth, actually looking like he had a smile on his face.

"I said play dead!"

Lewis took a step forward and got Jake in the mouth with a hot wet tongue.

And that did it. Jake stormed into the kitchen and ripped open the cutlery drawer. He found the big knife – the one his mother used to cut up chicken when she made that greasy slop called *coq-au-vin*. Jake pulled it out of the drawer, pounded back to the dog, and raised the knife above his head.

"PLAY DEAD!" he screamed at the dog.

Lewis's ears snapped back and he winced. He knew the boy, knew how he became when his voice changed, and he backed up.

Jake charged the dog, grabbed it by the ear, and opened its throat in a wide swipe of the knife.

The dog made half of a high-pitched squeal, backed up a single step, and collapsed to the deck. Blood pumped out in a rhythmic arc that shrank with each pulse of his dying heart and his legs cycled in a run because his body did not yet understand that it was dead. He looked up at Jake with his big brown eyes.

The boy bent over the dog and spit on it. "THAT'S HOW YOU PLAY DEAD!" he screamed and went back into the house, closing and locking the door.

Of course, his mother knew. She had always known about him. Known how he was. Who he was. But Jacob wouldn't listen. *He's had a tough start. Give him time. Give him a chance. Give. Give. Give.*

His father had ordered her to take Jake out for breakfast, maybe to a movie. And the whole time she had just stared at him, as if examining an insect under a lens, her mouth a hard line, her eyes just a little too narrow. He had eaten a spectacular breakfast with a hearty appetite and when he had asked for more pancakes because they were his favorite, she had run from the table and he heard her sobbing in the restaurant's bathroom.

After that morning she had always been afraid of him. And his parents' marriage began to fall apart; it looked like eventually his father would have to make a choice between him and his mother. He had been on the boy's side up until now, sticking up for him, trying to get her to give him a chance.

But it didn't take a scientist to figure out that he had burned all of his chances with her – every last one.

As his father began the difficult process of choosing sides, Jake felt the gap begin to widen.

So he decided to improve his odds.

83

Jake was very still, his mind's eye peering over one of the memory fences slapped up haphazardly between the different parts of himself. The images on the other side were spotlighted like exhibits in a museum – grotesque studies of a self he saw but did not recognize.

He drew the back of his hand across his mouth and it tasted of saltwater, tears, scotch, and vomit. Jake began to protest, to offer some kind of denial, but at that particular instant he saw something out of the corner of his eye, a glimmer on the staircase. He turned his head.

Jeremy sat on the bottom step, wearing the little hat with the dolphin embroidered on it. His son was smiling, hugging Elmo to his chest. He looked so happy. So alive. *So real.*

Jeremy lifted his little fist, opened and closed it in his own special version of a wave, then brought it back to Elmo. He flickered a little, like a distant television signal.

Tears filled Jake's eyes. He blinked and they fell away. When he opened them again, Jeremy was gone.

Hauser stood up, circled around Jake. "You sonofabitch."

Jake looked up, tried to focus on the man he thought of as some kind of an ally, some kind of friend. Did he not – could he not – see that this was a mistake? "I … I … didn't … I couldn't …"

"Yes, you could," Hauser bellowed. "YES, YOU COULD!"

Jake's defibrillator launched a bolt of electricity to his heart. He flinched, bit his tongue.

"You killed that woman and her child up the beach, Jake. You remember that?"

Jake shook his head. How could Hauser think that he had—?

But the compartments in his head were coming apart and the images were flowing together, creating pictures. Pictures that thrashed and screeched and bled. More pornography of the dead.

Jake had peeled Madame X, a squirming bag of shrieking bloody meat who had chewed off her own tongue. She had squealed and begged and bled and died in his hands. Jake Cole. The Bloodman.

The two television stations in his head were melding, knitting their separate signals into one program. The sequences they transmitted were still a little fuzzy, short on details. Except maybe the color red. There was plenty of that. More than enough to go around.

Hauser stepped to his right, blocking out Jake's view of Frank with the yellow foam cracking his head apart. "Carradine told me that they got an ID on Little X, Jake. His DNA was matched through a lateral connection."

"Through a sibling?" The only time children had their DNA on file was if they had been reported as missing and a sample had been provided to the bureau's CODIS databank – the Combined DNA Index System. CODIS contained nearly three million DNA samples from missing persons. But a lateral match meant that they were matched through a family member who had their

DNA in the CODIS databank – besides the missing persons section, CODIS contained nearly eight million genetic fingerprints of known offenders. As well as government and law-enforcement personnel.

Hauser's face pulled tight and he looked into Jake's eyes, the expression a cross between sadness and … what? Hauser walked over to Frank's corpse, still shifting from the expanding foam. "I know who they are. Madame and Little X."

Jake stumbled over and leaned against the island. "I don't want to know." The bright staccato of a rapid-fire slide show filled his vision. Faces developing out of shadows, like black-and-white photographs in a developing tank, growing clearer by the second.

Hauser shook his head, pulled two computer-printed photographs out of his pocket. He held them out, fanned wide like a pair of losing cards. Jake reached out, took them, and they slowly developed into faces. A woman. A boy. Beautiful. Alive.

His wife.

His son.

"No. No. Nononononononononooooooooooooooo."

Somewhere off in the distance he heard his son's voice screeching as someone took him apart with a knife.

Not someone.

Him.

The Bloodman.

Me.

"Jake, I never saw them. No one did. You've been in Montauk for two weeks. TWO WEEKS! Jesus. You killed your wife and kid, Jake. Kay and Jeremy. You fucking skinned your wife and son, you sonofabitch. What is wrong with you?"

Jake's chest thumped again but this was his adrenaline, not the Duracell. He held the photo, vibrating like a leaf in his hand.

He saw Kay smiling up at him, then a quick loop of tape played through his head, one where she was on the floor, howling.

"Those horsehairs we found all over the house? They were from a bow. A cello bow."

Jake could no longer see. His eyes had flattened into crystal lines. He saw light and dark and red but little else. "No. No. No. No." Over and over. Inside his head, the images were flashing in series now, each one bloodier than the last.

Then Kay's voice roiled up out of the dark, her screaming so intimately horrible that he clamped his hands over his ears to block it out. Only he realized that it was inside his head, and something about that made it all the more frightening. He began to scream, the sound echoing like a gored animal in a steel tank.

Hauser spat on the floor. "No one saw them, Jake, except you. That morning you and I were discussing Carradine, they were upstairs taking a bath, remember that? Sure, I heard water running. I heard a radio in the bathroom. But you know what I didn't hear, Jake? Splashing. Talking. Laughing. Or any one of the million other noises you hear when a three-year-old takes a bath. There was no one else here with you, Jake. You were alone with your eidetic memory. You can create crime scenes in your head. You can create anything in your head. You're like Dr. Frankenstein, blowing life into discarded pieces. You imagined your family."

Jake's chest filled with hot lava that seared his vocal cords shut, melted his stomach, sent a boiling burst of adrenaline up into his brain. He doubled over. "Stop this!"

Hauser's hand was on his pistol and his eyes were humorless old pennies behind the yellow shooter's glasses. "The two bodies in the Farmer house were your wife and child, Jake."

"I was with Kay and Jeremy this morning!" he screamed. "Someone took them!" And it sounded like a lie, even to him.

Hauser shook his head but the pennies stayed nailed to Jake. "No, Jake. The woman and child were your wife and son."

"That woman and boy died three nights ago, Mike! Kay and Jeremy disappeared yesterday!"

Hauser shook his head. "No, Jake. They died three days ago. I spoke to Carradine – the lab at Quantico matched the dead child's DNA to you. Well, half to you, anyway."

"I WAS WITH THEM TODAY!" … *wasn't I?*

"No, Jake, you weren't." Hauser shook his head sadly. "Over the past three days, no one's seen your wife or son."

"If they weren't here, who have I been talking to?" *Making love to?*

Hauser shrugged. "You don't act crazy. It's that memory of yours. Seems more like a curse than anything else. Carradine said you see things that no one else does. Maybe that's exactly what happened. You pulled them out of your memory."

Jake thought of the way his mother used to visit him after she died and his fingertips tingled like they were filled with spiders. "Why would they be at the Farmer house?"

"Wohl finally spoke to Mr. Farmer an hour ago. He's in St. Lucia. He said that the house was rented by Kay River for the first of September."

Jake was thumped in the chest again and the breath left him with an audible chug. "Do … you … realize … how … crazy … this … sounds?"

"*DO YOU?* You've been alone in here." Hauser paused, searching back through all the little things he had missed. "Remember the pizza delivery? You ordered a single one for yourself. And a Coke. Because you knew there was no one else here."

"That's not true, I called the place to complain …"

"Do you remember placing the order?"

"Sure I—" And then he realized that he didn't.

"You skinned your own family, then created a memory-generated model so you could—" Hauser paused, tried to understand the thought process involved. "You are so fucked it's not even funny."

Nobody's your kind of mean, Jakey. Spencer's words Teletyped across his mental TV screen. Spencer, who had not wanted to discuss Lewis. Because he knew. *Nobody's your kind of mean,* his no-longer-alive voice repeated.

Then came the images of Kay on the bed with him mere hours before. Then he thought about the empty handcuffs.

He remembered the beach yesterday, Kay holding his hand, Jeremy waving to the couple walking by.

The couple not waving back.

Kay – incredulous – waving.

And the couple ignoring her, too.

Why?

They could not see her.

Or Jeremy.

Because they *weren't there.*

"They weren't locals," Jake whispered. "That's why," this so small he hadn't said it at all.

"No one saw them in town in the past three days, Jake. No one. And your wife kind of stuck out. No one at the Kwik Mart on Twenty-Seven. No one in the Big Shopper or the Montauk Market saw them. Not the place that sells the Hasselhoff T-shirts." Hauser stopped, and for a second it looked like he stopped breathing. Then he filled his lungs with a great dirty gasp. "I don't want this. I don't want this more than anything in the world, Jake. But you did it. I see it starting to swing around behind your eyeballs. You've been in town for nearly two weeks. Two fucking weeks!

You rented the place up the beach to take care of your father – you came here *before* he had his accident. You think I'm making this up?"

Jake shook his head. "I got here three nights ago. The night Madame and … and … Jeremy … and …." His voice trailed off into a sob as the little men in his head pulled the chocks from the wheels and the memories began to roll slowly forward.

"You murdered your wife and son at the Farmers' house and you cleaned up. Because that part of you – the *bad* part – has been paying attention to what you know. *It* may have its secrets from you but you certainly have no secrets from *it*."

The pictures arrived from his data-recovery software. Hundreds. Thousands. Millions. Frame by frame by frame.

He threw up again, a dry wracking spasm that shook his chest. "I don't— What—? Oh, Christ. Fucking *kill me*!" The wind throbbed outside and somewhere off in the distance there was a crash of another house falling into the sea. "Please."

He remembered Kay and Jeremy on the deck the other morning, Kay so proud of her *Don't Hassel The Hoff!* T-shirt, Jeremy's little hat with the embroidered dolphin on it. How could she … how could his son …?

And he saw other, fragmented pictures.

That twitched and shrieked and splattered and kicked.

His stomach convulsed in another violent swirl of acid and reflex and he threw up again, doubling over and retching loudly. Only there was nothing left to come out but pain.

Hauser went on. "After your wife and son, you killed Rachael Macready and David Finch. Then you killed Mrs. Mitchell and her daughter. You were floating in the water to clean yourself off. And that poncho probably protected you from most of their blood in the first place."

Guess again, a little voice at the back of his head said softly.

Hauser's jaw pulsed like steel cable. "I found the portrait inside the beach ball that the little girl made – you left it in the garbage can in the interview room. You said it was no good, that we couldn't use it. Why was that, Jake?"

Hauser left the room, his boots thudding over sand, then thunking on the stone floor in the foyer. He came back with the steel polyhedron cradled under his arm like a football helmet. He stood on the raised step above the living room and tossed the frame to Jake. Jake snatched it in, hugged it to his chest, collapsed over onto it.

Hauser reached inside his poncho and pulled out the scissor-slashed skin of the beach ball that Emily Mitchell had constructed/channeled. He tossed it to Jake. "Put it together," he said.

It landed beside him, a little left of the can of spray-foam insulation that had done Uncle Frank in. Jake shook his head. Cleared his throat. Tried to speak. The words came out cracked, broken, like the rest of his insides. "She ... she ... m ... made a mistake. She didn't read my father's painting right. She did a portrait of—"

"A portrait of you, Jake. Not a mistake. Only you didn't figure it out, did you?" Hauser tried to look into Jake's eyes – into the man he had liked, the man who on the surface seemed like he had turned a poisonous past around and had built something for himself. Something beautiful.

He remembered hearing that every culture has a bogeyman.

Jake stared back, and his eyes were deep black; a red hemorrhage blossomed in his left, his right clear and bright.

"Your father wanted you to know that the Bloodman is you."

Hauser came down and took the big stainless pistol from Jake's holster. He backed up and emptied it into his palm. He dropped five of the .500-caliber cartridges to the floor and swept them away with his foot, into a puddle. He dropped the sixth into the cylinder, slowly spun it into place, and snapped the weapon shut.

"That's why you're so good at hunting killers, Jake. You understand their language because you're one of them." Hauser watched Jake, watched the memory walls in his skull come down one after another in the domino effect.

"Remember those two suitcases that disappeared from the Farmer house? The ones that you figured out from the indents on the carpet? Guess what?" He pointed at the corner where Kay's Halliburton – dented and peeking open like a clam – lay beside the cello case, covered in sand and garbage that had blown in. "There's the second one."

"What about Kay's cello? Why would she come up here for one day and bring her cello? She knew she'd have no time to play it. I bet we call the bus company in a few hours and no one will remember a woman with a cello, Jake. Kay and Jeremy came up in your car. That's why there's a baby seat in the back. You stayed at the Farmers' a little while. And then …" He let the sentence drop off. "Your father wasn't trying to warn you, he was trying to scare you away."

Images were jamming up in his brain, tumbling over one another to let themselves out. His father had loved him, had defended him. And when Mia had been murdered, he had given up, crawled into the bottle, and tried to forget that he was still alive. Only he couldn't stop painting because it was what he had been made to do. And in his painting, in his work, he had let it come out. He had loved his son, had not turned him in, but he had turned his back on the boy. *We do things for blood we don't do for anything else*, Uncle Frank had said over the phone.

Hauser held up Jake's big stainless .500. "There is one round in here." He tossed the pistol onto the counter and walked past Frank's body and stepped through a blown-out window into the rising day.

84

Jake stood out past the break of the surf in water up to his waist. What was left of Jeremy floated beside him, undulating in the swell like a rotting sea creature. He held Kay's flat, shredded hand. The wind was completely gone now and had he not known he was standing in the eye of a hurricane, he would have sworn that it was one of the most beautiful mornings he had ever seen.

Except for the skin of his dead wife and son floating at his side in the brown swells.

Back on the beach, the house was all but destroyed and something told him that the second part of the storm would finish what had been started here. It would wipe the whole place clean.

Jake remembered the men he had been. There had been some good in his life. Maybe more than a little. But it was canceled out by everything he had taken away. Mostly from himself.

He raised his wife's flattened hand and gave it a kiss, ignoring its smell. Then he kissed his little boy on the cheek, beside the hole where his ear had been.

Then he placed the cold wet barrel of the big stainless revolver against the roof of his mouth and angled it back, so it would do its job. He thought about the woman he had loved, about the boy they had made, and about how it had all amounted to nothing.

He closed his eyes.

And gently pulled back on the trigger.

Half an ounce of pressure later, Jake Cole became a ghost.

85

Hauser stood at the edge of the muddy embankment that used to shelve out onto a nice sand beach. In the early-morning light it was strewn with debris and flotsam, ranging in magnitude from a golf bag to an upside down forty-seven-foot Chris Craft Constellation that looked a lot like his boat. Probably was, if he wanted to guess. Only it was upside down. Not a good week, he realized. Then thought, *Fuck it*, and decided that he had earned himself a drinking problem.

He turned back to the house where Jacob Coleridge had made his contribution to American painting. He saw the concrete slab of the studio floor, pitted and scarred, the building pulled out to sea. All those paintings, all that creative genius, all that money, gone.

Some families run on love, some run on anger and madness, some run on worse things, Jake had said.

Worse.

Things.

What could be worse than this? Hauser wanted to know. He took in the world that the ocean had littered with all the things it didn't want, and the stretch of sand as far as he could see was scabbed over with insurance claims. He wondered if his house had made it through the night. His gun collection in the basement. Maybe it— And then he stopped. Because none of it mattered. Not anymore. And he had to save himself for Act II of the hurricane. In another few hours hell would be back.

Minus the Devil, this time.

He half slid and half fell down the new scoop of the beach. He had never really paid attention to the layout here before, but he was sure that the storm had pulled a sixty- or seventy-foot swatch of coast away.

The beach felt like another planet – one no human had ever set foot upon. Hauser was not interested in metaphysics, but he wondered how many people had had their lives irrevocably changed by the last two days of weather.

And worse things.

Sand clung to his boots with weak fingers as he moved down the beach, arms hanging loosely like the quarterback he had been so long ago. Above the gentle wind he heard the whine of an approaching siren – Scopes on his way.

Behind him, the ocean reached out and pulled the ghosts from the shallows, driving them to the bottom and dragging them out toward deep water with the rest of the trophies the storm had taken.

Author's Notes

Anyone familiar with the area of Long Island where this story occurs will notice that I have taken endless liberties with the locale – I have shifted roads, invented neighborhoods, fabricated streets, and created beaches that do not exist. This was done for the simple reason that I did not want any real-world locations associated with the fictitious events of this novel.

Also, the Southampton Sheriff's Department portrayed in this story is my own fabrication and has no bearing on any of the law enforcement agencies that serve the communities mentioned.

Acknowledgments

When it comes time to do the blood quantum for any novel, delineating patrimony can be difficult; for a first novel, whittling down the gene pool is impossible. But the following people stand out for going far above and beyond the call of duty:

My agent, Jill Marr, of the Sandra Dijkstra Literary Agency – she moves continents and commands the dead; Dr. Justin Frank – *bon vivant*, author, friend, driver of strange little cars, impresario, Chuck Close aficionado – a true 21st century Renaissance man; Sandra Dijkstra, the great Oz, pulling levers behind the curtain.

At my agency: Andrea Cavallaro for smuggling *Bloodman* over countless borders; Elisabeth James for her endless patience; Elise Capron for getting my manuscript to the right hands; Thao Le for her can-do attitude; Jennifer Azantian for dragging the cart up the hill each day.

At Thomas & Mercer: Andy Bartlett, for always making me feel like the only writer in the room; Victoria Griffith, for seeing something in my work that no one else could; and everyone at T&M who helped put *Bloodman* into a dust jacket.

About the Author

Robert Pobi dealt in fine Georgian antiques for thirteen years before turning to writing full time. He has fished for everything that swims – from great white sharks off Montauk to monstrous pike in northern Finland. He prefers bourbon to scotch and shucks oysters with an old hunting knife he modified with a grinder. In warm weather he spends much of his time at a cabin on a secluded lake in the mountains, and when the mercury falls he heads to the Florida Keys. The critical response to his first short story (written when he was twelve) was a suspension from school. Now he writes every day – at a desk once owned by Roberto Calvi.

Bloodman has been published all over the world.

Visit him at www.robertpobi.com.